The Loom • 베틀

강양욱 번역
(Charles Y. Kang)

Washington State University Bachelor
UC, Irvine Master
UC, Irvine Doctor of Philosophy

매실과 눈깔사탕 (Mesil and Eyeball Candy)
콩만큼 점수 받은 날 (A reward in the size of a peanut)
정담의 향기 (The Fragrance of a Warm Conversation)
시 한 송이 피워 (Growing a flower of poetry)
론 사이프러스 (Lone Cypress)
담쟁이넝쿨 (Ivy vines)
베틀 (The Loom)

The Loom 베틀

초판 1쇄	2018년 9월 10일
지은이	정순옥
발행인	김재홍
교정 · 교열	김진섭
마케팅	이연실
발행처	도서출판 지식공감
브랜드	문학공감
등록번호	제396-2012-000018호
주소	경기도 고양시 일산동구 견달산로225번길 112
전화	02-3141-2700
팩스	02-322-3089
홈페이지	www.bookdaum.com
이메일	bookon@daum.net
가격	12,000원
ISBN	979-11-5622-398-6 03810
CIP제어번호	CIP2018025136

이 도서의 국립중앙도서관 출판예정도서목록(CIP)은 서지정보유통지원시스템 홈페이지(http://seoji.
nl.go.kr)와 국가자료공동목록시스템(http://www.nl.go.kr/kolisnet)에서 이용하실 수 있습니다.

문학공감은 도서출판 지식공감의 인문교양 단행본 브랜드입니다.

한·영 에세이
Korean · English Essay

The Loom 베틀

정순옥 · Chung Soon-Ok

문학공감

책머리

한없이 부족한 제가 수필집 제3권 『베틀』을 한·영으로 상재(上梓)할 수 있게 된 것은 온전히 하나님의 은혜라 생각하고 영광을 올려 드립니다.

이 책을 상재하는 데 도움을 주신 문학평론가이시며 우리나라 문학계에서 서정수필의 거목으로 알려져 있는 존경하는 정목일 선생님께서 바쁘신 중에도 『베틀』에 대한 평설을 해 주셔서 한량없이 기쁜 마음입니다. 그리고 강양욱 번역 문학가, 강정실 수필가이시며 문학평론가, 언제나 내 수필의 첫 번째 독자가 되어주며 한국문학을 세계화하는 데 앞장 서가는 남편인 이병호 시인, 사랑의 편지 역할을 하는 가슴 따스한 정순자 언니와 함께 이 순간 호흡을 맞춰서 수필집 『베틀』을 만들어 낼 수 있어서 참으로 좋습니다. 가슴이 흐뭇하도록 삶의 희락과 행복을 느낍니다.

저는 낯선 나라에서 모든 것을 새롭게 시작한 미주이민 1세로서 열심히 살아온 모습을 한 편의 수필로 담아내고 싶습니다. 여러 모양의 삶이 조화를 이루어 한 역사를 이루어 간다면, 저의 삶도 분명히 후세에 가치가 있는 삶일 것이라는 생각이 듭니다. 미주이민 1세로 살아오면서 형성된 정서를 정제시켜서 글로 표현하고, 진실되고 향기로운 삶 속에서 인생의 가치를 깨달은 수필을 쓰고 싶지만 모든 것들이 미흡하여 저는 늘 졸작만 생산해 내는 느낌입니다. 그래서인지 저는 아직도 '수필가'라는 말이 송구스럽고 쑥스럽기만 합니다. 그래도 용기를 내어 글을 쓸 때는, 영원세계에서 나를 지켜보고 있는 사랑하는 사람들과 대화를 나누면서 글을 씁니다. 서로서로 얼굴을 대면하고 살았던 시절엔 무심히 지나쳤던 말, 제 가슴속에 묻혀있는 '사랑한다'는 말도 스스럼없이 할 수 있어서 좋기 때문이랍니다.

재미동포라는 카테고리 안에서 신앙인으로 살고 있는 저는 어떻게 하면 하나님께서 허락해 주신 이 땅에 사는 동안 아름답게 살 수 있을까를 고민하면서 사라져 가는 아름답고 정다운 한국어를 부여잡고서 수필을 쓰고 있습니다. 바람결에 따라 머리카락이 움직이듯이 제가 수필을 대하는 마음결에 따라 독자들의 마음도 움직일 것이라는 생각에 언제나 새로운 마음으로 정성을 다하여 수필창작에 임하려 합니다. 수

베틀

필은 일상생활과 가장 밀접한 글이어서 진솔하면서도 친밀하고, 독자에게 신선한 감동과 읽는 재미를 느끼게 할 수 있어야 함을 잊지 않으면서 말입니다.

앞으로 살아가야 할 인생 순례자의 길은, 아름다운 언어들을 보듬고 한국문학인으로 긍지를 갖고 문학을 즐기면서 행복하게 살고 싶습니다. 부족한 저에게 많은 지도 편달 부탁드립니다. 수필집 제3권, 『베틀』이 상재될 수 있도록 도와주신 교인들을 비롯해 문우들과 가족들…. 저와 인연을 맺고 사는 모든 사랑하는 사람들 중 특별히 강 회장님께 다시 한 번 진심으로 감사드립니다.

2018년 4월, 미국, 몬터레이

정순옥

목차

책머리 — 5

1부 | 단풍 바구니

이든은 신비로워 — 13
도라지 꽃, 위안부 — 17
이슬방울의 예쁜 꿈 — 22
사랑의 회초리 — 26
절규에 빛이 — 30
단풍 바구니 — 34
억센 머리카락 인생 — 38
하나님 아리랑 — 42
수상가옥 사람들의 꿈 — 46
내 사랑 한강 — 50

2부 | 베틀

감사한 은퇴 — 57
그리운 봉선화 — 61
냉이 향취 — 65
베틀 — 69
떡방아 — 73
아버지와 백로(白鷺) — 77
얼레빗 — 79
싸리문 — 84
빨래터 — 88
농촌의 등불 — 92

3부 | 눈꽃송이

그대로 좋아! — 99

성탄절 — 103

눈꽃송이 — 105

해피 리타이어먼트 — 109

좋은 글 — 113

큰일 났네! 속에 감춰진 진실 — 117

감사와 행복 품은 사돈들 — 121

양파가 날 울려 — 125

무궁화 — 129

그랬었구나! — 133

4부 | 몬터레이 아리랑

몬터레이 소나무 — 139

생명 — 143

몬터레이 아리랑 — 147

빗님이 오시네 — 151

바람 같은 사랑 — 155

디아스포라의 유랑 나이 — 159

꽃잔디 — 163

꽃밭 — 167

선교와 틀니 — 171

나는 보았네 — 175

평설 | 백의천사(白衣天使)의 일생으로 피운 삶의 꽃 — 181

| 1부 |

단풍 바구니

이든은 신비로워

나는 신비롭고 아름다운 이든을 바라보고 있어. 이든은 하나님이 최초로 창조해 준 축복의 땅, 낙원동산에서 영원히 죄에 물들지 않고 살기를 바라는 부모의 마음을 담은 이름이래. 이든 좀 봐! 오밀조밀하게 이목구비를 갖추고 여아로 태어난 이든은 너무나 신비로워 내 가슴을 요동치게 하잖아. 흐~음 싱그러운 아기 냄새, 너무 좋아.

샛별같이 반짝이는 새까만 눈동자와 촉촉이 젖은 앵두 같은 입술, 뽀오얀 우윳빛의 보드라운 살결이며 발그레한 볼과 얼굴 중앙에 오뚝 솟아 있는 코, 보송보송한 솜털이 가늘게 흔들리는 두 개의 귀를 가진 이든. 이 세상에 있는 신(神)의 창작품 중 가장 아름답고 신비롭게 창작된 이든을 볼 수 있는 축복이 나에게 주어졌어. 세상에 태어나자마자, 자기가 한평생 살아가야 할 세상이 그렇게도 궁금한지 두 눈을 초롱초롱 뜨고서 앙증스러운 손으로 살짝 입을 가리고 있는 귀여운 이든은 나의 첫 번째 외손주라구.

명주실보다도 더 보드라운 머리카락, 내 숨결에도 움직이는 가느다란 속눈썹, 젖내 같은 아기살 내음이 내 후각을 감미롭게 하는 부드럽고 은은한 향내를 풍기는 이든이 얼마나 사랑스럽고 신비스러운지 내 혼을 빼앗아 가버린 느낌이야. 하나의 생명으로 잉태되어 엄마 자궁 속에서 40주보다 빠른 38주를 보내고 6.15파운드로 해산의 고통을 감내하며 정상으로 태어난 외손녀. 보송보송한 솜털, 팔딱팔딱 뛰는 심장박동 소리, 새근거리는 숨소리가 내 가슴을 짜릿하게 해. 나의 핏줄의 인연으로 만나게 된 기쁨을 응~애! 하며 커다란 첫 호흡으로 대신하여 나를 행복하게 한 네가 너무 고마워.

몸에 뚫린 구멍으로 만들어진 동그란 두 눈, 오목하게 생긴 두 귀, 앙증스럽게 생긴 입은 세상과 아름답게 소통하면서 살았으면 해. 건강한 두 손은 좋은 일에 많이 봉사하면서 살기를 바라는 마음 간절하고. 아픈 사람의 상처를 어루만져 주는 사랑의 손, 두 손을 모으고 늘 기도하는 손이 되었으면 좋겠어. 골격이 튼튼한 두 발로는 무릎을 굳게 세우고 궁휼한 자를 찾아 나서는 발이 되길. 견고한 양어깨는 누군가가 힘들 때 기대도 좋을 인간의 향기를 풍기는 사람이 되었으면 좋겠네. 맑고 하이얀 얼굴은 천하보다도 귀한 한 생명의 환희를 품은 영혼의 은은한 미소가 가득하면 얼마나 좋겠나.

한민족의 유전자 세포를 지닌 이든은 행복한 마음으로 일생을 선하게 살아가리라 믿어. 한민족의 정서에는 낭만이 흠뻑 깃들어 있거든. 한순간을 귀하게 여기면서 아름다운 삶의 하모니를 이룬 꽃을 피울 거야. 오묘한 색채와 향기를 발하면서 말이야. 우주의 기운을 뿜어내는 바람과 공기와 햇빛 같은 자연과 더불어 순수한 삶을 즐길 수 있었으면 해. 귀엽게 옹알이를 시작하면서 말을 배우면, 아름다운 말, 남에게 격

려되는 말, 은혜스러운 말만 하길 바라구. 즐거운 목소리와 행복한 웃음소리가 늘 함께했으면 해. 하늘에서 들리는 신령한 음성을 들으며 하늘을 사모하면서 평화롭게 살다가 은총 안에서 귀천(歸天)하길 소망해.

아름다운 음악을 듣고, 작은 들꽃 속에서도 향기로운 꽃향내를 음미하면서, 마음이 행복해지는 정서를 지니고 살면 좋겠네. 때깔 고운 옷과 맛있는 음식을 먹으며 인생살이의 낭만도 즐기고, 희망찬 삶의 비전을 가지고 복스럽게 살기를 바라. 새파란 능금이 빨갛게 농익어 가듯이 날마다 생활이 싱그럽길 바라는 마음이야. 주위 사람들과 아름다운 인간관계를 형성하면서 보람있는 삶을 살았으면 좋겠어. 고독은 깨끗해지는 은총이라 하니 가끔은 그런 시간이 있어도 괜찮을 거야. '침묵은 금이다'라는 말도 있으니 자주 하는 게 유익하겠지. 진선미(眞善美)를 갖춘 아름다운 여성으로 한세상을 살면 얼마나 좋을까.

수많은 세포로 이루어진 뇌는 바른 생각만 하길 바라. 오장육부로는 뒤틀리는 남의 배고픔도 알아차리길 바라고, 꿈틀거리면서 축제의 소리도 낼 수 있었음 좋겠어. 마음속은 언제나 촉촉한 감정을 가지고 사랑의 꽃눈을 틔우는 이든이길 바라. 넓은 가슴을 활짝 열면 드넓은 우주의 신비를 흠뻑 받을 수 있을 거야. 혈액순환을 감당하는 붉은 피를 뿜어내는 심장은 언제나 뜨거운 가슴으로 내 이웃을 내 몸같이 사랑하는 마음이었으면 해. 사랑을 베푸는 데서 참 행복을 찾는 삶이 되길 간절히 바라는 마음이라구. 고귀한 생명이 깃들어 있는 붉은 피는 언제나 청량하고 신선하길 바라. 몸은 하나의 성전이라고 했으니 항상 건강하도록 몸 관리를 잘해야 할 거야.

뼈를 이어주는 골절마다 골수로 꽉 차서 원활하게 움직이는 것처럼,

인생살이가 모든 것이 풍요로워 순조롭게 살 수 있었으면 좋겠어. 삶을 대변하는 숨을 쉬게 하는 허파에 헛바람이 들지 않도록 세상살이에 매사에 겸손하도록. 인체의 기능이 쇠퇴해 가는 징조인 간이 부었다는 소리를 듣지 않도록 언제나 현명하길 바라. 콩팥과 요도와 배설구들이 힘을 합쳐 몸에 불필요한 요소들을 자꾸만 버리듯이 생활에 불필요한 요소들을 제거하면서 몸과 마음을 언제나 정화시키면서 살았으면 좋겠네. 신의 섭리로 이 땅에 태어났으니 진리 안에서 자유를 누리고 생명의 존귀함을 알고 매 순간을 의미 있고 소망이 있는 삶을 살기를-.

새로 태어난 사랑하는 내 외손주가 살아갈 이 세상이 죄가 사라지고 지상천국이 되었으면 하는 간절한 마음이야. 어쨌든, 아름다운 이 세상에서 공동체를 이루며 사는 동안 하나님 사랑 많이 받고, 이웃사랑 많이 하면서 행복하게 살기를 바라. 늘 기쁘고 행복한 마음으로 감사하면서 매일매일 살기를 기도해. 나에게 할머니 자리를 선물해 준 사랑스러운 사람으로 태어났음에 감격하여 또다시 나 혼자서 중얼거리네.
　"이든은 신비로워!"

도라지 꽃, 위안부

날카로운 비수가 꽂혀있어 함부로 접근할 수 없는 언어 '위안부'가 있다. 사람들은 '도라지 꽃'이라 부르며 접근한다. 잔인한 일본군화에 짓밟혀 으깨어진 순결한 몸과 마음을 다시는 돌이킬 수 없는 원한(怨恨)을 품고 살았던 조선의 언니들이다. "여자가 원한(怨恨)을 품으면 오뉴월에도 서리가 내린다"는 말이 있다. 한두 명이 아닌 수많은 위안부가 하늘 위에서는 고혼(孤魂)들이 땅 위에서는 노혼(老昏)들이 원한을 품고서 지금도 통곡하는 소리가 천지에 진동하고 있다. "왜놈들아! 역사를 왜곡하지 말고 위안부들에게 진심으로 회개하고 사과하라!

순결한 도라지들의 진실이 하늘에 닿아 천지가 화답하면 쓰나미 보다도 더한 천재지변(天災地變)이 일어날까 두렵다. 일본에서 천하 보다도 귀한 수많은 생명을 앗아간 쓰나미가 있었을 때, 한국이 제일 먼저 달려가지 않았던가. 일본은 잘못된 역사를 인식하고 인권을 짓밟고 성노예로 삼았던 비통한 위안부들에게 통곡의 피눈물로서 진심으로 사과하고, 한국과 역사적인 원수에서 현실적인 동반자로 거듭나야 한다. 새로운 인류 역사를 아름답게 창조해 나가기 위해서 말이다.

1937년 말부터 일본이 본격적으로 군(軍)위안소를 설치해 위안부를 기거하게 하면서 인권을 유린시키고 비인간적인 포악한 방법으로 성노예를 시켰다. 일제강점기 때, 가난하고 힘없는 우리나라에 아름다운 보라색 치마를 입고서 피어난 도라지꽃들이 심심산천에 살고 있었다. 도라지꽃은 세상에 태어난 햇수로 14살쯤 되면 너무도 예뻐서 산골로 나무를 하러 온 숫총각의 마음을 설레게 했다. 그렇지만 꺾지 않았다. 보기만 하여도 가슴이 울렁거리는 도라지꽃은 신성하기까지 하여 감히 접근할 수도 없어서였다. 그런데 그리도 어여쁘게 피어나는 도라지꽃들을 군화 신은 포악스런 왜놈들이 '죠센징'이라 부르며 사정없이 짓밟아 버렸다.

조선의 귀한 딸, 총각의 가슴을 설레게 하던 숫처녀의 처녀성을 그리도 더럽고 험악스러운 일본군화로 허물어 버려 치를 떨게 한 '위안부'가 역사에 있다. 늑골이 부러지도록 팽팽하게 저항해 봤자, 결국은 갈기갈기 찢어진 도라지 이파리들의 굵은 핏줄과 시퍼런 멍들만이 커억커억거리는 목울대로 파고들었을 뿐이다. 그 큰 고통 속에서도 생명을 포기할 수 없었던 것은, 고향에 있는 사랑하는 부모 형제가 보고 싶어서요, 악착같이 살아서 억울했던 삶에 대한 진실을 밝히고 말겠다는 희망이 있어서였다.

"위안부(慰安婦)는 제2차 세계대전 동안 일본군의 성적 욕구를 해결하기 위한 목적으로 강제적이거나 집단적, 일본군의 기만으로 징용 또는 인신매매범, 매춘업자 등에게 납치, 매수 등 다양한 방법으로 일본군을 대상으로 성적인 행위를 강요받은 여성을 말한다."라고 위키백과에

베틀

정의되어 있다.

이렇게 위안부의 구성원으로는 조선인을 포함한 중국인·필리핀·태국·베트남과 말레이시아 등 일본 제국이 점령한 국가 출신이 일본군에게 징발되었는데 생존한 사람들은 하루 30번 이상 성행위를 강요당했다고 증언하고 있다. 대한민국의 위안부 피해자들은 일본 정부의 사과와 진상 규명 및 적절한 배상 등에 대해, 1992년부터 현재까지 대한민국 주재 일본 대사관 앞에서 매주 수요일마다 항의하는 수요집회를 개최하고 있다. 현재 생존해 있는 일본군 위안부 피해자로는 김복동 할머니와 몇 분만이 증언하러 다니시지 거의 다 다른 세상으로 떠나버린 상태다.

일제강점기 시대에는 젊은 처녀는 영문도 모른 체 일본군이나 일본 순사들에게 붙잡혀 가면 국가를 위해서 솔선수범한다는 일본군 강제위안부나 정신대에 파견되어 일본 군인들을 위해서 몸을 희생해야 했다. 고향에 돌아오면 '화냥년'이라고 손가락질을 받아 가면서 살아가기 때문에 결혼 같은 건 아예 포기하고 살아야 했던 위안부들의 뼛속까지 깊이 박힌 울분을 어떻게 풀어 줄 것인가. 나는 지금도 우리 어머니의 음성이 귓가에서 생생하게 들린다. "…… 내가 오죽했으면 니 큰언니를 서둘러서 일찍 시집을 보냈껐냐~? 일본 군화 신은 군인들이나 순사들이 군대 트럭을 가지고 와서 얼굴이 핀만한 가시내들은 무조껀 끌어가서 일본군 강제위안부나 정대신로 집어넣어 부리면 왜놈들 성(性)노리갯감이 되어 버린단마려~. 하마트면 화냥년 소리를 들었을 낀다-, 그것보다는 나치 안 껐냐?"

위안부들을 피해서 뒷문으로 하버드 연설장에 들어서는 일본을 대표하는 아베 총리의 추접스런 행동에, 최초로 위안부 결의안을 회의에 올렸던 고인이 된 미국 레인 에번스 의원, 자국 출신 혼다 의원 등 인권 옹호자들에게 일본은 이미 무시를 당하고 있음을 직시해야 할 것이다. 일본이 세계적으로 인정받고 새역사를 창조해 나가는 성숙한 동반자로서 자격을 갖추려면 인권을 중요시하는 국가가 먼저 되어야 하지 않겠는가.

지금도 몸서리치도록 당한 수치 때문에 가슴이 아파서 세상을 향해 똑바로 눈을 뜨지 못하는 억울한 성노예 피해자, 위안부들에게 진심 어린 사과를 해서 용서를 받고 새로운 세대를 이어가는 양심적인 일본으로 거듭나기를 바라는 마음이 간절하다. 오늘날, 인권을 유린당한 여린 도라지들의 혼령(魂靈)이 생명으로 부활하여 인권을 존엄히 하는 미국 땅 공원에 위안부기림비로 저고리 치마를 입고 앉아 있다. 조상들이 지은 죄를 진심으로 뉘우치면 용서하고 포용(包容)해 주려고 그 당시에 입었던 넓은 치마폭을 입고 있으니, 이 좋은 때에 일본 아베 정부는 무릎을 꿇고 머리를 조아려 죄 사함을 받고 사랑의 구원함을 얻어야 하리라.

누가 알랴! 그 어느 날, 도라지의 알레르기가 있는 사람들은 불쑥불쑥 가슴의 빗장을 풀고서 잘린 꽃봉오리의 진한 향기를 풍기는 위안부들에 취해서 정신을 잃어버리고 말지ᅳ. 세상의 모든 만물은 자꾸만 움직이면서 변하지만, 진실만은 변하지 않는다. 그리고 참으로 공평하게 돌아간다. 하늘과 땅이 알고 있는 그 진실이 있다. 심심산골에서 아름다운 보라색으로 자란 여린 도라지들이 꽃을 피워 보지도 못하고 포악한 일본 군화로 검붉은 피를 토하면서 뭉그러져 버린 그 진실 말이다. 이 세상에서 진실을 이길 수 있는 것은 아무것도 없다. 진실을 사랑하는 세상 사람들은 촉구하고 있다.

"일본은 극악무도(極惡無道)하게 인권을 짓밟은 위안부들에게 진심을 다해 공식으로 사과하라!"

이슬방울의 예쁜 꿈

이슬방울에 맺혀있는 예쁜 꿈을 안다. 아름답고 영롱한 빛을 발해 내 마음을 위로해 주고 희망을 주었던 이슬방울 말이다. 한 편의 내 수필도 누군가의 마음을 위로하고 어떤 순간에도 포기하지 않고 희망을 품게 하는 축복의 통로가 되었으면 좋겠다.

성경 말씀 중『헐몬의 이슬이 시온의 산들에 내림같이』를 상고해 본다.

이슬방울은 햇빛이 비치면 수정체 물방울이 프리즘작용으로 오색찬란한 빛을 발한다. 이때 이슬방울의 예쁜 꿈을 영글게 된다. 내 수필도 세상의 빛으로 오신 이의 숨결로 신비로운 생명력이 있어 독자의 마음을 품을 때 내 수필의 꿈이 이루어짐을 안다. 이슬방울은 어두운 밤에 찬 공기에서 참으로 힘들게 수증기를 끌어내어 만들어진다.

따라서 내 수필도 머리가 쥐어짜지는 고통 속에서 한 편의 수필이 탄생한다. 이슬방울은 깊은 밤 허공 속에서 쥐어짜낸 미세의 이슬들이 서로 엉키면 크고 작은 이슬방울이 된다. 내 수필도 그렇다. 창작의 몸부림치는 고통 속에서 내 작은 생각과 언어들이 묶어지면서 만들어지는 것이다. 아주 작은 알갱이 물방울 이슬들이 서로 뭉쳐서 모습이 선

베틀

명한 이슬방울을 만들고 조그만 이슬방울들의 간격이 서로 합쳐지면 정말 놀랍도록 커다랗고 수정같이 맑은 이슬방울이 된다. 내 수필도 그렇다. 짧은 단어들이 모여서 만들어진 문장들이 또다시 합쳐져서 한 편의 수필이 구성된다. 독자에게 감명을 주려면 좋은 책을 많이 읽고, 생각을 많이 하고, 또 많이 써 봄으로써 문학과 만난 좋은 수필이어야 하기에 나는 매 순간을 수필과 함께하고 있는 기분이다.

이슬은 요술쟁이 같다. 미라클적인 생명력으로 무지개처럼 아름답던 모습에서 어디론지 사라졌다가 또다시 그 모습으로 태어나는 걸 보면 말이다. 수필도 그렇다. 금방 글 한 편 써 낼 것처럼 많은 생각이 떠올랐다간 어느새 모든 생각이 깡그리 사라져 버린 것 같으나 또다시 수필로 태어나니 말이다. 수필도 이슬방울처럼 수많은 세포가 있어 살아날 수 있게 하는 신선한 산소가 필요하다. 전능자의 선물인 맑은 산소가 있어야 생명의 언어들을 잉태할 수가 있지 않겠는가. 느낌이 들 수 있게 하는 생명의 언어들을 말이다.

나는 시골에서 많은 형제 중에서도 늦게 태어났다. 내가 부모님을 알면서부터 내 아빠 엄마는 이미 늙으신 분들이셨다. 그래서인지 부모님을 생각하면 대 식솔을 거느리며 힘들게 일만 하시는 불쌍한 분들이라는 생각에 안쓰러운 생각만 난다. 내가 중학교 졸업반 때였다. 시시때때로, 나는 고요한 새벽녘에 눈을 뜨면 텃밭으로 나가곤 했었다. 진학 문제로 고민에 차있는 나에게 자연은 참으로 좋은 친구가 되어주었다. 어느 날, 나는 토란잎 위에 송골송골 얹혀있는 수정같이 맑은 이슬방울이 바람결에 미련도 없이 또르르 굴러서 땅으로 떨어져 버리는 모습을 포착했음인가, 내 마음도 한없이 연약하여 땅으로 굴러떨어지는 것 같고 앞날이 캄캄했다. 나는 상급학교에 진학해서 좋은 책을 많이 읽고 글을 쓰고 싶은 배움의 열망이 있었는데, 내 의지하곤 상관없이 가정형편이 허락할 것 같지 않았다. 나는 침묵으로 일관했지만 정말 괴로웠다.

아, 그런데 말이다. 나는 신기한 일을 발견했다. 무채색의 이슬방울이 햇빛의 도움을 받으니 신비스럽게도 오색찬란한 색깔을 발했다. 나는, 그때 나를 위로해 주고 희망을 주고 싶어하는 이슬방울의 예쁜 꿈을 보았다. 무아지경(無我之境)이 된 내 마음을 그대로 품어주고 나에게 아름다운 꿈을 갖게 하고 싶어 하는 이슬방울의 예쁜 꿈을 말이다. 나는 진실로 누군가의 돌보심이 나에게 임할 것을 믿었고, 등 뒤에서 내이름을 부르시는, 어머니의 사랑에 넘치는 음성을 들을 수 있었다.

많은 세월이 흘렀다. 고국 텃밭 싱싱한 토란잎 위에 있다가 재미교포로 살아가고 있는 집 정원 파초 이파리에 이슬방울이 다시 살아나 있다. 내 수필도 그랬으면 좋겠다. 수필을 읽은 후 잊힌 것 같으나 어느때 다시금 생각이 나는 글, 나는 그런 수필을 쓰고 싶어한다. 어떤 순간에도 포기하지 않도록 나에게 희망을 준 이슬방울의 예쁜 꿈이 있었기에, 오늘날 내가 수필문학에 정진할 수 있지 않은가 싶다. 나는 더욱더 영혼을 투명케 하여 맑고 향기로운 수필을 쓰고 싶어 오늘도 간절한 소망을 기도드린다. 축복의 통로가 되는 수필을 쓸 수 있게 해 주시라고 말이다.

나는 평생토록 이슬방울의 예쁜 꿈을 가슴 속에 품고서 고마운 마음으로 살아가고 있다. 햇빛의 도움을 받아 신비로운 무지개 색상을 발

베틀

해 꿈의 통로가 되어 나에게 희망을 품게 했던 예쁜 꿈을. 항상 수필을 쓸 때마다 맑고 오묘한 사랑의 색채를 품은 생명체들이 살아 움직이는 수필을 나는 쓸 수 없는 걸까 고민하면서 부족한 내 생활을 반추(反芻)해 보곤 한다.

  누군가 나를 '수필작가'라고 불러줄 때는 쑥스러우면서도 어려운 시기를 용케도 잘 견뎌내는 힘을 전능자로부터 받아 꿈을 이룬 축복 받은 사람이라는 생각이 들 때도 있다. 그래서일까. 내가 만약 축복받은 사람이라면, 이슬방울의 예쁜 꿈을 품은 내 수필이 축복의 통로가 되었으면 좋겠다. 누군가를 감동을 줘 위로하고 희망을 주고 싶어하는 이슬방울의 예쁜 꿈을 전달해 줄 수 있는 축복의 통로 말이다.

사랑의 회초리

사랑의 회초리! 그 시대엔 있었다.

내가 교육을 받으며 자라나던 그 시대가 자랑스럽게 여겼던 말, 지금 시대는 거의 사라진 느낌이 든다. 그 시대에는 참으로 많이 사용했던 생활용어, 가난이라는 말과 함께 사용하던 참으로 귀한 교육용어였는데---. 한 시대를 견고하게 세워 준 버팀목이었는데---. 선진국 대열에 진입할 수 있는 오늘의 한민족을 만들어낸 밑거름이었는데---. 지금은 자꾸만 퇴색해 가고 있는 느낌이 들어, 나는 안타깝다.

"회초리 맞아라!"

내가 자라던 그 시대에는 가정에선 부모님으로부터, 학교에선 선생님한테서 수없이 들었던 교육용어였다. 사랑하는 마음으로 회초리를 들고서 내 앞에서 견고하게 말씀하시던 부모님과 선생님들이 있었기에, 행복하게 살 수 있는 지금의 내가 있어 나는 참으로 감사 또 감사하는 마음이다. 열심히 공부해서 훌륭한 사람이 되어야 가난에서 벗어나 잘살 수 있다. 부모님 말씀에 순종해야 모든 것이 잘되고 옳은 인생길을 갈 수 있다. 죽기 아니면 살기로 공부를 해도 모자랄 판에 게으름을 피

베틀

우고 숙제를 안 해온 너는 선생님의 회초리를 맞아야 한다. 새로운 시대를 이끌어 갈 새싹인 내 앞엔, 교육의 현장인 가정과 학교는 언제나 사랑의 회초리가 있었다. 그 시절엔 어느 사람도 사랑의 회초리를 비난하거나 잘못된 교육 방법이라고 윽박지르는 사람이 없었다. 사랑의 회초리를 맞은 사람들도, 그 장면을 목격한 사람들도, 그 이야기를 전해들은 사람들도 한결같은 마음으로 "너 잘되라고 그런 거야. 회초리 맞을 일을 했으니 그랬지─" 그뿐이었다.

일간지를 읽고 읽던 남편이 한숨 섞인 말을 한다.

"회초리가 사라져서 그래~. 나는 언제나 왼손엔 영어사전, 오른손엔 회초리를 들고 다녔는데───. 가정에서 자식이 자기를 낳아 준 부모님을 폭행, 학교에선 학생이 자기를 교육하는 선생님을 폭행, 어떻게 이런 사건들이 일어날 수가 있는지 교육현장이 염려스러워~."

첫 직장으로 고등학교 3학년 영어교사였던 경험이 있는 남편이 심각한 표정으로 말한다. 나도 회초리가 사라져 가는 후세들의 교육에 문제점들이 많음에 공감하면서 회초리를 생각해 본다. 교육을 받아야 할 시기에 올바른 길로 안내해 주던 회초리, 올바른 교육을 위해서 도구로 사용하는 사랑의 회초리가 지금은 어디로 사라진 것일까? 수많은 지폐 속으로, 여자들의 치마폭 속으로, 아니면 유행의 바람을 타고 어디론가 사라져 버린 걸까. 나는 사라진 회초리가 다시 교육현장에 의기양양하게 돌아오는 모습을 그려본다. 내 후세들의 앞날을 교육해 가는데 필요한 사랑의 회초리가.

우리 집 방문을 열면 커다란 거울 위엔 항상 사랑의 회초리가 놓여 있었다. 사랑의 회초리는 무언의 스승이었다. 회초리를 바라보면서 옳은 길로 가라는 우리 어머니의 지혜가 그 회초리에 응집되어 있었다. 그 사랑의 회초리는 우리 8남매를 건강하고 아름답게 키워내는 데 사용한 우리 어머니의 교육용 도구였다. 그 회초리는 우리 똑똑한 오빠가 만들어 놓은 회초리였는데 사연인즉 가난한 시대에 흔히 있을법한 일이었다.

어느 날, 오빠는 배가 고파 먹을 것을 찾다간 마른명태를 대청 마루방 벽장에서 찾아냈다. 가난한 시절 산골에 사는 한창 커 나가는 남아에겐 참으로 좋은 간식거리였다. 앗~뿔~사! 어머니의 허락 없이 공들여야 할 제사용 음식을 오빠가 뜯어 먹어 버렸으니 어머니의 놀람은 말할 수가 없었다. 남의 집에서 가져온 음식도 어머니가 주실 때까진 먹지 않고 기다리던 불문율을 오빠가 깨어버린 것이다. 이때 어머니는 오빠에게 잘못을 인정시키고 직접 회초리를 만들어 오라 하셨다. 그리곤 그 회초리를 커다란 거울 위에 올려놓으셨다. 그런데 어느 날 그 회초리가 사라져 버렸다. 어머니는 오빠에게 다시금 회초리를 직접 만들어 거울 위에 올려놓게 하셨다.

"회초리가 있다 해서 무조건 때리지는 않는다. 누구든지 매 맞을 짓을 했을 때만 사용할 것이다."라고 하시면서. 나는 단 한 번도 우리 어머니가 그 회초리를 사용하신 모습을 본 적이 없다.

우린 8남매가 함께 자랐지만 싸움을 한다거나 욕을 한다거나 큰소리로 언쟁하는 일이 없었다. 물론 의견 충돌이야 있었지만. 때때로 형제들이 모여서 가곡을 함께 부르거나 소설책에 나오는 주인공 이야기로 형제들끼리 의를 나누면서 아름다운 정서로 커 나갈 수 있게 돌보아

베틀

주신 어머니의 정성의 무기는 그 사랑의 회초리가 아니었나 싶다.

우리 어머니가 집에서 사용하시던 사랑의 회초리, 우리 남편이 학교에서 사용하던 사랑의 회초리를 나는 문화와 정서 차이가 많은 이국에 살면서도 선호했다. 무엇보다도 모국어를 계승(繼承)시키기 위해서 나는 우리 아이들에게 사용했지만, 요령이 부족해서인지 나에겐 안타까움만 줄 뿐이었다. 다행한 것은 늦게나마 딸 아이가 한국말의 중요성을 깨닫고서, "엄마, 회초리로 더 세게 때려서라도 한국말을 더 잘할 수 있게 만들지~." 하면서 아쉬움을 토로한다.

아이~휴, 엄마가 때렸다고 경찰 부르겠다고 할 때는 언제고? 딸은 배꼽이 빠지라고 웃으면서 저도 아기가 태어나면 사랑의 회초리를 들고서 교육할 거란다. 나는 벌써부터 내 사랑스러운 손주 뒤에 사랑의 회초리를 들고서 색색거리는 딸 아이의 모습이 그려진다.

절규에 빛이

빛이다. 절규 속에서 새 생명을 틔우는 것은. 절규는 새 생명이 틔우는 아픔의 순간이다.

딱딱하게 굳은 씨방이 터지는 엄청난 고통 말이다. 껍질을 깨는 고통이 없으면 어둠을 뚫고 희망의 새로운 싹이 세상 밖으로 나올 수 없음이다. 굳은 내면의 생각에 구멍이 뚫려 새싹이 틀 수 있게 한 것은 절규에 빛이 임함이리라. 그러니 절규(Scream)는 절망(Despair)이 아니라 희망(Vision)을 예고해 주는 신호라 말해도 좋을성싶다.

헬(Hell)조선! 탈(脫)조선! 돈 없고 배경도 없는 나는 어떡해?

요즈음 젊은이들 속에서 자주 튀어나오는 절규 소리란다. 지옥 같은 조선을 떠나고 싶다는 심정을 경악스럽게 표현한 말일 것이다. 휴~우 다행이다. 조선은 이미 지나간 시대의 대한민국 이름 아닌가. 현재의 우리나라 이름은 '대한민국'이다. 고희(古稀)를 바라보면서 재외동포로 사는 나는 그들에게 답을 해주고 싶다. "천국(Haven)! 대한민국, 대한민국에서 사세요."라고 말이다. 이 세상 어디를 가도 우리나라처럼 산천이 아름답고 사람들 정 많고 살기 좋은 나라는 없노라고 나는 단연히

베틀

말할 수 있다.

"젊은이들의 절규 소리에 잠을 잘 수가 없어요."

어느 날 내가 들은 대통령의 고민에 찬 음성이었다. 젊은이들이 경쟁의 전쟁터에서 현실의 위기를 모면하려고 몸부림치는 고통소리가 한 나라를 대표하는 대통령의 귀에 절규로 들렸다면, 절규에 빛이 임하고 있음을 말해 주고 있음이 아니겠는가. 나는 또다시 말해 주고 싶다.

"절규의 순간은 새 희망을 만드는 시간이요, 희망과 절망 사이에서 허우적거리려야 하는 기막힌 현실 앞에서 희망을 바라보라고."

과거 현재 미래가 아름답게 공존하는 우리나라는 대대로 비쳐오는 광태 나는 하얀 빛이 있는 나라가 아닌가.

이 시간 나는 노르웨이 화가, 뭉크(Edvard Munch, 1893~1910)의 절규(Scream)라는 그림이 생각난다. 사람의 엽기적인 모습을 그린 그림이다. 내 눈엔, 세상 소리가 너무도 괴롭게 들려 두 귀를 막고 두 눈을 부릅뜨고 입은 짝 벌렸지만, 소리도 낼 수 없을 정도로 괴로워 괴물 같이 일그러진 모습이 된, 정신착란을 일으키기 전의 현대인을 표현한 그림 같다. 하늘과 땅과 바다가 있는 이 세상 길을 혼자서 외롭게 걸어갈 때, 보일 듯 말 듯 신비한 석양빛을 지고 등 뒤에서 걸어오는 두 사람은 누구일까? 아마도 사랑하는 사람들이 절규의 순간을 안타깝게 지켜보고 있는지도 모르겠다는 생각이 든다. '절규'라는 그림은 어느 젊은 날 나의 모습을 표현해 준 것 같기도 하다.

"합격자 발표일이 내일인데 오늘 합격자 발표를 했군요. 그럴 수가 있나요?"

"왜, 못해? 지원자 전원을 합격시켜도 정원 미달인데, 뭣 하러 합격자 발표일을 기다려!"

"그럼 저는 어떻게 되는 건가요. 체력검사 때 시계 초침 소리를 잘 못 들었다고 의사진단서를 가지고 오라 해서, 별 이상이 없다는 의사 진단서를 가지고 왔는데요."

"합격자 발표를 끝냈으니 추가 합격자 발표는 없어!"

"네?"

요즈음 젊은이들이 고통스럽게 외치는 말처럼, 돈 없고 배경 없는 나는 불합격자일 수밖에 없었다. 학교 수익을 위해서 지금보다도 훨씬 더 편법과 불법이 심했던 반세기가 지난 그 시절에, 나 혼자만 제외하고 전원 합격을 시킨 내가 지원했던 교대의 역사가 목울대가 터지도록 피를 토해낸 내 절규 속에 잠재하게 된 것이다. 내가 꾹 참았던 감정을 터트리는 순간, 우주 만물 어디든지 공평하게 비치는 빛이 나를 도우셔서 새 생명의 싹이 트게 해 주셨음을 안다. 그 결과로 생명을 귀하게 여길 줄 아는 오늘날의 나로 생성(生成)되지 않았나 싶다.

1969년 처음으로 예비고사가 시행되었다. 예비고사란 수시로 바뀌는 문교부 정책에 의해, 지금 실시하는 수능시험의 옛날 방법이라고 말할 수 있겠다. 하얀 눈이 소복이 덮여 있는 예비고사 합격자 발표 장소에서 나는 눈을 비벼가면서 몇 번이나 합격자 명단에서 내 이름을 확인했다. 나는 얼마나 기쁘던지 '감사합니다'라는 말밖엔 나오지 않았다. 꽁꽁 얼어붙은 빙판 위와 밤새도록 내린 함박눈에 햇살이 비치니 눈부시게 하얀 설광(雪光)을 발산한 아름다운 겨울날이었다. 나는 은방울처

베틀

럼 고여 있는 내 눈물 속에서, 흙과 땀으로 얼룩진 얼굴인데도 활짝 웃으시며 하얀 옷이 너풀거리는 사이로 덩실덩실 춤을 추시는 늙으신 부모님의 모습이 아른아른 보였다.

"그 자리가 얼~만~데~" 길게 늘려 빼는 친구의 말이 날카로운 쇠꼬챙이 되어 내 가슴을 후벼대며 살이 찢어지도록 아프게 했다. 그 자리, 내가 있어야 할 자리를 확보하려면 엄청난 돈과 배경이 필요함을 늦게서야 터득한 나는 순진한 바보였을 뿐이다. 양지바른 동산 위 교정에서 피어나는 그윽한 아카시아 꽃향기 속에서, 졸업과 함께 취직이 보장되는 교육대학에 진학할 희망을 품고서 일 년 동안 지낸 여고 시절. 나는 쉬는 시간에도 오르간을 치고, 미술 공부인 데생 연습을 했었는데--. 고통 후, 나는 정원 미달인 어느 후기대학모집 국문과를 가슴에 품고 학비를 면제받을 수 있는 곳에서 대학과정을 마쳤다. 새 생명이 틔우는 아픔의 순간인 절규에 빛이 따뜻하게 비쳤기에 새로운 비전을 가질 수가 있었음을 믿는다.

이 시간 고통스럽게 절규하는 고국의 젊은이들은, 지상에서의 천국은 '대한민국'이요, 절규는 꿈과 희망의 새싹을 틔우는 아픔의 순간임을 깨닫고 밝은 내일을 꿈꾸며 살아가는 한 사람을 볼 수 있겠다. 나는 절규에 빛이 임하여 절망이 아닌 희망의 싹이 트이게 한 흔적을 지니고 순간순간을 감사한 마음으로 사는 사람이다. 그 빛은 삶을 사랑하는 자의 곁엔 언제나 임하고 있는 영혼의 참 빛이리라.

단풍 바구니

나는 만들고 싶다. 내 인생의 아름다운 단풍 바구니를.

초록색 나뭇잎들이 가을철이 되면 신비스럽게도 붉은색, 노란색, 갈색 등으로 물든 가을 정취 나는 단풍잎들을 대바구니 속에 차곡차곡 담아서 아름다운 내 인생의 단풍 바구니 하나 만들고 싶다. 내 인생의 추운 겨울이 되면 햇살 따사로운 이 가을에 만든 향기 있는 단풍 바구니를 보듬고서 하나하나 감상하면서 흐뭇한 미소를 지을 수 있게.

내 인생의 꿈인 참으로 아름다운 예쁜 색깔의 단풍잎을 만들려면 나는 더욱더 사랑스러운 자연을 아끼며 빛나는 햇살과 신선한 공기와 서늘한 바람 앞에 더욱더 겸허하게 서야 할 것이다. 기후 변화로 식물이나 나뭇잎들이 단풍이 들듯이 내 인생도 여러 가지 변화로 물들어 갈 때, 한 날을 살 수 있음에 감사하면서 정성을 다해 아름답게 살려고 노력하면 서서히 채색되어 가는 단풍잎처럼 고상한 색깔을 품은 인생단풍이 될 것 같다. 그러려면 나는 더욱더 아량 있고 인내하면서 내 주위에 있는 소중한 사람들에게 관심과 사랑을 베풀 줄 알아야 하리라. 그리고 설령 마음을 번거롭게 하는 사람일지라도 귀한 가을날 햇볕과 같

베틀

이 따스한 마음으로 품을 수 있어야 신기할 만큼 짙게 물든 사랑의 향기가 배어 있는 인생단풍이 만들어지지 않겠는가.

온갖 초목들이 조금씩 조금씩 연한 움이 돋아나고 싹이 트는 봄. 수액이 왕성하여 이파리들이 초록으로 짙게 물들이고 꽃이 피는 여름. 마른 갈바람에 초목들이 단풍으로 물들어 가는 가을. 그리고 수액의 흐름이 멈춰가기에 메마르고 차가운 겨울. 춘하추동(春夏秋冬) 사시절은 우주 만물의 기본적인 질서이기에 누구도 막을 수 없는 시간의 흐름이다. 인생살이도 사계절(四季節)로 나눈다면 나는 이미 가을이어서 단풍인생이라고 말할 수 있다. 한여름 햇빛 찬란한 시절에 핀 꽃들로 꽃바구니를 만들어 두지 못한 나는 이 가을에 곱게 참으로 곱게 물든 단풍잎들로 아름답고 풍성한 단풍바구니를 만들고 싶다. 가능하다면 가을 소풍을 즐기는 마음으로 천천히 단풍잎들을 행복한 마음으로 바구니에 담고 싶다. 추상(秋霜)을 거친 뒤에 화려하게 물든 단풍잎들은 참으로 아름다운 것처럼 내 인생에 된서리 맞아 빨갛게 물든 단풍잎들은 예술적인 색깔이 되어 어쩜 경이롭기까지 할지도 모른다. 가능하다면 이제 남은 시간은 흠 없이 곱게 물든 단풍잎이 되었으면 좋겠다. 추억 속의 샛노란 은행단풍잎처럼.

시시때때로 추억 속으로 나를 불러대는 예쁜 은행단풍잎은 내가 희망을 품고 다니던 초등학교 교정에 있었다. 은행나무가 두 그루 있었는데 우리는 부부 은행나무라고 부르면서, 조금 핼쑥해 보이는 나무는 남편이고, 풍성하게 보이는 은행나무는 부인 은행나무라 불렀다. 추운 겨울을 인내로 이겨낸 은행나무는 봄이면 연한 은행이파리 새싹을 내어 보는 가슴을 뛰게 하고, 여름이면 생동감 있는 초록빛 은행잎으로 무성해지다가 찬바람이 불기 시작하면 노랗게 물들기 시작하여 간밤에 무서리가 내리고 느닷없이 불어대는 세찬 가을 비바람에 미련도 없이 우수수 땅에 떨어진다.

그러면 은행나무 곁에 지나가던 사람들은 너나 할 것 없이 샛노랗게 물든 예쁜 은행잎에 감탄사를 보내며 땅에 떨어져 있는 은행잎을 서로서로 줍곤 했다. 여학생들뿐만 아니라 남학생들도 더 예쁜 은행잎을 고를라치면 익살스러운 친구들은 남학생들을 놀리기도 했다. 남자들이 무슨 짓 하는 거냐고. 그러면 남학생들은 "나는 사람이 아니냐? 우리 엄마 줄끼다." 하면서 더 예쁜 은행잎을 찾느라 공부 시작종 소리도 아랑곳하지 않았던 것 같다.

그런 날이면 우리 어머니도 틀림없이 노란 은행단풍잎 때문에 행복해하셨다. 내가 고른 은행단풍잎과 오빠가 주어온 흠 없이 샛노란 은행단풍을 번갈아 보시면서 옛 띤 소녀의 표정을 하시던 모습이 지금도 눈에 선하다. 한글을 그 당시에는 언문(諺文)이라 불렀는데, 우리 어머니가 서투르게 쓰시는 언문 살림살이 일기장엔 노오란 은행단풍잎이며 알록달록 예쁘게 물든 빨간색 단풍잎들이 노트 속에서 말려져 처음 모습대로 많이 보관되어 있었다. 그 예쁜 단풍잎들은 틀림없이 우리 아버지가 새봄이 돌아와 경칩(驚蟄)이 되면 언제나 문을 새 창호지로 바르실 때 단풍잎들을 문에 붙여 주시어, 우리 온 가족은 예술적인 자연을 즐기면서 살았었다. 나는 항상 문을 여닫을 때마다 마주 보는 처음 색깔처럼 고운 가을향기 품은 단풍잎들을 보면서 우리 부모님의 소박한 인생의 꿈을 헤아려 보았던 것 같다.

우리 부모님의 아름다웠던 인생단풍처럼 나도 내 인생의 예쁜 단풍

베틀

잎들을 만들고 싶다. 가을날 노랗게 물든 벼들을 추수할 땐 언제나 논 한 자락은 가난한 사람들을 위해서 그냥 놓아두셨던 우리 아버지. 얼마나 넉넉히 남겨 두셨느냐고 아버지와 일꾼들과 함께 즐거워하시던 우리 어머니. 다음 해엔 풍년이 들어 더 많은 벼를 들에 남겨 두어 누군가에게 더 많은 도움을 줄 수 있었으면 좋겠다는 아름다운 꿈인 노란 벼 단풍잎들을 가슴에 많이 품고 사셨던 우리 부모님. 이웃 사랑을 실천하시면서 아름답게 살았던 삶의 흔적이 아름다운 단풍이 되어 창호지 바른 문에 노랗게 빨갛게 물들어 자리하고 있어 많은 사람의 마음을 즐겁게 해 주었던, 지금도 내 눈에 아롱거리게 하는 그런 아름다운 단풍잎들이 나에게도 생겨났으면 좋겠다. 문풍지가 흔들리는 바람이 불고 싸락눈이 내리는 추운 겨울이 되면 문에 창호지로 덧입혀진 아름다운 단풍잎들을 바라보시면서, 동네 불쌍한 사람들을 걱정하시기도 하고 오손도손 새해의 희망찬 계획들을 세우시던 모습은 참으로 아름다운 단풍인생들 모습이셨다.

어느 사람도 거스를 수 없는 자연의 순리에 따라 찾아온 가을 인생에, 수액이 말라 땅에 떨어져 쓸쓸히 뒹굴면서 부서지는 소리만 내는 낙엽이 아니라, 인고의 삶 속에서 자연에 감사하며 이웃사랑으로 곱게 물든 부모님 같은 인생단풍잎들이 만들어졌으면 좋겠다. 한평생 노란 벼 단풍잎들과 벗 삼아 이웃들에 관한 관심과 사랑으로 이 세상에 산 삶의 아름다운 흔적들이 지금도 내 가슴 속에 단풍으로 남아 아름다운 것처럼. 이웃에 관해 관심과 사랑, 더하여 나를 버겁게 하는 사람까지도 곁에 있음에 감사한 마음으로 포용할 수 있다면 내 인생 단풍바구니는 더욱더 아름답고 풍성해질 텐데….

억센 머리카락 인생

드물게 보는 억센 머리카락이란다. 이 지역에서 멋쟁이 권사님으로 통하는 박 권사님이 손가락을 활짝 펴 풍성한 머리카락을 만지시면서 계속 말씀하신다. 한국전쟁을 겪으면서 사랑하는 많은 것들을 잃어 가슴 아프고 힘들게 살았던 한 여인의 억센 머리카락 인생이, 삶의 무늬가 되어 손가락을 따라서 잔잔한 수채화처럼 그려진다.

미용사가 그러는데 이렇게 억세고 숱이 많은 머리카락은 드물데. 태몽 꿈도 이상하게 부스스하게 털 많은 수탉이 우리 집 마당에 가득했다더군. 그래서 팔자가 센가 봐. 나는 이 사회에 죄를 너무 많이 지었어. 그래서 남은 인생은 죄를 갚으면서 살아야 해. 지금까지 내 인생을 인도해 주신 하나님께 감사하면서.

억세고 숱이 많은 머리카락은 화사한 미소에 곱게 화장한 얼굴과 조화를 이루어 지금도 하이힐을 신고 다니는 구십 수를 바라보시는 권사님을 멋져 보이게 하는 일등공신이다. 나는 가발로 착각할 만큼 풍성한 머리카락에 외모를 멋지게 꾸미고 다니시는 멋쟁이 권사님이 마음도 멋쟁이라는 생각이 든다. 아름답게 변화된 마음으로 숨기고 싶은

베틀

억센 머리카락 같은 인생사를 한 편의 드라마를 이야기하듯이 말할 수 있는 자유로운 마음이.

단발머리 여학생 시절, 어머니가 자궁암으로 하늘나라로 떠나버리신 세상은 공허했다. 그렇지만 윤기나는 긴 머리를 찰랑거리면서 이화여전 다니던 시절까진 이 세상에서 재물은 부러운 게 없었다. 은행을 가진 아버지가 계셨기에. 북한군이 불법 남침한 1950년 6월 25일 사변이 일어나기 전날도 애인과 함께 한강에서 배를 타고 청춘을 즐길 정도였다. 그 후 돌아오기만을 손꼽아 기다리다 노처녀가 되게 한 첫사랑은 많은 다른 대학생들과 함께 이북으로 끌려가 흑백사진 한 장만 남겨두고 지금까지 무소식이다.

아버지는, 은행은 인민의 피를 착취한다는 죄로 이북으로 납치된 후 무소식. 1953년 2차 후퇴 때 춘천이 회복되어 흩어졌던 가족도 찾고 여경으로 취직도 되었다. 그 시절에 억지로 선을 보아 약혼했던 남자에게 단 한 번 속살을 보여준 역사가 운명을 바꾸어 놓은 셈이다. 한국을 남과 북으로 갈라놓은 억센 철조망으로 된 삼팔선이 가까운 고지에서 군복무하고 있는, 결혼 날짜가 잡힌 약혼자를 찾아갔을 때, 이성(理性)이 마비될 정도로 아름다운 함박눈이 너무 많이 내려 여관에서 묵게 되어 일어난 일이다.

약혼자는 알고 보니 어느 마담과 동거하고 있는 사이였다. 미련도 없이 사주 보따리를 그의 누나 집에 갖다 주고서 새벽 4시에 서울로 올라왔다.

새로운 직장이 필요했는데 다행히도 예전에 알던 사람을 만나 부평에 있는 PX에 취직할 수 있었다. 영어가 부족하여 새벽 2시까지 공부하며 아침에 출근할 정도로 겨우겨우 직장생활을 유지해 나갔다. 청천벽력이랄까! 어느 날 임신 5개월이 된 것을 알았다. 낙태시키기엔 너무 늦은 시기여서 출산을 했는데 솟아낸 피보다도 더 붉은 상처의 흔적을 품고 여자아이가 태어났다. 설상가상으로 이 애가 소아마비를 앓아 3살까지 서지를 못했다. 장애아를 보듬고서 죄인처럼 사는 미혼모의 마음이 얼마나 괴롭던지 아이와 함께 자살을 시도해 보았지만, 그 짓도 못했다.

PX에서 열심히 일했더니 인정을 받아 육군 인사과로 이동되니 생활이 넉넉해졌다. 승진함에 따라 미군 부대 사무직에 일하게 되자 부하직원이 생겼는데 총각인 하사병이었다. 장애인 복지가 천국이라는 미국에 가면 장애인 딸을 잘 키울 수 있다는 주위 사람들의 권유에 힘입어 젊은 미국인 부하직원을 초대해서 딸아이를 보여주며 사정을 하여 결혼하였다.

미국에 와서 딸과 아들을 낳고, 소아마비로 고생하는 딸도 장애인 복지 시설이 잘 되어 있는 나라인지라 학교생활도 무난했다. 그런데 군대 생활을 하는 젊은 남편이 필리핀으로 파견을 나가선 바람을 피웠단다. 이유는 나이가 많고 상사였던 부인이 항상 어렵고 부담스웠다나.

결국, 남편과 이혼하고 혼자서 직장 생활하며 애들 셋을 아파트에서 키우는데 집이 있어야 자유롭게 살 수 있을 것 같아 새집을 산 것이 무리였다. 비행장 시큐리티 패트롤로 15시간씩 일을 해도 생활이 점점 어려워져 그 당시에 집세를 감당할 수가 없어 5년이나 따라다니면서 결혼하자고 졸라댄 이혼 남자와 재혼을 하게 되었다.

즐거운 마음으로 애들 셋 결혼시키고 노년의 행복한 삶을 선사해 준 남편은 세 번이나 심장 수술을 한 탓인지 어느 날 갑자기 심장마비로 세상을 떠나고 말았다. 박 권사님은 이 시절 유치원 시절부터 알기는 했으나 소홀히 했었던, 믿기만 하면 모든 사람을 사랑해 주시는 주님 곁으로 온전히 돌아와 신앙생활을 할 수 있게 됨이 너무나 행복하다고 하신다.

오늘날 박 권사님은 구속의 은혜에 감사하면서 신앙인의 본을 보이며 선한 생각 속에서 행복하게 사는 참 멋쟁이시다. 이 세상에서 숨 쉬는 동안에 한 가지 소원이 있다면 통일, 납북된 아버지는 돌아가셨겠지만, 첫사랑을 만나보는 일이다. 아름다운 추억이 깃들어 있는 흑백사진들을 보는 눈망울은 언제나 촉촉한 그리움으로 가득 차 있어 보는 이의 가슴을 아리게 한다. 전쟁으로 말미암은 이산가족의 슬픔을 어찌다 표현할 수 있으랴.

사랑하는 많은 것들을 조국에 남겨둔 채 이민생활 하는 나 자신을 본다.

날마다 알게 모르게 이 세상에 지은 죄가 너무 커 부끄러움에 눈을 들어 하늘을 우러러볼 수도 없는 나다. 하나님의 은혜가 없었으면 살아있을 수 없는 나다. 핏덩이를 토해낼 정도로 너무나 괴롭고 슬퍼서 뭉크의 괴로워하는 인물을 표현한 명화, 〈절규〉가 나 자신이라는 생각이 들 때가 있지 않았던가. 삶의 모양만 다를 뿐이지 공기를 마시듯 죄와 함께 살면서, 어렵고 슬프고 가슴 아팠던 일들이 더 심했던 내 인생살이가 한 편의 소설 같은 멋쟁이 박 권사님의 억센 머리카락 인생사에 오버랩 된다. 나는 어느새 손가락을 펴내 헝클어진 머리카락을 가르며 쓸어 올리고 있다. 머리카락을 감지라도 하듯이―.

하나님 아리랑

나의 일생은 '하나님 아리랑'이다.

하나님은 내가 믿고 사는 유일신(唯一神)이고, 아리랑은 우리나라 대표적인 민요로 하나님과 동행한다는 뜻이 내포되어 있다 한다. 그러니 하나님 아리랑은 '하나님, 하나님 한민족으로 살고 있는 저와 동행하여 주시옵소서'가 된다. 하나님 아리랑은 하나님을 믿으며 한민족으로 살아가고 있는 내 평생의 기도요, 삶을 요약한 말인 듯싶다.

우리나라의 대표적인 민요, 아리랑은 무슨 뜻인지 아직도 정확한 해석이 없다고 한다. 몇 가지 추측이 있는데, 아리랑에서 아리는 하늘을 뜻하는 '알'의 변음(變音)이고, 랑(郎)은 사내, 남편 외에도 '주인'이라는 뜻을 갖고 있다고도 한다. 나는 기독교인이라서인지는 몰라도 이 '하나님설'을 믿는다. '하나님 저희들과 동행하여 주시옵소서'라고 한다면, 아리랑이 따로 떨어진 민족정신이 아니라 견고한 믿음의 반석에 세운 민족정신이 살아날 텐데 하는 생각이 들어서다. 아름다운 아리랑의 음률 속에는 유일신의 마음이 투영돼 있음을 나는 항상 느끼곤 하기 때문이리라.

베틀

아리랑은 민족의 혼(魂)이 깊숙이 담긴 음률(音律)이다. 아리랑의 음률은 누에고치가 보드라운 명주실을 뿜어내듯이 한민족의 한을 풀어내는 듯하다. 수많은 아리랑은 언제 어디서나 흥얼거려도 가슴을 촉촉이 적시는 지역마다 다른 민족의 감정이 흘러나온다. 아리랑을 부르면 누군가가 그립고, 어디론지 떠돌아다니는 인생의 슬픔과 외로움이 가슴속에 저민다. 청천 하늘엔 잔별도 많고 우리네 가슴엔 희망도 많다고 아무리 힘차게 외쳐봐도 왜 그런지 눈이 촉촉이 젖어옴을 느끼는 게 아리랑이다. 그래서 난 외롭지도 슬프지도 않으려고 온전하신 하나님과 동행하고 싶어 '하나님 아리랑'을 부르나 보다.

헐렁해서 미끄덩거리는 검정 고무신을 신고 싸리문을 나서는 단발머리 소녀인 나에게 어머니는 재차 확인하신다.

"정말로 너 혼자서 그 머나먼 예배당을 다녀올 수 있단 말이여?

"으-으-ㅇ? 엄마. 나 혼자 갈 수 있어요."

어머니는 내 손에 빨강 앵두나 볶은 콩을 한 움큼 쥐여 주시면서 무슨 힘에 이끌리어 예배당에 가는지 모르겠다고 걱정하시면서도 못 가게 막으시지는 않으셨다. 나는 십 리도 훨씬 넘는 신암 예배당을 그 어린 나이에 강대미 언덕을 헐떡거리면서 오르내렸고 질퍽거리는 논두렁 밭두렁을 지나기도 하고 자갈이 깔린 신작로 길을 걸어서 혼자서 다녔는데도 외롭지 않았으니 하나님이 동행해주셨음이 아니겠는가. 생각건대, 하나님께선 나를 신앙의 도구로 삼으셨는지도 모르겠다. 특별한 날이면 마을 사람들과 어우러져 아리랑을 흥이 나게 부르면서 너울대는 춤사위로 내 마음에 사랑을 심어 주시던 우리 어머니도 기도생활을 하시다가 소천을 하셨으니 말이다.

1950년 한국전쟁, 그리고 휴전협정이 끝난 후의 농촌은 참으로 황폐하고 적막하기 그지없었다. 추수 후 논에서 자란 잡풀 씨를 손으로 훑어다가 죽을 끓여 먹으면서 목숨을 연명해 나가는 사람들도 있었다. 이런 시기에 가난한 농촌까지 찾아와 달콤한 초콜릿을 주면서 사랑을 베풀어 준 사람들이 있었으니 선교사들이었다. 내가 살던 지역에서는 '노랑머리 코 큰 사람들'이라고 부르면서 선교사들은 이상한 사람들이라 했다.

"예수쟁이들은 다 좋은데 소중한 조상님들한테 제사를 지내지 못하게 하니 큰일이란 말이여~" 하얀 한복을 입은 어른들한테서 흔히 듣는 말이었다.

6·25사변을 겪은 후, 내가 자란 지역에서는 나이는 상관없이 공민학교라는 것을 설립해, 애국가도 가르치고 한글도 가르쳤다. 나는 그곳에서 예배당에 가서 예수님을 믿기만 하면 구원받고 평생토록 행복한 마음으로 살 수 있다는 기쁜 소식을 들었다. 그 당시의 예배당은 어느 부잣집 대청마루나 어느 공공장소의 마룻바닥 아니면 천막촌이었다. 내가 처음 다닌 신암 예배당은 어느 부잣집 대청마루가 아니었나 싶다. 마룻바닥에 무릎을 꿇고 앉아서 예배를 드린 기억이 난다. 어른들이 기도를 시작하면 한없이 길게 해서 나는 꾸벅꾸벅 졸기가 일쑤였다. 가끔, 특히 크리스마스 때엔 코 큰 선교사님들한테서 선물 꾸러미를 받는 기쁨이 무척 컸다. 예배당 종소리는 시계가 없는 농촌에선 시간을 알리는 종소리이기도 했다. 그때 들은 탄일종(誕日鐘) 소리가 시시때때로 내 귓가에서 울리고 있다.

내가 살던 곳에는 내가 학업을 계속할 수 있는 유일한 중학교가 있있는데 불교재단에서 지었다. 그래도 나는 예배당에 가끔 다닐 수 있었으니 하나님이 동행해 주셨음이 분명하다. 여고 시절은 미션스쿨을 다닐 수 있었기에 참으로 좋았다. 나의 신앙의 비전은 신선했고, 믿음, 소망, 사랑을 실천하면서 아름답게 살고파 신이 나게 활동하면서 지낸 젊은 날이었다.

심금을 울리는 아리랑 가락을 잊지 못하고 사는 디지털 노마드의 삶은 언젠가는 은은한 조국의 향기 속에 묻혀서 살고 싶은 희망이 있기에 힘이 솟는다. 못 견디게 그리운 고향이 그리워서인지 나는 오늘도 몬터레이해변 꽃잔디를 보면서 내가 지어 부르는 몬터레이 아리랑을 부른 후엔, 하나님, 하나님 저와 동행하여 주시옵소서라는 뜻이 포함된 '하나님 아리랑'을 외치며 덩실덩실 춤을 추면서 삶의 현장 속에 합류하고 있다.

수상가옥 사람들의 꿈

푸~후~, 이럴 수가!

이 시간, 지구촌 어느 한 곳에서는 땅 위에서 사는 것이 평생 꿈인 사람들이 있다. 육지가 아닌 물 위에서 일생을 살아가고 있는 수상가옥 사람들이다. 물 위에 떠 있는 보트 안에서 평생을 살다가 죽어서까지도 결국은 수장(水葬)되어야 하는 이들의 안타까운 인생살이를 알게 된 후론, 날마다 드리는 나의 기도다. "창조주 하나님! 수상가옥 사람들에게 긍휼을 베풀어 주시어 지배하면서 살라 하신 축복의 땅 위에서 생활할 수 있도록 허락하시어, 그들의 꿈을 이루게 하여 주시옵소서."

내가 수상가옥 사람들을 처음으로 접했던 곳은 캄보디아 '벙 똔래 쌉' 호수에서다. 사람들은 쉽게 톤래 삽 호수라 부르는 곳 대부분이 '보트 피플'이라고 불리는 베트남 전쟁 후유증으로 생긴 난민들이란다. 1975년에 종식된 월남전쟁의 슬픈 역사를 가슴에 품고서 물 위에서만 살아야 하는 수상가옥 사람들. 땅 위로 발을 내딛는 순간부터 밀입국자가 되므로 다시 추방당하거나 아니면 감옥에 가야 하는 신세가 되기 때문에 평생을 수상가옥에서 산단다.

베틀

공산주의 체제인 크메르루주 정부에 혼란스러움을 느낀 사람들이 보트를 타고 고국을 떠나 와 캄보디아에 도착했지만, 캄보디아 정부에서 받아주지 않기 때문에 그냥 보트에서 생활할 수밖에 없음이다. 나는 나라 잃은 사람들의 슬프고 처량한 모습이 눈에 밟혀, 평화스러운 대지를 밟을 때마다 내 마음속에 있는 사랑의 흙 한 움큼씩을 보내주곤 한다.

수상가옥 사람들은 모든 생활을 보트를 타고서 한다. 옆집에 갈 때나 고기잡이 갈 때나 일단 자기 집을 나서면 여러 종류의 보트를 타고서 이동한다. 나는 단단한 땅 위를 밟지 않고 차를 타거나 배를 타거나 무엇이든지 움직이는 것을 타면 멀미 때문에, 수상가옥 사람들이 물 위에서 부유(浮游)하며 살아가는 생각만 해도 어지럽고 가슴이 아프다. 톤래 삽은 캄보디아 등 6개국을 거쳐 흐르는 메콩강 한 줄기에 신선한 물로 생긴 커다란 호수로 우기와 건기로 나누어지는 기후에 따라서 수위가 달라진다. 하루에 한 차례씩 세찬 비가 쏟아지는 거의 반년을 차지하는 우기가 되면 수상가옥 사람들은 한 곳에 머물 수가 없어 또다시 적당한 곳으로 보트를 옮겨서 견뎌내야 한단다. 살아가기 힘든 우기지만 그래도 고기를 많이 잡을 수 있어 생업이 거의 고기잡이인 이들에겐 축복이라 말할 수도 있노라 한다.

수상가옥은 친환경이 조화를 이루는데, 특별히 탁한 진흙탕 속에서도 아름다운 꽃을 피우는 연꽃이 군락을 이루고 있다. 그곳에서만 특이하게 잘 자라는 작은 핑크색 꽃봉오리를 터트리는 연꽃은 참으로 신비스럽고 아름다운 빛으로 피어난다. 그 연꽃들이 수상가옥 사람들의 배설물까지도 정화해, 그 물로 다시금 일상생활을 할 수 있다니 인간을 세세히 감찰하시는 하나님의 사랑이 임함이리라. 음료수만은 빗물을 받아 끓여서 마시거나, 봉사자들의 손길을 거쳐 육지에서 배달된 물을 마실 수 있다니 한 생명을 아끼면서 서로 더불어 살아가는 봉사자들의 아름다운 마음이 천사의 마음 아닌가.

나는 오늘도 캄보디아 커다란 호수에서 월남전쟁의 상흔(傷痕)을 갖고 사는 보트 피플들과 그 부근 물가 위 나무다리 집들 속에서 사는 사람들을 생각한다. 그리고 생명의 씨앗을 흙에 박고서 황토물과 사람들에게서 나온 오물과 심지어는 수장된 사람까지도 정화시키는 연꽃을 생각한다. 엄청난 비밀을 품은 듯이 은은한 향기를 내뿜으면서 수상마을 사람들의 주위에서 환한 미소를 짓는 연꽃은 내 마음까지도 밝게 해준다. 아름다운 연꽃 속에서 살기에 마음에 평화가 깃들어서인지 수상가옥 사람들의 행복지수는 의외로 높다고 한다. 행복은 외부적인 조건보다도 마음먹기에 달렸지 않다던가. 나는 가끔 수상마을 사람들에게 생명의 은인이 되는 연꽃을 생각하면서 한 줄기 식물보다도 못한 나 자신인 것 같아 부끄러워지곤 한다.

유람선을 타고서 현지인의 안내로만 접한 수상가옥 사람들이지만, 나는 멀리서 바라본 그들의 생활이 안타까워 주님에게 드리는 기도의 끈만은 놓지 않고 있다. 누군가의 욕심 때문에 선량한 시민이 피해를 당하고서 전쟁의 후유증을 감내해 내야 하는 수상가옥 사람들을 생각하면 너무 안쓰러웠다. 살육을 벌이는 전쟁은 성경에 나오는 우리 조상 카인과 아벨의 형제간의 생명의 피 흘림이 이어져 고금을 통해서 사라지지 않고 있으니 어쩌랴. 전쟁이 없고 평화만 존재하는 지상천국이 언제 오려나---. 어느 날, 월남 전쟁의 후유증으로 고통스럽게 사는 수

베틀

상가옥 사람들의 이야기는 역사 속으로 사라져 가고, 후세들은 전설처럼 아스라이 자녀들에게 이야기해 줄 수 있는 날이 하루빨리 왔으면 좋겠다. 기적 같은 일이 이 시대에 올 수는 정녕 없는 걸까?

보통 사람들에겐 땅 위를 걸어 다니는 일이 지극히 평범한 일이다. 그러나 수상가옥 사람들에겐 이루고 싶은 평생 꿈이다. 나는 오늘도 신비로운 흙 향기를 맡으며 포근한 땅 위를 걸으면서 멀리 지구촌 한곳에서 본 수상가옥 사람들을 생각한다. 날마다 소원을 허공 속에서 소리쳐야 하는 수상가옥 사람들을 위해서 실질적인 아무런 도움은 주지 못할지라도 따뜻한 마음으로 그들의 꿈이 이루어지는 날까지 기도만은 동참하고 싶다.

"전능하신 하나님, 수상가옥 사람들에게 축복의 땅을 밟을 수 있는 은혜 내려 주시옵소서!"

오늘도 나의 기도가 톤래 삽 호수에서 특이하게 잘 자라는 연꽃 대궁으로 뽑아 올려져 아름답게 피어나고 있음을 지구촌 서쪽에서 바라보고 있다.

내 사랑 한강

한강의 기적. 내 사랑 한강이 품고 있는 어휘(語彙)다.

내 가슴 속에선 언제나 '하면 된다. 할 수 있다'는 말이 나의 마음을 뭉클하게 한다.

내 나라와 나를 소통시키고 있는 한강은 대한민국 강원도 금대봉의 검룡소에서 발원되어 한반도 중부를 가로지르면서 서울을 지나고 태평양을 지나 기적적으로 재미한국인으로 사는 내 가슴 속까지 흘러들어와 머문다.

서울에서 사랑을 타고 내가 사는 현지까지 뻗쳐 온 한강 물줄기는, 내가 해외에서 재미교포라는 카테고리 안에서 살아갈 수 있는 영양수액을 공급받는 생명줄이다. 나는 생각만 해도 가슴 설레게 하는 내 사랑 한강물이 때론 생수가 되어 시원히 내 마음을 적셔주기 때문에 오늘도 생동감 있게 현지에서 살 수 있음을 안다.

기적을 일으키는 한강은 우리 민족의 가슴 속을 흐르는 영혼의 강이요, 내 사랑이다.

아~, 내 사랑 한강! 나는 생각만 해도 가슴이 벅차오른다.

베틀

지금은 제2한강의 기적을 바라는 세대에 살고 있다. 나는 이미 역사적인 한강의 기적을 체험한 세대를 살아온 것이다. 6·25, 4·19, 5·16, 새마을 운동, 월남 파병, 광주민주화운동, 88올림픽 등 최초의 여성 대통령.

시골에서 태어난 나는 줄곧 지방에서 생활했기 때문에 여고 시절에야 한강을 직접 눈으로 볼 수 있었지만, 한강은 서울을 대표하는 강(江)이요, 또한 우리나라를 상징하는 아름답고 보배로운 한반도의 중요한 강임을 듣고 배워서 잘 안다. 대한민국 국민의 한 사람으로서 내 사랑 한강이 품고 있는 '한강의 기적'이라는 말을 수없이 들으면서 지금껏 살아왔다. 오늘날 재미동포의 삶을 잇대어 가는 나의 가슴 속에도 조국의 혼이 서린 한강이 흐르고 있는 것이다.

열약한 김포 국제공항에서 비행기를 탄 후, 한강을 스쳐 지나오면서도 가슴이 막혀 사랑한다는 말도 못하고 안타까운 마음만 지닌 채 1970년대부터 나는 해외생활을 하고 있다. 그런데 지금은 자동차로 한강대교를 편안한 마음으로 지나 세계 최고의 인천 국제공항을 넘나들고 있다. 시대와 환경은 달라졌어도 한강을 말없이 바라볼 때마다 나는 왠지 모르게 가슴이 울컥해지면서 한없는 연민이 일곤 한다.

생각만 해도 내 가슴이 뛰는 한강. 보고 또 보아도 아름답기만 한 한강. 보고 있으면서도 또다시 떨어져 지내야 하는 아쉬움에 눈시울이 젖어드는 한강. 지금은 머나먼 곳에서 무사함을 비는 마음으로 그리움을 달래야 하는 한강. 한강은 내 영혼을 신선하게 해 주는 영원한 내 사랑이다.

한국전쟁 후 가난이 서러워 울던 시대로부터 새마을 운동 이후 경제

부흥이 급속히 일어나, 도움을 받는 나라에서 도움을 주는 나라로 변한 것을 한강의 기적이라 사람들은 말한다. 내 사랑 한강은 야경이 황홀할 정도로 아름다운 물줄기를 뿜어내 보는 사람으로 하여금 희망이 솟아나게 하지만, 때로는 피와 눈물이 섞여 있고, 뼈를 깎는 아픔을 감당해 내면서 조국을 위해 헌신하는 영혼들이 그 속에 있음을 나는 안다. 그러기에 한강은 살아 숨 쉬고 있고 영혼을 새롭게 하는 기적을 일으키는 강인가 보다. 난 지금은 미국에서 살고 있지만 언제라도 나를 품어 줄 한강이 있어 외로운 줄도 모르고 고단함도 잊고 감사한 마음으로 은혜답게 하루를 살아갈 수 있나 보다.

내가 우리 영토를 넓혀간다고 자부하고서 재미동포로 생활하기 시작할 무렵에는 미국 사람들은 이 세상에 대한민국이 존재한다는 사실도 잘 알지 못했다. 그럴 때마다 나는 지구본을 손으로 돌려 가면서 혀가 닳도록 우리 민족을 설명해야 했다. 그런데 88 국제올림픽 이후로는 대한민국의 위상이 높아져 전자제품 하면 코리아, 그리고 한강, 김치, 불고기라는 용어쯤은 거의 확실히 발음하는 사람들이 많아졌다. 근래에는 한국 최초의 여성 대통령이 미국의회 상·하원 합동연설을 영어로 한 데 대해 놀라는 사람들이 많다. 한국은 행복한 통일 여행을 꿈꾸고 있다는 비전이 있는 연설을 국제언어로 들으면서, 나는 제2의 한강의 기적을 이미 본 느낌이 들었다.

조국이 경제적으로 부강하고 든든해야 해외동포 생활이 수월하다. 십여 년 전에 있었던 LA 폭동 사건에서 본 것처럼 힘이 없어 억장이 무너지는 억울함을 당했음을 우리는 간과해서는 안 된다. 공식적으로는 한인들과 흑인들 사이에 갈등이 있어서 LA 폭동이 일어났다고 하

베틀

나, 사실은 그렇지 않았음을 현지 부근에서 사는 나는 알고 있다. 힘이 없는 민족이어서, 이민생활에서 오는 언어장벽 때문에 갖는 가슴에 서린 한(恨)을 긴 한숨으로 허공에 날려 보내 버려야 하는 억울한 희생자들의 모습을 나는 보았다. 모든 것을 포용하며 뼛골이 아프도록 노력하면서 열심히 사는 선한 재미동포들의 아픈 가슴을, 내일의 기적을 바라보고 있는 한강이 오늘도 어루만져 주면서 위로해 주기에 그래도 위안을 받으면서 희생자들은 살고 있음을 안다.

나는 한 사람의 인격을 소중히 여기며 서로 사랑하며 다른 인종과 잘 조화되도록 노력하여 화목하게 살기를 원한다. 나 자신이 진정으로 아름답게 변화되어 자랑스러운 재미한국인으로서 또다시 뜨거운 열정과 도전으로 내일에 대한 꿈을 안고 살아가는 그날이 오면, 나는 제2한강의 기적이 내 가슴속에서 일어났다고 말하리라. 인간의 힘으론 할 수 없는데 이루어지는 것이 기적이라 말한다면, 나는 신이 내려주신 축복이라 말하고 싶다. 나라에 공헌할 아무런 능력이 없는 약한 나지만 날마다 새로운 삶 속에서 지구촌 평화와 행복을 빌면 하늘이 웃는다.

이제는 인생의 가을 소풍을 즐기고 있는 시기여서인지, 땅에 떨어져도 줍고 싶은 빛깔 고운 단풍잎이나 노랗게 물든 은행잎처럼 살고 싶은 생각이 크다.

어느 날, 서울에 있는 내 사랑 한강을 보면 재미동포로 아름답게 살려고 노력했노라고, 이제는 단풍 같은 향기를 지니고 다시 찾아왔노라고 나는 말 하고 싶다. 내 가슴 속에 파묻혀 있는 그리움을 한강물에 와락 쏟아 부으면서-.

오! 내 사랑 한강.

| 2부 |

베틀

감사한 은퇴

참으로 감사한 일이다. 내가 정년퇴직을 생각하게 되다니-. 은퇴는 대략 육십 대에서 하는데, 언제나 비실비실한 내가 이 나이까지 살았다는 것만으로도 감사한 은퇴다. 나는 백의의 천사라고 불리기도 하는 간호사로서 세상에서 가장 귀한 생명을 다루는 의료계에서 사랑을 펼치려 노력하면서 살았는데, 이제는 은퇴를 생각하게 된다. 기적적으로 46년간을 병동에서 일할 수 있었던 것은 온전히 하나님의 은혜라 생각한다. 은퇴는 새로운 삶의 시작이라 하지 않던가. 나는 또 다른 새로운 삶을 위해서 씨를 뿌려 싹을 틔우고 잘 키워서 인생 이모작을 잘 결실하고 싶다. 은퇴 이후의 삶은 신앙을 가진 한국문학인으로서 긍지를 갖고 문학을 더욱더 사랑하며 이웃들과 아름답고 행복하게 살고 싶은 게 나의 꿈이다.

두 손으로 촛불을 받들고 하얀 유니폼을 입고서 간호사의 상징인 캡을 쓴 후, 나는 일생을 의롭게 살며… 나이팅게일 서약문을 엄숙한 모습으로 외우던 때가 1972년. 되돌아보면 참으로 멀고도 결코 쉽지만은 않았던 의료계 생활을 번 아웃(Burn out)하지 않고 봉직할 수 있었음은 보이지 않게 돌보아주신 손길이 있음을 믿고 살 수 있었음에 감사할 뿐이다. 잦은 교통사고가 있었음에도 불구하고 보람을 느낄 수 있는 간호사로서 정상적인 업무를 할 수 있었음에 감사한다. 현지 간호사 자격증을 따기 위해서 받은 정신적인 스트레스, 나만을 위해 살아온 듯한 사랑하는 아들을 하늘나라로 먼저 보내면서 받은 슬픔으로 죽고 싶은 유혹을, 구원받고 영원히 살 수 있는 신앙생활로 이겨낼 수 있었음에 감사한다. 피눈물이 나는 삶의 현장 속에서도 믿음 안에서 아름다운 인생살이를 하고 싶은 꿈이 항상 있었음에 감사할 뿐이다.

나의 처음 직장은 이십 대에 고국인 한국에서 5년을 전남 광주시에 있는 조선대학부속병원에서 지냈다. 졸업하기 전에 이미 취직시험에 합격한 젊음이 넘치는 낭만의 시절에 보낸 나의 첫 직장생활은 언제나 싱싱했다. 학교에서 배운 대로 정말 순수하게 나이팅게일 정신으로 환자들을 간호했다.

의대생들을 위해서 미리 신설한 의과대학 부속병원 병실에서 일하는 나는 첫 번째로 의대생들이 실습 나왔을 때의 감격을 잊을 수가 없다. 나는 첫 번째 직장에서 첫 번째 맞이한 크리스마스 때, 선물로 내과병동 의사들이 간호사들에게 선물해준 빨간색 토퍼론 스카프를 지금도 간직하고 있다. 아름다운 시절의 추억을 품고 있는 스카프는 신선하고 행복했던 시절을 추억하고 싶기에 나는 평생토록 간직하고 싶은가 보다.

나는 첫 직장에서 수간호사 시절에 결혼했고, 아들도 낳았다. 내 인생살이를 축복해 주고 격려해 주고 사랑으로 보살펴 주었던 반세기 전에 같이 일했던 동료들이 참 많이 생각난다. 어디에서 어떤 삶을 살고 있는지 궁금하고 아무쪼록 건강하고 행복하게 살기를 비는 마음이다.

다민족이 어우러져 생활하는 이민생활과 함께 삼십 대에 시작된 나의 새로운 직장생활은 언어와 환경에 적응하기에 바쁜 나날이었다. 지구촌 어디에서나 사람 살아가는 방법은 별다를 것 없다는 생각과 함께 빈혈이 날 정도로 욕망과 현실 사이에서 방황하기도 했다. 이 세상에서 가장 귀한 생명을 다루는 직업인지라 무엇보다도 사랑이 제일임을 절실히 느끼면서 글로벌 간호사라는 생각으로 열심히 일한 젊은 시절이다. 노스 홀리우드 커뮤니티병원(Community Hospital of North Hollywood)은 재미 동포로서의 꿈을 실현하기 위해서 시작한 첫 번째 나의 직장이다.

남편을 따라 이사하면서 쉽게 얻을 수 있는 직장은 몬터레이 파인(Monterey Pines SNF)이라는 양로병원이었다. 삶의 애환을 맛보면서 보낸 삼십 대, 사십 대, 오십 대 내 인생의 절반을 보낸 곳이다. 온갖 고난을 참고 견디면서 현지 정식 간호사(Resister Nurse)시험에 도전한 뒤, 1년에 2번씩, 8년 만인 16번째에 합격 통지를 받았을 때의 기쁨을 어찌 다 표현하랴. 내가 불이익을 당하면서도 하나밖엔 없는 사람의 생명을 귀하게 여기고 어머니처럼 한국 할머니를 간호해준 일은, 나는 역시 한국의 얼을 가지고 살아가는 한국인임을 스스로 굳게 느낄 수 있는 기회였다. 사람은 이 세상 어디에서나 자기가 살기 위해서 몸부림친다는 사실을 터득하기도 한 곳이다. 세찬 세상 바람에 꺾이지 않으려고 휘어지면서도 다시금 곧게 세워 견뎌온 세월이다.

나는 이제 육십 대로 은퇴를 준비하고 있다. 내가 이곳, 은퇴의 집 병동에서 파트 타임, 풀 타임으로 이십오 년을 지내고서 은퇴를 생각할 수 있게 된 것은 하나님의 은혜요, 만남의 인연을 갖은 때부터 나를 도와주고 있는 익스큐티브 디렉터 노마(Executive Director, Norma B) 덕분이라고 말할 수 있다. 내 동생이나 된 것처럼 오랜 세월 동안 나를 옆에서 보살펴 준 메리 안(Marry Ann)과 로웨나(Rowena)… 정말이지 수많은 동료들의 도움이 없었다면 오늘의 나는 없었을 것이다. 이 병원은 꽃이 많고, 깨끗하고, 사랑이 많은 곳이다. 내 생애에 잊을 수 없는 이곳엔 제이드 가든(Jade Garden)이 있는데, 5억 년 전의 숨결을 품은 옥수석이 운치 있게 모자이크된 뜨락에 조형되어 있어 뭇사람들의 사랑을 받고 있다. 수억 년 전에 형성된 옥수석의 침묵은 진실된 세월의 흐름 속에서 나도 영원 속의 한 점으로 이음새가 되고 있는 귀한 생명체임을 느끼게 해준다.

이제, 나는 은퇴를 생각할 수 있어 기쁘다. 미주이민 1세로 살아온 나의 삶의 흔적이 하나님 보시기에 합당한 삶이 된다면 얼마나 좋겠는가. 은퇴 후의 삶은 주위의 사람들과 사랑을 나누며 신앙을 가진 한국 문학인으로서 더욱더 아름답고 행복한 인생살이가 되도록 노력해야 할 것이다. 이 시간 나는, 지금까지 건강 허락해주시고 내 평생 직업이 생명을 귀하게 여기는 간호사의 삶으로 이끌어주신 하나님께 감사드리며 영광을 올려드릴 뿐이다. 어느 날이 될지는 모르지만 참으로 감사한 은퇴라 생각한다.

베틀

그리운 봉선화

봉선화.

왜 이리 고향의 봉선화가 보고 싶은 걸까? 내가 고향에 두고 온 것 중에서 가장 많이 생각나게 하는 꽃이다. 요즈음도 눈 감고 고향 생각을 하면 봉숭아가 터지고 눈 뜨고 숟가락을 만져도 따다닥 터지는 소리로 변한다. 손을 살짝이라도 대면 씨방을 터트리면서 반가움을 표시하는 봉선화 생각뿐이다.

어느 날부터 나는 재미동포 생활을 시작했는데 "이를 앙다물고 살아야 한다."라는 어머니의 말씀 따라 힘든 디아스포라의 삶에서도 고향을 잊지 않고 인내하며 살아야 했다. 그 힘의 근원은 어쩜 한여름날 뜨거운 뙤약볕 아래서 시들시들 처량한 모습이었다가도 밤이슬에 다시 힘을 얻어 살아났던 봉선화 때문이라 싶다. 아름다운 꽃을 피우고 나의 손톱을 빨갛게 물들게 한 봉선화. 어쩌면 어린 가슴을 신기함으로 들뜨게 했던 내 고향 봉선화의 혼이 내 가슴에 항상 잠재했기 때문이리다.

나는 오늘도 이곳에 있는 봉선화가 아닌 줄기를 따라 마디마디에 소박한 꽃을 피우는 그리운 내 고향 토종봉숭아나 접봉숭아를 찾아 눈을 크게 뜬다. 그리하여 귀를 나발통처럼 넓게 열고서 이리저리 헤맨다. 언젠가는 그리운 내 고향 봉숭아꽃을 이곳 뜨락에 심어 꽃핀 빨강·주홍·흰색봉숭아 얼굴들을 보면서 하루하루를 즐겁게 살고 싶은 소망이 있기에 그렇다.

　내가 살던 소쿠리 마을은 낮은 구릉과 산들로 둘러싸여 있어서 시골이라기보다는 산골에 가깝다. 나무가 많고 잡풀이 많아서인지 집 안에서 지네나 뱀들도 가끔 볼 수 있었다. 그런데도 장독대에 뱀이 들어갔다는 말을 들은 적이 없다. 어머니 말씀대로 신기하게 봉선화 꽃이 있는 곳엔 해충과 파충류들이 얼씬도 못했다. 그 탓에 마을 집집마다 장독대 둘레나 울 밑 이곳저곳에 봉숭아꽃이 심어져 있었다. 그야말로 소쿠리 마을 전체가 봉선화로 물들인 마을이었다.

　아름다운 정서를 제공해 주던 내 유년시절의 우리 집은 봄을 기다리는 아버지의 가슴에서부터 만들어지곤 했다. 봄이 오기 전 토담 아래에 있는 꽃밭은 겨우내 쌓아 두었던 땔감과 볏단이 치워지고, 아버지의 말씀에 오빠가 삽으로 땅을 깊게 판 후 흙을 골라 보송보송하게 만들었다.

　토담 아래 있는 꽃밭에 마지막 잔설이 녹아내리기 시작하면 어머니는 서랍 속에 고이 간직해 둔 봉선화 꽃씨와 다른 꽃씨들을 꺼낸다. 그리고는 언니에게 건네주면서 꽃밭에 심으라 하셨다. 언니는 물론이고 나의 손에도 호미를 쥐게 했다. 어느 사이에 꽃밭에 온 새언니랑 언니와 나는 촉촉한 땅을 호미로 파고 골을 만들었다. 우리는 봉선화 꽃씨를 구분해서 심고 곁에는 다른 꽃씨들도 함께 뿌리곤 했다.

다음 날부터 나는 매일 아침저녁 꽃밭에 새싹이 나오기를 고대하며 물을 준다. 일주일이 지나면 연초록 봉선화 새싹이 땅을 헤집고 고개를 쏙 내밀고 나온다. 그 경이로움은 이루 말할 수 없는 생명의 환희를 주곤 했다. 키도 아담하게 자라고 가지가지마다 이파리들이 무성하게 자란 후엔 옆구리마다 봉선화 꽃들이 맺히기 시작한다. 그런데 여름꽃들이 꽃망울을 터트리면서 활짝 피기 시작하면, 비바람과 소나기가 뭉친 태풍이 한 번씩 불어와 사정없이 후려치기도 한다. 때아닌 재난에 봉선화의 몸이 흔들리고 가지들이 시련을 이기지 못해 찢어져 피를 흘리기도 한다. 하지만 상처를 부여안고 수많은 역경을 견뎌낸 후 마침내 소담한 꽃을 피워 내는 행복의 화신, 그게 바로 봉선화였다.

우리 집 여자들은 한여름날을 골라 봉선화를 물들이는 날로 잡는다. 어머니는 시장에 가서 하얀 차돌 같은 백반을 사오신다. 새언니는 꽃을 따서 꽃물이 진하게 들도록 수분을 증발시키려고 시들시들하게 장독대 위에다 말린다. 언니는 텃밭에서 아주까리잎을 따고 굵직한 무명실 꾸리를 챙긴다. 나는 주먹만 한 돌을 야산에서 주워와 해가 질 무렵에 봉선화 꽃과 이파리 몇 개를 백반이랑 함께 넣어 토방에서 돌로 찧는다.

산골 집 마당 멍석 위에서 향기로운 모깃불을 켜놓고 저녁을 먹은 후엔 가족이 봉선화 꽃물들이기 위해서 고개를 맞댄다. 늙어 보이는 어머니도 "수줍은 처녀처럼 꽃물이 예쁘게 들어야 할틴디!" 하시면서 손가락을 내미신다. 새언니는 "우리 예쁜 아가씨들이 세상에서 제일 멋있는 신랑감을 만날 수 있도록, 첫눈이 올 때까지 봉숭아꽃물이 잘 들게 해 달라!"라고 익살스럽게 말한다. 그리고는 언니와 나의 손톱 위에 잘 찧어놓은 봉숭아꽃을 얹고서 아주까리잎으로 싸맨 후 물이 흐르지 않도록 새언니는 무명실로 꼭꼭 묶어 주었다.

그다음 날이면 아빠의 흐뭇해하시는 미소, 오빠들의 장난스러운 말, 손톱이 빨갛게 꽃물들인 보며 서로 즐거움을 나누었다. 이게 고향 소쿠리 마을 여름날의 낭만적이고 아름다운 풍광이었다. 이렇게 손톱과 발톱에 꽃물을 들이면서 가족 간의 사랑과 소중함을 느끼면서 행복했던 추억이다.

이제는 이를 앙다물고 살지 않아도 될 것 같다. 그래서일까? 내 가슴 속에 서려 있는 고향의 토종 봉선화를 내 눈으로 직접 보며 살고 싶어진다. 그리고 내 딸들의 손톱에도 봉선화로 꽃물을 들인 추억을 만들어 주고 싶어진다.

베틀

냉이 향취

냉이 향취가 나는 참 좋다.

내 후각(嗅覺)을 감미롭게 하는 봄나물인 냉이 향취 속엔 우리 시어머님과 시누님 그리고 시고모님의 사랑이 섞여 있다. 그래서 나는 더욱더 좋다. "애~야! 이 냄새 좀 맡어 보거라이 얼매나 향내가 좋으냐~. 냉이 향취가 좋지라우?" 정감있는 남도 사투리의 보유자이신 시어머님과 시누님이 번갈아 가면서 땅에서 뿌리까지 막 캐어낸 봄나물인 냉이를 내 코앞에 내밀면서 냉이 향취를 음미해 보란다. 시어머님과 나보다 연상인 시누님이 사랑의 손가락으로 캐어 낸 들풀 냉이 향취에 흠뻑 젖어 나는 행복에 취해 버렸다.

동서고금을 막론하고 고부간의 갈등이니, '시(媤)' 자만 들어도 몸에서 경련이 일어날 것 같고 참고 살기 힘들다는 이야기가 있다. 시어머니와 말다툼할 때 말리는 시누이가 더 밉다는 말도 있다. 그만큼 여자들에겐 출가해서 다른 환경에서 살아온 시댁 사람들과 조화롭게 살아야 하는 시집살이가 만만치 않다는 말이 되겠다. 결혼이라는 전환점에서 운명적인 만남의 고부간의 대화 소통법으로 나처럼 뭔가 잘 모르는 어수룩한 사람이 되어 보는 것도 좋을 것 같다는 생각을 해 본다. 내가 '시' 자가 앞에 붙은 시어머님과 시누님의 사랑을 무등산 자락에서 받은 이유는, 시골에서 살았는데도 '냉이'를 아리송하게 알고 있을 뿐인 내 성격 때문이었기에 말이다. 어리벙벙한 내 코앞에 냉이 나물을 들이대는 시어머님과 시누님은 확실히 나에게 가르쳐 주심에 흐뭇해하신 것이다. 어수룩한 나에게 뜻하지 않은 선물인 행복이 찾아올 줄이야.

무등산(無等山)의 봄은 정의(正義)의 정기(精氣)를 뿜어 내는 듯이 참으로 늠름하면서도 신선하다. 무등산을 바라보면서 사는 사람들은 광주 학생독립운동, 광주민주화항쟁 등 정의로운 일에는 목숨까지도 아끼지 않고 앞장서고 있음은 무등산의 신비로운 산세(山勢) 때문인지도 모른다. 그러면서도 한없이 여린 남도 소리꾼들의 노랫소리, 소화 기관인 뱃속이 아니라 사고(思考)하는 뇌 속 깊숙이 박혀 있는 실핏줄까지 팽대해져 머릿통을 휘두른 후 뒤통수를 날카롭게 친 울림으로 내는 떨림의 소리가 충장로에 있는 수많은 국악원에선 끊임없이 울려 나오고 있다. 너무도 황당하게 가슴에 상처받은 역사의 현장에서 소리꾼들이 아무리 소리친들 그 한(恨)을 어찌 다 품어 낼 수 있으랴. 그런데… 참으로 신기하다. 무등산 자락에서 자란 냉이 향취는 피비린내도 중화시킬 수 있을 만큼 놀랍도록 심오(深奧)해 모든 것을 껴안고서 은은한 향내를 발하고 있음을 나는 시어머님의 한없이 너그러운 사랑을 통해서 느끼고 있다. 시어머님 앞에 서면 나는 언제나 부끄럽고 죄송스러운 며느리임에도 불구하고 며느리 도리도 못한다고 원망하시기는커녕 무등산 줄기의 냉이 향취로 나를 흠뻑 사랑에 취하게 하신 시어머님이 아닌가.

나는 고마운 마음에 생(生)의 환희(歡喜)를 느끼며, 관용과 사랑을 베풀 수 있는 마음을 가질 수 있게 하는 기적의 냉이 향취에 놀라곤 한다. 냉이 향취가 배어 있는 무등산 정기에 휩싸여 있는 땅에선, 무조건 나를 용서해 주시고 사랑해 주시는 한없이 넓고도 넓은 가슴의 시어머님과 시누님 그리고 시고모님도 살고 계신다. 즐거운 마음으로 또다시 찾아오라고 나를 부르시면서.

무등산에 피어오르는 봄의 운기(雲氣)가 의연하게 대지에 드리워짐일까. 무등산 자락에 샛노랗게 피어나는 개나리꽃들이, 기억 속에 상처받은 영혼들을 위로해 주기 위해 하늘에서 막 하강(下降)한 선녀들의 옷자락같이 신선하고 아름다워서 바라보는 내가 숨도 제대로 쉴 수가 없었다. 이렇게 아름다울 수가! 하늘에서 내려온 선녀들이 무등산 정기에 매료되어 샛노란 개나리꽃으로 변해서 멋있는 산과 어우러져 그냥 사는 느낌을 주었다. 시누님이 나를 무등산 구경시켜 준다고 산 중턱까지 차로 드라이브시켜 주니 동심이 된 나는 무등산에 피어 있는 선녀들 옷자락 같은 샛노란 개나리 꽃구경에 옆에 계신 시어머님도 의식 못 할 정도로 환성을 지르며 참으로 행복해했다. 웬일이었을까? 나는 그때 느닷없이 냉이가 생각이 나서 무등산에 있는 냉이가 보고 싶다고 했다. 우리 시어머님과 시누이는 나의 말이 떨어지자마자 냉이를 찾기 위해 차에서 몇 번이나 내려 산속을 헤맸으나 못 찾고 결국 무등산 끝자락에 있는 밭두렁에서 냉이를 찾았다. 냉이는 산채가 아니고 들풀임을 늦게서야 깨닫기도 했다.

냉이는 봄바람에 잔설이 녹아내리기 시작하면 양지바른 언덕이나 밭두렁 논두렁에서 쑥이나 달래나 꽃다지들과 함께 자라나는 흔히 보는 민들레와 비슷하나 하얀색 꽃이 피는 아주 상긋한 향기를 천지에 내는 겨잣과의 두해살이풀이란다. 살아오면서 많이도 먹은 향기 좋고 맛있는 봄나물인데 나는 이름은 알면서도 모양엔 관심을 두지 않아 아리송했을 뿐이다. 냉이는 봄나물 중에서도 단백질이 많고 무기질이 많아 몸에 아주 좋은 친환경 건강식이어서 특히나 채식주의자들에게 꼭 권하는 봄나물이라나. 나도 건강해지려면 냉잇국을 먹어야 한다는 생각과 함께 우리 시어머님이 직접 담그신 맛있는 된장으로 무등산 줄기에서 캐낸 파릇파릇한 향기 좋은 냉이를 넣어 끓인 맛깔스러운 냉이 된장국을 먹고 싶다. 구순이 되시는 시어머님의 무릎이 관절염으로 아프셔도 무등산 자락에서 냉이를 발견하시게 되면 또다시 나를 위해 냉이를 손가락으로 후벼서 캐실 것이다. 나는 아는고로 미리부터 준비해야 할 냉이를 땅에서 캐낼 도구와 나물 바구니의 모양을 그려보고 있다.

"아무쪼록 시어머님과 시누님 그리고 자네, 냉잇국이 먹고 싶다고 나한테 진작 말하제 그랬능가–," 하시던 인자하신 시고모님. 언제나 내 위치의 도리(道理)를 못해 죄인 같은 내 마음은 아랑곳하지 않으시고 따뜻한 사랑을 주시기만 하는 시집 식구들과 함께 다음 해에도 또다시 무등산을 드라이브하면서 선녀들 옷같이 예쁜 개나리꽃도 구경하고 풋풋하고 상긋한 냉이도 캐서 맛있는 냉이 된장국을 끓여 먹었으면 좋겠다. 나는 오늘도 소박한 나의 꿈이 꼭 이루어지길 빌면서 새로 올 봄날을 기다리며 행복해하는 자신을 본다. '시(媤)' 자가 붙은 시어머님과 시누님 그리고 시고모님의 사랑이 섞여 있는 냉이 향취에 취해서.

베틀

철커덩 철거더엉.

오늘도 나는 베틀 위에 앉아서 고국을 떠나 다른 나라의 땅에서 살면서 이민자의 삶이라는 아름다운 피륙을 짜고 있다. 한국인이라는 근본이 되는 정적인 날줄 위에 이민자라는 동적인 씨줄을 북에 담아 적당하게 뿌려주면서 힘차게 피륙을 짠다. 희망에 찬 '미주한인'이란 정겨운 베틀가를 부르면서.

철커덩 철거더엉.

이민 초기의 나는 거칠고 까슬까슬한 삼대껍질을 벗겨서 만든 실로 피륙을 짜기 시작했다. 강하고 질긴 누런 색깔의 삼실을 북에 담아서 열심히 손놀림하면서 이민 시작의 피륙을 짜기 시작한 것이다. 참으로 어떻게 해야 하는지, 방법이 익숙지 못해서 당황할 때가 잦았다. 때때로 실이 끊어져서 다시금 이으면 그때마다 매듭이 생겼고 힘든 노동으로 한숨과 눈물이 흘러내려 내가 짠 피륙에 진한 얼룩이 지곤 했다.

새로운 자격증을 따는 데 있어 언어장애 때문에 갖은 고생을 했으며, 또 직장에서 교육을 받을 때도 몇 배나 더 노력해야만 했다. 답답한 가슴은 터질 것 같았고 움츠러들기만 하는 내 영혼의 고통 탓에 피륙이 고르지 못하고 울퉁불퉁했다.

그뿐인가! 햄버거와 커피를 즐기는 사람들 틈에서 빠져나와 신토불이 김치와 고추장을 찾아 먼 길을 다녀와 고향에 대한 향수와 연민, 눈물과 외로움으로 짠 피륙은 한없이 느슨했다.

나의 꿈나무인 아이들이 태어나서 학교에 가기 시작하니 또 다른 문제점들이 생겨났다.

아이들은 학교에 갔다 오면 자주 우울해하고 울먹거렸다. 친구들과 재미있게 놀고 싶은데 다들 피한단다. 친구를 붙들고 왜 그러느냐고 물었더니 자기는 놀고 싶지만, 부모들이 눈이 옆으로 째진 동양인들과는 놀지 말라고 했단다. 친구들로부터 상처받는 여리디여린 우리 아이들. 이민가정으로서 각박하기만 한 생활전선의 이중성에 시달리던 이민 초기의 삶, 무엇보다 경제적인 안정부터 찾아야 했다.

아이들 말에 북을 쥔 손에 나도 모르게 힘이 너무 들어가서 삼베실이 뚝 끊어져 버렸다. 다시금 실을 잇는 나의 손은 떨렸고 이은 자리는 또 다른 매듭으로 남았다. 북을 잡은 손과 베틀신을 신은 나의 발이 떨려서 제대로 고운 피륙은 짤 수 없었지만, 그래도 허리에 띤 베틀 띠를 더 단단히 묶어 가면서 피륙 올올이 땀과 인내와 희망을 섞어 무지개 꿈을 안고서 열심히 짜고 또 짰다.

이때는 내가 짠 천으로 옷을 해 입으면서 참으로 안타까운 심정에 실보다도 더 질긴 인내를 배웠다. 기다리므로 고달픈 이주민의 한 사람인 나의 베틀가를 부르면서.

철커덩 철거더엉.

베틀

어느 날부터인가는 하얀 목화송이에서 실을 뽑아낸 따뜻하고 푹신한 무명실로 피륙을 짜기 시작했다. 베틀신, 북 등 베틀에 딸린 기구들을 어떻게 이용해야 더욱더 아름다운 피륙을 짤 수 있는지 차츰 터득하고 있었다.

아이들도 이민가정과 현 생활의 이중성을 인정하고 지혜롭게 생활해 나갔다. 신 앞에 모든 인간은 평등하다는 중요한 진리를 알게 한 신앙 생활의 도움이 컸다. 나는 아이들을 위해 학교에서 내가 할 수 있는 자원봉사를 했다. 아이들이 노는 놀이터를 보살펴 주기도 하고, 미술 시간에 학부모 교사가 되어 동양화의 기본이 되는 사군자 그리는 법을 가르치기도 했다. 학교 오픈하우스 때 가보니 내가 지도해서 그린 학생들의 그림이 교실 한 면을 차지하고 있어서 마음이 흐뭇했다. 이 시기에 내가 짠 피륙은 매끄럽기 그지없었다.

철커덩 철거더엉.

나는 더욱 심혈을 기울여서 견고하고 탄탄한 하얀 무명천을 짰다. 나의 꿈나무인 자녀와 함께 행복한 나날을 꿈꾸면서. 그런데 또 한 번 내 인생의 뜻하지 않은 말할 수 없는 사고로 입은 상처 때문에 크게 구멍 뚫린 피륙은 다시는 회복될 수 없는 흠집으로 남아 있다. 응혈 된 피로 말미암아 피륙 일부분이 삭아져 버렸기 때문이다. 그래도 나는 묵묵히 베틀 위에 앉아서 새로운 피륙을 짜기 위해서 몸을 움직였다. 한 순례자 이주민인 나의 베틀가를 부르면서.

철커덩 철거더엉.

지금, 내가 짜는 피륙은 누에고치에서 실을 뽑은 보드라운 명주실에 상큼한 코발트색 물감을 들인 곱디고운 명주다. 이 명주 한 필을 다 짜고 나면 양장점에 맡겨서 예쁜 옷 한 벌 지어 입을 것이다. 소매가 긴 블라우스와 무릎을 덮는 에이라인 스커트를. 그리고는 아이들이 주관하는 즐거운 잔치에 참석할 것이다. 이 소망을 갖고 현대적으로 개량된 베틀 위에 앉곤 한다.

이제 우리 아이들은 이민 가정인 것조차 잊은 듯 이곳 미국생활에 동화되어 뿌리에 대한 정체성이 희박해지고 있다. 이 시대는 인터내셔널 시대란다. 나는 두렵다. 너무나 토속적인 내 예쁜 실크 옷차림이 아이들이 초대해 주는 세련된 이름의 파티에서 어색하거나 어울리지 않을까 봐.

그럼에도, 오늘도 나는 피륙을 짜는 힘과 능력이 있다는 것만으로 감사하면서 베틀 위에 앉아서 코발트색 명주를 짜고 있다. 영원세계에 계시는 우리 어머니나 할머니가 그랬던 것처럼, 아무쪼록 세상이 평온해져서 사랑스러운 자녀가 행복하게 살기를 염원하는 한 여인네로 신기하고 운명적인 나의 베틀가를 부르면서….

철커덩 철거더엉.

베틀

떡방아

정겹다. 쿵덕- 쿵덕- 떡방아 찧는 소리가.

하이얗게 부푼 떡쌀을 절구통에 넣고서 절굿공이로 절구질하는 소리가 장단 맞춰 들린다. 맛있는 떡으로 만들어지기 위해선 거친 쌀들이 절구통 속에서 찧어져야 한다. 더하여 떡가루가 고울수록 떡이 더 부드럽고 감칠맛이 있기에 빻은 떡가루를 체로 거르는 힘든 작업을 한다. 나도 내 인생의 맛있는 떡을 만들기 위한 고운 떡가루를 만들려면 더 많이 신앙인 떡방아에서 찧어지고, 잘 빻아진 고운 가루를 숭숭 구멍이 나 있는 얼정이 체가 아닌 이성의 가는 체로 더 많이 걸러내는 수고를 해야 할 것이다. 가벼운 고운 가루가 되어 바람을 타고 두둥실 하늘나라로 올라가려면.

내가 만일 사람들과 함께 으깨어지면서 사는 특별히 맛있는 인절미 같은 인생이라면, 혀끝에 걸리는 떡옴이 되지 않기를 소망하면서 오늘도 나는 내 인생의 떡방아를 찧는다. 쿵덕- 쿵덕-.

생각 속에 있는 나의 유년의 뜰은 언제나 아름답다. 그곳에는 언제나 우리 어머니와 새언니가 나를 위해 사랑의 떡방아를 찧으시던 곳이기 때문일 것이다. 보통 시골 생활에선 떡은 별미다. 나의 유년시절은 전쟁 후 참으로 힘든 시골 생활이어서 쌀농사를 짓는 사람들도 명절이나 특별한 날이 아니고선 떡이 먹고 싶어도 함부로 떡을 해 먹을 수가 없었다. 그런데도 가족들의 생일이나 내 생일은 어김없이 맛있는 떡을 먹을 수 있었던 건 내 생애의 한 축복의 측면일 것이다.

내 생일은 팥고물을 얹은 찹쌀 시루떡이 나를 행복하게 했다. 그리고 가끔은 인절미였는데, 물에 불린 찹쌀을 시루에 쪄서 그대로 절구통에 쏟아 부은 후 거친 떡쌀이 부서지고 으깨어져서 부드럽게 서로 찐득찐득 달라붙을 때까지 절굿공이로 찧은 후, 고소한 콩가루를 묻혀서 만든 떡이었다. 다른 떡과 달리 재래식으로 만드는 인절미는 언제나 두 명이 호흡을 맞춰야만 떡을 만들 수가 있다.

한 명은 떡을 치고, 한 명은 두리뭉실한 커다란 덩어리 떡에 물을 적셔주면서 잘 찧어질 수 있도록 이리저리 돌려주는 일이다. 새언니와 짝꿍이 되어 땀을 펄펄 흘리며 인절미를 만드신 어머니는 떡 맛을 보시면서 가끔은 얼굴에 못마땅한 표정을 짓기도 하셨다. 인절미에 떡쌀이 빻아지지 않은 옴이 너무 많아— 하시면서.

시골이나 산골 마당 한구석에 있는 절구통은 돌이나 나무 속을 파내 만든 생활도구다. 두텁고 기다란 나무를 손으로 잡기에 좋게 만든 절굿공이로 절구통에 들은 곡식을 쿵덕—쿵덕— 찧으면 원하는 만큼 곡식 껍질이 벗겨지거나 곡식이 바숴진다. 맛있는 떡을 만들려면 미리 쌀을 물에 담가서 불린 후 소쿠리에 담아 물을 빼고, 하이얗게 물에 부른 거친 쌀을 절구통에 넣은 후 절굿공이로 떡방아를 찧고, 더 부드럽고 고운 가루를 만들기 위해선 잘게 부서진 쌀가루를 고운 체로 몇

베틀

번이고 거르는 인내의 수고가 따른다. 이런 수고를 기쁨으로 감당하시면서 나의 생일을 위해서 맛있는 떡을 만드시고 위대하신 신神에게 나의 앞날을 기도하던 어머니의 정결한 모습이 눈에 선하다.

정성이 오롯이 담긴 그 아름다운 모습이 내 눈에 서릴 때면 나는 거친 내 말과 행동이 내 인생의 떡방아 속에서 더욱더 고운 가루로 찧어져야 한다는 생각을 한다. 그리고 맛있는 인절미같이 서로 찰떡 사랑으로 살아가는 오묘한 인생살이에서 깨어지지 않아 혀끝에 자극을 주는 떡옴같은 사람이 되지 않았으면 하는 소망이 크다.

쟁반같이 둥근 환한 보름달이 밤하늘에 휘영청 떠 있는 날은 나는 천연의 나라에서 떡방아를 찧는 옥토끼를 찾아 나선다. 커다랗고 밝은 보름달 속에는 계수나무 밑에서 옥토끼가 떡방아를 찧고 있다는 전래 동화가 있기에 나는 항상 그렇게 아름다운 모습을 달 속에서 찾곤 한다.

1969년 아폴로 우주선이 달 착륙했다는 충격적인 뉴스에 천연의 내 꿈의 나라를 파괴한 문명을 거부해 본 적도 있는 나. 한없이 신비하고 오묘한 아름다운 달나라에서 펼쳐보는 동심(童心)의 세계는 언제나 순수하고 아름답다. 내 꿈이 머물고 있는 그리도 순수하고 아름다운 내 꿈의 나라에서 살지 못하는 나는 몸과 마음이 세상 욕심으로 한없이 부풀고 거칠어져 있다.

오늘은 동심의 세계에서 살고 싶은지 오늘따라 더 밝고 커다란 둥근 보름달을 따다가 내 마음의 마당 한가운데에 내려놓는다. 나는 언제나 내 마음을 앗아가는 동화 나라 달 속의 신비한 옥토끼와 함께 신앙인 절구통으로 내 인생의 떡방아를 찧는다. 거칠어진 내 생각, 행동, 언어, 탐심, 교만 등을 집어넣고서. 신앙(信仰)의 떡방아로 찧고 또 찧고 이성

(理性)의 체로 거르고 또 거른다. 고운 가루로 떡을 빚어 제사를 드려야만 나를 빚으신 창조주께서 열납하시고, 흠향하실 것임을 알고 있기에. 떡옴이 있는 내 산 제물은 못마땅해 하심을 알고 있기에.

떡방아로 쿵덕 쿵덕 찧을 때 고운 가루로 부서짐은 얼마나 아름다운 아픔인가. 떡방아로 찧을 때 서로 으깨져 찐득찐득 붙음은 얼마나 아름다운 고역인가. 나는 그 아름다운 아픔과 고역을 은혜로 생각하고 기도하는 마음에 품곤 한다. 보통 사람인 나는 자유롭게 거주와 직장의 이동이 가능한 노마드 시대에서 인생살이 순례자의 길을 걷고 있다. 그러기에 나는 미세한 지체가 되어 시시때때로 새로운 많은 사람과 접촉하면서 공동체로 살아가게 된다.

지금은 떡방아를 요리조리 피해 깨어지지 않고 혀를 자극하는 인절미 속에 있는 옴같이 특별한 사람보다는 다른 사람들과 함께 으깨어져 찰떡 사랑으로 공동체 생활하기를 소원한다. 먼 훗날은 부서지는 아픔 속에서 고운 가루가 되어 하늘나라로 바람을 타고 두둥실 올라가고 싶은 열망이 크다. 그러기 위해서 나는 오늘도 내 꿈이 머물고 있는 천연의 나라에서 사는 옥토끼와 동무가 되어 소통하면서 내 인생살이 떡방아를 정겹게 찧는다. 쿵덕-쿵덕-.

*떡옴 = 떡가루를 만들 때 고운 가루 안 되고 토돌토돌 남아있는
       덩어리

베틀

아버지와 백로(白鷺)

어느 고을에 사라졌던 백로(白鷺)가 다시 돌아왔다는 소식에 내 가슴이 설렌다. 이 기쁜 소식을 들으니, 하얀 수염에 한복을 입으신 아버지께서 눈부신 깃털을 살짝 접고 청송(靑松) 위에 앉아있는 백로를 보시며 행복해하시는 모습이 한 폭의 신선도(神仙圖)처럼 내 눈에 아른거린다.

새해가 시작되면 아버지는 백로를 맞이하기 위해 발걸음을 앞동산으로 새벽 일찍이 수시로 옮기시는 모습을 볼 수 있었다. 날씨가 서늘해지자 어디론가 떠난 철새인 백로가 회귀본능(回歸本能)으로 다시 돌아올 시기가 되었다는 것이다. 백로는 길조(吉鳥)로 아버지의 좋은 친구다. 애타게 기다리던 친구 백로를 맞이한 날은 아버지의 얼굴은 온통 행복한 어린애처럼 싱글벙글이시다. '…백로가 왔어, 백로가— 올해도 좋은 일이 많을 거야~' 아버지는 너무도 기뻐서 울음소리에 가까운 목소리는 넓다란 아침마당을 진동시킨다. 아버지의 흥분된 소리에 가족들은 너나 나나 할 것 없이 마음이 들떠 환호하면서 앞동산으로 향한다.

어느 날이다. 마을 꼬마가 숨 가쁘게 아버지 앞에 달려와 떨리는 목소리로 제대로 말을 잇지 못하면서 보고한다. '… 사냥꾼이 초~ㅇ~으로 하늘로 날아가는 큰~새를 잡았어요. 논바닥에 떨어졌는데 피를 많이 흘리면서 퍼덕퍼덕거리다가 죽~었어요.' 그렇잖아도 총소리를 듣고 불안해하시던 아버지께서는 무슨 예감을 하셨는지 급하게 앞동산으로 뛰어가셨다. '날짐승을 잡는 몹쓸 놈의 사냥꾼이라니~ 백로가 무사해야 할 텐데.' 하시면서.

다음 날 아침, 아버지는 안심하신 표정으로 반가운 소식을 가족들에게 전해 주셨다. 백로 한 마리가 움직이지 않고 가만히 앉아 있고 한 마리가 날갯짓하며 주위를 맴도는 것이 아마도 알을 품고 있는 것 같다는 소식이었다.

나는 재외동포다. 그런데도 내 귀는 항상 고국을 향해 열려있고 마음은 고국에서 맴돈다. 솔바람 소리와, 솔향기가 자꾸만 나를 강대미 언덕 위로 이끈다. 정기 어린 모악산이 바라보이며 넓은 들판이 눈 아래 평화롭게 보이는 자연이 아름다운 강대미 언덕. 내가 어릴 적 꿈을 안고서 오르내리던 강대미 언덕에 백로가 서식한다는 소식은 언제나 들리려나-. 아버지와 백로가 대화를 나누면서 즐기시던 앞동산은 과수원으로 변한 지가 오래되었다 하니 백로가 찾아올 리가 없다. 그렇지만 아직도 사람의 정서를 키워주는 자연을 보유하고 있는 강대미 언덕은 소나무가 울창해지면 백로가 찾아들지도 모른다.

어느 날 나는 강대미 언덕 청송 위에 앉아 있는 백로와 대화를 나누면서 즐거워하는 백발의 나를 생각해 본다. 아버지와 백로처럼. 이루어질 수 없는 꿈이란 걸 알면서도 눈부신 백로의 아름다움에 넋을 잃고 앉아 있는 아름다운 풍광을 환상 속에서 그려만 봐도 나는 행복해진다.

베틀

얼레빗

옛날 어머니가 쓰시던 장롱 밑에는 공간이 있었는데 그곳에 항상 꼭 한 가지가 놓여 있었다. 대나무로 만든 머리빗 그릇이었는데 그 속에는 얼레빗, 참빗 그리고 머리 가르마를 타는 가늘게 잘 다듬어진 대나무 꼬챙이가 담겨 있었다.

얼레빗은 선이 굵고 엉성하고 간격이 넓게 만들어진 굵은 빗이고, 참빗은 가운데로 버팀목이 있어 균형을 잡아주면서 양쪽으로 촘촘하게 빗살이 선을 이루게 한 얇은 대나무 빗이다.

거울 앞에 앉은 어머니는 기다란 머리를 앞에서 뒤까지 대나무 꼬챙이로 한가운데 가르마를 타서 양어깨 앞으로 머리를 내려뜨린 후에 복잡한 생활을 가다듬듯 헝클어진 머리를 얼레빗으로 먼저 빗으셨다. 그리고 메마른 삶에 윤기라도 주려는 듯 동백기름을 손에 묻혀서 두 손으로 서너 번 문지른 후엔 머리카락에 촉촉이 바르신 후 천천히 꼼꼼하게 다시금 참빗으로 머리를 곱게 빗으셨다. 그 모습이 인생을 관조하는 듯한 여유로움으로 보였다.

그런 후엔 정성스럽게 빗겨진 머리카락 전체를 한 묶음으로 똬리를 틀어서 뒤통수에 붙이고 옥비녀, 은비녀, 금비녀를 번갈아 가면서 꽂은 어머니의 낭자 머리는 참으로 단아하고 아름다웠는데 가냘픈 여인의 고단한 삶이 빚어낸 영롱한 예술품 같았다. 한 가닥 흐트러짐 없이 곱게 빗어 낭자를 친 우리 어머니는 손거울을 들고서 요리조리 자신의 모습을 살펴보셨다. 아버지께서 곁으로 지나치시게 되면 "내 낭자 어때요?" 하면서 살짝 몸을 움직여 남편의 표정을 살필 때 어머니의 표정은 요염해 보이기까지 했다.

어느 날부턴가 늘 쓰시던 얼레빗이 하나둘씩 빗살이 떨어져 나가 엉성하여져 가는데도 어머니는 그대로 사용하셨다.

"머리빗이 오래 쓰니까 내 이빨처럼 삭아서 빠져나간다."

"엄마, 그럼 아버지가 장에 가실 때 새로 사오시라고 부탁하세요."

"애~애는 이렇게 쓸 수 있는데 뭐하러 새로 사느냐? 쓸 수 있을 때까정 써야지 무엇이든지 아껴야 살림이 되지 이까짓 것 별것 아니다 생각하고 그냥 버리기만 좋아하면 살림이 안 되는 것이여."

많은 자식을 키우시면서 일본강점기의 궁핍을 견디셨고 6·25 동란을 겪어내신 어머님의 몸에 밴 삶의 비결은 오직 '절약'뿐이셨으리라. 동란 이후의 가난을 이겨내기 위하여 나라에서는 절약정신을 기본으로 한 새마을 운동에 뒤따라 플라스틱 제품들이 물밀 듯이 쏟아져 나왔다. 첫째는 값이 쌌으며 엄청나게 질기고 다양한 모양과 색깔을 가진 플라스틱 제품 중에는 머리빗이 단연 판을 쳤다.

시장 입구나 가게 어느 곳을 가든지 흔히 눈에 띄는 머리빗이 어느 날 육교를 지나던 내 눈에 유난히 띄었다. 아니 마술에 걸린 것처럼 평

베틀

생 하나만 사면 끝이라고 떠들어대면서 머리빗을 두 손으로 세차게 밀쳐도 보이고 두들겨대기도 하면서 선전하는 머리빗 장수의 마법사 같은 흥미로운 소리에 흡입되었는지도 모른다. 나는 성글성글하게 빗살이 빠져있는 어머니의 얼레빗이 생각나서 얼른 하나를 샀다.

그리고 내 지갑에 넣고 다니기에 좋을 아주 작은 얼레빗도 샀다. 하나 사면 평생 쓸 수 있다는 말에 무엇이든지 아끼시는 어머니에게 적격이라는 생각이 들어서였다.

선물을 받으신 어머니는 기쁜 표정으로 받기는 하셨는데 사용하시지 않고 계속 대나무 향이 나는 이빨 빠진 얼레빗을 쓰고 계셨다. 그러나 나는 그 이유를 묻지 않았다.

그러던 어느 날이다. 어머니의 얼굴엔 희색이 만연하고 무척 행복해 보였다.

"느이 아버지가 무심한 것 같아도 내심 자상하시느니라. 얼레빗만 사와도 되는디."

5일 만에 서는 장날에 아버지께서 머리빗 한 벌을 새로 사 오셨다는 것이다. 남편의 사랑을 듬뿍 받은 아녀자의 행복스런 모습을 나는 그때 들뜬 어머니의 모습에서 처음 보았다. 앞머리 한가운데에 드러난 하얀 가르마와 하얀색 명주로 지은 치마저고리 한복을 곱게 입고 하얀 버선에 코빼기가 나온 하얀 고무신을 신은 모습이 어우러져 눈이 시릴 정도로 깨끗하고 단정한 어머니는 내 눈엔 이 세상에서 제일 우아한 미인이셨다.

그런데 어느 날 그러니까 아버지가 이 세상을 떠나신 후의 일이다. 한여름 몹시 따가운 날 시골 사람들이 말하는 호랑이 장가가는 날 소위 햇볕은 쨍쨍 쬐면서도 잠깐 동안 소낙비가 내리는 날이었다.

미장원이라고는 한 번도 가본 적이 없는 어머니가 신식바람이 났는지 아니면 남편이 없는 허전함에 견디지 못함이었는지 머리를 싹둑 짧게 잘라 버리고선 파마머리를 하셨다. 동그란 눈을 크게 뜨고서 기가 막혀 있는 막내딸의 표정이 멋쩍으셨던지 짧은 머리를 어색하게 쓰다듬으면서 "이젠 늙어가니 낭자 치기도 귀찮아서 머리를 잘랐더니 이렇게 더운 날인데도 시원하고 머리 빗기에 편해서 좋다." 하시며 내 시선을 피해버리셨다.

그 후론 어머니는 아버지가 사주신 대나무 얼레빗을 더이상 사용하지 않고 새로 산 빨강 플라스틱 머리빗을 사용하셨다. 한쪽으론 얼레빗 또 한쪽으론 참빗이 함께 있도록 만들어진 소위 신식 머리빗을.

머리에 착 달라붙어서 더욱더 까맣게 번들번들 윤이 나게 보이던 낭자 머리를 잘라버리고 푸수수하고 꼬불꼬불하게 지져 붙인 파마머리를 하신 어머니, 그날 나는 세월 따라 어쩔 수 없이 고운 자태가 무너져 내리는 어머니의 변색하여 가는 삶의 모습을 보는 것 같아 서글프도록 가슴이 아팠다.

지금은 어머니의 숨결도 낭자 머리를 위하여 어머니가 쓰시던 얼레빗도 사라졌지만, 어머니에게 선물하기 위해 플라스틱 얼레빗을 샀을 때 함께 샀던 내 조그만 얼레빗으로 상처받은 삶을 어루만지기라도 하듯 나는 가끔 부드럽게 머리를 빗곤 한다. 특히 어머니가 그리울 때면.

이 시간도 나는 대나무 향내에 동백기름이 배어서 반들반들 윤기가 나고 엉성엉성 빗살이 빠져나갔던 어머니의 혼(魂)이 어린 듯한 어머니의 손때 묻은 얼레빗이 눈에 어른거리고 참으로 사랑스럽던 어머니의

베틀

음성이 되살아난다.

"버리기만 좋아하면 살림 안 되는 것이여."

낡은 머리빗 하나도 함부로 버리지 않고 아끼고 절약하신 것처럼 우리 집 대문가에 찾아드는 불쌍한 사람들의 마음까지도 아끼고 함부로 저버리지 않은 아름다운 삶을 사셨던 어머니, 그분의 발자취를 생각하게 하는 오래된 내 얼레빗을 손에 들고서 나는 어떤 생활태도로 인생을 살아가고 있으며 내 딸에게 어떠한 아름다운 삶의 모습을 보여주고 있는 것인지 나 자신을 깊이 생각해 본다.

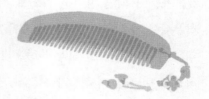

싸리문

눈에 삼삼하게 보이는 싸리문이 있다. 싸릿가지를 성글성글하게 엮은 싸리나무 울타리에 연결되어 출입할 수 있게 만든 빗장이 없는 낮은 문이다. 문이 울타리에 붙어 있을 수 있도록 새끼로 고리를 만들어 살짝 안과 밖을 구분해 놓았을 뿐인 출입문. 이웃과의 예의를 지키면서도 소중한 사람들 간에 서로의 얼굴을 볼 수 있어 정이 듬뿍 오가던 문. 시골 초가집 지붕과 함께 참 잘 어울리는 내가 언제나 간직하고 싶은 참으로 정겨운 고향집 싸리문이다.

이 싸리문은 아지랑이가 아물거리는 봄날이 오면 싸리나무 울타리에 노랗게 피어나는 개나리꽃처럼 나의 꿈도 피어나게 하던 문이다. 눈 부신 햇살이 싸리나무 울타리를 덮는 여름이 오면, 활짝 피어난 호박꽃 속을 넘나드는 벌, 나비처럼 나도 활기차게 집 안팎을 드나들게 하던 문. 가을이 되면 싸리문 밑으로 뒹굴던 낙엽이 좋아서 맴돌다 가기도 하는 문. 겨울이면 함박눈을 맞으면서 나를 포근히 기다려 주었고, 싸리문 주위의 잔설은 모악산 봉우리에 있는 잔설을 불러내어 서로 화답하면서 내 가슴에 정서가 서리게 하던 문이다.

베틀

야산의 맑은 정기를 품은 싸리나무 울타리에 연결된 싸리문은 나즈막해서 사람들이 오가다가 한 번쯤 고개를 돌려 바라보게 된다. 그러면 울 안에 있는 사람도 마주 보고서 정답게 인사를 나눌 수 있었던 아주 사랑스러운 문이었다. 시골 인심이 듬뿍 배인 쑥떡을 담은 그릇을 들고서 문고리를 살짝 벗기고 들어서는 친구가 반가워 멍멍개도 꼬리를 치며 반가워하던 싸리문이 고향에 있었다. 너와 나의 한계성만 살짝이 알려 주고서 수시로 드나들 수 있도록 나즈막하게 만든 싸리문은 나의 마음에 자리하고 있는 평화로운 문이다.

고학년이 되어 도회지로 주거지를 옮겼다. 내 눈에 띄는 드높은 돌담들, 시멘트블록으로 쌓아 올린 높은 담장 위에 날카롭게 깨진 유리조각이나 철조망이 있는 담벼락을 따라 달린 육중한 나무나 철제 대문은 소름 끼치게 무서웠다. 빈부의 차이를 말해 주기라도 하듯이 불법 침입자를 막기 위해 빗장으로 꼭꼭 잠근 높다란 대문은 사람들의 인심이 차가워져 가는 모습처럼 보여 내 마음속도 답답하고 차가워졌다. 나는 기와지붕과 함께 빗장이 단단히 걸려 있는 대문 안에 사는 사람을 보고 싶어도 문을 두드릴 용기가 없어 망설이면서 시골집 싸리문을 그리워했다.

많은 세월이 지나 미국에 오니 집집마다 사립문이 없어 참 좋았다. 문 걸어 잠그는 소리를 듣지 않아도 되는 넓은 초록색 잔디밭에 확 트인 공간이 가슴을 시원하게 해 주었다. 활짝 열린 공간은 이웃 간에 쉽게 소통할 수 있어서 좋을 거라 생각했다. 그런데 꼭 그런 것만은 아님을 알았다. 서로 바쁜 시간에 쫓기다 보니 서로 얼굴 보기도 힘들고,

얼굴을 본다 해도 서로의 문화가 다르니 별 할 말이 없다. 그리고 집이 너무도 개방되어 있어 지나가던 개가 똥오줌을 누고 가는 일이 잦았다. 그뿐만이 아니었다. 눈에 보이는 사립문이 없을 뿐이지 방문은 이중으로 잠겨 있는 집이 많고, 어떤 집은 전기 시설로 불법 침입자를 막고 있는 집도 있음을 알고 난 뒤, 나는 우리 집 정원에 빗장이 없는 나즈막한 싸리나무로 엮어 만든 싸리문이 있었으면 좋겠다는 생각이 들곤 했다. 이웃과 다정스럽게 대화를 나눌 수 있게 만들어진 빗장이 없이 고리만 걸어 둔 아늑함을 주는 싸리문. 사회생활도 마찬가지로 무한정 자유가 허락되는 것 같으면서도 오롯한 대화를 나누기가 힘든 이방인의 생활이 아닌가 싶다.

상긋한 향기가 나는 귀여운 분홍색 싸리꽃이 만발했다 떨어질 때면 마을 누군가의 집에서 새 싸리문이 만들어지던 고향 마을이 눈에 선하다. 지금은 이중문화 속에 살지만, 어느 날엔가는 우리 집 앞뜰에 나즈막한 싸리문이 만들어지는 꿈을 가져 본다. 어느 사이에 내 마음도 낮은 싸리문이 되어 누구라도 정겹게 맞이하고 싶어진다. 너와 나의 한계성은 분명히 있되 자유롭게 드나들 수 있는 정서적인 싸리문이 내 이민생활에도 있었으면 좋겠다. 꼭꼭 문빗장이 잠긴 육중한 대문보다는 싸리나무로 성글성글하게 엮은 싸리문에 문고리만 살짝 걸쳐 있으면 얼마나 좋은가!

내 가슴 속에 있는 싸리문 너머로 나를 찾기 위해서 기웃거리는 이웃들의 따스한 모습이 아른거린다. 누군가의 발걸음 소리가 점점 더 가까이 들려오는 듯하다. 사람들이 도란도란 이야기하는 소리도 들리는

베틀

것 같다. 바람이 불면, 마른 싸리나무 가지들이 서로 부딪치면서 사각사각 소리를 내는 아름다운 자연의 소리도 들리는 것 같다. 빗장이 없는 싸리문은, 나에게 아름다운 이웃들과 오손도손 정서적인 소통을 하면서 행복하게 사는 방법을 알려주고 있다. 소싯적 그리움이 서린 싸리문을 내 가슴 속에 달게 되니 이리도 포근하고 평화스러운 것을….

싸리문은 생각만 해도 인정스런 이웃의 따스한 입김이 이마에 스치고, 정다운 웃음소리가 귓가에 들린다. 너와 나의 한계성만 구분해 두고 가까운 정을 나눌 수 있는 싸리문. 세상살이의 즐거움을 주는 싸리문을 생각만 해도 나는 즐거워진다.

빨래터

이곳이다. 빨래터. 우리나라가 백의민족(白衣民族)이 된 원천(源泉) 말이다.

지금은 사라져 가는 우리나라의 아름다운 생활풍경엔 여인네들의 삶의 터전인 빨래터가 있다. 동네 우물가에나 물이 흐르는 시냇가, 또는 저수지에서 여인네들이 모여 앉아 더러워진 옷가지들이나 각종 물건을 깨끗하게 씻어서 다시금 새롭게 사용할 수 있게 만들어 내는 곳이다. 우리 민족이 순결한 백의민족으로 불리게 한 아름다운 생활풍경이다. 순결하고 정갈한 마음은 순백의 한복을 즐겨 입던 우리 조상들이 물려 준 정신유산이다. 세계 어느 나라를 가도 우리 민족처럼 깨끗하고 단아한 미(美)를 창출해 내는 민족은 없다. 물에 빨고 빨아서 더러워진 옷가지들을 깨끗하게 만들고, 또다시 양잿물로 삶아서 밝은 햇살 아래서 광택을 내게 하는 빨래터가 있어서가 아니겠는가.

여인네들이 모여 앉아서 일상생활의 이야기꽃을 피우던 빨래터가 자꾸만 그리워지는 요즈음이다. 아낙네들의 사랑방 같은 빨래터에 가 보고 싶다. 내 마음을 정결하게 하고 싶을 때는 더욱더 그렇다. 수많은 여

베틀

인네들이 모여 앉아서 빨래하는 곳. 특히 전주천을 따라서 있는 빨래 터에서 빨래한 후에 큰 가마솥에 양잿물을 넣고 푹푹 삶아진 하얀 무 명 이불 홑청을 햇빛 아래서 바람에 말리는 모습이 보고 싶다. 나는 학창시절 대부분을 전주에서 보냈기에 전주천을 자주 보면서 살았다. 가장 아름다운 여고 시절에 전주천 둑을 따라서 맑은 물과 빨래터를 바라보면서 자주색 교복 치마 속으로 미풍을 맞으며 홀로 걸을 때 느 꼈던 그 상쾌하고 즐거웠던 기분은 내 평생 지니고 싶은 행복함이다.

시냇가에서 여인들이 모여 앉아 빨래하는 모습을 담은 그림, 박수근 화가의 〈빨래터〉를 늘 생각한다. 한국사람이 그린 그림으로는 가장 비 싼 가격으로 경매에서 팔렸다니, 우리 민족성을 대변해 주는 그림이 아 니겠는가 싶다. 한국적인 화강암 질감으로 한국적인 소재를 그린 화가, 참 자랑스러운 화백은 빨래터를 통해서 우리 민족의 순결하고 정갈한 마음을 말하고자 함이 아니었을까. 조선 후기의 화가 단원 김홍도나 혜원 신윤복의 빨래터에서는 서민의 애환보다는 풍류적인 색채가 많은 걸 보면, 여인네들의 흥미로운 얘깃거리들이 많이 오가던 곳이기에 그 랬을 성싶다. 여인들이 긴 머리카락을 감기도 하고 달빛에 속살을 내 놓고 목욕을 하기도 했기에 남정네들이 기를 쓰고 훔쳐보고 싶기도 했 을 거다. 시집살이의 고충으로부터 사랑방 이야기까지 끝없이 펼쳐지는 이 빨래터. 한 가정을 꾸려나가는 여인들이 더러워진 옷가지들만 빨아 내는 것이 아니라 삶에 찌든 몸과 정신적인 찌꺼기들까지 정화하는 곳 이었기에 여인네들의 삶의 터전이요, 우리나라가 백의민족이 된 원천이 아니겠는가.

백의민족이면서도 동방예의지국인 우리나라는 빨래터에서도 은근한 예의가 있다. 냇가에서 맑은 물길을 따라 빨래를 할 수 있는 돌을 차지할 때도 서로서로 배려하여 자리에 앉는다. 흰색이나 비교적 가벼운 빨래를 하는 사람은 물줄기 위쪽에 앉고, 옷에서 물감이 빠지거나 똥이 묻은 기저귀를 빨 때는 아래쪽으로 앉는다. 그뿐인가! 시집살이의 한을 풀어내면서 빨랫방망이로 빨래를 후려칠 때는 옆 사람이 다치지 않도록 가급적이면 조금 떨어진 곳에서 한다. 정감 넘치는 우물가에서 빨래할 때는 줄줄이 골을 내어 우둘투둘하게 만들어진 빨래판 위에서 빨래에 비누 칠해 북북 문질러 얼룩을 빨기도 한다. 어느새 깨끗하게 빨아진 빨래를 펼쳐서 바라보는 여인네의 마음이 빨래보다도 더 맑고 깨끗해져 서로 만난다. 이 깨끗해진 마음이 살아 움직여 나라를 형성하는 가족들을 돌봐왔기에 우리나라가 백의민족이라 칭함을 받지 않았나 싶다.

지금 시대는 세탁소나 대부분 가정엔 세탁기가 있어 기계로 빨래를 한다. 그 시간에 대부분의 주부들은 조용한 시간을 가져서도 좋지만, 빨래터에서 느끼는 풋풋한 삶의 향기를 맛볼 수가 없어 외로워지기가 쉽다. 이 시간에 책을 읽거나 노래를 듣거나 하면서 정신을 정화하지만 팽팽한 삶의 리듬이 주는 맛이 없어선지 나는 가끔 빨래터가 그립다. 촌스럽다는 말을 듣는 게 일쑤인 나는 지금도 하얀 목화솜 이불을 선호한다. 때에 따라서 이불 홑청에 표백제를 넣고 빨아 인스턴트 풀을 뿌리고 다리미로 다린 후에 덮을 때 들리는 바삭거리는 소리는 빨래터에서 바람에 빨래 말리는 소리로 살아난다. 삶의 향기가 풀풀 살아나는 정갈스러운 소리로 들어내 마음도 하이얀 목화꽃처럼 아름답게 피어나고 깨끗해지는 기분이다.

베틀

빨래터의 여인네들은 가족들을 사랑하는 마음으로 옷에 묻은 때와 얼룩을 인내를 갖고 힘들게 주물러 씻어내면서 어느 사이에 마음의 때와 얼룩들도 함께 씻어낸다. 깨끗하게 빨래를 하는 정성스런 마음은 진실한 삶의 발견으로 목화꽃처럼 순수하고 아름답게 인생의 꽃을 피워 내고 있음이다. 더러워진 옷들을 빨고 또 빨아 깨끗하게 만드는 빨래터에서 만나는 마음들이 모이면 우리들의 인생살이도 깨끗해지지 않겠는가. 백의민족답게 모든 사람들이 몸도 마음도 생활도 항상 정갈했으면 좋겠다. 가끔 세상살이의 찌들은 옷을 빨고 싶어 전주천에 있는 빨래터가 생각날 때는 하얀 이불 홑청이 바람에 날리고, 빨랫방망이 소리, 빨래하는 아낙네들의 수런거리는 소리들이 내 귀를 즐겁게 해 준다. 그리고 내 마음이 아름다운 목화꽃처럼 하얗게 부풀어 오른다.

빨래터가 그립다.

농촌의 등불

어두움 속에서 빛을 발하여 누군가의 꿈을 이루게 하는 농촌의 등불이 있다. 낮에는 초가집 처마 밑에서 침묵으로 누군가를 기다리는 아름다운 모습을 품고도 있다. 직사각형 모양으로 사면엔 유리로 덮여 있고 아래로는 나무 받침을 만들어 호롱불을 놓을 수 있게 조립해 손으로 들 수 있도록 만든 조명기구다. 반세기 전에 주로 농촌에서 사용하던 등불이어서 지금은 골동품상에서도 발견하기가 어려울 것이다. 나의 소망인 이 나이에 알맞은 아름다운 인생살이를 생각해 보면서, 유년시절의 아름다운 흔적으로 내 가슴 속에 아름답게 새겨 있는 농촌의 등불 같은 삶이 좋겠다는 생각을 해 본다. 어두운 곳에서 헤매는 사람에게 밝은 빛을 주어 꿈을 이루게 하고, 필요치 않을 때는 침묵으로 도움 줄 사람을 기다리는 아름다운 모습의 농촌의 등불 말이다.

밝은 햇빛이 서산으로 뉘엿뉘엿 넘어가기 시작하면 농촌의 마당은 어두움이 서서히 몰려오기 시작한다. 이때에, 시골집 처마 밑에 걸려 조용히 휴식을 취하고 있는 등불은 밝은 빛이 필요한 사람을 위하여 불이 켜진다. 대부분은 저녁이 되어가는데도 아직도 일을 끝내지 못하

베틀

고 마무리 작업을 하는 농민들을 위하여 이 등불은 넓은 마당을 밝히게 한다. 특히나 추수의 계절을 맞이하여 타작을 기다리는 볏단들이 산더미같이 마당에 쌓여있는 날은, 농촌의 등불도 최선을 다하여 농민들의 아름다운 꿈을 이루어가는 데 앞장선다. 가을 들판에서 거둬들인 황금색으로 탱탱하게 영글은 벼들을 타작마당에서 벼훑이로 한 줌씩 잡고서 후드득! 훑어낼 때 농부들의 꿈도 벼 낱알들과 함께 톡톡 튀어 오른다. 농부들은 이마에 환한 미소를 띠고 큰소리로 소리 내여 웃으면서 일을 하다가도 어두움이 밀려오기 시작하면 마음이 조급해지고 손놀림이 빨라진다. 이때에 농부의 꿈을 이루어 가는 수고와 노력을 위로하며 어두움을 물리치는 길잡이가 되어 환한 빛을 힘껏 발하는 농촌의 등불은 숭고하기까지 하다.

전기 시설이 없던 때, 추억 속 농촌의 등불은 참으로 귀한 생활의 조명 도구였다. 우리 집 처마 밑에 걸려있는 직사각형 등불도 호롱불을 넣어 두고선 언제나 사용했다. 이 등불은 필요에 따라서 호롱에 불이 켜지고 수시로 옮겨 다녔다. 주로 처마 밑에서 사용되지만 때로는 부엌으로 옮겨지고, 화장실 갈 때도 사용되고, 어떤 때는 내 책상 위로도 옮겨졌다. 이 등불이 참으로 귀하게 쓰일 때는 식구 중에 누군가가 밤에도 집에 돌아오지 않을 때다. 사랑하는 사람을 마중 나갈 때 손에 들고서 동네 어귀까지 나간다. 특히나 아버지가 5일 만에 서는 원평시장에 가신 날은 우리 가족들은 처마 밑에 걸려 있는 두 개의 등을 찾아 호롱에 기름을 채우고 불을 켠다. 그리고 가족들은 두 편으로 갈라서 아버지를 마중 나간다. 왜냐하면, 마을로 들어오는 길이 두 길이 있어, 어느 길로 오실지 모르기 때문이었다. 한 길은 자갈이 깔린 비포장

신작로를 따라오다간 새장터 골목길로 들어오는 길인데 시간이 많이 걸린다. 다른 길은 뜸북새 우는 꼬불꼬불 좁다란 논둑길을 걸어 집으로 오는 길인데 강대미 언덕을 오르려면 숨이 가빠도 조금은 빠른 길이다. 우리 가족들은 직사각형 등불을 손에 들고서 자칫 넘어질 수도 있는 위험한 곳을 비켜 걸으면서 원평장터에서 늦게 돌아오시는 아버지를 마중 나가곤 했다.

어두움이 온 세상을 덮고 있을 때, 원평 오일장에 나가신 아버지를 마중하러 내 손에 들고 있는 사랑의 향기를 발산하고 싶어하는 농촌의 등불은 모악산이 보이는 강대미 언덕에서 깜빡인다. 낮에는 나즈막하고 두리뭉실한 산들이 구릉지를 이루고 구릉지들이 또 다른 능선을 이루어 출렁이는 물결같이 생동감을 주는 가운데서 우뚝 솟아 정기를 뿜어내는 모악산이 보이는 마을 언덕 위다. 동네 어귀 들녘엔 홍자색 자운영 꽃이 무리로 피어나 가슴을 설레게 하는 참으로 아름다운 자연환경을 이루고 있는 곳이다. 모악산 바라보고 웃으며 굳세게 자라기 위해서 오르내린 언덕 위, 어스름 속에서 등불을 들고 아버지를 기다리는 마음은 추워서 오돌오돌 떨리는 몸과는 달리 훈훈했다. 아버지는 어두움 속에서도 탁 트인 벌판 너머로 멀리서 깜빡이는 등불을 보고서 가족이 기다리고 있음에 반가워서 오시고 있음을 기분 좋은 큰소리로 알려주셨다. 사랑하는 아버지를 기다렸다가 포근한 품에 행복하게 안길 수 있었음은 어두움 속에서 장애물을 비켜갈 수 있도록 발길을 밝혀 준 고귀한 농촌의 등불이 있어서였다. 농촌의 등불은 사랑하는 사람들의 무사한 재회의 꿈을 이루게 도와준 것이다.

베틀

나는 오늘도 마음속에 있는 등불을 들고 동구 밖 언덕에서 사랑하는 아버지를 기다리는 모습이 수시로 떠올라, 나를 행복하게 하는 서로 살펴주는 농촌의 등불 같은 사람들이 모여 사는 아름다운 세상을 꿈꾼다. 이 시간도 나는 어두움 속에서 빛을 발하는 등불을 들고 서서 사랑하는 사람의 발자국 소리를 기다리는 기분이다. 주위가 캄캄해서 어느 방향으로 어떻게 가야 할지를 몰라 서성일 때 길을 밝혀 주면서 위로와 희망을 주는 등불. 누군가의 꿈을 이뤄주기 위해 기다림의 아름다운 모습을 품고 있는 등불. 등불은 내가 남을 위해서 들고 있거나 누군가가 나를 위해서 스스로 들고 있을 때는 생각만 해도 안심이 되어 좋다.

이 나이에 알맞은 아름다운 삶의 모습은, 어두움 속에서 빛을 발해 누군가에게 꿈을 이루게 하고, 더 밝은 빛이 있을 때는 자신을 드러내지 않고 처마 밑에서 침묵으로 시간을 관조하며 누군가의 필요함을 기다리는 농촌의 등불 같은 모습이 아닐까 생각해 본다. 내 가슴 속에 옛날의 아름다운 삶의 흔적이 되어 그리운 사랑의 무늬로 판화처럼 남아 있는 농촌의 등불 같은 삶의 모습 말이다. 남은 나의 인생살이가 아름다운 농촌의 등불 같은 인생살이가 된다면 얼마나 좋겠는가.

| 3부 |

눈꽃송이

그래도 좋아!

내 친구 무명초의 떨리는 음성이 내 가슴을 찡하게 한다.

"미안, 미안, 너무도 무심해서 정말 미안해. 30년이 넘게 함께 살아오면서 아직도 이름을 몰라. 너를 무명초라 불러서."

무명초는 내가 무심해도, 자기 이름을 내 마음대로 지어서 불러도 날마다 보는 것만으로 만족하고 내가 그래도 좋다고 단호히 말한다. 나 자신이 생각해도 참으로 한심한 년데, 내 무심함과 허물을 덮어 주는 무명초에게 참으로 미안하고 고마울 뿐이다. 무명초는 나와 날마다 얼굴을 수없이 대면하면서 침묵의 대화를 즐기는 친구다. 우리 집 거라지에서 살고 있는데 옆에는 항상 행운목이 자리하고 있다. 행운목은 누군가 나에게 알려주어서 알고 있고 무명초는 그 사람도 이름을 모른다는 바람에 지금까지 나도 모르고 있는 것이다.

아마도 내 이민생활의 역사를 거의 알고 있는 무명초일 것이다. 꼭 이름을 알아야 한다면 지금이라도 꽃집에 가서 알아보면 될 테지만 그럴 필요성을 느끼지 못했기에 30여 년이란 세월을 이름을 몰라 무심한 나는 그냥 무명초라 부르고 있는 것이다. 예쁜 꽃을 피워 내 시각을 즐겁게 하면서 내 마음을 들뜨게 하는 꽃나무도 아니고 그렇다고 맛있는 열매를 맺어 내 입맛을 돋워 줄 나무도 아니고 한결같은 푸름만 간직한 상록수기에, 나는 사실상 무언가 이루고 싶은 내 꿈을 무명초에 걸지 않았기에 무심했는지도 모른다.

사무실 같은 실내에서 흔히 볼 수 있는 무명초는 대나무 비슷하게 생겼고 꽃은 피지 않고 늘 초록 이파리만 달고 있는데 기다란 이파리 가운데로 하얀 선들이 나란히 개가 줄지어 안정된 조화를 이루기 때문에 거기에 아름다움이 있는 것 같다. 지금 나와 함께 있는 무명초는 제2세가 된다. 제1세는 이미 이 세상에 존재하지 않는다. 그러니까, 나의 초창기 이민 시절에 처음으로 집을 사서 집들이할 때 누군가로부터 받은 선물이다. 나는 둘이 나란히 있어 한 쌍의 부부 같은 이 무명초를 햇빛이 잘 드는 2층 배스 실에 두고서 커다란 화분으로 갈아 주었더니, 꼭 자기들 닮은 개의 새끼도 치고 쑥쑥 잘 자라나 키가 천장에 닿으려 했다. 나는 물을 줄 때마다 부모와 두 자녀가 똑같이 생겼다는 생각을 하곤 했다. 세월이 지나니 제2세가 되는 두 개의 무명초는 싱싱하게 잘 자라고 제1세가 되는 부부 무명초는 희끄무레하게 빛도 바랜 것 같고 억세고 키만 멋없이 너무나 자라 천장을 찌를 것 같은 불안감을 주었다. 나는 마침내 새끼 무명초가 더 잘 자랄 수 있는 환경을 조성해 주기 위해서 부모 무명초를 잘라 주었다. 부모들은 언제나 자식을 위해 희생하게 된다는 생각을 하면서. 그리고선 내가 새집으로 이사 할 때, 무명초 화분 위에 누군가가 준 예쁜 조개껍데기들을 함께 넣어 옮겨왔다.

지금 나와 함께 지내고 있는 제2세 무명초는 웬일인지 후계자가 나오지 않고 있다. 하루에도 몇 번씩 얼굴을 대면하면서도 무심한 척 그저

베틀

일주일에 물 한 번 주고 가끔 미라클 영양분을 줄 뿐이다. 내가 선뜻 행동으로 옮기지 못하고 있는 이유가 있기는 있다. 나는 웬일인지 화초를 잘 가꾸지 못한다. 나는 내심 화초를 잘 키우겠다고 정성껏 물도 주고 거름도 주는데 대부분 너무나 물을 많이 주어 물창이 들거나 거름을 너무 많이 주어 몸에 상처를 받은 화초들은 결국은 나를 떠나 버리고 만다. 그럴 때마다 적당한 환경을 조성해 주지 못한 내 잘못에 가슴이 아프고 내 정성과 꿈이 한꺼번에 사라져 버려 나는 허탈감에서 허우적거린다. 더 예쁘고 관심이 많은 화초일수록 빨리 내 곁을 떠나고 만다. 그래서 나는 가능하면 무명초에 신경을 안 쓰려 하는 것이다. 얼굴을 더 오래도록 보고 싶어서, 내가 사는 동안 날마다 침묵의 대화를 나누고 싶어서. 그런데 나는 오늘에야 ~ 참으로 오랜 세월을 지낸 후에야 내 커다란 허물을 찾아냈다. 화분 안에, 내 눈에 예쁘게 보인 조개껍데기를 놓았으니 무명초가 숨도 제대로 못 쉬고 제2세도 가질 수가 없었던 것이다. 내 이 한없는 무심함과 커다란 허물을 어쩌랴!

내 이민생활의 희로애락을 잘 알고 있는 내 친구 무명초는 속내를 잘 드러내지 않는 내 마음을 잘 알고 있다. 그래서 내가 이름을 알려고 하지도 않고, 새 환경으로 조성해 주지 않고 무심한 것도 관계치 않고 나를 지켜보면서 사랑만 하는 것이다. 나는 오늘 새삼스럽게 내 친구 무명초에게 내 무관심과 허물을 말하면서 무척 미안해하고 있을 때, 무조건 '그래도 좋다'고 무명초는 나를 안심시킨다. 정말 위로가 되는 말이다. 특이한 내 사랑 방법을 알고 있는 무명초의 너그러움이 어쩜 우리가 삼십여 년이 넘게 같이 있을 수 있게 한 보이지 않는 힘이었는지도 모르겠다. 나는 사실 무명초가 생명을 유지 하고 내 곁을 떠나지 않는 것만으로도 참으로 좋다.

　나는 무명초보다도 더 많은 관심과 사랑을 주면서, 좋은 거름과 물도 자주 주고 아름다운 열매를 보리라는 내 꿈을 안고서 5년 전에 심었던 사과나무를 오늘은 유심히 들여다봤다. 아뿔싸! 지금쯤 열려 있어야 할 사과가 단 개도 열려 있지 않았다. 작년엔 서너 개가 열렸기에 올해는 더 많은 사과가 열리면 사랑하는 사람들과 즐거움을 함께하리라는 기대가 많았었는데---. 나는 내 정성 어린 사랑과 꿈이 무너지는 허탈감에 빠져 나도 모르게 "무심한 것~."했다. 그런 후에 사과나무를 쳐다보니 가슴이 뜨끔할 정도로 너무도 슬퍼 보인다. 나는 그때 무명초가 떠올랐다. 내 커다란 허물과 무심함을 탓하기는커녕 '그래도 좋아' 하면서 나와 함께 지내는 것만으로 행복해하는. 나는 사랑이라는 이름으로 집착했던 나 자신이 몹시 부끄러워졌다. 남에겐 너그러운 마음으로 나의 무심함과 허물을 용서받기를 좋아하면서도 남에게는 옹졸했던 나의 마음까지도.

　나는 얼른 사랑스러운 얼굴로 사과나무에 다시 말한다.

　'그래도 좋아!'

　이 말은 무명초가 내 가슴을 찡하게 감동하게 한 말이다.

성탄절

예수님의 탄생을, 기독교가 기념하는 2014년째 성탄절이 돌아오는 12월 25일이다.

우리가 사용하고 있는 달력이, 예수님 탄생을 기점으로써 만들어졌기 때문에, 서기 몇 년이라는 대신에 기독교에서는 '주후' 몇 년이라고 많이 사용하고 있다. 그래서 올해의 성탄절은 주후 2014년 12월 25일이 되는 것이다.

죄에 빠져 죽을 수밖에 없는 우리인데, 예수님이 흘리신 십자가의 보혈 공로로 말미암아 우리들의 죄가 대속되었음을 의미한다.

천지를 창조하신 하나님께서 독생자 예수 그리스도를 이 땅에 보내 주시어 불쌍한 인간들에게 새 생명 허락하시고, 하늘나라에 갈 길을 내어 주셨다. 우리 인간이 신의 세계에는 갈 수 없기 때문에, 예수그리스도께서 인간의 모습으로 오신 것을, 신학적 용어로는 성육신(聖肉身) 되시어 오셨다고 한다. 그날이 바로 성탄절, 온 세계가 공통적으로 사용하고 있는 크리스마스다.

종교적인 차원을 떠나서, 성탄절은 세계적인 공휴일이다. 일 년 중에

단 하루만 쉬는 가게도 성탄절에 문을 닫는다. 그만큼 성탄절은 온 인류가 기뻐 찬송하는, 특별한 의미가 있는 날이기 때문일 것이다.

성령으로 잉태한 예수님은 이스라엘에 있는 '베들레헴'이라는 작은 성 어느 마구간에서 요셉과 마리아를 육신의 부모로 두고 태어나셨다. 예수님의 마지막 생에는 죄 없으신 몸으로 침묵으로만 고통을 참으시고 고난의 십자가 위에서 못 박혀 돌아가시어, 우리 죄를 대속해 주신 온 인류를 위한 온전한 사랑이셨다.

예수님을 맞이하는 오늘날의 나의 모습은 어떠한가! 나는 참으로 부끄러운 존재일 뿐이다.

세상의 명예나 물질같이, 우선 나에게 좋은 것으로만 기쁨과 행복을 느끼기보다는, 진리의 말씀인 성경 말씀대로 순종하면서 하나님의 품 안에서 사는 것만이, 참 자유를 얻고 진실한 기쁨과 행복을 누릴 수 있다는 것을 알면서도 기독교인의 도리인, 세상의 빛과 소금의 역할을 감당하지 못하고 있어 부끄럽다.

전형적인 크리스마스 색깔인 빨강과 녹색은 그리스도를 통한 영원한 삶을 상징하는 녹색이고, 예수님이 십자가에서 흘린 피는 붉은색으로 상징화된다.

빨간색과 초록색 이파리가 있는 포인세티아가 곳곳에 장식되어 있는데, 불쌍한 영혼들을 위한 나의 기도가 부족하여, 예수님이 그곳에 찾아오실 것 같지 않은 생각을 하면, 죄가 되어 나는 마음이 괴롭다.

예수님이 이 땅에 태어나신 기쁜 성탄절을 맞이하면서, 내 삶을 다시 한 번 정리해 본다.

베틀

눈꽃송이

하얀 눈꽃송이- 삶의 환희를 느낀다. 하늘에서 사뿐히 내려오는 하얀 눈송이도 아름답지만, 하늘에서 펑펑 내려와 겨울나무 위에서 겸손하게 군락을 이루어 만들어진 눈꽃송이는 참으로 더 아름답고 성스럽기까지 하여 신에게 감사의 기도가 절로 나온다. 나는 내 일생을 통해서 아무리 노력해도 이렇게 아름다운 눈꽃송이를 단 한 번만이라도 피워 낼 수 없는 연약한 인간이기에, 신(神)이 만들어 낸 미(美)의 완성품을 감상하는 것만으로도 행복한 은혜라 생각한다. 나에게 삶의 환희를 준 눈꽃송이처럼 나도 한평생 살면서 누군가에게 하얀 눈꽃송이가 될 수는 없는 것일까. 내가 소녀에서 처녀로 생리적인 탈바꿈 할 때 삶의 환희를 준, 겨울 마당에서 보았던 아버지의 참사랑이 모여 만들어진 겸손하고 탐스러운 하이얀 눈꽃송이처럼 말이다.

내가 살고 있는 미국은 땅덩어리가 넓어서인지 사계절을 동시에 맞이하고 있다. 겨울철에도 꽃이 피는 캘리포니아에 살고 있는 나에게 동부 보스턴에서 살고 있는 문우, 언제나 친절한 금자 시인한테서 참으로 멋진 설경을 담은 사진들이 카톡으로 왔다. 우~후~와, 정말 멋있다. 너무너무 멋진 사진 속의 설경을 감상하는 내 심장에 새로운 세포들이 살아나 통통 뛰는 것 같이 감동을 주는 수많은 사진 중 내 마음을 앗아가 버린 사진, 사철나무 위에서 눈꽃들이 고개를 숙이고 겸손하고 성스럽게 피어 있는 눈꽃송이다. 참으로 아름답다는 느낌 속에 나의 사랑의 계절에 보았던 삶의 환희를 준 눈꽃송이가 눈에 어린다. 첫눈이 수북이 내린 그 해, 시골집 마당에서 아버지의 겸손한 참사랑이 피워 낸 탐스럽고 성스러운 하이얀 눈꽃송이가.

시간에 흔들리며 떠오르는 결코 잊을 수 없는 초가집 속에서의 설렘과 교회당 모퉁이에서 서럽게 울던 하얀 눈물을 추억 속에서 펼쳐본다. 노년이 되어서도 표현하기가 조금은 쑥스러운 여성만의 특성인 매달 치러야 하는 생리가 있다. 온몸의 신경이 떨리는 설렘과 부끄러움 속에서 초경을 맞이했다. 아랫배가 더부룩하고 아파서 잠을 이룰 수가 없을 때 발견한 붉은 초경의 놀람과 가슴 두근거림은 나에게 추위에 얼어붙어 손이 닿는 순간 쩍쩍 들러붙는 느낌을 주는 방문 고리를 만지게 했다. 밖으로 나오니 낮부터 조금씩 흩날리기 시작한 첫눈이 함박눈으로 변해 평화가 고요하게 넘치는 넓은 마당에 내리고 있었다. 뭇사람들의 사랑을 받는 함박눈이 하늘에서 내려와 겨울나무에 겸손하게 차곡차곡 쌓여 만들어지는 환상적인 하이얀 눈꽃송이에서 나는 신기하게도 삶의 환희를 느끼고 있을 때, 아버지의 음성이 들렸다. " 야~아, 첫눈이구나. 첫눈이 이렇게도 많이 내리는 모습은 처음인 것 같다." 내가 화장실에 가는 것을 알아챈 아버지가 나에게 안도감을 주시기 위해서 안방 문을 열면서 조금은 흥분된 어조로 하신 말씀이다.

베틀

전깃불도 없던 시골집엔 뒷간 혹은 '칫간'이라고 불리는 화장실이 본채와 멀리 떨어져 있었다. 넓은 마당 한구석에 있는 재래식 화장실은 밤이면 사람들이 말하는 몽달귀신이 나올 것 같아 늘 머리가 쭈뼛쭈뼛해지고 무서워서 혼자서는 못 간다. 우리 집에선 밤이 되면 달항아리처럼 예쁘게 생긴 요강을 마루 한쪽에 늘 두고 있기에 소변은 문제가 없었는데, 대변을 보려면 언제나 아버지가 마당에 서 계셨다. 내 사춘기 때, 초경이 시작된 그 다음 날도 나는 잠을 설치고 요강 위에 앉아 있으니 뭉클하게 핏덩이가 배출됨을 느꼈다. 첫 경험이라 나는 무척 당황했고 이른 아침이 되면 아무도 모르게 요강을 비우리라는 생각으로 마음을 진정시키려 해도, 부끄러움에 얼굴이 후끈거리며 가슴이 두근두근하며 온 신경이 곤두세워져 안절부절 새벽을 기다렸다.

방문 창호지가 환해 질 무렵 나는 가만히 얼음장같이 차가운 무쇠 방문 고리를 열고 방을 나섰다. 그때에 아버지의 헛기침 소리도 들렸다. 나는 설광 속에서 뽀독뽀독 눈 위를 걷는 소리를 혼자 들으며 요강을 비우기 전에 먼저 화장실로 향했다. 재래식 화장실인지라 두 다리를 구푸리고 앉아서 볼일을 보면서 함박눈 구경을 할 요량으로 듬성듬성하게 짜인 화장실 판잣문 사이로 밖을 내다보았다. 아뿔싸, 아버지가! 처음으로 내 눈에 확 들어온 모습은 아버지였다. 하이얀 한복을 입으신 아버지가 달항아리 같은 요강을 두 손으로 보듬고서 고개를 조금 숙인 체 조심조심 하이얀 눈이 소복이 쌓인 마당을 가로질러 화장실로 향하고 계셨다. 순간적으로 나는 느꼈다. 아버지가 아무도 모르게 내 붉은 피가 오줌에 섞여 있는 요강을 비우려고 화장실 옆 회색 재가 있는 곳을 향하고 있음을. 나는 그때 따스하면서도 속 깊은 아버지의 참

사랑이 모여 겸손하게 피어난 하이얀 눈꽃송이를 보았다. 나는 요강을 보듬고 있는 아버지를 보면서 나와 성(性)이 다른 남자라서 부끄러우면서도, 겸손한 하이얀 눈꽃송이로 보이는 아버지를 보면서 왠지 모르게 참사랑을 받고 있다는 행복감과 생의 환희를 느꼈다. 그리고 그런 일이 있었음을 아무한테도 내색하지 않으신 진실된 사랑이 보석으로 변해 내 가슴속에서 아름답게 빛나고 있다.

　내 생애에 아버지께서 피운 눈꽃송이처럼 겸손의 아름다운 꽃을 피울 수 있다면 얼마나 좋겠는가. 나는 미주이민 다음 해에 세상을 떠나신, 사랑한다는 말 한마디도 해 드리지 못한 소중한 아버지를 그리워하면서 교회당 모퉁이에서 서럽게 울었던 그 시절을 상기해 본다. 이 세상에서 참사랑이 무엇인가를 몸소 실천해 주셨던 겸손한 하이얀 눈꽃송이, 아버지를 영원세계에서 만나면 나는 꼭 말하리라. "첫눈이 그리도 많이 내렸던 그날, 내 붉은 초경의 부끄러움을 어느 사람에게도 내색하지 않았던 속 깊은 은밀한 사랑을 나는 알고 있었노라고. 추워서 오돌 거리던 겨울날, 부끄러움에 움츠려진 나의 가슴속에 참으로 겸손한 모습으로 소담스러운 하얀 눈꽃송이 되어 피어난 아버지의 참사랑은 신기하게도 나에게 삶의 환희를 주었노라고."

베틀

해피 리타이어먼트

"해피 리타이어먼트! 은퇴를 축하합니다."

"네, 네, 감사합니다. "

요즈음 노신사 얼굴이 싱글벙글한다.

은퇴를 축하해야 하나요, 젊은 여집사가 조심스럽게 내 귀 가까이에서 묻는다. 옆에 있는 또래 집사가 어느새 알아듣고는 바로 대답한다.

"어~머 당연하지요."

또 다른 여집사는 꼭 그렇지만은 않은 것 같단다.

나에게도 묻는데, 솔직히 나는 잘 모르겠고 감사한 마음으로 노신사의 얼굴을 바라다본다.

은퇴에 대한 다양한 의견들이 있지만, 노신사는 어쨌든 규칙적인 생활을 해야 하는 직장생활에서, 자유롭게 시간을 활용할 수 있는 무직장(無職場) 생활인이 되니 그리도 좋나 보다. 연세가 많아 판단력이 떨어져 쉬어야 하는 정년퇴임이란 걸 까맣게 잊고 말이다. 어쨌든 은퇴는 제2의 인생을 살아가게 되는 참으로 중요한 시점이 아닌가. 좋은 생각들과 아름다운 앞날을 계획하는 노신사는 대학에서 35년 4개월을 가르치다가 은퇴했다. 그뿐인가! 고국에서 5년 동안 교육자로 직장생활을 한 것을 합치면 40년을 넘게 제2세들을 위해서 교육현장에서 수고했으니 경이롭기까지 하다.

은퇴하면서 만든 시다.

「은퇴」 이병호

대학에서 강산도 3번 반 변하게 가르치다가 때가 되어 손을 떼다 / 그동안 받은 스트레스와 긴장도 눈 녹듯 녹아가고 / 시간은 화살처럼 너무 빨리 날아가는데 / 괴로움도 어려움도 산들바람에 실어보내고 / 새로운 제2의 인생을 설계해 본다 / 그 세월에 희로애락도 많았는데 / 가르치는 즐거움 속에서 나도 모르게 / 머리가 희끗희끗 희어졌나 보다 / 양어깨에 건강과 소망을 메고 터벅터벅 걸으며 / 걸어온 길 뒤돌아 보지 않고 앞을 향하여 / 인내는 쓰지만 그 열매는 단것처럼

1978년 9월 28일, 그날을 상기한다. 미국이민 바람이 세차게 불던 시기였다. 사랑하는 많은 것들을 고국에 남겨두고 김포국제공항에서 미국이민 길에 오른 날이었다. 무엇보다도 돌 지난 지 얼마 되지 않는 사랑하는 아들을 부모님께 맡기고서 국외선 비행기 트랩을 밟는 그의 마음은 무거웠을 것이다. 다행히 하나님이 동행해 주신다는 믿음이 있어서 안심은 되었겠지만, 넓은 대지에서 원대한 꿈을 펼치고 싶은 욕망이 살아 꿈틀거리는 시기였다. 그는 미지의 세계에서 받아야 할 고통보

베틀

다도 모든 일에 긍정적이고 개척정신이 투철했다.

그는 교육청에서 보조교사 자격시험을 치르고 집 부근 중고등부에서 영어선생을 한 2년을 했는데, 좋은 기회가 있어 국방대학 한국어과에 취직되었다. 그게 인연이 되어 31년이 넘게 일하다가 교수직을 정년퇴임 하게 되었다.

노신사가 되어 은퇴하니, 사람들이 모이는 곳에서 심심찮게 은퇴한 사람들의 보편적인 모습들이 대화 중 거론된단다. 규칙적인 직장생활을 안 하니 자유로워 보인다. 외모에 신경을 덜 쓰기 때문에 조금은 추하게 보인다. 흰머리가 많아져 은발색 머리거나 아니면 거의 다 염색머리다. 은퇴한 노인들은 물기 없이 말라가는 나무처럼 피부가 각질화되고 말라가기가 쉽다. 어디 그것뿐인가, 아버지나 어머니라는 호칭보다는 할아버지, 할머니라는 호칭을 많이 듣는다. 육신이 쇠퇴해 가니 안경, 틀니, 보청기 같은 건강보조기를 점차 사용하게 된다. 무엇보다도 외로움을 느낄 때가 많단다. 세끼를 집에서 먹는다 하여 '삼식'이라는 별명을 듣기 쉬운 남자 은퇴자들이 가장 싫어하는 것은 부인이 부엌에서 곰탕 끓이는 뒷모습이라고 한다. 곰탕을 많이 끓여 냉장고에 넣어둔다. 그리고는 부인은 동창생 모임이네, 외국여행이다, 하면서 마음대로 돌아다닌다. 이렇다 보니 남편은 혼자서 시간을 보내야 하니 외로울 수밖에 없을 것이다.

나는 생각해 본다. 외로움을 느끼지 않으려면 욕심을 버리고 항상 누군가를 도와주며 살아야 한다. 사랑스러운 가족의 일원으로서 행복하게 살기 위해 기도가 중심점이 되어야 한다. 잔소리가 아닌 은은한 인간의 향을 풍기는 행동과 언어를 해야 할 것이다. 무엇보다도 취미생활을 하면 건강을 유지하고 외로울 시간이 없을 것이다. 노신사는 은퇴하기 전이나 다름없이 항상 바쁘다. 하고 싶은 취미생활이 많아서다. 성경 읽기, 골프, 붓글씨 쓰기, 무엇보다도 좋은 시를 쓰기 위해서 독서를 많이 해야 하니 심심할 시간이 없다. 왜 이렇게 시간이 빨리 가는지 모르겠다고 푸념 아닌 푸념을 하곤 한다. 어쩌면 하고 싶은 일들을 하면서 사니 인생의 가치를 높이고 행복한 삶이 되나 보다.

사랑의 밥주걱을 힘있게 들고 성도들에게 밥을 퍼주는 '밥퍼장로'라고 쓰인 에포론을 입고 있는 노신사는 나의 남편이고 이병호 시인이다. 접시 위에 송골송골 퍼담은 밥 알갱이들이 하얀 함박꽃으로 변해 '해피 리타이어먼트'라고 함성하는 듯하다.

베틀

좋은 글

좋은 글은 어디에 있을까. 나는 좋은 글을 찾기 위해 이 시간도 술래가 되어 꼭꼭 숨은 좋은 글을 찾아 나선다. 소싯적에 친구들과 즐기던 숨바꼭질을, 지금은 좋은 글과 하고 있다.

"너는 생각이 많아 좋은 글을 쓸 수 있을 거야."

시골 할머니, 늙은 우리 어머니의 이 한 마디가 올무가 되어 나를 수필에 매이게 하고 있다. 문우 중에는 명성 높은 교수들한테서 문학수업을 받은 후에 문학인이 되었노라고 은근히 자랑하지만, 나의 문학에는 흙과 함께 평생을 보내신 우리 어머니일 뿐이다. 흙은 모든 생명을 잉태해 내는 자궁이며 사랑의 근본임을 알게 해 주신 우리 어머니는 내가 책 읽는 모습을 보시면서 행복해하셨다. 내가 즐겨 읽었던 책들 중엔, 심훈의 상록수, 이광수의 흙, 펄 벅의 대지, 박경리의 토지 등 대부분이 흙을 대상으로 쓴 글들인 걸 보면 내가 시골 태생이고 흙과 함께 살아온 농부의 딸이었음을 말해 준다. 좋은 글을 쓰려면 좋은 인격체를 가져야 함을 몸소 실천해 보여주시던 어머니가 말씀하신 좋은 글을 나는 아직도 쓰지 못하고 있음은 내 인격이 부족함이어라. 아름다운 인생살이를 해야 살아 움직이는 삶 속에서 사랑의 향기를 뿜어내는 꽃 한 송이 같은 수필을 쓸 수 있을 텐데….

좋은 글이란 무엇이라고 정확한 대답을 한마디로 말할 수는 없겠고 여러 의견들이 있을 뿐이다. 그중에서도 나는 작가의 혼(魂)이 담긴 글이 독자와 소통이 잘 되는 좋은 글이라는 의견에 마음이 많이 간다. 아무리 화려한 문체와 해박한 지식을 넣어 한 작품을 완성했다 해도 독자가 무슨 뜻인지 이해하기가 어려우면 좋은 글이라고 말할 수 없을 것 같다. 꽃은 누군가가 이름을 불러 줄 때 비로소 꽃이 된다는데 글도 누군가가 읽고 감동을 할 때 좋은 글이 아니겠는가. 이 세상에 있는 수많은 문학인이 좋은 글을 쓰기 위해서 이렇듯 고민할 때는 삶의 참 의미를 깨닫기 위함이 아닌가. 삶의 참 의미는 무엇인가. 나는 그 대답을 수필을 쓰면서 조금씩 조금씩 찾아가고 있는 느낌이다. 마음의 눈을 활짝 열고 아름다운 세상을 사랑으로 바라볼 수 있을 때 좋은 글이 쓰이리라.

좋은 글이란 독자가 감동을 느끼는 글, 향기가 나는 글, 사랑을 느끼게 하는 글, 삶에 대한 애착을 깊이 느끼게 하는 글, 감사가 넘치게 하는 글 등등 삶에 대한 깨달음을 느끼게 하는 감동스런 글이어야 함이 틀림없다. 이론적으로는 알기에 정말 힘들어서 수필 한 편을 쓰긴 하지만 아직도 이렇다 할 작품 하나 쓰지 못하고 있으니 나는 어쩌랴.

"어머니! 어떻게 하면 좋은 글을 쓸 수 있을까요?"

내가 아무리 여쭈어 봐도 우리 어머니는 미소만 짓고 계신다. 이렇게 고민에 빠지도록 진솔한 삶의 이야기를 쓰는 수필에 나는 왜 매달려 있는지 모르겠다. 내가 좋은 수필을 쓰고 싶다면, 나는 먼저 삶이 향내

베틀

가 나야 하고, 삶이 투명해야 하고, 삶이 아름다워야 하리라.

　나는 오늘도 좋은 글을 쓰지 못하는 나 자신을 보면서 내 인생살이를 되돌아본다. 맑고 빛나는 생활이 아니었기에 좋은 글을 쓸 수가 없는 나 자신에 괴롭다. 모든 것들은 욕심에서 오는 것, 불필요한 것들을 버려야 하리라. 투명한 거울을 보면서 잡티가 없이 투명한 글을 쓰고 싶은 마음이 인다. 아름다운 꽃을 보면서 꽃처럼 아름답고 향기로운 한 편의 아름다운 수필을 쓰고 싶다. 모든 오물들을 말없이 포용해주는 넓은 초록빛 바다를 보면서 세상을 품을 수 있는 마음이 생기게 할 수 있는 좋은 글을 쓰고 싶다. 드높은 파아란 하늘을 올려다보면서 가슴이 확 트이는 시원스런 글을 쓰고 싶어진다. 하얗게 피어나는 목화송이처럼 부드러운 글을 쓸 수는 없는 것일까. 멀리서 들려오는 은은한 종소리나 그윽한 풍경소리를 닮은 글을 쓸 수 있다면 얼마나 좋을까. 잘 발효되어 맛있는 고추장처럼 맛깔스러운 수필을 쓰고 싶어 고민에 빠진다. 특히 나는 농부의 딸로 태어나서인지 모든 것들을 받아들여 따스한 빛을 받아 다시금 보송보송한 흙으로 변해서 새로운 생명을 신비하게 탄생시키는 흙의 사랑을 쓰고 싶다. 한없는 흙의 사랑을, 받을 수 없는 자격인데도 받고 사는 한량없는 빛의 은혜를 수필이라는 장르를 통해서 독자들과 공감하고 싶어 막히지 않은 소통의 통로로 나는 쓰이고 싶다. 그러기 위해서 나는 열정을 갖고 인내하며 열심히 수필 쓰기를 연마해야 하리라.

　순수한 내 삶의 흐름을 자연스럽고 진솔하게 표현해서 독자와 소통하면 좋은 글이 되리라. 문학의 한 장르인 수필은 우리네 인생살이의 생활기록이면서도 인생의 아름다움과 소중함 그리고 가치 있는 삶을 찾아내고, 나아가서는 꿈이 있는 인생의 정서를 생명력이 있는 문장으로 표현하면 좋은 글이 되지 않겠는가 싶다. 숨어 있는 인생살이의 아름다움들을 많이 찾아내어서 수필이라는 이름으로 활짝 피워 내는 통로로 내가 쓰임 받으면 얼마나 좋을까. 오늘도 세계 각처에 있는 문학인들은 너나 나나 할 것 없이 어떻게 하면 좋은 글을 쓸 수 있을까 고민하면서 펜을 잡을 것이다. 때로는 무엇 때문에 이렇게 고생스런 일을 하는지 자문하기도 할 것이다. 그러면서도 쓰지 않고서는 못 견디게 하는 마음, 나는 그 마음이 이 지구의 한구석에 사랑을 심으며 평화를 기원하는 마음이라 생각한다. 이러한 마음들이 세상을 아름답게 하는 데 쓰임을 받고 있지 않은가.

나는 오늘도 어머니가 말씀하신 좋은 글을 쓰려면 내 인생살이가 더욱더 아름다워져야 한다는 것을 알면서도 그렇게 살지 못함에 부끄러움을 느낀다. 할 수만 있다면, 가슴에 사랑만 품고 살아 소중한 인생살이에서 얻어지는 느낌들을 수필에 담아내어 독자들과 소통하면서 살고 싶다. 내 인생의 꿈인 듯이 좋은 글을 쓰고 싶어하는 내 가슴에 은혜의 단비를 촉촉이 내려주시라고 간절한 소망의 기도를 두 손 모아 드린다.

베틀

큰일 났네!
속에 감춰진 진실

큰일 났네~, 최순실의 말. 진실은 반드시 밝혀질 것입니다~, 박근혜 전 대통령의 말. 유치한 막장드라마를 보고 있는 듯한 느낌을 주면서 대한민국을 떠들썩하게 한 박근혜-최순실 게이트 국정농단 사건의 주된 말이다. 두 사람이 말한 큰일 났네! 속에 감춰진 진실이라는 것이 무엇을 의미하는지 나는 참으로 아리송하기만 하다. 최순실-박근혜 국정 농단은 촛불시위로 시작해 박근혜 전 대통령을 탄핵으로, '사람이 먼저고 희망이다'를 외치는 문재인 새 대통령이 당선됨으로써 일단은 마무리된 우리나라 역사상 으레 없는 국민 정서를 훼파시킨 비선 실세의 국정농단 사건이다.

'허접한 여자와 국정운영, 탄핵당해도 싸다'는 어느 정치인의 말과 청와대에서 오랫동안 박근혜 전 대통령의 시중을 들어 주었던 김막업 씨의 인터뷰 중 '배우지 못한 나보다도 더 불행한 사람'이라는 말이 귓가에서 맴돈다. 박근혜-최순실 국정농단 사건에는 공주와 시녀 사이도 같고, 둘이서만 공유하고 있는 어떤 특별한 비밀이 있는 것 같기도 하여 참으로 묘한 관계로 보이는 둘만의 사이에서 최순실이 비선 실세로 사익을 취하고 국정농단을 했다는 것이다. 이 사건의 중심부에는 최순실의 딸 정유라가 있다. 생물학적 아버지라고 부르는 정윤회와 최순실의 시험관 시술 아기라고 하는데 항간에서는 독신인 박근혜 전 대통령과 측근인 영생교주 최태민 사이에서 난 딸이라는 악성 루머도 있다. 정유라는 삼성 그룹으로부터 지원을 받아 아시아 경기에서 금메달을 딴 승마선수, 이대 부정입학, '돈도 실력이다'는 말을 SNS에 올려 국민들의 공분을 샀던 국정농단 중심에 있는 인물이다.

2016년 가을, JTBC언론사 손석희 앵커가 태블릿PC를 화면에 보여주면서 국정농단 사건을 언급했다. 그 후, 이대 총장 등 관련된 사람들이 줄줄이 감옥으로 행하고 있는 이 사건은 박근혜 전 대통령, 국정농단 주범인 최순실, 뇌물죄로 구속된 글로벌 회사인 삼성 부회장 이재용, 불륜 관계로 시작되어 사건이 터졌다고 하는 고영태, 사건 제보자 노승일, 박영수 특검팀에 도우미라는 별명이 붙기도 한 장시호, 블랙리스트 작성 중심인물이라는 전 비서실장 김기춘, 전 문화체육부장 조윤선, 이 사건을 계속 추적하고 있는 안민석 국회의원 등 사건에 연루된 사람들이 수없이 많음에 놀랍다.

호스트바, 무당, 굿, 필러시술, 대포폰, 태반주사, 백옥주사, 뇌물횡령, 직권남용……. 세월호 7시간의 행적까지 난잡하고 희한한 언어들도 수없이 쏟아져 나와 국민들의 자존감을 사정없이 추락시킨 국정농단 사건이다. 박근혜 물러가라는 광화문 촛불집회에 맞서 박근혜 전 대통령을 나라로 표현하면서 보호하려는 태극기 집회가 생겼다. 세계의 하늘에 힘차게 펄럭여야 할 한국인의 얼이 담긴 태극기는 조국의 얼굴인데, 정치판 싸움에 사용되는 것이 코아메리칸으로 살고 있는 나에겐

베틀

참으로 못마땅하다.

역사 속에서 선덕여왕 이후로 소중한 여성대통령으론 처음인 박근혜 전 대통령은 불통 대통령, 수첩공주라는 말을 들으면서 시녀 같은 존재라는 최순실과 진실이 아닌 가식으로 인연을 맺고 살아온 값을 단단히 받고 있는 건가. 한 나라의 대통령의 딸로서 부귀영화를 누리며 공주처럼 살다가 대통령까지 지낸 사람이 국정농단의 주범으로 두 손에 수갑을 차고서 국민들과 세계 언론 앞에 나타난 모습은 참으로 참담하다. 헌법을 가장 잘 지켜서 국민들에게 모범을 보여주어야 할 헌법에 따라서 된 대통령이 헌법재판소에서, 헌법 정신을 지킬 수 없는 대통령이라는 불명예를 안고 8:0이라는 전원일치로 탄핵 소추안 결의에서 이정미 헌법재판소 소장 대행으로부터 '박근혜를 파면한다'는 말을 들은 역사상 처음으로 파면당한 대통령이 되었다.

새마을 정신을 외치면서 근대사를 이룬 박정희 대통령과 국민 어머니로 통했던 육영수 여사의 삼 남매 중 큰딸로 태어나 청와대에서 살다가 부모들이 총탄에 맞아 쓰러진 뒤, 세월이 많이 지나 제18대 대통령으로 당선되었으나 임기도 채우지 못한 채 대통령 탄핵이 된 박근혜 전 대통령. 수많은 사람의 열광과 환호 속에서 국익을 위해서 나라와 결혼했다고도 말한 박근혜 전 대통령이 나라의 최고의 통치권자로서의 명예가 한순간에 추하게 떨어지는 애잔한 모습을 보며, 동시대를 살아온 사람으로서 인간적인 연민을 느낀다. 그리고 나는 진리의 말씀인 성경 말씀을 되뇌어 본다. 부귀영화를 누렸던 솔로몬 왕의 입을 통해서 오늘날 나의 가슴 속에 깊게 박혀 주시는 하나님의 말씀, '…… 모든 것이 헛되고 헛되고 헛되도다.'

법 미꾸라지로 알려진 우병우 전 민정수석은 교만한 자세로 두 팔짱을 끼고서 레이저 눈빛을 쏟아냈다 하여 국민들의 분노를 자아내고 있다. 혼란한 정국으로 상처받은 국민들의 마음속에 대통령에 대한 존귀함이 얼마나 살아 있을까. 정치란 수많은 백성들을 행복하게 해 주는 것이라고 알고 있는 평범한 한 시민으로서의 바람이 있다면, 우리의 후세들이 크면 대통령이 되고 싶다는 아름다운 꿈과 희망을 가질 수 있는 나라로 회복되었으면 좋겠다. 미국에서 상하원들의 기립 박수를 받으면서 영어로 연설해 자긍심을 심어주던 대통령의 모습을 다시 볼 수 있었으면 좋겠다.

박근혜-최순실 게이트 국정농단의 중심이 된 큰일 났네! 속에 감춰진 진실은 정말 무얼 말하는지 아리송하기만 하다. 추운 겨울날 태극기와 성조기를 들고서 박근혜 대통령을 지지했던 국민들도, 박근혜 탄핵을 외치며 촛불을 들었던 국민들도 모두 민주주의를 열망하는 꿈을 지닌 애국자들이 아니겠는가. 하루빨리 엮였다는 매듭이 풀려 진실이 밝혀지고 정의가 살아남는 아름다운 고국이 되기를, 포용과 사랑으로 행복이 넘치는 자유민주 공화국인 대한민국이 되기를 진심으로 소망하며 전능자의 한량없는 은혜를 간구하는 나의 마음을 태평양 너머로 보낸다.

베틀

감사와 행복 품은 사돈들

감사와 행복을 품고 있는 사돈들을 만났다. 사돈들은 내가 부모가 되었을 때부터 보고 싶었던 반가운 사람들이다. 두 딸, 해미와 해련 덕분에 나는 사돈들을 만날 수 있어서 한량없이 기쁘기만 하다. 사돈(査頓)이란 서로 혼인한 남자와 여자 측의 가족 간을 말하기에, 두 딸 해미와 해련이 결혼을 함으로써 나에겐 자연스럽게 사돈들이 생긴 것이다. 2015년 3월, 우리 부부는 두 딸 부부와 사돈들과 합심으로 만복의 근원이 되시는 하나님께 영광을 올려드렸을 때, 나는 가슴이 뭉클해지면서 눈시울이 뜨거워짐을 느꼈다. 내 생애에 이렇게 행복한 시간이 또 있을까 싶을 정도였다.

우리 부부에게 있는 두 딸은 첫 번째 딸 이름은 해미(海美), 둘째 딸 이름은 해련(海蓮)이다. 두 살 터울이 채 안 되기에 연년생이나 다름없다. 그래서인지 어떤 사람들은 쌍둥이처럼 닮은 면이 많아서 누가 누군지 모르겠다고 말하기도 한다. 언니와 동생이 똑같이 미키마우스 옷을 입고서 찍은 사진은 어머니인 나도 가끔은 헷갈린다. 언뜻 보기에 그럴 뿐이지, 사실은 많은 차이가 있다. 우선 생김새가 큰딸은 아담하고,

작은딸은 키가 크다. 큰딸은 있는 대로 적응하며 양보심이 많은 성향이며, 작은딸은 남을 위해 주면서도 자기 몫도 챙기는 성향이다. 서로 다른 면이 많지만, 자매라서인지 아무래도 닮은꼴인 두 자매는 결혼도 비슷하게 했다.

두 딸 시부모와 시형인 사돈들이 서로서로 손을 잡고서 동그랗게 원을 그리면서 감사기도 시간을 줬을 때, 나는 얼마나 감사한지 시간이 멈춰도 좋을성싶었다. 그날을 위해서 지금까지의 내 인생을 열심히 살아온 듯싶다. 옛말에 "변소와 사돈은 멀리 있는 게 좋다"는 말이 있다. 고약한 냄새가 나는 변소나 껄끄러운 사돈은 꼭 필요하면서도 가까이에 있으면 부담스러워서 하는 말이었으리라. 그런데 지금은 모든 문화가 편리한 세대로 변해가면서 반대가 되어가고 있다. 변소가 안방으로 들어와야 좋고, 사돈들과는 가족처럼 지내는 게 좋으니 말이다.

큰딸 해미는 출가하면서 자연스럽게 박씨 가문으로 흡수되고, 작은딸 해련이는 구씨 가문으로 흡수되었다. 요즈음은 사위를 배 안 아프고 거저 얻은 아들이라 한다. 우리 부부는 두 딸이 혼인하게 됨으로써 사랑스러운 아들을 하나도 아니고 둘이나 인생의 선물로 받게 되었다. 큰 사위 이름은 성찬, 작은 사위 이름은 요셉이다. 사돈댁들에게 "이렇게 귀하게 잘 키운 아들을 저희 부부에게 사위로 맞이하게 해 주심을 진심으로 감사한다."고 말씀드렸다. 사돈댁들도 똑같은 말을 되풀이해주셨다. 우리 사돈들은 나처럼 힘든 해외이민 1세를 살아오신 분들이고, 사위들은 두 딸처럼 코아메리카 이중문화 속에서 꿋꿋하게 자란 미주이민 2세들이다. 비슷한 환경 속에서 살아온 사람들끼리 혼례를 통해서 사돈의 인연을 맺게 되니 마음이 편하고 즐겁다.

베틀

결혼이란 남녀 두 사람이 만나서 부부의 연을 맺는 행사다. 혼례라는 말을 많이 쓰던 옛날 시대엔 얼굴도 안 보고서 결혼한 후에, 첫날밤에야 비로소 신랑·신부가 서로서로 얼굴을 보았다는 웃지 못할 이야기도 있다. 어느 쪽이 얼마나 되는지 자로 재고 저울질하던 중매결혼시대에서 차츰 자유결혼시대로 지금은 연애시대라 한다. 지금은 갈수록 생활하기가 편리해져서 무결혼을 선호하는 사람들이 많아진다 하니 다음 세대는 결혼문화가 어떻게 형성되어 갈 것인지 아리송하다. 나는 이 중 문하 속에서 힘들게 자란 두 딸이 삶의 주인공이 되어 행복하게 살겠노라고 적령기에 사랑하는 배필을 만나서 결혼하게 되어 너무도 감사하다. 하나님이 두 사람이 한 몸을 이루어 행복하게 살라고 부부의 연을 맺어주셨으니 허락해주신 땅 위에서 검은 머리가 파뿌리 되도록 백년해로하면서 행복하게 살라는 주례사의 말씀을 들으며 결혼하는 딸들을 바라보는 나의 마음은 고마운 마음으로 흐뭇할 뿐이다.

우리 딸들은 아빠 엄마와 팔짱을 끼고서 은은한 꽃향기가 흩날리는 아름다운 꽃길을 사뿐사뿐 걸어 야외결혼식장에서 결혼식을 올렸다. 곱게 단장한 머리 위에 쓴 나비처럼 하늘거리는 하이얀 베일 속에 드러난 순결한 얼굴이 천사처럼 아름답다. 결혼하는 순간처럼 언제나 순결하고 고운 마음으로 부부가 서로서로 사랑하며 행복하게 살기를 간절히 바라며 딸을 사위에게 넘겨준다. 행운아인 딸들을 며느리로 받아들이겠노라고 사랑스럽게 안아주는 사돈들에게서 훈훈한 정이 흐른다. 이젠 끊임없는 기도 외엔 모든 것들을 사돈들에게 넘겨야 한다. 평생토록 딸들 앞에선 겸손히 기도하는 이 세상에서 제일 좋은 어머니로 남아 있기 위해서라도 말이다. 언제나처럼 결혼식을 알리는 결혼행진

곡 소리에 내 신경세포가 팽대해지면서 찌르르 눈시울이 뜨거워지는데 "엄마. 우린 영원한 엄마 딸~!" 하는 고운 음성이 귓가에 맴돈다. 시원하면서도 허전한 나의 눈 속엔 아직도 어여쁜 색동옷 입은 어린 딸들이 시집가서 아름다운 미래의 꿈을 지혜와 인내로 펼쳐 나아가는 두 딸이 되기를 염원할 뿐이다.

한민족의 정서와 문화가 서린 야외폐백실에서 우리 부부와 사돈들은 결혼서약을 끝내고 양가 부모님에게 고맙다는 인사를 하는 들꽃처럼 청초한 결혼한 자녀에게 고운 밤과 대추를 던져준다. "자아~. 아들 딸 많이 낳고 행복하게 잘 살거라." 결혼한 자녀가 보자기를 펼쳐 들고서 축복을 다 받겠노라고 아우성이다. 사돈들의 즐거운 웃음소리가 아이들의 결혼식을 진심으로 축하하는 마음을 노래하는 듯하다. 사랑하는 딸들이 결혼하는 시점에서 반갑게 만난 사돈들은 내가 팍팍한 이민생활에서 낙타처럼 메마른 모래땅 사막길을 걷다가 찾은 오아시스에서 만난 사람들 같다. 나는 감사와 행복 품은 사돈들과 함께 남은 나의 인생 여정을 도란도란 얘기를 나누면서 즐겁게 함께 걷고 싶은 심정이다.

눈을 들어 하늘을 우러러보니 눈이 시리도록 청명하고 참으로 아름답다.

베틀

양파가 날 울려

    속상하다. 콧잔등이 시큰해지며 눈물이 난다. 눈시울이 쓰리고 붉어지면서 속울음이 기어이 터트려지고 만다. 나는 부엌에 있는 수돗물을 틀면서 소리친다. 양파가 날 울려! '양파 핑계 대고 많이 우세요~' 나를 어쩔 줄 모르게 하는 그 목소리, 바로 오장육부가 뒤틀리기라도 하는 듯 어지럽게 한 그 사람이 아닌가. 어떻게 내 마음을 알았을까 그리고 그 위로의 말은 또 뭐람, 묘연해진 내 머리가 종잡을 수 없이 혼란스러워진다. 부족한 신앙의 한복판에 서서 내 영혼을 살리기 위해 안간힘을 쓰고 있는 내 가슴에 소금 알갱이들이 엉켜 뭉쳐지고 있음을 느낀다.

    나는 짭짜름한 눈물을 삼키면서 교회 친교실 벽에 걸려 있는 달력을 본다. 매운 양파 물과 눈물로 범벅되어 흐릿해진 내 눈동자에 침묵의 언어인 십자가의 모습이 아른거린다. 아~ 사랑의 완성! 거듭나지 않으면 새 생명으로 태어날 수 없는 것! 내 가슴을 휘~잉 하고 세찬 바람이 지나가면서 내 가슴 속에 있는 소금 알갱이를 깨부수는 기분이다. 세상에서 소금의 역할을 하려면 하얀 소금은 깨어지고 부서지는 아픔이 있어야 맛을 내고 부패를 막는 방부제 기능을 할 수 있지 않은가.

짭짜름한 소금물이 성수가 되어 눈물 콧물로 내 몸속에 저려 있는 속상함을 시원스럽게 헹궈준다.

인생살이에선 어디에서나 나 아닌 남과 어우러져 살아갈 때 이기적인 생각을 버려야만 아름다운 인간관계를 유지할 수 있음을 안다. 특히나 영원한 생명을 갈구하는 신앙생활을 공동으로 해 나가려면 무시당해도 묵묵하고 부서져도 두렵지 않은 겸손이 필요하다. 하나님의 선물인 주위 사람들과의 아름다운 인연을 위해 선한 일만 하면서 생활하고 싶지만 그러지 못할 경우도 있다. 조직으로 일하다 보면 계획에 없던 일들이 옆구리를 치고 들어오는 경우가 있다. 이럴 땐, 의견이 분분하고 억양이 거칠어지고 시끄럽다. 자기의 의견과 다르면 심하게 쏘아댈 일도 아닌데 남의 가슴에 구멍을 뚫을 만큼 큰 소리로 자기의 입장을 표명하기도 한다. 말과 혀를 조심하라며 언어생활의 중요성을 수없이 강조하신 성경 말씀을 알면서도 자기의 감정을 조절하지 못하여 서로의 가슴에 상처를 내고 만다.

아무리 사실이라도 날카로운 언어로 크게 바락바락 악을 쓰면, 듣는 사람은 언어폭력에 심장이 쿵쾅 거리고 마음에 구멍이 뚫리도록 상처를 받는다. 육체적인 고통은 시간에 묻혀 잊히지만, 말로 받은 상처는 마음을 훼파해 다시금 원상태로 치유되기가 어렵다. 흔적 탓에 서로의 틈새로 살며시 스며드는 서늘한 감정의 바람이 있기 때문이다. 한 번 상처받은 아픈 마음은 아무리 노력해도 원상태로 될 수가 없기에 말 한마디도 실수하지 않도록 참으로 조심해야 할 일이다. 한마디 언어에도 꽃처럼 색깔도 있고 향기도 있을 터이니 아름답고 희망을 주는 말만 했으면 좋겠다. 누군가에게 위로가 되고, 꿈꾸는 삶을 가질 수 있도

베틀

록 한 마디라도 따뜻한 마음으로 표현하는 고운 언어를 구사해서 사용한다면 얼마나 좋겠는가.

신앙인의 인품은 기도와 공동체의 생활에서 연마되고 원만해지기 때문에 소금이 깨어져 짭짤한 성수로 변한 눈물 콧물로 마음을 정화시키고 용서하는 슬기로움이 필요한 것만 같다. 그리고 모든 문제는 나의 어리석은 과실 때문이라고 치자. 도움과 이해와 따뜻한 사랑을 원한다면 내가 한 걸음 밑으로 내려서서 인내와 성찰과 겸손한 자세를 취하는 수밖에 없다. 죄 없으신 예수님의 수난을 생각하면 우리가 받는 마음의 상처는 점 하나에 불과하지 않겠는가. 새 생명을 열망하는 신앙 생활에서 내세의 행복을 확신하는 기쁨이 크지만, 그보다도 지금 따뜻한 가슴으로 사랑을 나누는 행복이 빠진다면 무슨 의미가 있겠는가 싶다. 좋은 인연을 가진 사람끼리 겸손과 온유한 마음으로 화목하게 살기 위해서 자기 자신을 인내로 연마하여 남에게 도움이 되는 것도 하나의 소금의 역할이 아니겠는가.

나의 보호막이 되어 남모르게 내 속에 잠재해 있는 속울음을 눈물 콧물이 되어 배설시키게 한 양파는 둥근 모양의 채소다. 까고 또 까도 똑같은 모양의 양파는 아삭아삭하고 달콤하면서도 매운맛을 내며 특이한 향기도 있다. 종류에 따라 조금씩 다르긴 해도 자극적인 냄새를 내며 최루성 물질로 바뀌는 이황화프로필알릴과 황화알릴이라는 효소가 있어 칼로 껍질을 벗기거나 요리를 할 때 눈의 점막을 자극하여 몹시 쓰리고 아프다. 무슨 양념에도 조화를 이루어 다양한 맛을 내는 채소류 양념이다. 나는 가능하면 많은 종류 중에서 맛도 순하고 독한 맛도 덜 하는 양파를 구하기 위해서 노력하지만, 양파란 근본적으로 단

맛과 매큼한 맛이 함께 공존해 있음을 안다. 사람에게도 장단점이 있듯이 말이다. 경천애인(敬天愛人)을 마음속에 품고 사는 신앙인의 태도를 망가뜨리지 않기 위해서 안간힘을 쓰며 양파를 다루면서 성도들의 성품과 소금의 역할을 생각해 본다.

내 안에 쌓인 못된 감정이 변하여 응집된 하얀 소금이 하얗게 부서져 녹아, 짭짜름한 눈물로 변하여 흐르며 겸손해질 때 영혼의 하이얀 기도꽃으로 피어난다. 이 기도꽃이 세상을 조금이라도 아름답게 만들어 가는 데 쓰인다면 얼마나 고마운 일인가. 우리는 작은 노여움에 소중한 사랑을 잃기가 쉬운데 가능하다면 마음이 욱신거리도록 아파도 인내로 이겨 남을 품어주는 것이 세상 속에서 소금의 역할을 하는 게 아니겠는가. 부족한 생각과 어눌한 말투로 남의 핀잔을 받은 날은, 자신에 대한 실망이 깊어져 부끄럽고 우울한 감정이 되어 죄로부터 자유로워지기가 쉽지 않다. 어금니를 깨물며 견뎌냈으나 더는 견딜 수 없는 침묵을 눈물 콧물로 감정을 시원하게 터트린다. 나는 신앙인으로서의 꿈을 이루기 위해 양파를 핑계 삼아 울게 한 성도에게 고맙게 생각하기로 한다. 그리고 마음을 활짝 열고 큰 소리로 외친다.

"양파가 날 울려!"

베틀

무궁화

무궁화(無窮花)는 1948년 정부가 수립되면서 광복절에 정식으로 지정된 대한민국 국화(國花)다. 나는 대한민국 사람이어서인지 무궁화가 무조건 사랑스럽고 좋아진다. 무궁화는 내 인생의 친구요 반려자이기도 하다. 나는 태아(胎兒) 때부터 이순(耳順)을 넘긴 지금까지 무궁화와 함께 살고 있다.

내가 태어나고 어린 시절을 보냈던 농촌 우리 집 텃밭 울타리는 무궁화 나무였다. 우리 어머니가 하루에도 몇 번씩 드나드는 시골집 텃밭 울타리 무궁화는 생명의 환희를 말해 주는 듯 싱싱하고 아름다웠다. 무궁화 나무가 줄지어 있는 울타리 밑으로 작은 도랑이 있어 언제나 물이 졸졸 흘러내려 흙이 촉촉이 물기에 젖어서였으리라. 이른 아침에 이슬을 머금고 피어나는 무궁화 꽃은 언제나 나에게 신선함과 삶에 대한 희망을 품게 했다. 초봄에 연둣빛으로 돋아나는 무궁화 이파리는 우리 가족의 무공해 건강식 반찬거리였다. 무궁화는 아욱과 식물이어서, 연한 이파리들을 물에서 하얀 거품이 일도록 손으로 비벼서 씻은 후에 마른 멸치 넣고 된장국을 끓이면 아주 구수하고 맛있다. 무궁화는 일제 강점기 시절에도 6·25 시절에도 우리 민족들과 고난을 함께하면서 이파리는 육체에, 꽃은 영혼에 밝은 내일에 대한 희망을 준 고마운 꽃이다.

여름이 되면 무궁화 꽃이 피기 시작하는데 피고 지고 또 피고 가을이 깊어질 때까지 피고 진다. 꽃 수술에 입 맞추길 좋아하는 벌, 나비 덕분에 꽃가루받이가 잘 돼 분홍색, 하얀색, 보라색 등 조화를 이루어 여러 색깔을 볼 수 있다. 그중에서도 하얀색 무궁화는 옥양목 한복에 꽃자주 옷고름을 단단히 맨 우리 민족의 여인같이 단아하고 고결한 자태이다. 그리고 일편단심 우리 겨레만 사랑하며 지키고자 하는 지조(志操)를 보여주고 있다. 신비로운 소리를 내는 나팔같이 생긴 기다란 꽃 수술이 황금가루가 넘쳐남은, 언젠가는 우리 겨레가 자랑스러운 세계 최고의 경제국가가 될 것임을 나팔 불고 있음이 아니겠는가. 그뿐만이 아니다. 무궁화 꽃송이마다 안으로 들어갈수록 더 짙은 색깔을 나타내 우리 국민의 내면이 옹골짐을 말해 주고 있다. 이러한 연유로 무궁화는 우리 겨레를 상징해 주기에 가장 적합한 꽃임이 틀림없다.

한 송이의 무궁화 꽃은 청순한 얼굴로 아침에 피었다가 저녁이면 오므라들고 마는데, 또 다른 꽃들이 잇대어 피어나기 때문에 날마다 새로운 꽃들을 볼 수가 있어 영원히 지지 않을 꽃 같은 느낌을 준다. 아마도 우리 눈에는 보이지 않지만 전능자의 보살핌이 우리 겨레를 계속 보살펴 주고 있음을 믿게 하기 위함인가 싶어진다. 화려하지도 밉지도 않아 수수하게 보이는 해맑은 무궁화는 어느 누가 돌보지 않아도, 뜨거운 뙤약볕 속에서도 겸허하게 은근과 끈기로 살아남아 줄기차게 연연히 피어난다. 많은 슬픔과 고난을 이겨낸 우리 국민성을 닮은 꽃이

베틀

기에 민족의 무궁한 발전과 번영을 기원하는 마음을 담아 우리 겨레의 상징인 국화(國花)로 정했으리라.

　내가 아메리칸 드림을 안고 고국을 떠나 올 때였다. 2세들의 교육을 위해서 평생토록 교육계에서 헌신하신 우리 시아버님께서 동양화한 점을 선물로 주셨다. '무궁화, 무궁화 우리나라 꽃…'이라는 노랫말이 적힌 가벼운 그림 한 폭이었지만 그 뜻을 아는 나에겐 참으로 무거운 생각이 들었다. 해외에 나가서 살지만, 한민족의 얼을 언제나 가슴에 품고 살라는 시아버님의 뜻을 알았기에 나는 가슴판에 깊이 새겼다. 지금도 나는 그 감격의 순간을 잊지 않고 나 자신뿐만 아니라 자녀에게도 수시로 무궁화는 대한민국을 상징하는 꽃임을 일깨워 주곤 한다. 고국에서 떠나 올 때 가지고 온 무궁화 그림은 방문을 열면 볼 수 있는 자리에서 거실로 옮겨 놓았다. 우리 집을 방문하는 사람은 누구든지 좀 더 가까이 볼 수 있게 옮겨 놓았더니 역시 잘했다는 느낌이 들 정도로 사람들의 관심사가 되고 있다. 나는 무궁화가 얼마나 사랑스럽고 아름다운 꽃인지, 얼마나 인간들에게 이로움을 주는지를 혀가 닳도록 이국 사람들에게도 자랑하곤 한다.

　요즈음 내가 살고 있는 지역에 무궁화 나무가 늘어나고 있어 나는 가슴이 뿌듯하다. 이제 우리 민족은 삼천리강산에서 사는 것만이 아니라 세계 각국에서 힘찬 생명력으로 살아가고 있다. 해서 우리 겨레의 심성이 담긴 무궁화를 아끼고 사랑해서 보급하는 일에 힘써야 하지 않겠는가 싶다. 나는 우리 겨레의 꽃을 번식시키려고 꼬마 무궁화들을 후세들을 키운 것처럼 아름다운 꿈을 품고 정성을 다해 가꾸고 있다.

한국인의 얼과 기상 속에 은근과 끈기로 살아 숨 쉬는 소중한 무궁화, 그 혼(魂)의 영향을 받아 나도 이렇게 힘든 해외동포 생활을 이겨내고 있지 않겠는가. 화려하지 않고 천박하지도 않아서 수수한 무궁화, 나를 닮은 것 같아 더욱더 정감이 가고 사랑스러운 걸까. 나는 무궁화와 함께 날마다 생활할 수 있음에 행복하다.

우리나라는 아직도 동족 간의 6 ·25 전쟁 후 휴전 상태에 있다. 무궁화의 얼을 지니고 사는 한 민족들이 하루빨리 통일의 꿈을 이뤄 화려한 무궁화 꽃동산을 만들고 서로서로 얼싸안고서 얼씨구 좋구나! 둥둥 춤을 추어야 하리라. 우리나라 강산 여기저기에 피어나는 무궁화가 이제는 지구촌 이곳저곳에서 피어나니 한량없이 기쁘고 즐겁다. 나는 이 세상에서 사는 날까지 나의 사랑 무궁화처럼 수수하고 소박한 아름다움과 은은한 향기를 지니고 사람들과 화합하면서 살고 싶은 소망이 크다. 한민족의 얼이 살아 숨 쉬는 한 그루의 강인한 무궁화가 되어 광활하고 기름진 이 땅에 굳건히 뿌리를 내리면서. 햇빛과 물과 공기가 되어주는 사랑하는 사람들과 함께 호흡하면서 말이다.

베틀

그랬었구나!

"아— 그랬었구나! 그래서 내가 양초를 좋아하지 않는 이유를 알았
다고."

나는 신기한 것을 발견이라도 한 듯이 흥분된 어조로 중얼거리면서
손뼉을 치니, 무언가 막혔던 것이 순식간에 시원히 뚫리는 기분이었다.
나는 수십 년 동안 잊어버리고 산 일인데, 참으로 우연히 내가 양초를
좋아하지 않는 이유를 알아낸 것이다.

"이 초 향기 좀 맡아봐, 흠— 너무도 좋다. 라일락 꽃향기야."

사랑하는 친구가 예쁜 코를 벌렁거리면서 양초 향내를 몽땅 오목하
게 생긴 콧속으로 빨아드릴 듯이 냄새를 맡더니, 내 앞으로 내밀었다.

"나는 초 냄새를 별로 몰라. 좋아하지도 않고."

친구가 초를 내 앞으로 내미는 찰나에, 나는 순간적으로 친구를 밀
쳐버렸다. 향기에 매료되어 들뜬 친구의 감정도 아랑곳하지 않고, 듣기
에 민망스러울 정도로 퉁명스럽게 말하면서.

그 순간에 나는 내 오른손 안쪽으로 촛농이 떨어져서 굳어버린 듯
이 울퉁불퉁하게 생긴 흉터를 본 것이다. 내 과거사를 들은 친구는, 무

안해하던 표정을 짓고 '그랬었구나!' 하면서 내 잘못된 행동을 너그럽게 용서하여 주었다.

얼마 전에도 비슷한 일이 있었다. 촛대를 사 들고서 우리 집을 즐겁게 오신 속 깊은 초강 언니한테 나는 별로 달갑지 않게 말했다.

"나는 초를 별로 좋아하지 않는데— 촛대 사왔네."

"그래?"

어쩜 좋아, 내가 왜 이런 말을 했을까. 서운한 표정의 언니를 보면서 나는 바로 후회했지만, 이미 내 말은 공중으로 쏘아버린 화살과 같았다. 나는 실수를 하고 만 것이다.

"촛대가 참 예쁘네, 언니가 만들었어? 사람들이 보이는 곳에 두고서 오래도록 잘 간직할게."

나는 어색한 분위기를 얼버무리고 말았다. 나는 안다. 지금은 멀리 떠나 살고 계시는, 촛불을 두 손으로 받들고 서 있는 수호천사같이 신실한 도예가 언니가, 내 과거사를 알게 되면 틀림없이 나를 이해하여 주실 것이다. 그랬었구나— 하시면서.

그러니까, 지금 시대보다도 훨씬 더 전력이 덜 풍부했던 시절이었다. 내가 가장 지겹게 살았던 여고 졸업반 시절이기도 하다. 그 시절엔, 밤 늦도록 전등불을 켜놓고 공부하기엔 엄청난 전기세도 부담스러웠을 뿐만 아니라, 절약시대의 국가에 대해서도 미안한 일이었다. 그래서, 호롱불보다는 편리한 촛불을 켜놓고 공부할 때가 많았다.

그날도 그랬다. 내가 오른손을 촛불에 덴 날도. 피곤했던 나는, 앉은뱅이책상 위에 촛불을 켜 놓고서 시험공부를 하다간 잠이 들어 버렸다. 내가 무언가 타는 냄새에 놀라서 눈을 떴을 땐, 책상 위에 놓인 양

베틀

초가 다 타고 조금 남은 촛물이 나무책상을 태우고 있는 순간이었다. 나는 얼마나 놀랐던지 엉겁결에 오른손으로 촛불을 덮는 순간에, 뜨겁게 녹아내린 양초가 내 손에 달라붙어서, 피부가 홀랑 벗겨져 버릴 정도로 데어 버린 것이다. 나는 손에 화상을 입고서 고생한 후로, 아픈 상처에 대한 흔적을 남긴 양초에 대한 거부감이 마음속 깊은 곳에 잠재해 있었나 보다. 양초가 있는 곳에선 어느 사이엔가 내 몸이 움츠러지고, 도사려질 정도로.

근래에 난 오른손에 있는 흉터를 볼 때면, 초와 관련해서 내 생활을 반추시켜 보곤 한다.

파르르 떨면서 꺼져가는 순간까지, 자기 몸을 태워서 한 줄기 빛으로 남을 밝게 해주는 촛불 같은 인생을 사는 사람들이, 이 세상에는 헤아릴 수 없이 많다. 나는 비록 그런 사람은 되지 못할지라도, 적어도 '그랬었구나-'하고 남의 형편과 사정을 이해하여 주는 너그러움은 있어야 할 것 같다. 완전히 이해하지 못한 오해로 남의 마음을 어둡게 하지는 말아야겠다는 생각이다.

누구든지 무슨 문제가 발생하였을 때는 실수한 일도 있을 것이고, 어쩔 수 없이 저지른 일도 있을진대, '그랬었구나-' 하고 나는 더욱더 넓은 마음으로 이해하고 받아들이는 관용을 베풀어야 할 것이다. 나의 잘못과 실수에 남이 나를 용서해 주고, 이해하여 주기를 바라는 마음처럼.

더불어 살아가면서, 밝은 세상을 만들어 가려고 노력하는 사랑스러운 한 사람인 내가 되려면.

| 4부 |

몬터레이 아리랑

몬터레이 소나무

내가 '몬터레이 소나무'라고 이름 붙이고서 20여 년 동안 친구처럼 지내는 노송(老松)이 있다. 언제나 나를 다정하게 반겨주며 생활의 지혜를 날려주는 참으로 고마운 나무 친구다.

하늘을 향해서 쭉쭉 뻗어난 나뭇가지에 짙은 초록 색깔의 뾰쪽뾰쪽한 이파리가 촘촘하게 달려 있는데 많은 세월이 흘렀어도 한결같이 짙푸르기만 하다.

몬터레이 지역에 있는 소나무들은 자세히 보면 종류가 조금씩 다르다. 어림잡아 대여섯 종류는 되는 것 같다. 같은 종류인데도 토양과 온도와 바람맞는 환경에 따라서 조금씩 모양이 다르다. 고국에 있었을 때 무더기로 산에서 보아온 바늘같이 생긴 이파리를 가진 뭉실뭉실하고 큰 솔방울을 달고 있는 '몬터레이 파인'이라 불리는 소나무가 있는가 하면, 잣나무같이 생긴 작달막한 이파리가 질서정연하게 하늘을 향해서 쭉쭉 뻗쳐 있고 작은 솔방울을 달고 있는 내 친구 같은 '몬터레이 사이프러스'가 있다.

'몬터레이 사이프러스'인 나의 친구 노송은 창조주의 아름다운 창조물로 몬터레이 지역에 살고 있음을 자랑스럽게 여기면서 이곳 관광객들에게 즐거움을 선사하는데 한 몫을 담당한 거칠고 비비꼬인 삶의 흔적이 더해짐에 따라서 더욱더 멋이 있어 가는 내 친구 '몬터레이 소나무', 환경에 굴하지 않는 의연한 자세에 모두 감탄한다. 나는 시간이 지남에 따라서 사람들에게 더 많은 기쁨을 주는 내 나무 친구를 볼 때마다 '나도 저렇게 나이가 더해갈수록 남에게 행복을 줄 수 있을까?'고 민해 본다.

사이프러스 트리는 몬터레이의 상징수이다. 그래서 관공서에서 관리가 대단하다. 내 친구 몬터레이 소나무에도 어느 날 보니 동전 같은 것에 '2200'이라고 번호가 쓰여 있었다. 내 친구 나무도 이 고장에서 보호를 받고 있는 걸 직감할 수 있었다. 또 그것은 아름다운 몬터레이의 위상을 높이기 위해서 오랜 풍파를 견딘 후에 받은 '훈장'처럼 보였다.

내 친구 '몬터레이 소나무'는 참으로 의젓해서 나의 문제를 무엇이나 해결해내는 '해결사' 같다. 어떨 땐 풀리지 않는 문제를 내어놓고 해결 방법을 물어본다. '어떻게 해야 하나?' 나는 내 작은 팔을 다섯 번이나 벌려야 안을 만큼 덩치가 큰 백 살도 넘은 내 친구 노송에 포근한 엄마 품에 얼굴을 파묻듯이 가만히 얼굴을 대고선 귀를 기울인다. 그러면 내 가슴속으로 은밀한 소리가 들려온다.

"좀 더 기다리고 좀 더 참으면 안 되겠니? 좀 더 마음이 너그러워지면 좋겠다. 좀 더 사랑하는 마음을 가질 수는 없겠니? 나는 하루 이틀이 아닌 수많은 세월 동안 온갖 어려움을 이겨내면서 이렇게 든든하게 내 자리를 지키고 있지 않니? 비바람에 찢겨 내 몸에 이렇게 많은 상처가 남아 있고 내 몸에 이물이 들어와 나를 부식시키고 심지어는 나

베틀

와는 하등 관계도 없는 식물이 내 약한 부분을 파고들어 와 제집인 양 살고 있어도 나는 받아주었단다."

날마다 잇대어지는 내 이민 역사도 몬터레이 소나무와 함께 이곳에 뿌리를 내리고 있음을 느낄 수 있다. 그래서인지 내 친구 몬터레이 소나무는 우리 한인 이민사 백 년을 기념하는 잔치로 감개무량해 하는 나를 이해하여 주는 것 같다. 하와이에 있는 사탕수수 농장으로 첫 이민을 시작으로 우리 한인들이 몇 년 전에 겪은 가슴 아픈 LA 폭동사건을 결코 잊지 못하지만 그래도 굽히지 않고 다시 굳세게 일어나는 삶의 모습을 내 친구 몬터레이 소나무는 대견해하는 듯하다. 오늘날 우리 2세들은 떳떳하고 활기 있게 각종 분야에 진출하고 있다. 언론계나 의학 분야, 또는 정치마당으로도 도전하는 한인들을 흐뭇해하는 나에게 내 친구 몬터레이 사이프러스는 동참해주는 기분이 든다.

그 어느 날 내 친구 노송을 만나러 가는데 노란 줄로 바리케이드가 쳐져 있고 그 안쪽으로는 많은 잘린 가지들이 놓여 있었다. 각질화되고 생명력을 잃은 가지들이 몸통에서 떨어지면 지나가는 사람들이 다칠 우려가 있어 산림관리인들이 미리 몸단장을 시켜주는 것이었다. 어쩔 수 없이 늙어 가면 누군가의 도움이 필요하게 된다는 자연의 섭리를 일깨워주었다.

몬터레이 세계에서 가장 살기 좋은 곳일지도 모른다는 착각을 일으킬 정도로 참으로 아름답고 아담한 관광 휴양도시다. 사시사철 날씨의 변동이 심하지 않고 공기가 맑아서인지 사람들은 온화하고 맑은 눈동자를 가졌다. 날개를 달고서 하늘을 날 듯한 생명력 넘치는 늘 푸른 사이프러스 트리, 꿈의 궁전 같은 고풍스러운 집들이 줄을 지어 아기자기한 도시들을 만든다. 해변을 따라서 절묘한 바위절벽과 어우러져 피어 있는 분홍색 물감을 뿌려놓은 듯한 황홀하리만큼 아름다운 매직 카펫 꽃, 널따란 태평양 한가운데로 놀랍도록 커다란 붉은 해가 떨어지는 신비스러운 낙조는 관광도시 몬터레이가 뿜어내는 아름다움의 극치이다.

이토록 헤아릴 수 없이 많은 아름다운 것 중에서 특히 내 친구 '몬터레이 소나무'가 없어선 안 될 만큼 정이 든 것은 그는 내 호흡에서 나오는 김치 냄새를 맡아주고 나는 그의 치즈 냄새에 적응해갈 수 있도록 틈만 나면 몸을 접촉하고 대화를 나누면서 화합을 이루어가기 때문이다.

어느 날 생명력을 잃어서 잘려나간 노송의 가지 위에 물새 한 마리가 쉬고 있다. 그 물새가 남들의 도움을 받을 정도로 나약해지고 굵은 뼈만 남은 핏기 없이 앙상한 어깨인데도 온 힘을 다해 몸을 버티고 있는 모습이 2세들을 위한 밑받침이 되어주기 위해서 희생하고 있는 이민 1세들의 모습을 보는 것 같기도 하고 몬터레이 한인사회를 위해서 알게 모르게 힘쓰는 일꾼들을 보는 것 같기도 해 마음이 뭉클했다.

오늘도 오래된 나의 친구 '몬터레이 소나무'를 찾았다. 자꾸만 머리카락이 작아지는 노인네처럼 내 친구 노송도 해마다 초록색 이파리들이 줄어들고 거칠어져 우둘투둘해도 늠름히 더 깊은 뿌리를 내리면서 몬터레이 위상을 높이고 있다. 나는 참으로 듬직하고 변함없는 친구 노송을 만져도 보고 눈을 들어 올려다보며 두 팔 벌려 안아도 보았다.

그때에 강렬하게 들리는 해송(海松)의 맥박 소리가 나에게 어떤 삶의 희망을 주었다. 그리고 '몬터레이 소나무'는 이렇게 말하는 것 같았다.

"나는 푸르게 살리라. 너도 푸르게 살아라. 우리는 푸르게 살아야만 한다."

베틀

생명

　살아 움직이는 모든 것엔 생명(生命)이 있다. 성경에는 말씀으로 천지를 창조하시고 하나님의 형상대로 흙으로 빚어진 사람에게 생령(生靈)을 불어넣어 주어 생명이 있게 하셨다고 쓰여있다. 생명은 인간이 범할 수 없는 오묘한 신(神)의 영역이다. 이 세상 어느 누구도 생명만은 만들 수 없다. 생명은 창조주가 생명체를 가진 피조물에게 유일하게 이 세상에서 살아갈 수 있게 한 선물이다. 생명은 이 세상을 살아가기 위해 부여받은 단 한 번의 귀중한 선물이기에 참으로 감사한 마음으로 소중히 해야 한다. 세포 속에서 생명력이 자연히 소멸될 때까지 말이다.

　생명은 세월의 통로다. 과거, 현재, 미래를 이어주는 통로가 있다는 사실은 얼마든지 인격을 발전시킬 수 있는 원동력이 되지 않겠는가. 과거를 회상하면서 오늘은 좀 더 알차게 살려고 노력하고 오늘을 보면서 내일에 대한 희망도 품어 볼 수 있겠다. 나는 참으로 귀한 생명이 있는 이 순간 사랑하는 사람들과 이 지구촌에 사는 불쌍한 사람까지도 다 함께 어울려 더 깊고 넓은 마음으로 아름다운 인생살이를 하고 싶다. 나에게 새 생명을 허락해 주실 존귀하신 분 앞에 서는 날까지.

생명은 싱그럽고 아름답다. 봄이 되면 연두색 새싹들이 무거운 흙덩어리를 들어 올리면서 생명의 축제를 열겠노라고 아우성이다. 여름이 되면 세상은 온통 진초록으로 생(生)을 찬미한다. 가을이 되면 알록달록 각종 아름다운 색깔로 현란한 결실의 잔치를 베풀며 노래한다. 겨울이 되면 침묵으로 아름다움을 유지한다. 생명은 사시사철 싱그러운 아름다움을 품고 있다.

생명은 신비롭다. 아기가 엄마 젖을 찾고 웃고 울 때 신비스러움을 느낀다. 자그마한 지렁이가 몸이 두 동강이가 나도 꿈틀거리는 생명력을 볼 때 참으로 신비롭지 않은가. 작은 씨앗이 적당한 물과 온도와 영양분 속에서 새싹이 나고 꽃이 피고 열매를 맺을 때 생명의 신비스러움을 느낀다. 생명의 꿈틀거림은 무생물에서는 찾을 수 없는 생명의 신비로움이다. 불가사의(不可思議)로 알려진 피라미드나 앙코르와트와 건축물은 웅장하고 경이롭지만, 무생물이라서인지 생물인 작은 들꽃 초록 꽃대에서 연분홍 꽃눈이 터져 나오는 살아 움직이는 생명의 신비로움은 못 느낀다. 생명은 생물에서만이 느낄 수 있는 신비로움이기 때문일 것이다.

생명은 감사함과 행복이다. 아침에 잠에서 깨어나 눈을 떴을 때, 숨을 쉬는 허파의 바람소리와 심장이 뛰는 맥박소리를 감지할 때 얼마나 감사하고 행복한가. 사랑하는 사람들을 생각할 수 있고 느낄 수 있으니 얼마나 감사하고 행복한가. 어제 일을 기억할 수 있고 또 내일 일을 생각할 수 있으니 얼마나 감사하고 행복한 일인가. 생명은 순결한 마음으로 살 수 있도록 기회를 주니 얼마나 감사하고 행복한가.

생명은 끊임없이 움직이며 스스로 변한다. 생명이 있는 곳엔 생동력

베틀

이 있어 움직이기 때문에 언제나 다른 모습으로 변한다. 무생물은 타인에 의해서 변하지만, 생물은 자체 내에서 변한다. 나는 생명이 있는 사람이니 나 스스로 노력하고 전능자의 도우심을 받도록 기도하면서 나 스스로 영혼이 아름답게 변화하도록 노력해야 한다. 호흡이 있는 동안 광채가 나는 영혼이 되도록 부지런히 연마(研磨)해야 할 것이다. 내 안에 생명이 있으니 시시각각으로 진실한 사람으로 변해 갈 수 있는 소망이 있어서 좋다.

생명은 향기롭다. 풋풋한 삶의 냄새는 기분을 좋게 한다. 성실하게 사는 평범한 일상생활에서 풍겨 나오는 삶의 향기는 생명의 꽃이다. 남을 도와주면서 내는 사랑의 향기는 가슴 속에서 오래도록 머물러 생의 기쁨을 더해준다. 움직이면서 생성되는 생명의 향기는 활력소가 되어 앞날에 대한 희망을 품게 한다. 신선한 풀 냄새, 향기로운 꽃내음은 생명의 향기로 배어 나와 이 세상을 생기있게 해주고 있지 않은가. 나도 인간의 자애로운 향기를 낼 수 있다면 얼마나 좋을까.

생명에는 소리가 있다. 참으로 신비한 소리다. 내 핏속에 들어 있는 생명은 팔딱거리면서 소리를 내고 있다. 건강관리사 노릇을 하는 모양이다. 이웃을 사랑하라고 소리를 한다. 미운 사람을 용서하라고 소리를 낸다. 모든 것들을 좀 더 포용하라고 소리를 낸다. 무언가 인간다운 일을 하라고 소리를 낸다. 물 흐르는 소리, 뭉게구름이 퍼져가는 소리, 바람 소리…, 자연의 소리보다도 더 멋있는 삶의 소리를 내라고 말한다.

생명은 환희(歡喜)다. 생(生)과 사(死)의 갈림길에서 선택된 생명(生命)은 환희의 극치일 것이다. 죽음의 골짜기에서 빠져나와 숨결을 느꼈을 때의 삶에 대한 기쁨은 천하보다도 귀한 생명임을 자연적으로 느끼게 되는 희열이다. 생명은 가슴 뛰는 환희요 죽음은 절망이다. 어느 누가 환희를 마다하고 절망을 좋아하겠는가.

생명은 유한하다. 하루살이 곤충도 있고 백 년쯤 사는 사람도 있고 몇천 년을 사는 나무도 있지만 언젠가는 무생물이 되어 퇴색하여 갈 것이다. 영원한 생명을 얻고 싶다면 믿음으로 사는 길밖엔 없다. 생명을 주신 창조주를 믿으면 이 세상에서 인생살이가 끝나고 다른 세상으로 가는 날 새 생명을 영원히 부여받게 될 것이다. 생명(生命)은 유한한 우리 인간에게 이 순간이 참으로 귀중함을 자연적으로 느끼게 해 준다.

나는 귀중한 생명(生命)이 있으니 이 세상에서 사는 동안 사랑으로 이웃들과 함께 어우러져 기쁘고 행복하게 인생의 향연(饗宴)을 즐기고 싶다. 이 시간, 생명이 내 핏속에 도도(滔滔)히 흐르고 있음을 영육(靈肉)으로 감지하면서 은총 입은 눈을 들어 하늘을 우러러본다.

베틀

몬터레이 아리랑

아리랑 아리랑 아라리요
아리랑 사랑스런 디아스포라
이 세상을 밝게 하는 한민족이라서
무궁화 피는 바닷가를 사랑하네
(후렴) 아리랑 아리랑 아라리요
아리랑 몬터레이 바닷가를 걸어가네

아리랑 아리랑 아라리오
아리랑 디아스포라 코아메리카
이 세상을 아름답게 하는 한민족이라서
봉선화 피는 바닷가를 사랑하네

아리랑 아리랑 아라리요
아리랑 별처럼 꿈이 많은 디아스포라
이 세상을 향기롭게 하는 한민족이어서
분홍꽃 피는 바닷가를 사랑하네

나는 오늘도 내가 작사한 '몬터레이 아리랑'을 흥얼거리며 아름다운 몬터레이 바닷가를 걷는다. 몬터레이 아리랑은 고국에 대한 그리움이요, 내가 한민족임을 자랑스럽게 생각하면서 긍지를 가지고 살 수 있게 하는 내 영혼의 자부심이다.

오늘도 날마다 한민족의 혼(魂)이 담겨 있는 몬터레이 아리랑을 은물결이 일렁이는 태평양 바닷가에서 부른다. 아리랑을 부르면 바다 저너머로 그리운 목소리들이 파도를 타고 끊임없이 들려준다. 나는 혼자 노래를 불러도 혼자가 아니다. 한민족의 혼들이 일제히 나와 함께 합창한다고 느끼기 때문이다. 이렇게 나는 내가 힘있게 살 수 있는 에너지를 몬터레이 아리랑을 부르며 충전시키면서 살아가고 있다. 그리운 사람들의 음성을 태운 파도가 밀려왔다 밀려가는 몬터레이 해변가에서 말이다.

아름답게 살고자 하는 꿈을 안고서 디아스포라 미주이민자로 살아가고 있는 세월이 고국에서 살았던 세월을 뛰어넘었다. 하지만 아직도 나는 현지 생활에 서먹서먹할 때가 많다. 참으로 열심히 살아가고 있지만, 이민 광야에서 부닥쳐야 하는 언어와 보이지 않는 인종차별로 해고 정리를 감당해야 하는 서러움을 왈칵 쏟아 내야 하는 고통이 있다. 때로는 공평하지 않은 처사에 맞설 배짱도 없는 약함을 한탄하기도 한다. 외롭고 텅 빈 영혼이 되어 사랑으로 채우고 싶은 목마름이 있지만 뜨거운 가슴을 열어 주는 사람을 못 찾아 누구나 마실 수 있는 영원한 생명수에만 의존하면서 살 때도 있다. 아마도 나는 누군가도 나처럼 상처받고 쓸쓸하고 가슴이 허허로워 사랑에 갈증을 느끼고 있는 사람들과 함께하기 위해 수필 쓰기에 고민하고 있는지도 모른다. 정녕 나는

베틀

가슴의 답답함을 풀어줄 수 있는 시원한 바람 같은 글을 쓸 수는 없는 것일까 싶다.

현대인들의 새로운 삶의 패턴인 자유롭게 새로운 터전과 직장을 찾아 창조의 삶을 살아가는 디지털 노마드 시대에, 디아스포라 미주이민자의 삶을 사는 나는 사람 옆에 있어도 때로는 외로움을 느끼면서 산다. 외로움에 더하여 사랑하는 사람을 상실할 때 가슴 저미도록 슬픔이 깃든 고통 탓에 영혼이 피를 토하는 비명은 참으로 참담하지 않는가. 날마다 나의 생활에서 의사소통이 부족하여 이민 광야에서 쓰러지는 들풀과 같이 쓸쓸한 내 정서와 국경과 언어를 초월하여 피나는 노력으로 일구어 가는 이민자의 삶의 희로애락을 생각하면 왠지 모르게 눈시울이 뜨거워진다. 하지만 나는 이 시간도 코아메리카로 행복하게 살아가기 위하여 용기를 잃지 않고 재외교포라는 카테고리의 길을 걷고 있다. 내 한(恨)과 꿈(vision)이 섞인 몬터레이 아리랑을 부르면서 말이다.

지금은 글로벌시대다. 지구촌의 아름다운 곳을 여러 방법으로 볼 수가 있지만, 눈으로 보기에 좋아 즐거움을 주는 내가 사는 몬터레이에는 관광객들의 가슴을 뛰게 하고 가슴에 새겨져 남을 만큼 아름다운 꽃들이 많다. 어쩌면 아름다움의 극치를 이루는 연분홍 카펫꽃이 만발하는 세계적인 휴양지 17마일 드라이브 코스, 야생화가 지천에 피어 있는 환상적인 빅베어를 바라다본다. 그 환상은 그리운 사람을 손꼽아 기다리면서 아침저녁으로 그 길을 걸어서 반드시 온다는 전설이 있는 아리랑 품은 소천재가 보이는 소쿠리 마을, 가슴 속의 서러움을 몽땅 쏟아 붙고 싶은 한강이 된다. 그렇지만, 나는 향수에만 젖어 있지 않고 디아스포라 미주이민자로서 아름답게 살고 싶은 꿈을 안고서 삶의 현장을 힘차게 누비고 있다. 지금 이 시간이 가장 귀하고 중요함을 알기에 말이다.

오늘도 나는 태평양 바닷가를 걸으면서 몬터레이 아리랑을 부른다. 참으로 많이도 불러온 몬터레이 아리랑이건만 오늘따라 왜 이리도 내가 밟고 있는 땅의 이름이 낯설게 느껴지는지 모르겠다. 나는 얼마큼 더 이민생활을 해야 고향에서 즐겨 부르던 아리랑을 잊을 수가 있을까. 아련히 떠오르는 고국의 사랑하는 사람들의 모습이 내가 불렀던 아~리~아~리 아리랑 소리와 함께 내 가슴을 후비고 들어온다.

언제나 나는 가슴 속에 자리하고 있는 조국의 아리랑 곡에 내가 작사한 내 영혼의 자부심을 표현한 아리랑을 부를 수 있음에 감사하지만, 오늘은 웬일인지 똑똑하지 못함에 조금은 처량한 생각이 바보처럼 든다. 사랑스러운 삶의 흔적을 남기기 위한 꿈을 안고서 피눈물을 삼키며 가슴 아픈 디아스포라 코아메리카로 살아가는 내가.

고국에 대한 그리움을 품고서 몬터레이 아리랑을 부르는 내가 말이다.

베틀

빗님이 오시네

"오! 이제서야 빗님이 오시네~."

후드득~ 후드득! 양철 지붕 위로 떨어지는 빗방울 소리에, 우리 부모님들은 너무 좋아 맨발로 마당으로 뛰어나가 하늘을 향해 두 손 뻗고 함성을 하시던 모습이 내 눈에 어린다. 얼마나 애타게 기다리던 빗소리였으면 과묵하신 우리 아버지께서도 '이젠 살았다'고 하시면서 그리도 좋아하셨겠는가.

오랜 가뭄 끝에 들리는 빗소리는, 농부이신 우리 부모님들에겐 가뭄 속에서 목숨을 살리는 생명의 소리였던 것이다. 그냥 단순한 비가 아니라 '빗님'이라고 부르면서 기뻐하시던 우리 부모님들의 울음에 가까운 감격의 음성이, 지금도 하늘에서 내려와 내 가슴을 타고 발끝까지흘러내리는 기분이다. 나는 그때 인간은 범할 수 없는 신의 영역을 절실히 느꼈었다.

그 빗님이 하늘에서 땅으로 떨어지는 소리가 점점 커져 주룩주룩 내리기 시작하면 해야 할 일이 있었다. 집안에 있는 그릇 중 물을 담을 수 있는 그릇 모두를 내어다가 처마 밑에 놓는 일이다. 처마 밑으로 흘러내리는 물을 모든 그릇에 받아 두었다가 빨래도 하고 청소하는 데도 사용했다. 빗소리가 들리면 모든 것들이 풍요로워지고 생기가 돌았다. 두레박으로 물을 조금씩 떠올리던 우물은 빗물로 넘쳐나고, 마을 사람들은 농기구를 들고서 비를 흠뻑 맞으며 들녘으로 나가는 소리로 부산했다. 가뭄 속에서 빗소리를 생각하며, 나 자신을 생각해 본다. 꼭 필요한 소리를 내지 않아 내가 어느 누군가의 가슴을 새까맣게 태운 적은 없는지….

빗님이신 빗소리는 계절을 알리는 소리이기도 하다. 봄에는 보슬비로 산천초목들을 싱싱하게 눈을 트이게 하고, 여름날엔 소낙비로 무성하게 자라게 하고, 가을날엔 가랑비로 아름다운 색깔로 물들게 해 정서를 주고 겨울날엔 진눈깨비로 벌거벗은 나목이 되어 또 다른 계절을 기다리게 하는 인내를 준다. 이렇게 계절을 따라 알맞게 내리는 단비는 사람의 마음을 아늑하고 감미롭게 하여 낭만적인 정서를 주기도 한다. 빗소리가 들리면 좋은 음악을 틀어 놓고 추억 속에 있는 사랑했던 사람과 우산 속에서 속삭였던 사랑의 말들을 다시 들어 보기도 하고 상념에 젖기도 한다. 주룩주룩 내리는 빗소리는 마음이 차분해지며, 더러워진 몸과 마음도 씻겨서 정화되는 기분이다. 적당하게 주룩주룩 내리는 단비는 참으로 듣기 좋은 소리다. 나도 누구를 위해서 아름다운 소리가 되었으면 좋겠다.

빗님이신 빗소리가 천둥·번개에 휩싸이게 되고 사나운 바람에 휘몰아치게 되면 폭우로 변한다. 폭우가 많이 쏟아지면 결국 홍수가 되고 만다. 빗소리가 넘쳐나면 인명피해, 재산피해가 이만저만 아니다. 내가 살던 고장에선 홍수가 나면 허술한 오두막집은 지붕이 날아가 버리기도 하고 아예 흙탕물에 휩싸여 집이 무너져 냇가로 둥둥 떠내려가기도 한다. 홍수로 냇물을 건널 수가 없어 학교에 갈 수 없어서 학교는 휴학하고 빗소리가 멎기를 기다린다. 이래저래 빗소리가 너무 오래 나면 장마철이 되어 빗소리가 지긋지긋해지고 모든 활동이 줄어드니 싫어질 수밖에. 내 소리는 어떤가. 지나치게 소리를 많이 내어 남에게 피해를 준 적은 없는가. 너무 지나친 빗소리 때문에 일어나는 홍수는 너무 빗소리가 들리지 않은 가뭄 때보다도 더 심각한 피해를 낸다고 한다. 남에게 지겹게 들리는 내 소리가 애타게 기다리는 내 소리보다도 더 좋지 않다는 말이 아니겠는가.

내가 사는 미국, 몬터레이뿐만 아니라 지구촌 곳곳에 물 한 방울이 아까울 정도로 지독한 가뭄이 들어 난리다. 이런 와중에서도 새로운 친구인 정원에 있는 선인장은 이슬만 먹고도 빨갛고 노랗고 하얗게 아름다운 꽃들을 피워 바라보는 나를 행복하게 해주니 고맙기 그지없다. 각종 미디어에선 가뭄이 들어 지구촌이 신음하며, 애가 타는 사람들의 마음을 대신해 주기에 바쁘다. 나는 쩍쩍 가라진 논 위에서 푸석푸석한 흙을 만지며 타는 농작물을 고통스럽게 바라보고 있는 늙은 농촌 할아버지 사진이 실린 기사를, 눈물 때문에 시야가 흐려져 더는 읽을 수가 없다. 그 늙은 할아버지는 곧 우리 아버지이기 때문이다. 물이 있어야 농사를 짓는 시골에선 농부들이 얼마나 애가 탈까 생각만 해도 내 목이 탄다.

오직 하늘에서 떨어지는 물로만 농사를 짓는 천수답(天水畓)을 가지고 있는 산촌 농부들은 날마다 하늘만 바라보고 살고 있음을 안다. 물이 고여 있는 웅덩이라도 있는 논은, 두레박으로 물을 길어 올려 농사를 지을 수가 있어 최상급의 농토다. 피부가 까맣게 타고 피부 껍질이 벗겨지는 뜨거운 뙤약볕 아래서, 양쪽으로 노끈이 달린 커다란 두레박으로 웅덩이에서 물을 퍼 올리는 농부들에겐 빗님이신 빗소리가 신의 소리 같으리라.

상사병이라도 걸린 듯이 주룩주룩 내 가슴에 내리는 단비 소리가 참으로 듣기에 좋다. 나도 가뭄과 홍수의 틈새에서 아름다운 단비 소리로 남에게 정서를 줄 수 있는 단비 소리를 닮은 소리를 낼 수 있었으면 좋겠다. 나는 어느 사람을 위해서 참으로 꼭 필요한 소리가 되어 봤던가. 내 정서까지 메말라 가는 심한 가뭄 속에서 나는 내 인생길에서 낸 소리를 생각해 본다. 내 소리가 있어야 할 곳에서 묵묵부답하여 남의 가슴을 태우게 한 적은 없는지, 내 소리가 너무 커서 남에게 진저리가 나게 들린 적은 없는지를 말이다.

적당한 시기에 주룩주룩 내려 산천초목을 살리고 희망을 주고 아름다운 정서를 주는 반가운 단비 소리 같이 나도 누군가를 위해서 꼭 필요한 소리가 될 수 있다면 얼마나 좋을까. 그러나저러나, 빗님이신 빗소리를 언제나 들을 수 있단 말인가. 성경에 나오는 엘리야 선지자의 간절한 기도에 구름이 일어나 여호와의 능력이 임하여 비를 내리게 한 것처럼, 이 세대에도 누군가에게 임(臨)하시길 간절히 기도하는 마음이다.

시방(時方), 으~응? 정말로 빗님이 오시네.

베틀

바람 같은 사랑

내 안에 바람 같은 사랑이 있다. 생성하는 자극으로 지금까지 나를 살게 해 준 것이다. 그것은 일 년 사시사철 나의 몸을 스치는 바람 같은 사랑이다. 육안(肉眼)으론 볼 수 없지만, 느낌이나 소리로 그 흔적을 보면 알 수 있다. 바람이 지나간 흔적과 쓰러진 들풀들을 보면서 알 수 있는 것처럼 말이다.

바람 같은 사랑은 봄에는 꽃향기로, 여름날에는 소나기로, 가을날에는 나락 익는 냄새로, 겨울에는 함박눈으로 내 가슴 깊은 곳을 파고든다. 그렇기에 내 가슴은 바람 같은 사랑이 지나간 흔적으로 운치와 멋이 있는 신비스런 삶의 무늬가 만들어지고 있음을 본다. 때로는 다른 방법으로 내게 온다. 바람 같은 사랑은 봄날에는 미풍으로, 여름날에는 회오리바람으로, 가을날에는 사그락거리는 갈바람 같기도 하다. 그러다가 겨울날에는 휭~! 하며 나목(裸木)을 사정없이 후려치는 칼바람으로 온다. 이렇게 바람 같은 사랑은 온 천하의 사계절 사이를 휘젓고 다니며 인생만사(人生萬事)라는 물감으로 내 몸과 삶 곳곳에 그림 그리기를 즐기고 그 흔적을 고스란히 남기고 있으니 어쩌랴 싶다.

또 있다. 바람 같은 사랑은 내 관절 마디마디에 찾아들어 숭숭 구멍을 뚫어 놓는다. 내가 자존심을 버리고 사랑을 찾아 헤매다 지쳐 침대에 누운 날에는 바람 같은 사랑이 내 관절을 쑤셔대며, 심한 통증까지 수반해 내 몸에 거(居)하고 있노라 외친다. 그러다가는 또 한 번씩 바람 같은 사랑은 날카로운 송곳처럼 내 가슴을 파고들어 심장 세포 사이를 후비고 다닌다. 이때 나의 가슴은 멍글멍글한 피보다도 더 빨간 응어리가 요동친다. 엄청난 고통에 아파하는 나를 아랑곳하지 않고 말이다. 나는, 이때 인생사의 무늬가 심장 부위에 빨갛게 새겨져 있음을 느끼게 된다.

바람 같은 사랑은 또 이렇게 말한다. "나는 한 곳에 머물 수 없는 속성을 가졌노라."고. 그러면서 또다시 나에게 "나를 한곳에 온전히 머물러 있기를 바라는 것은 너의 욕망이며, 욕망은 집착에서 온다."라고 말한다. 그래도 나는 한곳에 머물러 있을 수 없다지만, 잡아두고 싶은 집착까지 어떻게 버릴 수가 있겠는가. 집착은 영원히 소유하고 싶은 욕망이기에, 근심과 굴레 같은 삶일지라도 어쩔 수가 없을 것이리라. 바람 같은 사랑은 또다시 이렇게 말한다. "움직이는 사랑을 붙잡으려 하지 말고 온전히 놓아 버리고 자유인으로 살라."고 한다. 그러나 나는, 언제나 내 몸을 스쳐 가는 바람 같은 사랑인 것을 알면서도 치마폭을 팽팽히 넓게 벌려 잠시나마 품어 보고 싶어 한다. 그러면서 느낌으로 알 수 있는 바람결 같은 사랑과 함께 빙글빙글 돌고 싶어 안달까지 한다.

향기로운 꽃 바람이면 좋겠다. 아니다. 나를 감싸버리는 회오리바람 같은 사랑이 좋겠다. 하지만 바람 같은 사랑만 움직이지는 않을 터, 이 세상에 있는 모든 것들이 영원히 움직이지 않고 그 자리에 머물러 있

베틀

는 것이 있던가. 그렇다. 모든 것은 움직이며 변한다. 내 마음도 마찬가지다. 영원불변한 것은 이 세상에 존재하지 않는다. 오직 하늘나라에 계시는 유일신(唯一神)뿐이다.

바람 같은 사랑은 구태여 모습을 보이려 하지 않는다. 느낌으로나 소리로 보이지 않고 내 곁에 잠시 머물다가 스쳐 간다. 보이지 않는 마음을 품은 바람 같은 사랑이기에 나는, 더욱더 그리워하는지 모르겠다. 마법의 열쇠를 쥐고 있는 듯한 바람결 같은 사랑은 내 가슴을 풀어놓은 날에는 중구난방으로 내 몸을 쑤시며 막무가내로 파고든다. 때로는 허파 깊숙이 파고들어 오는 바람 같은 사랑 때문에 호흡곤란에 생겨 혼미해질 때가 있다. 이미 예민해진 나는 빨리 내 몸을 스쳐 가라 고함친다. 내 심장의 피가 펄펄 끓어올라 모세혈관들이 다 충혈되면 터져버릴 수도 있을 테니 말이다. 가끔은 바람 같은 사랑은 뇌신경 세포 속을 후비고 들어와 기어코 내 꿈길까지 요동치게 한다. 결코, 나를 떠나버릴 수 없는 존재임을 각인시켜 주려는 듯이 말이다.

사랑이란 이름 앞에 수많은 언어를 붙이고 나의 마음속을 들여다본다. 부모 사랑, 친구 사랑, 자식 사랑, 첫사랑……. 모든 사랑은 한곳에 머물지 않는 바람의 속성을 가졌기에, 나는 바람 같은 사랑이라 부른다. 내 코에 생기(生氣)가 들어올 때부터 함께 살아온 인연이 없었다면 결코 살 수 없는 바람 같은 사랑이다. 늘 내 곁에 있어도 그리움을 품고 다니는 바람 같은 사랑은 내 영혼의 그림자처럼 줄기차게 존재한다. 내 인생을 행복하게 해 주는 큰 보배라는 생각에 붙잡으려 하면 바람 같은 사랑은 어느 사이에 저만치 떠나고 만다. 어차피 내 곁을 스쳐 가기만 할 바람 같은 사랑이라면, 나는 미련없이 보내야 하리라 싶다. 자

유로운 삶을 누리며 신선하고 행복한 마음으로 돌아다니기를 빌어주어
야 하지 않겠는가.

　바람 같은 사랑은 나의 목울대를 겁나게 훑어 내리던 날. 저울질하
던 잘난 집안, 학벌, 앞에서 그리도 무정하게 나를 등지고 가더니만,
무슨 일인지 백만 송이 장미를 들고 돌아왔다. 떠돌아다니다가 우연한
기회에 백만 송이 장미를 스치게 되면서 변화된 진실한 사랑을 보여주
고 싶은 생각이 들었나 보다.

　허공을 휘저으며 헤매고 다닌 고단한 흔적이 나를 가슴 아프게 해,
나는 애써 침묵으로 품어 준다. 아마 백만 송이 장미꽃 향기 속에서
아름다운 세상을, 아름다운 수필처럼 살다가 바람 같은 사랑과 함께
먼 길을 떠나고 싶은 내 마음을 이제야 알았나 보다. 알면 뭣 하나. 어
차피 내 곁에 머물지 않을 바람 같은 사랑인 것을. 그래도 바람 같은
사랑이 좋은 걸 어쩌랴. 나는, 모악산 하얀 갈대밭에서 덩실덩실 춤추
던 바람결 같은 사랑이 마냥 좋기만 한 것을.

　그래도 내가 살아갈 수 있음은, 바람 같은 사랑이 언제나 내 곁을 스
치며 생(生)의 자극을 주기 때문이 아니겠는가. 내가 영원히 붙들 수 없
는 바람 같은 사랑, 그럼에도 내 인생과는 뗄 수 없는 참 인연이다. 바
람 같은 사랑은 오늘도 백만 송이 장미꽃 향기로 내 몸을 스친다.

　바람 같은 사랑은 멋있고 운치 있는 내 인생의 무늬를 신비하게 그려
가고 있는 느낌이다.

베틀

디아스포라의 유랑 나이

나이란 떠도는 게 아니지 않는가.

그런데, 디아스포라 미주한인 이민자로 살고 있는 나의 나이는 움직이면서 떠도는 나이다. 이름하여 나만의 신조어로, 유랑나이라 말해도 좋을성싶다. 이중문화권 속에 살다 보니 내 나이가 역동성이 있어 떠도는 유랑 나이가 된 느낌이다. 유랑나이라 생각하니 자유스러운 것 같으면서도 한 곳에 머물지 못하는 안타까움이 서린다. 유랑 나이는 이방인 인생의 연륜(年輪)을 아름답게 그리기 위해 항상 움직여야 하나 보다. 미주한인 이민역사는 디아스포라 이민자의 꿈이 서려 있는 유랑나이가 옮겨진 나무의 나이테처럼 여러 모양으로 아름답게 연륜을 쌓아가는 데 한몫을 하지 않나 싶다. 다른 문화이기에 존재할 수 있는 디아스포라 유랑나이는 각종 아름다운 색깔을 띠고 디아스포라 삶의 신비로운 나이테를 만들어 가는 자양분이 돼준다. 이방인의 자유가 서려 있고, 미주한인 이민역사가 담겨있는 보배로.

신원과 정신 상태를 파악하는 데 가장 중요한 것은 이름, 생년월일이라.

어느 날, 진료실에서 백인 의사가 나의 신상문제를 묻는다. 당신 나이가 몇 살이요? 음~당신 한국전쟁 아나요?

나이를 묻는데 한국전쟁을 아느냐고 따지듯 묻는 나의 생뚱맞은 질문에 의사가 눈을 똥그랗게 뜨고서 나를 바라본다. 그리곤 또 묻는다.

당신 나이가 몇 살이냐고 물었소. 학창시절에 한국전쟁에 대해서 배우지 않았단 말이요? 노! 라고 대답하는 의사에게 나는 말한다. 아마도 배웠지만 잊어버렸겠지요. 1950년이라오. 나는 한국전쟁이 일어난 그 해에 태어났지요. 그래서 66살이 되는데, 법적으로는 65살로 되어 있지요. 아~니네요. 내일 모레 이틀이 지나야 내 생일이니 오늘 나이는 미국식 나이로 64살이네요. 한국식 나이로는 67살이라오. 내가 살아남을 수 있었던 것은 미국이 한국전쟁을 도와주었기 때문이지요. 지금은 한국전쟁을 도와주었던 나라에서 내가 살고 있으니 고마운 마음뿐이죠.

진료하기 위해서 신원파악을 하던 의사가 무언가 말을 하려다 미소만 지어 보인다. 아마도 한국인으로서의 정체성을 확고히 하려는 나의 속마음을 읽었는지도 모른다. 나는 고국의 존재조차 생소해하는 이민국의 한 사람에게 나의 조국을 알리고, 한국전쟁 때 우리를 사랑으로 도와주었던 우방국의 후손에게나마 고마움을 전할 수 있었던 것은 유랑나이 덕분이라 싶다. 현지에서 살아온 세월이 고국에서 살았던 세월보다도 훨씬 더 많은 시간이 흘렀는데 고국의 정서와 타국의 정서가 유랑나이에서 만나고 있음을 느낀다. 유랑나이는 한국인의 정서를 간직하고 싶어하는 이방인의 마음속에는 항상 존재하고 있음이다.

베틀

때때로 나는 한국식 나이, 미국식 나이의 문화적인 차이로 일어나는 나이 때문에 내 나이도 잘 모르는 사람이 될 때가 있다. 언제나 움직이는 유랑나이가 디아스포라의 삶을 살고 있는 미주한인 사이에 상당히 많이 있음을 안 후엔 화젯거리가 되기도 한다. 전쟁 때는 늦게 호적을 올리는 바람에, 업무과실 등 여러 이유들이 많다. 초창기 하와이이민 땐 결혼식을 먼저 서류부터 작성하는 과정에서 다른 사람의 생년월일이 법적으로 자기 생년월일이 된 경우도 있단다. 문화적인 차이로 생년월일을 서류에 기록하는 과정에서 자신이 생년월일을 틀리게 적는 경우도 있다. 이래저래 새로운 것을 창조해 내는 유랑나이가 디아스포라 미주한인 이민사회에 많이 존재하고 있음에 놀랍다. 삶의 리듬이 있는 디아스포라의 유랑나이는 고국의 문화와 이방나라의 문화가 만나고 있음을 말해 준다.

한 사람의 존재가 알몸으로 이 세상에 나온 건 단 한 번 뿐이기에 생년 월일은 고정되어 있어야 하지 않겠는가. 그런데 유랑나이는 역동력이 있어 한 곳에 머물 수가 없다. 양력 음력이 엇갈려지는 2월이 생일인 나는, 한국식 나이 속에서도 무척 헷갈리고 호적상의 나이, 미국식 나이 때문에 나이가 헷갈려 실제의 나이를 말하지 못할 때가 더러 있다. 그래도 세월은 흐르기에 디아스포라 미주한인으로 살아온 이민 역사는 자꾸만 연륜이 쌓여가고 있음을 안다. 디아스포라의 꿈을 이루기 위해 잠을 잘 시간이 없어 화장실에서 몇 분 동안 꾸뻑 졸음으로, 마른 빵을 흘러내리는 짭짤한 눈물에 섞어 차 안에서 먹으면서 또 다른 직장으로 향하던 이민생활도 함께 어우러진 신비한 색채를 내면서.

아메리칸 드림을 이루기 위해 정확한 생년월일도 간직하지 못한 채

타국생활의 밑바닥을 훑으며 위태위태 살아온 세월. 아무리 어려운 일을 당해도 괜찮아질 거라고 스스로 위로하며 인내로 살아온 세월. 관중 속의 외로움 속에서 속울음을 토해낼 곳을 찾던 고통의 세월. 널따란 사막길에서 애타게 오아시스를 찾던 심정의 세월. 더욱더 아름답게 살기 위해 몸부림치는 정서와 희로애락이 어우러진 여러 색깔이 곰삭아 이민자의 나이테가 만들어지면 영원히 남을 신비스러운 미주한인 이민역사가 형성되지 않겠는가. 디아스포라의 유랑나이는 과거와 현재와 미래를 잇대어 소통시키는 세월 속을 쉬지 않고 떠돌아다니면서, 자리를 옮겨온 이민자의 가슴 속 나무에 나이테를 그리는 자양분이 되고 있다. 생활이 삭혀진 신비스런 색깔로 변해서 미주한인 이민생활의 역사를 세월의 연륜(年輪)으로 해마다 채색하면서 말이다. 디아스포라의 유랑나이는 이방인의 자유가 서려 있고 미주한인 이민 역사가 담겨있다. 참으로 귀중한 보배가 아닌가.

베틀

꽃잔디

　꽃잔디! 예쁘디 예쁜 이름에 가슴이 뛴다. 이 아름다운 꽃 이름을 처음으로 한국문학인 문우에게서 들었을 때 나는 얼마나 기뻤는지 모른다. 꽃잔디는 영어로 아이스 플랜트(Ice plant), 혹은 매직 카펫 (Magic Carpet)이라고 부른다. 나는 한국문인중한 사람인 강정실 선생이 아이스 플랜트를 '꽃잔디'라고 불러주었을 때, 한국어의 아름다움과 언어미학에 얼마나 놀랐는지 모른다. 몬터레이 해변가에서 시시때때로 꽃잔디를 볼 때마다 예쁘고도 고귀한 이름을 나에게 알려 준 문우가 고마울 뿐이다.

　꽃잔디를 나에게 말해 준 강정실 선생님은 현재 한국문인협회 7대 미주지회 회장으로 활약하고 있다. 활동이 미약하여 문인들도 잘 알지 못했던 문학단체, 한국문인협회 미주지회를 활성화 시키려고 문단 운영에 활화산 같은 열정으로 온 정성을 쏟고 있다. 한 번 하겠다고 결심한 일은 무슨 조건에서도 약속을 지킬 줄 아는 신뢰를 주는 사람이다. 십여 년 전 여름날, 비행기를 타고 문학행사에 참석하기 위해서 공항에 내렸을 때, 그 당시 한국문인협회 수필분과 위원장으로 활동하고 있는 문우를 처음 만난 것이 인연이 되어 지금까지 문학의 뜨락에서 함께 활동하고 있다.

어느 문학행사에서 문우들과 이야기 중에 강 선생처럼 빠르게 문학에 대한 폭을 넓히고 모든 분야에서 신동에 가까울 정도로 다재다능한(多才多能) 사람은 재외동포 사이에서 그리 흔치 않다는 얘기를 한 적이 있다. 수필가, 사진작가…… 지금은 문학평론가로 왕성한 활동을 하고 있다. 새로운 삶을 탐구하는 기행수필집 〈렌즈를 통해 본 디지털 노마드〉로 유명하다. 수많은 문학강연과 영한으로 잡지를 발행하는 데 선구자 역할을 하고 있고, 문학에 뜻이 있는 사람들에게 문학에 대한 꿈을 갖도록 도와주는 보기 드물게 앞서 가는 문학인이다. 이렇게 재치있는 한국문학인이기에 '매직 카펫'이라는 이름에 한국말로 아름답고도 귀한 새로운 꽃 이름인 '꽃잔디'란 이름을 창출해 내지 않았나 싶다. 꽃 이름에서 아름답고 보드라운 소리가 들리는 이 기발하고 신선한 언어를 모르고 살아온 우둔함에, 나는 언어라는 도구로 작품창작을 하는 문학인으로서 부끄러움을 느낀다.

꽃잔디는 얼마나 아름다운지 한 번 보고 난 사람은 반해서 또다시 찾아오는 사람이 많다. 햇살 따사한 날은 꽃잔디에 드러누워 사랑을 속삭이고 싶은 충동을 느낄 정도다. 내가 이곳에 와서 본 꽃들이 수십 년이 지났는데도 지금까지 변함없이 피고 진다. 꽃이야 새로운 꽃이겠지만 뿌리는 같은 뿌리일 것이기에 참으로 신기한 생각이 든다. 사라지지도 않고 더 많아지지도 않고 그 모습 그대로의 면적에서 살고 있으니 말이다. 몬터레이 바닷가에 있는 꽃잔디는 사계절 귀여운 초록색 이파리들을 겨드랑이에 다랑다랑 달고서 땅을 부드럽게 덮어 주며 뻗쳐 나가는 줄기를 볼 수 있다. 꽃계절이 되면 그 줄기 따라서 수많은 자그마한 꽃들이 분홍색으로 보드랍고 앙징스럽게 피어나, 그 아름다움으로 보는 사람들의 마음을 앗아가곤 한다. 몬터레이는 겨울철에 잠깐 비가 내릴 뿐인데도 아름다운 꽃잔디를 볼 수 있는 것은 보이지 않게 돌보시는 손길이 있음을 감지할 수가 있다. 밤이면 짭조름한 바닷물을 끌어 올려 물안개로 꽃을 살리시는 그 손길은 만물을 세심하게 돌보고 계시는 창조주 하나님이 아니고 누구시겠는가!

나는 생명의 환희를 맛보고 싶으면 관광지인 몬터레이 해변가 사랑공원을 찾아 꽃잔디를 본다. 꽃철이 되면 화사한 꽃들의 웃음에 즐겁고, 꽃들이 피고 진 후엔 앞날의 새로운 희망을 품고서 차분히 인내로 살아가는 모습이 정겹다. 생명이 있는 아주 예쁜 꽃잔디는 내 인생살이의 동반자라고 할 수 있다. 나는 이 꽃잔디와 함께 웃고 울면서 살아온 기분이다. 세월 따라 나는 자꾸만 주름이 늘어 가는데, 꽃잔디는 변함없이 싱싱한 몸매로 보는 사람들을 즐겁게 해 주고 있다. 외모야 자연의 섭리에 따라서 어쩔 수 없이 변해 가지만 내면은 변함없이 진실한 아름다움을 유지해야 한다는 교훈을 나는 꽃잔디에서 배우곤 한다.

사랑스런 꽃잔디 곁에 있으면 나도 사랑스러운 사람이 되는 기분이다. 해마다 분홍꽃이 피고 지는 꽃잔디와 함께 살면서 나도 변함없이 사랑받을 수 있는 사람이 되었으면 좋겠다. 아름다운 꽃잔디를 보면서 살아갈 수 있음에 감사하며 진솔하게 오늘과 내일을 잇대어 살고 싶다.

아름다운 꽃을 피워 대지를 아름답게 하는 꽃잔디처럼 나도 아름다운 마음의 꽃을 피워 사람들을 품어주어야 하리라. 내 주위에 꽃잔디가 있어서 나는 참으로 행복하다. 그리고 이렇게 아름다운 꽃이름을 지어 준 한국문학인 문우에게 늘 고맙게 생각한다. 잔디 같은데 꽃이 핀다 해서 '꽃잔디'라 한단다. 참으로 예쁘고 고귀한 꽃이름, 꽃~잔~디.

베틀

꽃밭

꽃밭이 나를 부른다. 시시때때로 나를 불러댄다. 천지가 화합(和合)하는 소리를 들으란다. 나는 즐거운 마음으로 꽃밭을 만나러 간다. 꽃밭은 정말로 아름다운 풍광 속에서 천지가 화합하는 소리를 내고 있다. 신기하고 아름다운 하모니로 온 우주가 서로 어우러져 사랑하며 즐거워하는 소리를 내고 있다. 아름다운 풍광 속에서 천지가 화합하는 소리 가운데 내가 있으매 참으로 행복하다.

꽃밭은 파아란 하늘과 땅 사이 우주 공간에 있다. 신선한 공기와 시원한 바람이 꽃밭을 스치고 있다. 보드라운 아지랑이가 눈에 아물거리는 봄날이 오면, 겨우내 꽁꽁 얼어붙었던 땅을 헤치고 새 생명인 꽃나무들이 여기저기서 연초록으로 태어난다. 신록의 계절 여름이 오면 온갖 나무 이파리들이 싱싱하게 초록으로 물들고 꽃들은 향기를 뿜어내며 활짝 피어난다. 가을이 되면 진한 꽃물 뚝뚝 떨구어 내면서 땅에 떨어진다. 겨울이 되면 꽃나무들은 벌거숭이가 되어 침묵으로 새봄을 기다린다. 꽃밭은 봄 여름 가을 겨울 사계절의 변화를 포근하게 품고 있다. 생명력이 있는 자연을 사랑할 수 있도록 하는 꽃밭은 늘 정신적인 안정감을 주고 온유하게 한다. 꽃밭을 가꾸다 보면 어느 사이에 내 마음도 가꾸어짐을 느낄 수 있다.

꽃밭에는 나를 행복하게 해 주는 여러 종류의 꽃들이 있다. 특히나 새언니에게서 나던 코티분 냄새가 나는 장미꽃 향기가 내 코를 사로잡는다. 올해는, 여름날 손톱에 물들이던 봉숭아가 우리 집 꽃밭에 있게 되어 가슴 설레는 유년시절의 행복함을 만끽하고 있다. 우리나라 꽃, 무궁화가 있어 나를 안심시키고, 아버지의 여린 사랑에 가슴이 저려 뜨거운 눈망울로 보았던 송정리 도롯가에 흐드러지게 피었던 코스모스가 다시 태어나 환하게 웃고 있다. 몬터레이 해변을 아름답게 하는 분홍색 꽃잔디도 있고, 잎과 꽃이 서로 그리워만 하지 만나지는 못하는 애달픈 설화를 품고 있는 상사화도 있다. 아~ 무엇보다도 보드라운 꽃잎이 망울망울 피어나 꽃대궐을 이루는 복숭아꽃 살구꽃도 우리 집 꽃밭에 있어 나를 행복하게 해 준다. 내가 꽃을 바라보면서 누군가를 생각하며 사랑의 얘기를 나눌 때면 꽃은 이미 나를 사랑하고 있노라고 화답해 준다.

꽃밭은 나에게 인연이 있는 그리운 사람들을 추억 속에서 만나게 한다. 사랑하는 부모 형제들을 만나 목소리를 듣게 하고 체취를 느끼게 한다. 육의 세계와 영의 세계가 한 자리에서 만난다. 알래스카 앵커리지 위디어 선착장에는 '천 개의 바람'의 원주민의 시가 돌비석에 있다. 이 시는 생계를 위해 고기잡이하다가 바람을 만나 바다에서 돌아오지 못한 영혼들을 위로하기 위하여 위령탑으로 세워져 있는데, 그 영혼들이 천 개의 바람으로 다시 태어나 내가 서 있는 꽃밭으로 바람을 타고 찾아옴을 느낀다. 세월호에 이름을 새긴 못다 핀 아름다운 꽃들의 영혼도 은은한 향기를 내며 예쁜 꽃으로 다시 피어남을 가슴으로 느낀다. 일제강점기 때 성 노예로 고역을 받고서도 무참하게 매장당한 위안부 혼령들이 나비로 화해 향기로운 꽃밭으로 날갯짓하며 찾아드는 느낌이 든다. 보드라운 흙을 매만지면서 흙을 밟고 사는 것이 평생소원인 수상가옥 사람들의 소원이 신비스런 흙냄새로 화해 내 허파 깊숙이 파고든다. 꽃나무들에게 물을 주면서 생명을 잉태해 내는 땅의 힘을 말씀해 주시던 어머니를 생각한다. 꽃밭은 언제나 신비한 새 생명의 환희와 향기로 가득하며 우주 만물이 서로 화합하는 소리로 가득하다.

꽃밭엔 벌, 나비, 새들뿐만 아니라 호미와 삽으로 흙을 파다 보면 땅 밑으론 지렁이와 들쥐들이 찾아와 생활함을 볼 수 있다. 꽃밭은 뭇 생명체들이 살아가기에 좋은 터전이다. 생명의 근원인 흙과 평화의 원천인 공기가 함께 공존하는 곳일뿐더러 생활의 활력소가 되는 꽃들의 향기가 있어 무릉도원이기 때문일 것이다. 육체는 흙으로 만들어졌고 또 언젠가는 흙으로 돌아가리라는 생각 때문인지 흙을 대하면 언제나 편하고 포근한 느낌이 든다. 인간과 자연이 어우러져 함께 살기에 좋은 꽃밭엔 낮에는 햇빛이 밤에는 빛나는 별빛이 평화롭게 내려와 앉는다.

꽃밭은 어렸을 때부터 늘 함께해 온 나의 생활공간이다. 그래서인지 눈을 감아도 나를 부르는 소리가 들린다. 어두운 밤이 우리들의 만남을 방해할 때는 나는 꽃밭을 내 눈 속으로 끌어들여 대화한다. 나는 침대에 누워서도 꽃들의 향기를 맡으며 꽃의 이파리들의 움직임을 보고 있다. 적당한 자리로 옮겨줘 호흡하기에 좋게도 하고 서로 어우러져 지내기에 편안하게도 해 준다. 고요가 서린 조용한 아침엔 침묵과 꽃향기가 어우러져 내 영혼을 정화시킨다. 나의 소중한 인생을 생각하게 하고 내 삶을 의미 있고 향기롭게 하고 싶어 묵상하는 자세가 된다. 수수한 자세로 아름다운 인생살이를 하고파 나는 늘 꽃밭에 머무는지도 모른다. 꽃밭을 예쁘게 가꾸고 싶은 염원이 삶의 기도가 되기도 한다. 꽃밭을 가꾸다 보면 어느 사이에 내 가슴이 꽃밭이 되고 있음이다.

꽃밭에선 우주 만물의 화합하는 소리가 융성하다. 인간과 신의 세계가, 이 세상과 영원의 세계가, 과거와 현재가, 인생의 희로애락이, 육체와 영혼이, 자연의 변화가… 꽃밭에 어우러져 있다. 하늘과 땅이 뻥 뚫려 우주의 만물이 화합하는 소리가 이렇게 신비롭고 아름다울 수가! 경이로움과 설렘으로 꽃씨를 뿌리고 꽃나무들에게 물 주고 잡풀을 뽑다 보면 서너 시간이 훌쩍 지나가 버린다. 꽃밭은 살아서 숨 쉬며 수시로 나에게 천지가 화합하는 소리를 듣게 해 나의 삶을 더 풍요롭고 생기가 있게 한다. 나는 수시로 생명의 근원이 되는 뽀송뽀송한 흙을 만지며 자유와 평화가 깃든 꽃밭과 함께 소중한 인생살이를 즐길 수 있음에 감사하며, 사랑하는 지구촌 모든 사람과 함께 꽃들의 향기에 취하고 싶은 마음에 머문다. 꽃밭에서 생성되는 천지가 화합(和合)하는 아름다운 소리를 온 세상 사람들이 다 함께 들을 수 있다면 얼마나 좋겠는가.

베틀

선교와 틀니

선교와 틀니는 무(無)에서 유(有)를 창출해내는 새로운 삶의 신비로운 기적을 볼 수 있다. 꼭 있어야 할 곳에 없어서는 안 될 무언가를 있게 하여 정상적인 생활을 할 수 있도록 도와주는 사랑이란 아름다움이 서려 있어서다. 심사숙고해 보면, 원래는 있었는데 무슨 이유론가 사라져 버린 본래의 모습을 되찾게 도와주는 아름다운 손길이리라. 선교와 틀니는 누군가를 즐겁게 하는 마력의 힘이 있어 요즈음 나는 생각만 해도 즐겁다. 선교지에서 틀니 때문에 유쾌한 시간을 가졌던 일을 생각하면 혼자서도 웃음이 나올 정도로 즐거운 마음이 된다. 우리의 구원자이신 예수님을 모르는 곳에 복음을 전하는 선교와, 이가 없는 곳에 가짜 이를 만들어 끼운 틀니는 새로운 삶에 대한 아름다운 꿈과 희망을 주는 신비로움이 있어 행복한 인생살이에서 꼭 필요하다는 생각을 한다.

2017년, 7월 24일, 새벽 일찍이 모여서 드린 예배는 '우리가 밟는 땅이 거룩한 땅이 되기를 원하오며, 우리가 만나는 사람들이 거룩한 사람들이 되기를 소망합니다'라는 선교의 비전이 탁월하신 임진태 목사님의 간절한 기도가 가슴을 뜨겁게 한다. 아주 작은 겨자씨 한 알 같은 복음을 뿌리면 새롭게 태어날 것이라는 믿음을 갖고 사랑하는 마음으로 선교에 대한 소망을 하늘에 두는 선교팀들. 내가 40여 년을 바라보면서 섬기고 있는 '몬터레이 중앙 장로 교회'는 태평양 바닷가를 정원으로 두고 있는 참으로 아름다운 교회다. 교회문을 열어 놓고 강단 위에서 앞을 바라보면, 널따란 태평양 푸른 바다 위를 유유히 나르는 물새들의 모습과 함께 드높은 푸른 하늘이 한눈에 들어오기에 감탄사가 튀어나오며 아름답게 천지를 창조하신 하나님께 저절로 찬양을 드리게 되는 참으로 보배로운 교회다.

멕시코를 차로 갈 수 있는 캘리포니아여서 우리 교회 선교팀들은 신앙의 꿈을 키우는 청소년들까지 모두 자동차로 움직일 수가 있게 되었다. 국경지대를 넘어 멕시코에 들어서면서부터는 전화도 쓸 수 없고 GPS도 쓸 수가 없어 내가 탑승한 차는 길을 잃고 방황하게 되었다. 순간적으로 멘붕 상태에서 언어가 통하지 않아 몸짓으로 길을 묻다가, 조폭 같은 사람도 만났고 돈만 뜯어가려는 나쁜 사람도 만났다. 다행히 순발력 있는 애디 권사님의 기도를 들어주신 하나님의 은혜로 참으로 선한 사람을 만나 무사히 선교팀에 합류한 기쁨이라니ㅡ. 멕시코 단기선교 팀장인 윤 권사님은 이산가족의 만남이라고 울먹인다. 본인이 의사인데도 아파서 몇 개월 동안이나 교회에 나오지 못했던 윤 권사님이 아니었던가. 멕시코 선교로 인해서 행복 호르몬인 엔도르핀이 솟아났는지 다시금 교회로 나올 수 있음과 동시에 선교팀장의 역할을 당당히 할 수 있게 되었으니 병든 자를 낮게 하는 하나님의 섭리요 은혜가 아니고 무엇이랴.

베틀

멕시코 앤세나다에서 한국의 건강미를 보여주는 태권도를 세계에 알리면서 선교사역을 감당하고 계시는 고센(Goshen)교회 이동훈 목사님을 만나니 모든 문제는 해결. 우리들은 하나님께 예배를 드린 후엔 각자 몸을 씻어야 하는데 수도꼭지는 있는데 물이 나오지 않고 있다. 이 년 동안이나 가뭄이 들어 물이 나오지 않고 있단다. 식수는 사서 먹거나 정부에서 조금씩 배달해서 먹고 허드렛물은 시내에서 구해 온단다. 목욕은 할 수도 없고 화장실에 물이 없어 시내에서 구해온 물을 바가지로 조금씩 떠서 처리해야 하는데 참으로 어려운 일이다. 소변은 별문제가 없지만, 대변은 참으로 난감하다. 누런 똥이 변기에 가득해도 물이 없으니 어찌하는 수가 없다.

　나는 합숙소에서 언제나 웃음거리를 품고 다니는 애디 권사님과 둘이만 있을 기회가 있었다. 재미있는 똥 얘기를 해 주시겠다면서 왈~ 친구가 비데를 몰랐던 시절, 유럽여행 중에 호텔에서 두 개의 변기 중 예쁘고 깨끗한 변기에 대변을 봤는데 변비가 심했던 터라 똥 덩어리가 돌덩이같이 딱딱하고 굵어서 흘러가지 않더란다. 아침에 잠에서 깨어 다시금 보니 똥 덩어리가 그대로 있어, 할 수 없이 손바가지를 만들어 똥을 퍼서 커다란 변기에 넣어 흘려보냈단다. 호텔 직원을 부르자니 동양 사람들의 무식함이 탄로 될 것 같아 창피해서 할 수 없이 두 손으로 똥을 퍼서 비데에서 변기로 옮겼다는 얘기다. 그 사건이 너무도 재미있는지 입을 벌리고 웃으시면서 나에게 들려주시는 권사님의 입을 보니 앞니가 하나도 없다. 나는 틀니를 빼놓은 그 모습을 보는 순간 너무도 우스워 배를 쥐어 잡고 뒹굴거리면서 큰소리로 웃다가, 순간적으로 틀니를 할 연세에도 훗날에 후회하지 않기 위해서 어려운 선교지에 앞장

서신 권사님이 경이로운 생각이 들었다.

선교지에서 항상 새롭게 배우고 느끼는 것은 남을 먼저 생각하는 배려다. 언제나 배려하는 마음은 주위 사람들을 기쁘고 행복하게 한다. 우리가 단기 선교를 한 멕시코 앤세나다는 너무도 궁핍한 생활을 하는 사람들이 사는 지역이기에 정부에서 배급을 나눠 준단다. 그런데 어떤 사람들은 그 배급 받은 물건을 자기 형편보다도 더 못한 환경에서 사는 사람들을 위해서 교회로 들고 온다는 것이다. 참으로 남을 위한 배려심에 감동의 눈물이 난다는 이 선교사님의 말씀이다. 남을 먼저 생각하는 배려심에 관한 얘기를 듣는 선교팀들의 마주치는 눈빛이 새롭게 빛난다.

이방인들에게 복음을 전하는 선교나, 이가 빠졌거나, 이를 제거한 사람들에게 박아넣는 틀니는 없어서는 안 될 무언가를 있게 하여 아름다운 삶을 영유하게 한다. 나는 한국전쟁 이후에 고국에서 만난 선교사님들이 그리도 부러웠었는데 지금은 나에게도 그 역할을 허락해 주신 하나님께 감사드린다. 그리고 틀니 때문에 자유롭게 큰소리로 마음껏 웃을 수 있는 환경을 허락해 주신 하나님께 감사드리는 마음이다. 즐겁고 재미있는 일이 아닐 수가 없다. 남은 인생살이를 더욱더 아름답게 하기 위해서는 주위 사람들을 기쁘고 행복하게 하는 배려심을 갖고, 새 생명을 잉태한 씨앗 한 알을 뿌리는 선교를 나는 이빨이 없어져 틀니를 끼기까지 지속해야 하리라.

베틀

나는 보았네

온갖 소리 속에서도 생명으로 통하는 구원의 소리, 복음의 씨앗이
싹트는 소리에 귀 기울이고 기뻐하는 사람들을 나는 보았네.

우리 교회가 '비전 트립'이라는 이름 하에 선교비전을 가지고 계시는
임 목사님을 비롯한 해외단기선교 팀이 7명으로 구성되었다. 오래도록
열방을 품에 안고 기도로 준비해온 해외 단기선교지로 태국과 캄보디
아가 결정된 후에는 현지 언어로 율동찬양도 배웠다.

태국에서는 예수님 찬양 예수님 찬양ㅡㅡㅡ/싼선 프라남 싼선 프
라남ㅡㅡㅡ을, 캄보디아에서는 좋으신 하나님 ㅡㅡㅡ/쁘레아 뜨룸 러어
나ㅡㅡㅡ를 부르기로 결정했다. 내 생전에 처음으로 신앙간증문도 작성
해 보는 기회가 주어졌다. 각종 멀미로 고생하는 나에게는 미국에서
태국까지 17시간 정도 비행기를 타야 한다는 것이 퍽 부담스러웠다. 언
제나 비닐봉지를 남몰래 내 몸에 지니고 다녀야 하는 고통이 내 평생
이어지고 있으니 말이다. 그런데 태국 치앙마이에 도착했을 때까지 속
만 울렁거렸지 토하지 않았다는 사실은 틀림없이 전능자의 보살핌이 있
었음이어라.

내가 처음으로 밟아 보는 땅, 태국은 여유롭고 평화로운 느낌이 들었다. 세계적으로 행복지수가 상위권에 속하는 나라여서인지 사람들의 표정이 온화하고 밝아 보인다. 일 년 내내 따뜻하고 습한 열대 기후에 우기로 접어들어서인지 주룩주룩 쏟아지는 빗방울에 산천초목들도 물기가 촉촉이 젖어있어 싱그럽게 보이니 부러운 생각마저 든다. 오랫동안 심한 가뭄으로 가슴까지 탔던 캘리포니아에서 지내다가 오랜만에 본 빗줄기여서 그럴 것이다. 만나는 사람들은 두 손을 기도하듯이 모아서 가슴과 턱 부분에 대고 인사하는 '와이'라는 태국 전통 인사법이 퍽 친근하고 즐거움을 느끼게 한다. 불교 국가인지라 가는 곳마다 황금불탑 같은 불교문화가 융성함을 볼 수 있다. 나는 내세를 위해 현실을 희생하리만큼 강한 불교적 관습과 문화 속에서 사는 사람들 틈에서 구원의 소식을 전하는 황 선교사님을 만났다.

구원의 소식을 듣고서 어두웠던 과거사를 접고 새 생명으로 태어나 청소년 재활 센터 'Jasper'에 사는 젊은 청소년들을 보면서, 나는 황 선교사님이 날마다 하나님께 드린 눈물의 기도를 생각한다. 선교사님의 기도 응답 속에서 복음의 씨앗이 싹 트고 자라나는 모습을 나는 현지에서 본 것이다. 태국에는 복음의 씨앗을 뿌리기 위해서 코끼리에게 그림을 그리도록 훈련하는 조련사보다도 더 힘든 인내와 땀방울로 기도드리고 있는 황 선교사님이 있음에 감사할 뿐이다. 깊은 산 속에서 황톳길 계단을 씩씩거리면서 한없이 올라간 뒤에서야 만날 수 있는 높은 곳에 최초로 지어진 교회엔, 현지 목사님을 시무하실 수 있게 하신다. 교회에서 사랑의 종소리가 멀리멀리 퍼져 나가고 있음에 행복해하시는 귀하신 황 선교사님의 얼굴에 하얀 광채가 난다.

베틀

나는 지금도 사상적 혼란 속에서 온전한 자유를 위해 분투하는 소리 없는 아우성이 들리는 것 같은 나라가 있어 애처롭다. 전쟁의 아픔과 피눈물이 너무도 많은 나라, 화장실이 없는 가정이 많고, 사람들도 동물들도 뼈가 앙상하게 드러나도록 말라 보이는 '캄보디아'다. 나는 이 땅 위에 신의 섭리가 있음을 믿는다. 이 세상 사람들은 누구나 자기가 섬기는 신이 있다고 한다. 심지어는 자기 자신이 신이라고 말하는 사람도 있지 않은가. 나는 사람의 작품이라기엔 너무 감탄스러운 캄보디아의 보물인 광대한 앙코르와트 고대 사원에서, 머리는 안 보이고 코브라 뱀 꼬리만 꿈틀거리면서 하늘을 날 것 같은 건축양식을 보면서, 자신을 희생해서 인류를 구원해 주신 예수님의 생애와 자기 자신을 위해서 많은 사람을 희생시킨 권력의 사람을 생각한다. 이런 땅 위에서 예수님의 모습을 닮으려고 자신을 희생하면서 복음을 전하는 김 선교사님을 만났다. 한 발자국을 뗄 때마다 기적이 일어나기를 간절히 기도드려야만 하는 고충을 안고서도 밀알처럼 복음의 싹이 돋아나는 영혼들을 보는 즐거움으로 거의 한평생을 해외선교사로 지내신단다.

캄보디아엔 사람이 동물 취급받았던 슬픈 역사가 그리 오래되지 않았음을 말해주는 듯 아직도 옷을 만들었던 천 조각들이 땅 위로 삐져나와 있어 걷는 발에 밟히는 킬링필드가 있다. 지금은 이름을 바꾸어 '힐링필드'라 한다. 1975년 호메르 정부가 들어서고 'Re-education campaign'을 벌이면서 수많은 지식인을 때려죽인 섬뜩한 인간의 허연 두개골들이 7층에 진열되어 있다. 심지어 어린아이들은 두 발을 손으로 휘어잡은 후 거꾸로 들고서 머리통을 나무에 후려쳤단다. 그 뻘건

피가 낭자한 참혹한 모습을 품은 커다란 나무는 지금도 말없이 그 자리에 무성히 서 있다. 나는 그 나무 위에서 우리를 구원해 주시기 위해서 죄 없이 참혹하게 돌아가신 십자가상 위의 예수님을 본다.

씨엠립 부근 메콩강 일부에 배수가 잘 안 되어 거대한 습지대를 형성하면서 생긴 '벙 톤레 쌉' 호수는 대부분이 베트남 전쟁의 상흔으로 남은 가슴 아픈 베트남 난민들인 '보트피플'들이 살고 있다. 뭍으로 발을 내딛는 순간 밀입국자가 되기에 평생토록 보트 위에서만 살다가 생을 마감하는 사람들이다. 그 지역에서만 잘 자라는 특이한 연꽃이 황토물을 정화해 주어 그 물로 수상가옥 촌사람들이 생활할 수 있단다. 대부분이 민물 생선을 잡아 생활하는 그 불쌍한 사람들에게 구원의 손길을 주는 한국교회 이름이 눈에 띄니 얼마나 가슴이 후련하고 기쁘던지— 캄보디아는 잠을 잘 수 없게 하는 돼지 멱따는 소리, 도마뱀들의 찍찍거리는 소란스런 소리, 새벽 불경 소리——— 각종 소리 속에서도 복음의 싹트는 소리가 들린다. 그리고 내 관심이 머무는 곳에 그 소리에 기뻐하는 선교사님들의 표정이 보인다.

베틀

백의천사(白衣天使)의 일생으로
피운 삶의 꽃

백의천사(白衣天使)의 일생으로피운 삶의 꽃
- 정순옥의 수필세계

• 鄭木日(수필가. 한국문인협회 부이사장)

1 ─────────────────────────────

재미 수필가 정순옥 님의 세 번째 수필집 『베틀』 원고를 읽게 된 일
도 인연이 아닐 수 없다. 정순옥 님은 2009년 월간 〈한국수필〉지의 신
인문학상을 수상하여 본격적인 수필작가로 나서게 되었다. 그 당시 필
자가 한국수필가협회 이사장으로 〈한국수필〉 발행인을 맡고 있었으므
로 심사에 참여한 기억이 떠오른다. 세 번째 수필집의 서평을 쓰게 된
것도 어쩌면 인연이 아닐 수 없다. 간호사이며 수필가로서 최선을 다한
삶에 경건함과 감사의 마음을 느낀다.

질병으로 고통을 받는 환자들의 생명을 지키는 간호사로서 시간을
쪼개어 자의식의 촛불을 밝혀 수필을 써온 삶에 온정을 느낀다. 평생
을 환자들의 질병과 고통을 치유하는 간호사의 소임을 다한 인생에서
따뜻한 인간애와 맑은 미소가 풍겨져 옴을 느낀다. 그의 수필에선 간
호사로서의 직무를 다하는 책임과 기도가 담겨 있다. 그의 수필은 편
안하게 그리움을 전해 주는 듯 다가오며 따뜻한 손길로 쓴 자신의 삶
의 고백이며 기도가 담겨 있다.

수필을 쓰려면 마음속에 촛불을 켜야 한다. 촛불이 켜진 자리가 자신을 만날 수 있는 중심점이다. 작가인 내가 주인공인 나를 살피고 있다. 사색의 한복판에 앉아야 한다. 그곳에 내면의 얼굴을 들여다 볼 수 있는 마음의 거울이 있다. 마음의 거울이 깨끗하고 청결하여야 영혼의 모습을 바라볼 수 있다. 사소한 일상의 흥미와 쾌락에 빠져서 수필을 쓰지 못한다면, 자신의 내면을 볼 수 없고, 삶의 발견과 의미도 놓쳐버린다.

정순옥은 '백의천사'로 부르는 간호사로 몸과 마음이 아픈 이들을 치유하는 일에 평생을 바쳐온 사람이다. 그의 수필 또한 마음의 치유를 위한 손길이 아닐까 싶다. 수필은 자신의 체험에 대한 기록만은 아니다. 체험을 통한 인생의 발견과 삶의 깨달음을 피워내는 일이다. 자신의 모습을 담아내려면 먼저 마음에 묻은 '탐욕'이라는 때, '성냄'이란 자국, '어리석음'이란 먼지를 씻어내야 한다. 마음이 맑고 깨끗해야만 자신의 영혼을 비춰 볼 수 있다. 수필쓰기는 자신의 마음과 영혼을 들여다보며 쓰는 삶의 진실이 아닐 수 없다. 인생에서 향기가 나야만 마음에서 향기가 난다. 그런 마음의 상태이어야 향기로운 수필을 쓸 수가 있다.

수필의 바탕은 진실과 순수이다. 수필가는 부단히 마음의 때와 얼룩과 먼지를 닦아내야 한다. 마음의 연마, 인생의 연마가 있어야 제 모습을 들여다 볼 수 있다. 수필만큼 삶을 확장시키고 스스로 깨달음에 이르게 하고, 영원과 대화할 수 있는 벗은 없다. 수필은 마음을 맑게 해주며, 안정과 평화를 안겨준다. 수필은 고백과 토로를 통해 갈등, 반목, 대립, 원한, 열등감에서 벗어나게 하는 치유사(治癒使)가 돼주기도 한다.

수필쓰기를 통해 얻는 기쁨은 스쳐가는 시공간을 보면서 인생을 발

베틀

견하고 있다는 자각이다. 수필을 쓰면서 이 순간 심장의 고동소리를 듣고, 영원의 숨결을 의식할 수 있음은 얼마나 다행한 일인가. 수필쓰기는 살아 있음의 지각이요, 그 표현이 아닐 수 없다. 수필가는 원대한 꿈과 패기를 자랑하지 않는다. 소박하고 진실한 삶의 의미를 꽃피우려 할 뿐이다. 수필쓰기는 진실의 숨결, 인생의 발견, 미학의 창조, 의미의 부여가 아닐까. 스스로 한 송이씩의 인생이라는 의미의 꽃을 피워내는 일이다.

2 ───────────────────────────────────────

재미동포들의 수필을 보면 고향에 대한 향수와 그리움이 많은 부분을 차지하고 있음을 본다. 비록 몸은 떠나 이국에서 살고 있을지라도 자신이 태어나고 자란 조국과 고향을 어찌 잊을 수 있으랴. 아마도 숨을 놓을 때도 조국과 고향에 대한 향수를 버릴 수 없을 것이다.

봉선화.
왜 이리 고향의 봉선화가 보고 싶은 걸까? 내가 고향에 두고 온 것 중에서 가장 많이 생각나게 하는 꽃이다. 요즈음도 눈 감고 고향 생각을 하면 봉숭아가 터지고 눈 뜨고 손가락을 만져도 따다닥 터지는 소리로 변한다. 손을 살짝이라도 대면 씨방을 터트리면서 반가움을 표시하는 봉선화 생각뿐이다.
어느 날부터 나는 재미동포 생활을 시작했는데 "이를 앙다물고 살아야 한다."라는 어머니의 말씀 따라 힘든 디아스포라의 삶에서도 고향을 잊지 않고 인내하며 살아야 했다. 그 힘의 근원은 어쩜 한 여름날 뜨거운 뙤약볕 아래서 시들시들 처량한 모습이었다가도 밤이슬에 다시 힘을 얻어 살아났던 봉선화 때문이라 싶다. 아름다운 꽃을 피우고 나의 손톱을 빨갛게 물들게 한 봉선화. 어쩌면 어린 가슴을 신기함으로 들뜨게 했던 내 고향 봉선화의 혼이 내 가슴에 항상 잠재했기 때문이리라.

나는 오늘도 이곳에 있는 봉선화가 아닌 줄기를 따라 마디마디에 소박한 꽃을 피우는 그리운 내 고향 토종봉숭아나 접봉숭아를 찾아 눈을 크게 뜬다. 그리하여 귀를 나발통처럼 넓게 열고서 이리저리 헤맨다. 언젠가는 그리운 내 고향 봉숭아꽃을 이곳 뜨락에 심어 꽃핀 빨강·주홍·흰색봉숭아 얼굴들을 보면서 하루하루를 즐겁게 살고 싶은 소망이 있기에 그렇다.

내가 살던 소쿠리 마을은 낮은 구릉과 산들로 둘러싸여 있어서 시골이라기보다는 산골에 가깝다. 나무가 많고 잡풀이 많아서인지 집 안에서 지네나 뱀들도 가끔 볼 수 있었다. 그런데도 장독대에 뱀이 들어갔다는 말을 들은 적이 없다. 어머니 말씀대로 신기하게 봉선화 꽃이 있는 곳엔 해충과 파충류들이 얼씬도 못했다. 그 탓에 마을 집집마다 장독대 둘레나 울 밑 이곳저곳에 봉숭아꽃이 심어져 있었다. 그야말로 소쿠리 마을 전체가 봉선화로 물들인 마을이었다.

아름다운 정서를 제공해 주던 내 유년시절의 우리 집은 봄을 기다리는 아버지의 가슴에서부터 만들어지곤 했다. 봄이 오기 전 토담 아래에 있는 꽃밭은 겨우내 쌓아 두었던 땔감과 볏단이 치워지고, 아버지의 말씀에 오빠가 삽으로 땅을 깊게 판 후 흙을 골라 보송보

베틀

송하게 만들었다.

토담 아래 있는 꽃밭에 마지막 잔설이 녹아내리기 시작하면 어머니는 서랍 속에 고이 간직해 둔 봉선화 꽃씨와 다른 꽃씨들을 꺼낸다. 그리고는 언니에게 건네주면서 꽃밭에 심으라 하셨다. 언니는 물론이고 나의 손에도 호미를 쥐게 했다. 어느 사이에 꽃밭에 온 새언니랑 언니와 나는 촉촉한 땅을 호미로 파고 골을 만들었다. 우리는 봉선화 꽃씨를 구분해서 심고 곁에는 다른 꽃씨들도 함께 뿌리곤 했다.

— 〈그리운 봉선화〉의 일부

〈그리운 봉선화〉엔 고향에 대한 향수가 담겨 있다. '그리운 고향집'을 떠올리는 추억 속에 먼저 떠오르는 것이 '봉선화'이다. 특히 여자일 경우는 더욱 그러리라 생각된다. 다른 꽃들은 눈으로 보고 즐기는 것이었지만, 봉선화만은 손톱에 물을 들이던 체험의 기억이 남아 있다. 고향과 어린 시절을 떠올릴 적에 선명히 떠오르는 추억의 꽃이다. 봉숭아 꽃잎을 찧어 손톱에 물을 들이는 체험을 통해 여성다움의 첫 표현을 드러내던 모습이 떠오른다. 손톱에 붉은 봉숭화 물을 들이는 것은 여성으로서 처음 시도하는 아름다운 치장의 시발점이 아닐 수 없다. 그때의 기억은 어릴 적 모습과 함께 고향을 떠올리게 해주곤 한다.

〈그리운 봉선화〉에서 저자는 고향의 봄을 그려 놓고 있다. 화려하고 장식적인 봄맞이가 아닌, 어릴 적에 고향에서 체험했던 자연 속의 봄을 그리고 있다. 봄이면 언니와 함께 땅을 파고 꽃씨를 심던 추억의 장면을 봄철이면 회억(回憶)해내곤 하는 것이다.

〈그리운 봉선화〉 속에는 꽃씨를 심는 모습만 있는 게 아니라, 못 잊을 고향과 어릴 적의 봄의 추억과 그리움이 담겨 있다. 외로운 이국에서 경험하지 못한 고국의 옛집에서 체험한 봄의 향기와 그리움을 담아 놓은 작품이다.

3 ———————————————————————————

정순옥의 수필은 미국 생활에서 현대의 삶의 모습을 통한 체험과 사유를 담아내기보다는 모국의 고향에서 지내던 추억담을 담아내고 있음을 본다. 미국의 이민자로서의 삶과 체험을 통한 인생의 발견과 체험을 통한 깨달음을 어떻게 꽃피워 내고 있는 것일까. 저자는 궁금증을 〈베틀〉이란 작품을 통해 명료하게 보여주고 있다.

철커덩 철거더엉.
오늘도 나는 베틀 위에 앉아서 고국을 떠나온 다른 나라의 땅에서 살면서 이민자의 삶이라는 아름다운 피륙을 짜고 있다. 한국인이라는 근본이 되는 정적인 날줄 위에 이민자라는 동적인 씨줄을 북에 담아 적당하게 뿌려주면서 힘차게 피륙을 짠다. 희망에 찬 '미주한인'이란 정겨운 베틀가를 부르면서.
철커덩 철거더엉.
이민 초기의 나는 거칠고 까슬까슬한 삼대껍질을 벗겨서 만든 실로 피륙을 짜기 시작했다. 강하고 질긴 누런 색깔의 삼실을 북에 담아서 열심히 손놀림하면서 이민 시작의 피륙을 짜기 시작한 것

베틀

이다. 참으로 어떻게 해야 하는지, 방법이 익숙지 못해서 당황할 때가 잦았다. 때때로 실이 끊어져서 다시금 이으면 그때마다 매듭이 생겼고 힘든 노동으로 한숨과 눈물이 흘러내려 내가 짠 피륙에 진한 얼룩이 지곤 했다.

새로운 자격증을 따는 데 있어 언어장애 때문에 갖은 고생을 했으며, 또 직장에서 교육을 받을 때도 몇 배나 더 노력해야만 했다. 답답한 가슴은 터질 것 같았고 움츠러들기만 하는 내 영혼의 고통 탓에 피륙이 고르지 못하고 울퉁불퉁했다.

그뿐인가! 햄버거와 커피를 즐기는 사람들 틈에서 빠져나와 신토불이 김치와 고추장을 찾아 먼 길을 다녀와 고향에 대한 향수와 연민, 눈물과 외로움으로 짠 피륙은 한없이 느슨했다.

나의 꿈나무인 아이들이 태어나서 학교에 가기 시작하니 또 다른 문제점들이 생겨났다.

아이들은 학교에 갔다 오면 자주 우울해하고 울먹거렸다. 친구들과 재미있게 놀고 싶은데 다들 피한단다. 친구를 붙들고 왜 그러느냐고 물었더니 자기는 놀고 싶지만, 부모들이 눈이 옆으로 째진 동양인들과는 놀지 말라고 했단다. 친구들로부터 상처받는 여리디여린 우리 아이들. 이민가정으로서 각박하기만 한 생활전선의 이중성에 시달리던 이민 초기의 삶, 무엇보다 경제적인 안정부터 찾아야 했다.

아이들 말에 북을 쥔 손에 나도 모르게 힘이 너무 들어가서 삼베실이 뚝 끊어져 버렸다. 다시금 실을 잇는 나의 손은 떨렸고 이은 자리는 또 다른 매듭으로 남았다. 북을 잡은 손과 베틀신을 신은 나의 발이 떨려서 제대로 고운 피륙은 짤 수 없었지만, 그래도 허

리에 띤 베틀 띠를 더 단단히 묶어 가면서 피륙 올올이 땀과 인내
와 희망을 섞어 무지개 꿈을 안고서 열심히 짜고 또 짰다.

- 〈베틀〉 일부

미국에서의 이민생활은 개척의 생활사가 아닐 수 없다. 이국의 땅에
뿌리를 내리기 위해서 몸과 정신을 다 쏟아야만 했다. 삶의 모습이 다
른 이국에서 적응력을 지니기 위해서는 모든 것들을 배워야만 한다.
이민가정의 어려웠던 삶을 극복하기 위해서 모든 노력을 경주한 삶의
고백을 토로하고 있다. 〈베틀〉이란 작품을 보면서 미주 한인들의 자립
을 위한 노력과 노고를 실감하게 된다. 근면과 성실로 직장에서 인정
을 받아야 하며, 미국사회의 질서에 부응하는 삶을 보이며 뿌리를 내
리기까지 최선을 다해야만 했다. 미국 사회에 정착한 한국인들은 근
면, 성실을 바탕으로 꾸준한 노력을 보여줌으로써 안정의 기틀을 마련
하고 있다.

4 ―――――――――――――――――――――――――――

정순옥의 수필에선 한국의 농경시대 풍경과 체험들이 선명하게 그려
져 있다. 농경시대와 산업시대를 거치면서 사라지고만 삶의 모습들이
한 장의 흑백 사진처럼 보여주고 있다. 어쩌면 미국 이민자이기에 기억
속에 선명히 남아 있는지도 모른다. 오늘의 젊은이들도 한국의 농경시
대와 산업화시대의 삶의 풍경과 모습을 알지 못한다. 정순옥의 일생에
서 가장 큰 변환은 미국 이민이었다. '간호사'란 천직이 있었기에 가능

베틀

한 일이었다. 간호사의 손만큼 거룩한 손도 없다. 어쩌면 진실한 간호사는 평생 동안 '손의 기도'를 드리지 않을까 생각한다.

부디 내 손을 깨끗하게 해 주소서.
욕망에 눈이 어두워 무엇이라도 갖고 싶어
안달을 부리는 손이 되지 않게 하소서.
아침마다 손을 씻는 것만이 아니라,
마음의 손을 씻게 하소서.

그 손으로 영혼을 씻게 하소서.
고통을 받는 사람들의 이마를 짚어줄 줄 아는
손이 되게 하소서.

— 필자의 '손의 기도' 일부

평생 동안 질병으로 고통받는 환자들을 돕는 백의 천사로서 살아온 정순옥 간호사이자 수필가의 일생에 감명과 은혜가 흐르고 있음을 느낀다. 미국 이민자로서 새로운 삶을 개척하고 간호사로서 본분을 다한 모습이 아름답게 다가온다. 특히 수필가로서 자신의 삶과 인생을 담아낸 기록정신이 돋보인다. '수필'이야말로 유한한 인생의 유일한 영원장치임을 알고 있다. 깨어있는 자의식과 삶의 의미를 '수필'로서 꽃 피워내고 있는 저자의 앞날에 축복과 문운을 빌며, 이번 상재하는 세 번째 수필집 『베틀』이 독자들에게 큰 사랑을 듬뿍 받길 바란다.

한·영 에세이
Korean · English Essay

베틀
The Loom

정순옥 · Chung Soon-Ok

문학공감

Introduction

It is purely God's grace and I glorify his name that an author like me who lacks indefinitely could publish her 3rd essay book 『The Loom』 in both Korean and English.

I am eternally grateful that the literature critic and one of the most prominent experts in the field of lyrical essay, Mr. Cheong, Mok-Il, took the time out of his busy schedule to review my book 『The Loom』 . I feel blessed that I could work with Mr. Kang, Yang-Wook, the translator, Mr. Gilbert Khang, the essayist and a literary critic, and the poet and my beloved husband, Mr. Lee, Byung-Ho, who is always my first reader and who is at the forefront of the globalization of Korean literature, Ms. Chung, Soon-Ja, my sister who plays the role of my love letter in creating this book 『The Loom』 . My heart is filled with happiness and the sorrow of life.

As a 1st generation of Korean American immigrants who had to start everything again in a foreign country, I tried to describe my dearest effort living in this country in the form of an essay. I think when all forms of life contribute to making history in harmony, my life will surely be worthwhile for our posterity. Though I have refined and written the sentiment formed throughout my life as a first-generation Korean American and have always tried to write essays that emphasize the value of a true and aromatic life, nothing feels good enough that I feel like I am not a good writer. Thus, I still feel embarrassed and humble to be called an 'essayist.' But when I work up my courage and sit on my desk, I write by communicating with my loved ones who have been watching me over from the eternal world. That is because I can freely say words that have rarely come out when I was living with them face-to-face: the words that have been buried deep in my heart, 'I love you.'

As a Korean American and as a believer of God, I write essays, holding on to the beautiful and loving Korean language that is sadly disappearing in our younger generations, and constantly think about how I can live a beautiful life while living in this land God has allowed me. As the hair moves along with the wind, I believe the way I approach essays will also move the minds of my readers, and I shall always try to create an essay with a new heart and soul. At the same time, I shall never forget that an essay is the closest thing to an everyday life, and it should be honest as well as intimate and make the reader feel refreshed while having fun.

As for a pilgrimage path to life, which has yet to come, I hope to embrace beautiful languages, have pride as a Korean literary scholar, and live happily while enjoying good literature. I humbly request guidance as well as encouragement. My third essay book 『The Loom』 is finally published and I would like to express my sincere gratitude to my church members, my literary friends, and my family members. Once more, I would like to thank those who have been loving and supportive of my work, especially Mr. Gilbert Khang.

April, 2018,
Chung, Soon-Ok
Monterey, USA

contents

Introduction — 193

CHAPTER 1 | My autumn-colored basket

Eden is mysterious —201
The Balloon Flower, the Comfort Women — 205
A beautiful dream of a dewdrop — 210
The cane of love — 214
The Light in the Cries — 218
My autumn-colored basket — 222
The life of a woman with a wild, wiry hair — 226
God Arirang — 231
Dreams of people living in the floating village — 235
My love, the Han river — 239

CHAPTER 2 | The Loom

A grateful retirement — 247
Garden Balsam — 251
The fragrance of shepherd's purse — 255
The Loom — 259
Rice-flour Mill — 263
Father and a white heron — 267
Earl-leh byt(Korean wide-tooth comb) — 269
Ssari door — 274
The Wash Place — 278
The lamp in a farming village — 282

CHAPTER 3 | The Snowflakes

It's okay! —289

Christmas — 293

The Snowflakes — 295

Happy Retirement — 299

Good writing — 303

The hidden truth in 'We have a big problem!' — 307

The grateful and always happy Sadons — 312

These onions are making me cry — 316

Mugunghwa(Rose of Haron) — 321

That was why! — 325

CHAPTER 4 | Monterey Arirang

Monterey Cypress tree — 331

Life — 335

Monterey Arirang — 339

Sir. Rain is coming.. — 343

A love that is like the wind — 347

Diaspora nomadic age — 351

The Flower Grass — 355

The Flower Garden — 359

Missionary and dentures — 364

I saw — 369

Review | Growing the Flower of Life as an Angel in White — 375

| CHAPTER 1 |

My autumn-colored basket

Eden is mysterious.

I am looking at the mysterious and beautiful Eden. Eden, originally a blessed land created by God, is a name representing the wish of parents for the baby to not be tempted by sins in this paradise. With all her features, such as ears, eyes, mouth, and nose, so elaborate, Eden is mysterious, and she makes my heart flutter. Ummm~ What a scent of the irresistible baby smell, it is so good.

Eden, with her deep black eyes that twinkle like morning stars, her moist cherry lips, the soft milky skin, the flushed rosy cheeks, the pointy nose, her fine soft hair, and her two ears that move gently. It is a true blessing to see one of the most beautiful and mysterious God's creatures ever created. As soon as she's born, she opened her eyes as if she was curious of the world she was to live in for the rest of her life, while gently covering her mouth with her hand. Such beautiful Eden is my first granddaughter.

Her hair softer than silk, her fine eyelashes that gently move to my breath, her baby skin that smells like mother's milk, her delicate fragrance that sweetens my sense of smell, all of these cannot be more lovely and mysterious it feels they steal my soul every single time. Conceived as a whole life, spending 38 weeks, which is less than 40 weeks, in her mother's tummy, she was finally born as a normal girl weighing 6.15 pounds, going through the pains of being born. Such fluffy soft hair, 'thump thump' the sound of her beating heart, her breathing sound makes my heart go electrifying. I am so thankful for your first breath going 'Waa Waa' to signal the joy of a blood relation, which made me so happy.

I want you to live a beautiful life, communicating with the world, with your two big eyes, two dented ears, and your pretty mouth. With your two healthy hands, I sincerely hope that you can volunteer for many good causes. The hands that can soothe the wounds of the sick, I want your hands to be ones that are joined together and pray all the time. I want your feet with strong bones to keep your knees straight and search for those who are compassionate. I hope your two strong shoulders to be able to lend for those who are in need to cry on and give a pleasant scent of human. How great would it be if your clear and white face to continue to be full of such gentle smiles that contain the joy of life, which is more important than anything under the sky? Since she has the DNA of the Korean race, I trust that Eden will be good-natured with a happy heart.

The emotions of the Korean people contain an abundance of romance. Respecting each and every moment, you will bloom flowers that will be in harmony with your beautiful life. Radiating a delicate color and fragrance. Along with the wind, air, and the nature like the sunlight which contain the energy of the universe, I want you to enjoy a pure life. When you begin to coo and gurgle and learn to speak a language, I hope you can only say beautiful words, words that will encourage others and feel gracious. I hope your happy voice and happy laughs will always go together. Listening to the spiritual voice from the sky and living peacefully with God, I hope you can one day go back to the heaven in grace.

Listening to beautiful music, enjoying the fragrant smell of flowers among the little wildflowers, I hope you can live with emotions that will make you happy. Wearing fine clothes and eating delicious food, I want you to enjoy the romance of life with a helping and giving heart having a vision of a good life. As apple becomes ripe turning from green to red I hope your life to be full of freshness. Having a beautiful relationship with the people around you, I hope you to live a meaningful and fruitful life. As people say loneliness is a blessing to cleanse soul, having such moments every now and then should be beneficial. As the saying 'silence is golden' it will be beneficial to remember this more often than not. How wonderful it would be if you can live in this world as a beautiful woman who also possess the truth, goodness, and beauty?

I hope your brain, which consists of an uncountable number of cells, only thinks of good and just thoughts. I hope you can sense the hunger of others, which can twist and tear one's internal organs, and wiggle your body to make sounds of festivals. I hope you become Eden who possesses warm feelings in her heart and blooms a flower bud of love. When you open up your heart, you will receive the infinite mysteries of the universe. Your heart which governs the circulation of the blood pumping red blood remains warm and can love your neighbors as you do yourself. It is my sincere hope you find true happiness by giving love. I hope your blood which is the basis of a precious love remains refreshing and clean. As your body is your temple, you shall need to take care of your body and your health.

As every joint that connects the bones is filled with bone marrow to make us move freely, I hope your life to be as smooth and worry-free. I hope you can be humble in your daily life and not be full of yourself and empty hopes. I hope you don't get too bold but stay wise. As the kidneys, the urethra, and cytopyge all work together to get rid of unnecessary elements in our bodies, I hope you can purify your body and mind by getting rid of many unnecessary things in your life. You were born here as God intended, and I hope you enjoy the freedom under God's truths, know the value of life, and live every moment in your life with hope. I hope this world where my beautiful granddaughter will live in will be free of sins and become the heaven on earth. At any rate, I hope God will love and bless you as you live and form a community in this beautiful world, and that you live happily and love your neighbors. I will pray every day and night that you will always be thankful and live with joy and happiness. As I become deeply moved once more for your being born a such lovely person and allowing me to become a grandmother, I am mummering to myself. "Eden is mysterious!"

The Balloon Flower,
the Comfort Women.

There are words with a sharp dagger inserted in them for which they cannot be approached casually, the 'Comfort women.' People cautiously approach the words, sometimes referring them as the 'balloon flowers.' With their bodies and minds stamped on mercilessly by the boots of the armed forces of Imperial Japan, they were the Joseon's sisters who have had to live with deep enmity all their lives. There's a saying in Korea "When women bear enmity, a frost will fall down even in May or June." More than just a few, the countless number of comforting woman, as souls in the sky and old here on Earth, are still wailing with their enmity whose echoes vibrating the heaven and earth. "People in Japan! Stop distorting history, and repent and apologize sincerely to the comfort women!"

I am afraid of potential natural disasters that can be even worse than tsunamis when the truths of the innocent balloon flowers reach the sky as heaven and earth respond. When the tsunami hit Japan in recent years and took many lives more precious than anything under the sky, was it not Korea that ran to its aid first?

Japan must realize and correct the wrong history and apologize to the comfort women whose human rights and dignity were trampled on and were used as sex slaves, and it must form a new practical partnership with Korea despite having been historical enemies. This is to create beautifully a new human history in a joint effort.

As Japanese military established comfort stations since the end of 1937, they began violating human rights and deploying sex slaves in the most inhumane and violent way imaginable. During this Japanese colonial era, there were many young girls wearing purple dresses living in many parts of our poor and powerless country. When they turned 14 years old, those balloon flowers would be so pretty, it would flutter and steal the hearts of many young boys. But the boys would never violate them. The baloon flowers were too pretty, even holistic, to even look at directly, that they would never dare to even approach them. But those savages in military boots tramped on the beautifully growing balloon flowers mercilessly, calling them 'Josenjin.'

The precious daughters of Joseon, the virgins who fluttered many young boys in our country, whose virginities were stampeded by the Japanese military boots, are in the history of 'comfort women.' Despite their resistance suffering broken ribs, the thick veins and deep bruises of the leaves of the balloon flowers would only suffocate their choking necks. It was their wanting to see their parents, brothers, and sisters again, alive, in their home country that they did not give up living, as well as their dreams of revealing the truths of their captured lives.

Wikipedia defines comfort women as "women and girls who

were abducted under Imperial Japanese rules or lured with false promises of jobs or higher education to be forced into sexual slavery for the Imperial Japanese Army in occupied territories before and during World War II in order to satisfy the sexual needs of the Japanese soldiers."

Most of these women were from countries occupied by Japan, such as Korea, China, the Philippines, Thailand, Vietnam, Malaysia, the survivors of the camps testify that they were forced into sexual acts more than 30 times a day. The comfort women who have survived have been protesting in front of the Japanese embassy in Seoul, Korea every Wednesday since 1992, demanding an apology from the Japanese government as well as a probe and appropriate reparations. Nowadays, only a few remaining survivors, such as Ms. Kim, Bokdong, are alive who can even testify, since most of the victims have since passed away.

During the period of Japanese occupation, young girls would be taken away by Japanese soldiers or police without knowing what would happen to them, and they would be incarcerated in comfort stations to serve the sexual needs of the Japanese soldiers. When they returned home, they would be ridiculed as "Hwa-nyang girl (slut)" and most of them would give up having a normal life and being married one day, having to store their anger deep within them that would never be resolved. I still remember my mother saying this as if it was yesterday. "…. Do you know why your older sister got married at such a young age? If I hadn't made her, she could've been taken away by the police and become a sex slave for the soldiers at the comfort stations~. She could've been labeled as Haw-nayung girl-. Wasn't she better off marrying at a young age?"

Japan must understand that its country and its cowardly tactics, such as Japan's Prime Minister Shinzo Abe entering Harvard University through a back door to avoid activists and student protesters, are being noticed by numerous human rights activists, such as Representative Lane Allen Evans, a comfort woman advocate and the major force behind the 'comfort women' resolution in Congress, as well as representative Michael Honda. Shouldn't Japan become a country that values human rights first and foremost in order to become a nation that is respected and creates a new history?

For the victims who still cannot face the world face-to-face due to the shame and horrors of being forced as sex slaves, I sincerely hope for a new conscientious Japan that is capable of apologizing for what they have caused to the comfort women to be forgiven by the world and that educates their new generations. Today, the ghosts of the fragile balloon flowers whose human rights and dignity were violated are reviving as comfort women memorial statues in various parks, wearing long skirts, here in the United States, a nation that values human and civil rights. They are wearing skirts with long width, ready to forgive and embrace the Japanese people for the crimes committed by their ancestors as long as they sincerely repent. The Japanese government should seize this opportunity and keel down for forgiveness and savation of love.

Who knows! Someday, those with allergies to balloon flowers may black out with their bolts down in their hearts due to the strong fragrance of the flowers of the comfort women~. All things in the universe change, except truths. And everything is fair. There is a truth that the heaven and earth know. The truth that the beautiful purple flowers in the deep mountains who had not even had a chance to bloom to be trampled on by the boots of the imperial armies of Japan, vomiting dark blood only to be crushed again permanently. There is nothing in this world that triumphs truths. People on this earth who love truth are urging.

"Japan must sincerely and officially apologize to the comfort women whose human and civil rights were stamped on heinously!"

A beautiful dream of a dewdrop

I know a beautiful dream born in the dewdrop. I am talking about the dewdrop that shined a beautiful and bright light to console my soul and gave me hope. I hope my essays can become also a passage of blessings that can comfort those who never give up under any circumstances. I recall the words of the Bible "Like the dew of Hermon that came down upon the mountains of Zion."

When the sunlight shines on dew, the light escapes the dewdrop in many beautiful colors due to the prism effect. At this very moment, a beautiful dream of the dew drop becomes materialized. I believe when my essays capture the hearts of the readers with the mysterious power of life of the one who came to the world as a light, it would fulfill my dreams as an essayist. Dew drops are made after a hard work when the night condenses moistures out of the cold air in the form of droplets. My essays are also born after the head-crushing pains. During night times, the tiny water drops mingle with one another to form the dew. So do my essays. Through the creative pains, my thoughts and words comingle to create a piece of essay. Tiniest water droplets combine themselves to form a clear dewdrop, and those drops sometimes form to produce an even bigger ones. So are my essays. Short words gather together to make sentences, and they in turn form an essay. In order to create essays that can leave a profound impression on my readers, I feel like I am constantly living with essays every minute of my day whether it is reading good books or thinking and writing a lot.

Dewdrops are like magicians. With the miraculous survival instincts, they disappear from its beautiful rainbow-like form only to be reborn to the original form. Essays are exactly the same. Many thoughts and ideas come into my mind as if I could whip out a beautiful piece only to disappear altogether, and finally reappear in the form of an essay. An essay also has cells like dew and requires fresh air to enable them to stay alive. Wouldn't God's gift such as fresh air be needed to conceive the language of life? The language of life that enables our feelings.

I was one of the youngest in my many siblings. So, when I knew them as my parents, they were already old folks. For this reason, when I think of my parents, I begin to feel sorry for them for having to always work hard to support our big family. It was when I was in my graduating class in middle school. Every now and then, I would wake up early in the morning and I would head out to the calm field. Because I was at a crossroad to determine about which school to go, the mother nature acted as a good friend of mine at the time. One day, I observed the moment when a dewdrop, which was clear as a crystal, rolling over a taro leaf following the wind and hit the ground with no regret. As if my weak self was falling over to the ground, I felt devastated without knowing what to do. I wanted to go to a good school and had the desire to read good books to continue my writing, but I felt like my parents could not afford me financially for such an opportunity. I did not raise my concerns to my parents, but it was a period of agony for me.

Ah, but something happened. I saw the marvelous moment. A colorless dewdrop with the help of the sun started shining mysterious colorful rays. In that moment, I saw a beautiful dream of the dew which wanted to help me and show me hope. I truly believed that someone would take care of me after all, and at that moment I heard the lovely voice of my mother from behind, calling my name.

Many years have passed. A dewdrop on the taro leaf in my hometown is revived as a new one in my garden here in the States. I wish my essays could be like a dewdrop. I have always wanted to write essays that people read once and then they would forget about them, but only to resurface at some point in their lives. I believe that I can completely devote myself to writing because of the beautiful dream of the dewdrop that day, which gave me hope of never giving up under any circumstances. I pray today as usual to cleanse my soul and to be able to write clear and amorous essays. That my essays can be the passage of blessings for those who read them.

I am thankful having lived all my life, having never forgotten the beautiful dream of the dew. Such a beautiful dream that was the passage of hope, beaming mysterious rainbow colors with the help of the Sun. I always agonize and reflect my life when I write essays if I could ever write that permeates mysterious and lively colors of love. When people refer to me as an 'essayist,' I become shy and remind myself that I am truly blessed that God has given me the conviction to overcome any obstacles of life. Perhaps that is why. I am truly blessed, and I would like my essays to become a passage of blessings like dew with beautiful dreams. The kind of passage of blessings that delivers beautiful dreams of dew that wish to console and give hope.

The cane of love

The cane of love! Such an expression existed in the early years. The expression that the era that I was educated in was actually proud of, but now almost extinct. In those times, they were the everyday terms that were used often, and they were such precious educational terms along with the word 'poverty--.' It was a support that firmly founded an era -- . It was the foundation that created the Korean people of today who join the ranks of developed nations -- . It is regrettable that such beautiful meaning is being slowly lost.

"Get the cane!" In those times when I was growing up, we would hear those educational terms countlessly from our parents at home and from our teachers at school. I feel thankful that I am who I am now due to the parents and teachers who firmly held the canes of love for me. You must study hard and become a good person in order to become well-off and out of poverty. You should obey your parents if you want everything to turn out alright and if you want to stay on the right path of life. Being lazy and failing to complete homework at a time when you should study like your life depends on it should require a cane! As a sprout to lead a new era, there was always a cane of love ready for me at various sites of education, such as home or school. In those times, no one would dare to complain and criticize using a cane on students as a wrong educational tool. Even the students who got the cane, those who witnessed the scene, or the people who heard about such incident, would all say "That was for your own good. You deserved to be spanked." Nothing further would be said of this.

My husband says a few words with a sigh as he is reading his daily papers. "That's because we don't use the cane~. I always carried a dictionary in my left hand and a cane in my right hand--. Violence at home by the children against their parents, violence by the students against their teachers, I am very concerned of these incidents happening at sites of education~." My husband who had worked for 3 years in high school as an English teacher at his first job says in a concerned voice. As I agree that there are many problems in educating our future generations where the role of cane is disappearing, I think of the roles of cane. Where has the cane of love gone, the cane that led us to the right way, the cane of love that was used as a tool to give them the best possible education?

Perhaps it has disappeared into money, or into women's skirts, or to someplace else under the wind of fashion. I picture the days of the glorious return of the cane in triumph into the field of education. The necessary cane of love to educate our future generations.

When I opened my door at our house, I would see the love of cane on top of the giant mirror. The love of cane was our silent teacher. Our mother's wisdom for us to always move forward in the right path was concentrated in the cane with the sight of it. Such cane of love was my mother's educational tool to raise the eight of us siblings in a healthy and beautiful environment. That can was one that my bright older brother made, and the story of how it came to be was a common occurrence in a poorer era.

One day, my older brother was hungry and was looking for something to eat and found dried pollack in the closet of the main wooden-floored room. It was such a good snack for a boy who was living in the mountains and who was growing up rapidly during the time of poverty. Oh~My! As he ate the food for the ancestral rites without my mother's permission, it goes without saying that my mother was stunned. My brother just broke the unwritten rule of having to wait to eat the food given to us from others until she gives it to us. In that moment, she made my brother aware of his mistake and ordered him to make the cane himself. And then she placed the cane on top of the big mirror. One day, she found out the cane was missing, and she again made my brother make another one and put it on top of the mirror. "Just because the cane is there doesn't mean I'll be using it without merit. I will only use it if its use is warranted," she said. In fact, I never saw my mother use the cane on us.

Although us eight siblings grew up together, we never got into a fight, used vulgar words, or raised our voices against each other. Of course, there were times when we had arguments. Every now and then, I think that perhaps the weapon of her devotion that allowed us brothers and sisters to get together and sing together or share the brotherly and sisterly love talking about the story of the main characters in a novel was the cane of love. We preferred to use the cane of love, like the one my own mother used at home and the cane of love my husband used at his school, even here in the United States as well, where there are many cultural and emotional differences. I used it especially in an attempt to inherit my native language to my children, but perhaps I lacked the right parenting technique, and I always felt I was inadequate. To my relief, my daughter realized the importance of learning Korean language albeit at a later age and are now expressing regrets. "Mother, you should've helped me become more fluent in Korean even if that meant you had to use the cane more frequently."

Oh~ Whew, she must have forgotten that she used to threaten me to call the police for using the cane. She would laugh her head off and told me that she would use the cane of love herself to educate her own child. I can already picture my daughter steaming, standing behind my lovely granddaughter, holding the cane of love in her hand.

The Light in the Cries

It is a light. That blooms a new life from cries. Cries are the moments of pain when a new life is born. I am talking about the unbearable pain of hardened ovaries bursting. Without the pain of breaking the shells, new buds of hope cannot burst into the world out of the darkness. Drilling a hole in the hardened one's thought would be the light shining on the cries. Thus, one could see that screams are not despairs but signal hopes and visions.

Hell Chosun, Exit Chosun! What should I do without money and a good background? These are the cries from our young people. It is a shocking expression that represents the minds of our young people wishing to leave Chosun which they believe is becoming a hell. Whew, what a relief. Chosun is the name of Korea from the past era. The present name of our nation is "the republic of Korea." As I am approaching the age of seventy living as a Korean American, I would like to answer for them. "Heaven! Korea, Live, Korea" I can definitively say that nowhere in this world there is a good country like ours to live in with a beautiful scenery and with people who are as warmhearted.

"I cannot sleep because of the screams of our young people." It was the voice of our president who had full of concerns for them. If the struggling sound of agony of our young people, who wish to escape the current crisis in a battlefield of extreme competition, was heard as a cry to the ears of the president who represents our country, it must be saying that a light is shining on the cries. I want to tell them again. "The moment of scream is the time when a new hope is created, and in this grim reality where you have been floundering between hope and despair, you must look at hope." Isn't our country, where the past, present, and the future are all coexisting, a country that has been shined on with bright lights for generations?

At this hour, the painting by a Norwegian painter, Edvard Munch, titled 'scream' comes to my mind. It is a painting that depicts the strangeness of people. To my eyes, the painting seems to speak about a modern man who is about to become mentally ill with his ears covered and his eyes and his mouth wide open, because the sound of his surroundings is so painful. While he is walking alone on this bridge of life with the sky, land, and the sea in the background, who would be these two people, barely visible against the mysterious setting sun, walking towards him? Perhaps they are people who love him and are regrettably watching the moment of his pain from behind.

The painting 'scream' also seems to be telling a story of my younger self. "They were supposed to announce the successful applications tomorrow, but it seems they already did it today. How could have this happened?" "Why not? The number of applicants didn't even meet the quorum so what was the point of waiting for the announcement?" "But what about me? I was told to bring a note by the officials since they failed to record my times correctly during the physical examination, so here I brought the note." "Well, the process is now over, so there would be no further announcement!" "What?"

As young people often painfully say these days, I had to become a failure for not having money or a good background. During the time, more than half a century ago, when unlawful processes and expedients were more rampant than present days, this incident of every applicant for the education university getting in except myself has resided in me along with the scream loud enough to cough blood and lose my voice. The moment I let my suppressed feelings explode, I know the light that shines fairly on all things in this universe helped me and put forth out buds of a new life of mine. As a result of this, I suspect that I have become the present me who treasures life.

The first preliminary college entrance examination was introduced in 1969. It was the old day's version of the current SAT. It was at the site, which was covered in a blanket of white snow, the results of the test-takers were posted, and I had to rub my eyes many times to make sure my name was actually on the list. It was and I was so happy, I couldn't say anything except 'Thank you'. When the light shined on the frozen road and on the snow that had fallen the night before, it was truly a beautiful winter day radiating a brilliantly white snow light. Though my tears formed like a silver ball, I saw an image of my parents whose face were stained with soil and sweat, smiling and dancing joyfully between white clothes. "How much was that spot worth?~" These words of a friend of mine came like a sharp iron stick to me, tearing the flesh out of my heart. That spot, to be in that spot, people would have typically spent an enormous amount of money and a good background, and I was such a naïve fool to not have realized the situation till much later.

On a sunny hill, amid the fragrance of acacia flowers blooming on the campus of an all-female high school, I practiced my organ and drew all day, even during recesses, in hopes of going to an education college that would have guaranteed me a job after graduation. After the pain, I applied to and accepted from a second group of universities as a Korean literature major, and I was able to graduate with a full scholarship. I believe I could form a new vision because the light shined warmly on my scream that moment of pain, which brought forth a new life.

To all the young souls in Korea suffering and screaming in pain at this moment, I want to tell them that the heaven on earth is 'Korea', and the scream is only the moment of pain that blooms the buds of dreams and hope. I have been living every moment of my life with gratitude for I have seen the light shining on my scream and the resulting bud of hope, not despair. This light is the true light for the soul that stays with those who love and treasure life.

My autumn-colored basket

I would like to make it. An autumn-colored basket of my life. When the green leaves mysteriously turn to red, yellow, and brown colors, I would like to put them neatly in a bamboo basket, creating a beautiful autumn-colored basket of my life. When the cold winter of my life arrives, I would like to enjoy the fragrant basket I made with similes in this sunny autumn weather.

If I wish to make a truly beautiful autumn-colored leaf, which has been a dream of my life, I shall take care of the lovely nature and stand more humbly before the bright sunshine, fresh air, and the cool breeze. As my life changes its colors slowly, just like as seasons change and plants and leaves change their colors, when I live each day trying my best to live gracefully and to its fullest, my life will be like that of an autumn leaf with elegant colors. To make this happen, I shall have to learn to be more tolerant and patient and give more attention and love to those who are precious to me. And even if someone becomes a nuisance to me, shouldn't I embrace them with love like the rare autumn sunshine if I wish to make an autumn leaf of life created with a deep scent of love?

The spring when all sorts of green plants and trees bud and

grow little by little. The summer when the leaves turn dark green and flowers bloom as the sap is strong. The autumn when the trees and plants change to autumn colors from the fall breeze. The winter when everything becomes dry and cold as the sap stops flowing. Since the four seasons are the basic order of things in the universe, it is the flow of time that no one can stop. If we could divide our lives into four seasons, I would say my life is currently in autumn, full of autumn leaves. If I had failed to make a basket of flowers which bloomed in the bright summer sun, I would like to make a basket plentiful of autumn leaves in this beautiful autumn. If possible, I would like to fill the basket with autumn leaves slowly as if I was enjoying the fall picnic. Just as the leaves turn to beautiful colors after going through the hardship of autumn, perhaps the red leaves of my life from the early frost will have an artistic color and become holistic. If possible, I would like the rest of my life to be without further blunders and become like a beautiful and colorful autumn leaf. Just like the bright yellow gingko autumn leaf in my memory.

The pretty ginkgo leaves, which call to my memory from time to time, were plenty to be found in my elementary school yard where I was a young girl full of dreams and hope. There were two ginkgo trees on the campus, and we called them the couple ginkgo trees, where the slightly thin one was the husband and the one that was fuller was the wife. In the spring, the ginkgo trees, which patiently overcame the cold winter, would make many hearts leap as they produce tender leaves sprouts; in the summer, they grow to be full of lively green leaves, and when the chilly wind starts to blow, the trees turn yellow and the leaves would fall on the ground seemingly without any regrets by the strong autumn rain and the wind from the night before. Then people walking by the ginkgo trees would be fascinated by the bright fallen yellow leaves and rush to pick up the leaves from the ground. Not only the girls, but also the male students would pick them up only to be made fun of by other playful classmates. Then the insulted boys would say "Am I not a human? I am giving this to my mom." This way, we would continue to search for even prettier ginkgo leaves, completely ignoring the sound of the school bell.

On such days, the yellow ginkgo leaves would surely make my mother happy. I still remember the face of my mother looking at the ginkgo leaves interchangeably that my brother and I had picked out for her, like a happy young girl. In the early days, the Korean language were also called "unmoon", and inside her housekeeping book written in poor unmoon were the yellow ginkgo leaves as well as red maple leaves, dry and kept in their original form. And those pretty leaves were surely used by our father as new decorations on the door in the spring time, and as such our whole family lived enjoying the artistic nature. Any time I was opening and closing the door decorated with the autumn leaves full of delicate autumn fragrances, I must have tried to guess my parent's simple life dreams.

I want to make pretty autumn leaves of my life as my parents did for theirs. When my father harvested the rice plants on autumn days that were ripe in yellow, he would always leave a patch of rice in the field for the poor. My mother would also look happy along with my father and the workers, asking him how much he had left behind for them. My parents who lived with beautiful dreams - the yellow rice autumn leaves - always hoped the following year's harvest would be even greater, so they could leave even more rice in the fields to help more people. The traces of life of my parents, who lived beautifully while practicing the love of neighbors, all have become the beautiful autumn leaves, finding their new places on the changho paper on the doors in bright yellow and red colors, and I sincerely hope to experience those beautiful autumn leaves as well. When the winter comes, as the cold winds would shake doors and the snow pallets were falling, our parents would be looking at the beautiful autumn leaves on the changho paper of the doors, worrying about the people who were less fortunate than us or making hopeful plans for the next year, and that was the image of a truly beautiful autumn-leaf life.

In the autumn of life that follows the force of nature that no one can resist, not as a leaf just fallen on the ground and broken, I want to be an enduring autumn leaf like that of my parents' who were always appreciative of nature while loving their neighbors. The traces of befriending the yellow rice autumn leaves all their lives and loving and caring for their neighbors have left as the autumn leaves in my heart. If I could embrace my neighbors with gratitude as well as those who have given me a hard time, the autumn-leaves basket of my life will be even fuller and more beautiful...

The life of a woman with a wild, wiry hair

It is an unusually wild and wiry hair. Deaconess Park, who is known in this town as a fashion expert, tells me this over and over while fixing her hair with her fingers. The life of a woman with a wild wiry hair, who has lived with the pains of going through the Korean war and losing loved ones, has becomes a pattern of life and is being drawn like a calm water painting along her fingers.

Her hairstylist says she has rarely seen a woman with such thick and full hair. Deaconess Park says her mother had a dream when she had her, in which a flock of roosters filled the front yard of her house. Perhaps that's why she was born with such a tough ill fate. She keeps saying that she's sinned too many times. So she'd spent the rest of her life paying back for her sins, thanking God for guiding her throughout her life.

However, her wild thick hair goes well with her face and gorgeous smiles especially when she wears a light make up, and that is the major reason why she looks amazing in her heels for a woman going on almost 90 years young. I think not only she is beautiful outside with her rich hair that sometimes tricks people into thinking that it's a wig, but she is also beautiful inside. I am referring to her beautiful heart that freely shares her wiry-haired life like it's a story from a TV drama.

When she was in school wearing a bobbed-hair, the world around her was void for her mother passed away with a uterine cancer. But until she was in high school, then wearing a long hair, she says she was at least well-off. She had a rich dad who owned a bank. On the day before June 25th, 1950, when the North illegally invaded the South, she was on a boat on the Han river enjoying youth with her boyfriend. Afterwards, her first love was captured to North along with many of his friends from college, and with an anticipation of his return made her wait until she was an old maid, with no news from him since and having only one black-and-white photo of him.

Her father was kidnapped to North being accused of his bank fleecing the people and he was nowhere to be seen since. In 1953, Chuncheon was reclaimed and she was able to find her families separated since the beginning of the war, and she started a job as a policewoman. Then when she shared her bed with her fiancé whom she met with an intention of marriage, her life changed upside-down forever. It was a day when the snow was falling down senselessly, forcing her to stay at an inn, and she was visiting her fiancé whom she was to marry and was serving military duties near the 38th parallel that divided Korea into North and South.

Her fiancé was secretly living with a lady who owned a coffee shop. At that moment, she left all she had brought that day to his sister's place and without hesitation returned to Seoul at 4 in the morning.

She needed to find a new job, and luckily, she met an old acquaintance whom she had known before and got her a job at PX in Bupyong. To get better with her limited English, she would study at night until 2 in the morning and get up only after a few hours of sleep to head for work. What a lightning in a clear sky! Not long after, she found out she was 5-month pregnant. She had to keep the baby since it was too late to get an abortion, and with a red scar darker than blood, a baby girl was born. To make matters worse, the baby contracted polio and she couldn't walk until she was 3 years old. It was too painful to be living as a single mother in those times with a handicapped child, so she even thought of committing a suicide.

She was recognized for her hard work at PX and was promoted to human resources in the Army, which resulted in a comfortable, well-off life. As she was further promoted to an office job, she was given a junior staff under her, a lower-rank male officer who was younger than her. At the suggestion of people around her that the United States had the state-of-art welfare system for handicapped children and that her daughter could receive proper treatments that she desperately needed, she proposed persistently and married the junior staff.

As they moved to the United States, the couple had two children of their own and her first child was transitioning to her new life and new school in the States due to a superb welfare system for the handicapped. But her husband ended up cheating on her in the Philippines while he was deployed there. His reasoning was apparently that his wife being older and having a higher rank than him was something he found to be uncomfortable and difficult to overcome.

In the end, she ended up divorcing him, raising the three kids by herself living in an apartment. Purchasing a house for the three kids to play in put a strain on her finances. Working as a security guard patrolling at an airport for 15 hours a day was not enough to raise the three kids and pay the mortgages, so she married a divorced man she had her eyes set for 5 years.

Her three children were now happily married, and her life seemed to be going well, but her husband died after having gone through three heart surgeries. Deaconess Park says she feels great joy being back in the arms of Christ and staying active in Church, for which she believed sporadically since she was in kindergarten.

Deaconess Park nowadays lives stylishly as a model Christian, being thankful for the grace that she now belongs to God. Her one wish while she is still breathing in this world would the unification of the two Koreas, and although her abducted father has most likely passed away, she would hope to meet her first love once again. Her teary eyes looking at those black-and-white pictures, longing to see them again, makes it disheartening to watch for everyone. How could one express in words the pains and sorrows of being separated from one's own family due to a war?

I am looking back at my own life who lives as an immigrant here in the States who has also left many things I once loved.

I have a hard time looking at the sky due the shame from all the sins that I've committed knowingly and unknowingly every day. Without God's grace, I would not have been here. Being constantly in pain and a sorrowful state to the point of vomiting blood clots, sometimes I think the Edvard Munch's famous painting "The Scream" could have been about my story. Although the timeline and shapes were different than hers, my life story of constantly living in sins as naturally as I am breathing is being overlapped to that of Deaconess Park. Without noticing, I am caressing my tangled hair with my fingers. As though I was feeling my hair - .

God Arirang

My whole life has been 'God Arirang.'

My god is one and only God I believe in, and Arirang is the folk song that best represents our country, whose meaning is said 'to accompany God.' Thus, God Arirang becomes 'God, please accompany me who lives as a membe of God's nation."' It is likely that God Arirang is a summary of my life and my life's prayer as someone who believes in God as the Korean race.

As the representative folk song of our country, it is said that there is still no exact interpretation of the meaning of Arirang. There are few theories, that Ari means 'Good' and rang 'Dear.' Ari of Arirang originates from 'Al' which means the sky, and Rang means 'Man,' 'Husband' as well as 'Master'. Perhaps it is due to the fact that I am a Christian, but I believe the theory of Rang representing 'God.' When we sing 'God, please be with us,' I believe that our national sprit that is built on the rock of solid faith would revive. That is because I always feel that the spirit of one God is reflected in the beautiful melody of Arirang.

Arirang has a tune that deeply contains the spirit of its people. Arirang's melody beautifully untangles the deep sorrows of the

Korean people as if a silk worm builds its cocoon. Many versions of Arirang, when hummed anytime, anywhere, bring out the warm feelings in our hearts that are different from various parts of our country. When I sing Arirang, I miss someone, and the sadness and loneliness of life that have been wandering around seep into my mind. No matter how loudly I shout to the world, "There are many stars in the clear sky and many hopes in our hearts" Arirang always makes me shed tears for some reason. Perhaps that is why I sing 'God Arirang' to be with God and not feel lonely or sad.

Mother wants to make sure for a bobbed-haired girl wearing a lose black rubber shoe, leaving the ssari door.

"Do you think you can really make it to that chapel so far away all by yourself?"

"Ayeee? Mom, I can do this."

Mother would worry what mysterious force was leading me to go to the chapel, but she would never stop me from going, putting a handful of red cherries or roasted beans in my hand for a snack. I would walk up the river hill at such a young age all by myself, walking up and down the path to the Shin-am chapel that was easily a few miles of travel on foot, walking through the muddy rice paddies and along the new path of gravels, but one thing I was not was feeling lonely at any moment, since God was walking alongside with me. Come to think of it, God must have used me as a tool of faith. My mother, who would sing Arirag along with the people in the village and danced joyfully on special days, having planted love in my heart, had since lived a life of faith until she passed away.

After the Korean War, which started in 1950, and the subsequent truce agreement, the countryside was truly desolate and bleak. Some people would survive on the scattered seeds left in the rice fields that they picked up after the harvest season to make rice soup. In this period, there were people who came to our poor village and showed love by giving us sweet chocolates, and they were the missionaries. The people in my village would call them 'yellow-haired, big-nosed people' and point out their weird requirements. "I like them Jesus followers, but keeping us from performing ancestral rites for our grateful ancestors can't be right ~' often say the village seniors in white Hanbok.

After the 6.25 war, our village founded an open public education center where anyone can attend regardless of his or her age, and taught, among other things, the national anthem and the Korean language. I first learned of the happy news at the school that if you go to the chapel and believe in Jesus then you can be saved and live happily forever. At the time, a chapel was merely any place where people could gather, such as the bamboo-floored living room of a wealthy family's house, a hall in a public building, or even inside a tent. I believe the Shin-am chapel started out in a living room of a house from a wealthy family. I vividly remember kneeling in worship on its wooden floor. When adults started praying, which felt it would never end at the time, I would begin to doze off and sleep. Every now and then, especially on Christmas, I would be as happy as a puppy to receive presents from the big-nosed missionaries. The bell at the chapel was used to signal time in our town since we did not have one in the village. I remember the sound of Christmas bells, which still rings in my ears from time to time.

Where I lived, there was only one middle school for the kids in the village who wanted to continue their studies, and it was a school established by a Buddhist Foundation. Since I could still attend the chapel, God must have been with me the whole time. In high school, I liked that I could go to all-girls missionary school. My vision for faith was fresh, and those were lively young happy days, practicing faith, with hope and love.

The life of a digital nomad that cannot erase the sad but beautiful melody of Arirang gives me hope that wishes to live in the gentle fragrance of my hometown. Since I am yearning for my home country above anything else, today I am joining the scene of life, looking at the flower grass alongside the Monterey beach, after singing my Monterey Arirang and shouting 'God Arirang' announcing my intention to walk with God, while dancing joyfully.

Dreams of people living
in the floating village

Oh my, what on earth!

At this moment, there are people in a remote village whose dreams are to simply live on land. It is the people who have been living on water in floating houses their entire lives. As I had learned of the tragic lives of people who had to live on water on small modified boats only to die and buried in water again, I pray to God everyday as follows. "Dear heavenly father, please have mercy and compassion for those who are living in the floating village and allow them to live on the land of blessing you told us to occupy and multiply and make their dreams come true."

It was at the 'Boeung Tonie Sap' lake in Cambodia where I first saw the people who have been living on the floating houses. The locals simply refer the lake as "Tonie Sap" and the people as the "boat people" and they are the refugees from the aftermath of the Vietnam war. With the sad history of the Vietnam war, which ended in 1975, the boat people have had to live on water in the Tonie Sap lake. From the moment they step on the ground they would officially become illegal aliens only to be deported or to confined in jail, they have had no choice but to live on the floating houses. Due to the sheer number of people who opposed the Khmer Rouge government in a communist regime and fled their mother country by boat and arrived in Cambodia, the Cambodian government denied admitting most of these people on their shores, which had forced them to live on water. I could never forget the sad and pitiful sight of the people who have lost their country, and I now send a handful of soil of love in my heart whenever I land on a peaceful land.

The people living on the floating houses depend on boats for all living activities. Whether it is visiting neighbors or to catch fish, to leave their houses they must use boats of many different kinds. Since I suffer from severe motion sickness, whether riding in a car or a boat, thinking of having to live on a floating house makes me nauseous and even painful. Tonie Sap is a giant lake formed by the fresh waters flowing from the Mekong river travelling 6 countries, including Cambodia, and depending on the seasons, such as rainy or dry seasons, its water levels can vary drastically. When the rainy season arrives in which the rain pours mercilessly once every day for almost half a year, these people must hop on a different boat and move to a safer place. This season makes the lives of the boat people especially hard, but since most of these people catch fish for a living, lots of rain could be argued a blessing for the abundance of fish during the fishing season.

The floating houses are built harmoniously with the surrounding nature, and the lotus flowers which bloom even in the thick of mud have formed a colony around the houses.

The local flower that flurishes in the lake blooms small pink-color flower buds is mysterious and rekindles in a beautiful light. These lotus flowers purify the excrement of the people who live in those houses, which allows them to use the water again to live their daily lives; it must be God's love who inspects our daily lives in full detail. For drinking water, they collect and drink the rain water by boiling it, or the bottled water is delivered from land by volunteers; the beautiful hearts of the volunteers who treasure each and every life are the hearts of angels.

Today as usual, I think about the boat people living in the giant lake in Cambodia, who have been carrying the scars of the Vietnam war, as well as the people living nearby the lake. I also think about the lotus flowers that have been planting the seeds of life in the mud, purifying the feces as well as the dead people in the water. As if carrying a great deal of secrecy, emitting a gentle delicate fragrance, the lotus flowers that show the bright smiles near the people living in the floating houses also brighten my mind. Perhaps it is because they are living among the beautiful lotus flowers along with their peace of mind, I am told that the happiness index of these people on the floating houses is unexpectedly high. Happiness must truly depend on the mind, not the external materials. Sometimes I am reminded of the lotus who is a life saver for these people living in the floating village and become ashamed of myself who does less than a piece of stem plant.

Though I had encountered the people from afar from a cruise ship with the help of local guides, I felt great sympathy of their lives, and I have never stopped my prayers to God. Due to the greed of an individual, the fact that innocent people on these floating houses have had to suffer and endure the aftermath of the war makes my heart ache. The wars that bring forth killings of lives have stemmed from the bloodbath of our ancestors Abel and Cain in the Bible and have continued since to the present days. When will the heaven on earth arrive here where there is no war but only peace ---. Someday, I hope the story of the people who live on these floating houses due to the aftermath of the Vietnam war fades into history, and I also hope that the day when the future generations could tell their children these stories comes soon enough. Could such a miracle happen in this generation?

For most of us, walking on land is such a normal and routine activity. But for the people living on these floating houses, it is their ultimate dream. I can't help but think of these people living in the floating village whom I saw from a corner of the world, when I smell the mysterious smell of the earth and walk on the warm ground. Even though there is nothing practical that I can do for them, I would like to participate in prayers for the people living in the floating village until they can live on the land of blessings, whose wishes have always come back as empty echoes each day. "Dear almighty God, please allow the people on the floating houses with your grace to step on the land of blessings!"

Today I see from this western part of the world that my prayer blooming mysteriously as a beautiful lotus flower in the Tonie Sap lake.

My love, the Han river.

The miracle of the Han river. That is the vocabulary that my lovely river brings out to me.

In my mind, the words "You can do it" touches my heart more than anything else.

The Han river, which communicates me with my home country, originates its source from the Geomnyongso pond in Geum-dae-bong, Gangwon Province, South Korea, and flows through the central part of the Korean Peninsula, passing through Seoul, eventually finding its way to the Pacific and even to my heart who lives in the United States.

The stream of the Han River that runs in Seoul and flows with love to where I live is a lifeline that carries the nutrition to my soul to live in the category as Korean Americans here in the United States. I understand that the reason I can live actively here is because the Han River, that excites me at the mere thought of it, cleanses my soul as if it's pure natural water.

The Han river that enabled the miracles of Korea is the river that runs through the hearts of our people, and it is my love.

Oh, my love, Han River! Thinking about you swells my heart

with joy.

Now we are living in an era awaiting the second miracle of the Han River. Growing up, I had already witnessed the historical miracle of the Han river. 6·25, 4·19, 5·16, the new community movement, the dispatch of our troops to Vietnam, Gwangju democratization movement, the Seoul Olympics in 1988, and the first female president.

Since I was born in the country and spent most of my childhood in rural areas, I could only see the Han river for the first time in person when I was a student at an all-female high school. But the Han river is not just a river that represents Seoul but is the one that signifies the beauty of our country. As a citizen of the republic of Korea, I've heard numerous times the phrase "the miracle of the Han River" as long as I've been alive. As someone who is living with the generations of Korean Americans, the river, which holds the spirit of our country, runs through my heart.

Since I boarded the airplane at the Gimpo International airport and flew over the Han river, I have been living abroad from the 70's, having never been able to express my love for the river and feeling sorry for it. Nowadays people cross the river on the Hangang bridge by car and fly through the Inchon international airport, which is undoubtedly the best international hub in the world. The times and the surroundings may have changed, but anytime I look at the river quietly, I feel uneasiness and sympathy towards the river that defies logic.

The river that excites my heart for even thinking about it. The river so beautiful no matter how many times I've seen it. The river that makes me shed tears in my eyes when I realize I would have to be apart from it again. Now I can only wish the river the best from far way to calm my yearning. The Han river is my eternal love that rejuvenates my soul.

After the Korean war, people refer to "the miracle of the Han river" as the transformation from an era of suffering from extreme famine and needing help from other nations to the era of helping other countries due to the economic recovery in such a short period of time that the world has rarely seen. My love, the Han river, displays an amazing scenery at night, captures people's attention and provides them with hope with its beautiful stream of water, but at the same time it possesses the sweat and blood of the souls who sacrificed their youth to the country and overcame unimaginable challenges. That is why the Han river is alive, breathing, and rejuvenates the spirits of the Korean people. Though I currently live in the United States, I am thankful for each day, never feeling lonely or exhausted, due to the Han river that keeps me in its open arms.

As I started my life here as a Korean American and I was becoming proud of myself thinking I was expanding our nation's territory, the truth is most of the people here weren't even aware the existence of our country. In those instances, I would pull out the globe to show them where our country was and give them a lengthy lecture about our people until my tongue would go numb. This all changed after the Seoul Olympics in 1988 and when the status of our country was elevated. Nowadays, many people would not hesitate to buy electronics made in Korea, and I see a lot of people who can correctly pronounce the Han river, Kimchi, and Bulgogi. There were some people who were surprised when the first female president of South Korea gave a speech in English in front of the congress. As I was listening to the speech about how we as a nation have a vision to unify the two Koreas, I felt like I was witnessing the next miracle of the Han river.

The lives of the Koreans who live overseas become easier when their mother land becomes wealthier economically. As we witnessed through the L.A. riot in 1992, we should not overlook the reality and those dejected feelings we felt at that moment in time because we were powerless. Officially, the riot is portrayed as the culmination of the rising tension between the Koreans and the African Americans, but due to being at the ground zero at the time, I know that the explanation is far from the truth. As powerless immigrants and due to the language barrier, which comes from living in a foreign country, I've seen countless times the dejected faces of the victims who have had no choice but to let go of their resentments and to store deep within them. So I know that the Han river comforts all of us living in the United States, who are surviving and trying their best to embrace all challenges and soothe the pain of day-to-day life.

I wish to live in harmony, comingled with all races, respecting one's personality and loving one another. When the day comes when I am truly transformed and can live in hopes and dreams of tomorrow while still challenging myself with a fiery passion, I shall say the second miracle of the Han river has occurred within me. If a miracle occurs that is out of our control, I'd like to say it's a blessing from God. I may be a weak individual who does not have the ability to contribute directly to our nation's well-being, but the heaven will smile upon me for wishing for a peace on earth and happiness everyday.

Since I am at a stage where I intend to enjoy the fall picnic of life, I wish to live like a pretty maple leaf or ginkgo leaf that people love to pick up from the ground.

Someday, I'd love to tell the lovely Han river in Seoul that I've tried to live beautifully as a Korean American, and that I've come back carrying the scent of a maple leaf. Pouring over the longing that's been buried deep in my heart into the river-.

Oh! My love, the Han river.

| CHAPTER 2 |

The Loom

A grateful retirement

I am beyond thankful. I am actually thinking of retiring from my profession-. Most people retire at the age of around 60, and it will be such a graceful retirement for someone like me who has never been that strong all her life. I am a nurse, which is sometimes called as the White Angel, and I have spent my life spreading my love and devotion to the medical field to treat the most precious thing in the world, life, and now I am thinking of my inevitable retirement. I believe it was entirely God's mercy that I have been able to work in hospitals for over 46 years. Isn't it often said that the retirement is a new beginning of one's life? I want to plant the seeds well for this new life of mine and harvest its fruits successfully. My dream after my retirement is to live happily and beautifully with my neighbors, as a proud Korean literary scholar and as a believer.

It was 1972 when I held the candle with my two hands and put on a white uniform and a cap, the symbol of a nurse, memorizing "May my life be devoted to service and to the high ideals …" from the Nightingale Pledge. In retrospect, I must be thankful to the invisible hand that I was never burned out from a career in the medical field, which I had to take the long road at times and successfully fulfilled the pledge I read in 1972. I am grateful that I could continue my career as a nurse despite numerous accidents in my life. The mental stress I've had to endure to obtain the local nursing license, the temptation of suicide from sending my beloved son to heaven, who seemed to have only lived for me, I am thankful that I survived all these hardships and be saved for eternal life. I am also thankful that I have always kept a dream of living a beautiful life in faith even in the midst of my shedding tears of blood.

My first job was in my twenties, where I spent 5 years of my professional life, at the Chosun university hospital in South Gwangju, South Korea. Since I was already offered the job before graduating college, my career in Gwangju was always refreshing in the romance of my youth. As I had learned in school, I always treated my patients with the spirit of Nightingale. As I had worked in the university hospital that was created for the incoming medical students, I cannot forget the feeling of being deeply moved when the first year medical students came out to practice at the hospital for the first time. I still have the scarf the doctors at the internal medicine gave us as a Christmas gift in my first year. Perhaps I wish to keep the scarf forever because it has memories of my beautiful days that I want to hold onto for the rest of my life. It was during my first job as a nurse when I got married and had my son. I still remember my colleagues who worked with me for over a half a century ago, who always blessed, encouraged, and deeply cared for me with love. I wonder where they are all now, and I wish them nothing but a happy and healthy life.

My new work life, which began in my thirties along with my multi-ethnic life as an immigrant, was beyond busy trying to adapt to the new language and the new environment. Thinking that the way people live here on earth is no different, I would suffer from anemia wandering between desire and reality. As I held a job dealing with life, the most precious thing in this world, I worked hard like I was a global nurse. The Community Hospital of North Hollywood was my first job here in the United States, which helped me realize my dream as a Korean-American.

As I moved around following my husband, a job I found here in Monterey was at Monterey Pines Skilled Nursing Facility for elderly people. It is a place I spent half of my life in my 30s, 40s and 50s, while experiencing the sorrows of life. After taking the exam for the registered nurse for the 16th time, twice a year for 8 straight years, going through all kinds of hardships, no words could express the joy I felt when I finally received the letter of acceptance. There were times when I had to choose between practicing nursing and being compassionate for my patients. Despite backlashes, the fact that I valued life of a human being and taking care for a Korean grandmother like she was my own mother was an opportunity which made me realize that I was indeed a Korean living with the spirits of Korea. It was also a place where I learned that people struggle to live everywhere in this world.

I am now in my sixties and getting ready for my retirement. It's truly God's grace that I am thinking of retiring after 25 years of working both part-time and full-time in this hospital for elderly people, not to mention the help of the executive director, Norma

B, whom I had a good relationship from the moment we met. I would not have been able to work here as long as I did without the help of many of my colleagues, Mary Ann, who is like my sister, and Rowena. This hospital is full of flowers, is clean, and lots of love. There is Jade Garden here, which I won't forget for the rest of my life, famous for and loved by people for a mosaic decorated with a crystal stone formed 500 million years ago. The silence of the stone, formed hundreds of millions of years ago, makes me feel like a precious creature as a juncture in eternity in the true passage of time.

Now, I am grateful that I can begin to think about my retirement. How wonderful would it be if the rest of my life as a first generation of Korean Americans could look suitable to God? Once I retire, I shall try to share my love with others and have an even more beautiful and a happy life as a religious Korean literary scholar. At this moment, I only thank God and give my sincerest honor to him for allowing my health and guiding my life as a nurse who values life more than anything. I don't know when it will be, but when the time comes, I believe it will be such a grateful retirement.

Garden Balsam

Why is that these days I am missing the garden balsams in my hometown so much? It is the flower that I long for the most among all things I have left behind in my hometown. When I close my eyes and think about the hometown from my childhood, the garden balsam pops and even the sound of them popping can be heard when I open my eyes and grab a spoon. These days are all about the garden balsam that pops its ovary even with the slightest touch, expressing its happiness.

I began my immigrant life here in the United States many years ago, and I have lived it patiently, despite the harsh reality of the Korean diaspora and never forgetting my hometown, with a motto "Live your life with your mouth clenched" preached by my mother. I imagine the source of such resilience came from the garden balsams that suffer miserably throughout the day from the scorching summer sun, only to rejuvenate at night with the help of evening dew. The garden balsams that bloomed beautiful flowers and dyed my fingernails red. Perhaps the sprits of the garden balsam from my hometown that captured my childhood curiosity has always resided in me throughout the years.

As usual, today I am looking for the garden balsams from my hometown, that are not native to here, that bloom humble flowers at all the joints along its stems. I search for them everywhere with my ears wide open like a horn. My wish is to grow the garden balsams from my native country here in my back yard and live happily everyday looking at the faces of the red, scarlet, and white flowers.

My hometown was surrounded by low hills and mountains, so it was more like a mountain village rather than a countryside. Due to the abundance of trees and weeds, we would sometimes encounter centipedes or snakes in our yards. But I never heard of the snakes sneaking into our crocks. Like mother always said, the reptiles and the insects would never dare to be near the garden balsams. For that reason, in each household we could see the garden balsams blossoming near the crocks or under the fences. In a sense, the entire town would be dyed with the garden balsam flowers.

Our house, which has provided me with warm feelings throughout my childhood years, would become busy each year with my father's heart and dedication to prepare for the upcoming spring. Before spring arrives, the firewood and sheaves of rice that had been sitting by the mud walls all winter would be removed, and under his command, my older brother would plow the ground to make it more fluffy.

When the remaining now starts to melt away under the mud walls, mother would bring out the garden balsam seeds as well as from other flowers' that had been stored carefully inside her drawer. Then she would hand them to my older sister and tell her to plant them in the flower garden. She would make both of us hold a short half-moon hoe in our hands. In no time, we would plow the moist ground with the hoe and make a small valley. We would separate the garden balsam seeds from the rest and plant them side by side.

From the very next day, morning and night, I would water the seeds hoping to see sprouts dig themselves out of the ground. After about a week, light green colored sprouts would show their heads from ground. Seeing this gave me immense delight would be an understatement. Once they become tidy enough and the stems are full of green leaves, then it's time for the flowers to bloom. Then, just when the summer blossoms have finally begun, a typhoon carrying winds and rain would stop by and exert its force on them showing zero mercy. Such an unexpected disaster would have the garden balsams hold on to their dear lives, swinging left and right and sometimes torn and bleeding. But what incarnation it was when they overcame the obstacles and produced the modest flowers; that was the garden balsam.

The women in our family set one summer day in each year to dye our nails with garden balsams. Our mother would go to the market and buy some white rice, which looks like white pebbles. My sister-in-law would pick out the garden balsam flowers from our garden and dry the leaves on the stone crocks to speed up the process. My sister would pick out the castor bean leaves from the vegetable garden and bring out the spindle of machine cotton. I would pick up rocks that are the size of my fists, and pound on the garden balsam flowers and a few of their leaves in our mud-floored room from early evening.

After finishing dinner on the straw mat laid out in the front yard, lighting up an aromatic smoke, which smells like fresh grasses, to fend off the mosquitoes, we would all gather around it to dye our nails with the garden balsam. My old mother would offer her hands saying, "It better be a pretty color!" like a shy single woman in a worrisome tone. The sister-in law says in a wishful tone "I want this to turn out beautifully so that you all can find the most handsome husband in the future!" Then she would put the well pounded garden balsam flowers on each of our nails and wrap our fingers with castor bean leaves and finally tie them firmly using the machine cotton thread.

The next day we would all enjoy a playful day with dad would showing big smiles on his face and our brothers being brothers, and our nails dyed in bright red. This was a typical romantic and beautiful scenery of my hometown. I still hold those precious memories of being happy and feeling loved from my family dying our nails with the garden balsams.

Now I am at a point where I don't need to live my life with my teeth clenched. Could this be why? I would like to live with the Korean garden balsam from my home country again, which has lived only in my heart for a while. And I wish to give my daughters the same memories I had of dying nails with garden balsams

The fragrance of shepherd's purse

I love the fragrance of the shepherd's purse.

In the fragrance of the shepherd's purse that sweetens my sense of smell are the mixture of love from my mother-in-law, sister-in-law, and my aunt-in-low. That's why I adore the smell even more. "My daughter~! Come smell this. How sweet is this smell~. Isn't the smell of this shepherd's purse amazing?" My mother-in-law and sister-in-law each offers me in their lovely southern accents to savor the smell of the spring shepherd's purse with its root that's just been dug up. Being totally immersed by the fragrance of the shepherd's purse that has been hand-picked by my mother-in-law and my sister-in-law, who is older than me, I become intoxicated with happiness.

In all countries and across all ages, the conflicts between the mother-in-law and her daughter-in-law and the stories about having the in-laws causing convulsion in one's body and mind are prevalent. Some even would say that they hate their sister-in-law even more when quarreling with their mother-in-law. Such stories paint the reality that for newly-wed women living harmoniously with the in-laws is no easy feat. Sometimes I believe being naïve, which is me, is not so bad at a turning point called marriage. The reason I was loved by my in-laws, especially my mother-in-law and my sister-in-law, at our place near Mudeung Mountain was because of my personality and because I was raised in a rural area and yet I barely knew of plants like the 'shepherd's purse.' An opportunity for them to teach me about something that they knew of, such as the shepherd's purse in front of me, must have made them feel pleased. Who would've thought that a pleasant surprise of happiness would find its way to a simple-minded person like me?

The spring of Mudeung Mountain is dashing as well as refreshing as if it is possessing the spirits of justice. The fact that the people who lived watching Mudeung Mountain rushed to Gwangju Students Independence Movement and Gwangju Democratization Movement without a care for their safety could have been due to the mysterious features of the mountain. At the same time, soft singing voices of the traditional singers in Namdo, singing not with the stomach – the digestive system – but with the sound vibrating off of the back of the brain while the small veins deep inside are swelling enough to wrap around the head, are echoing continuously from the National Classical Music Institutes in Chungjanno. How could one possibly bear all the sorrows that are deeply ingrained in our hearts and minds with mere songs from these singers at this historical site? Then... a truly amazing thing happened. Through the endless, generous love of my mother-in-law, I realized the scent of the shepherd's purse from Mudeung Mountain is mysterious and profound enough to even neutralize even the stink of blood. I feel ashamed and sorry when I am with my mother-in-law, yet she has never blamed me once for being such a lousy daughter-in-law and overpowers me with love through the scent of the shepherd's purse's stem. Feeling grateful, I feel the joy of life and be amazed by the scent of the shepherd's purse that enables us with such generosity and love. In the area surrounded by the sprits of Mudeung Mountain, my mother-in-law, the sister-in-low, and the aunt-in-law still live there. Always telling me to visit them any time.

Could it be that the warmth of the spring is all over the place in Mudeung Mountain? I was in awe that I had a hard time breathing because of the forsythia flowers near the entrance of the mountain that were so fresh and beautiful like the skirts of angels who just descended from heaven. What magnificent scenery it was! It looked like the angels from the sky were fascinated by the vital force of the Mudeung Mountain that they all decided to turn into the yellow forsythia flowers and to live in harmony with the mountains. When my sister-in-law drove me around the hillside of the mountain to show the Mudeung Mountain, I became so happy I completely forgot about the mother-in-law who was sitting next to me in the car and shouted with joy. Whatever could have been the reason? I suddenly thought of the shepherd's purse, and I had to tell them I wanted to see one in Mudeung Mountain. As soon as I told them, we all got out of the car and looked for one all over the mountain, but to no avail, only to find one in a farm near the foot of the mountain. I realized that the shepherd's purse is a wild herb found in the fields, not in the mountains.

The shepherd's purse typically grows on a sunny hill, on the bank around a field, or on a ridge between rice paddies along with mugwort, wild chive, and the whitlow grass. It may look like the typical dandelion but lives only two years or so to produce white flowers with amazing aroma. It was always confusing to tell apart since I had never paid attention to its shape, although it was the spring greens with a great smell that I love to eat all the time. The shepherd's purse is one that is highly recommended among all spring greens for being a healthy food due to its high protein and mineral contents, especially to those who are vegetarians. Thinking I should try shepherd's purse soup more, I am craving for a tasty sheperd's purse bean paste soup made with amorous sheperd's purse picked out fresh from Mudeung Mountain and the bean paste she made. Though she's over ninety years old with bad knees from arthritis, I know she personally picks out shepherd's purses near the Mudeung Mountain using nothing but her hands. Knowing this, I am already picturing the tools and the basket to bring the shepherd's purse home with in my head.

"By all means, mother, sister, and you, why didn't you all tell me sooner that you'd want to have a sheperd's purse bean past soup?" says the always freindly aunt from my husband's side. I hope to drive around the Mudeung Mountain next year with my in-laws, who have shown nothing but love with open arms to someone who has not done her part, and sightsee forsythias that are pretty like the clothes the Taoist fairy would wear. We can then pick out fresh sheperd's purse and afterwards make a delicious soup with it. Today I pray that my simple dream would come true and I am happily waiting for the opportunity. Being intoxicated by the fragrance of the sheperd's purse that contains love from the in-laws, my mother-in-law, sister-in-law, and my aunt-in-law.

The Loom

Clink Clank.

Today as usual, I sit in front of my loom and continue to weave a piece of an immigrant life in a forieign country apart from my own. I weave proudly a piece of fabric with my Korean root in the longitude and an immigrant life in the latitude. Singing my favorite loom song 'Korean American.'

Clink Clank.

In my early days as a new immigrant, I wove fabrics using thread made of rough skin from a Samdae tree. Using the yellow, strong, and durable thread from Samdae tree in the basket, I started weaving the beginning of the life as a Korean-American. More ofen than not, I was at a loss not knowing what to do and how to find better methods. Sometimes the strings would break only to be reconnected creating knots, and the fabrics would be stained with my sighs and tears resulting from hard labor.

Due to the language barrier, I went through significant hardship in getting a new certification, and I had to try extra hard during the orientation at my job. Many times, I felt like my heart would burst out, and due to the pain of my soul huddling itself up, the fabrics were never pretty or even.

That's not all! Removing myself from the people who enjoy hamburgers and coffee and coming back from my hometown searching for Kimchi and red pepper taste, the fabrics woven by the longing, love, tears, and loneliness for my hometown were indefinitely loose.

When I had my children, who are my hopes and dreams, and they began to go to school, other problems began to prop up.

When they came home from school, they would often show depression and tears in their eyes. They wanted to play with friends in school, but they would say everyone was avoiding them. When I asked them what was going on, they would say that their parents told them to not play with oriental kids with "Asian Eyes." Oh my poor kids, hurt from their own friends. In the first years of living in the States as immigrants having to make ends meet every day, we had to be financially stable first above anything else.

With what my children told me, I lost control of the loom, and the hemp thread broke when too much force was applied to it. My hands that were connecting the thread again trembled and another knot was created. With the news, I couldn't possibly continue to make fine cloths with the trembling hands and my feet in the way, but I had to march on and continue on with my weaving loom with the sweat, patience, hope, dreaming the dreams of a rainbow.

At this point of my life, I had to weave my own clothes, feeling pitiful and learning patience that is stronger than the thread. As a worn-out immigrant, feeling exhausted from the waiting and singing my loom song.

Clink Clank.

At some point, I started weaving clothes using warm, soft machine cotton from white cotton balls. I was also getting accustomed to the ins and outs of my loom in order to weave better and beautiful clothes.

My kids started to become wise and understand the duplicity of the lives at home and outside. The important truth that we are all equal under God was a big help. I volunteered at my kids' schools at every opportunity I could grab. I would look after the kids playing at the playground. I would volunteer to be a parent-teacher in a drawing class helping kids draw combretum indicum, which is the basis of oriental painting. It would make me feel proud of myself when I saw the paintings of the students I had taught decorating one side of the classroom in a school open house. At this point of my life, the goods woven by me were silky smooth.

Clink Clank.

Now I was more dedicated than ever to weave the finest clothes using a white solid, strong cloth. Dreaming of happy days that will be shared with my children. Then, an unspeakable accident that no one could have anticipated caused a giant hole in the fabric of my life as a scar that could not be undone. Still I returned to my loom without uttering a word and started weaving a new piece of cloths. Sing my loom song for an immigrant pilgrim.

Clink Clank.

Now, the fabric I am weaving is made from a very fine silk

freshly dyed in cobalt. When I am done with the weaving, I will bring it to a boutique and have them make fine clothes for me. A long-sleeved blouse and a skirt that covers up to the knees. And I will attend a party hosted by the kids. With this dream, I still sit in front of my loom that has now been modified with modern technologies.

Nowadays, our kids often forget that we had started as immigrants and have completely assimilated into the American way of life, losing a sense of the Korean root. They often say that we now live in an international age. I am a bit afraid. Would showing up to the kid's party in my traditional silk clothes create an awkward moment?

Even so, I am thankful that I still have the energy and the ability to weave on my loom, and so I continue working on my cobalt colored silk fabric. As my late mother and late grandmother had always done, hoping that my lovely children would live happily on this planet filled with peace and love, while sinning my loom song.

Clink Clank.

Rice-flour Mill

What an affectionate sound. Kung-dduk, Kung-dduk, the sound of rice milled into flower.

The sound of white rice-cake being milled by a pestle in a large mortar can be heard in rhythm. To make a delicious rice-cake, the rough rice must be pounded in the mortar. Since the finer the rice flour is, the tastier the rice-cake becomes, the hard work of straining rice flower through a sieve must be performed. For me to make delicious rice-cake of life of my own, I shall be refined in the religious mortar, and must be strained through the fine sieve of reason with no big holes in it. To ascend into heaven like the fine flour in the wind and to live a life, like that of a delicious injeolmi cake living amongst people, I am pounding on the mortar of my life, hoping I won't turn into dduk-om* that is hard to swallow beyond the tongue. Kung-dduk! Kung-dduk!

The front yard from my youth, now only in my memories, is always a beautiful place. Perhaps that is because it was the place where my mother and sister-in-law would mill the rice in the mortar for me. Usually in the country, a rice-cake is a delicacy. When I was young, it was a particularly a difficult time being right after the Korean war, so even those who harvest rice couldn't afford to make rice-cake on a regular basis unless it's for holidays or for special occasions. Thus, the fact that we could have delicious rice-cake on birthdays, including mine, was one of the blessings I enjoyed in my childhood.

On my birthdays, steam rice cakes with adzuki bean paste on top always made me happy. Sometimes it would be an injeolmi cake, which is a rice cake made with glutinous rice, soaked in water and steamed in a Siru steamer. Once it's poured in the mortar, it would be milled using pestles until the rice becomes sticky enough, after which the sweet bean power is applied on it. Unlike other rice-cakes, injeolmi cake can only be made with two people who keep in steps using traditional methods.

One person would pound on the rice-cake, and the other person would wet the cake and move it around for the other person holding the pestle could do so evenly. After my mother and sister-in-law sweated a bunch to make injeolmi, sometimes my mother would taste the cake and make a frowny face. "There are too many ohms in the cake," she would complain.

Mortars can commonly be seen in the front yards in the country or mountain villages and are useful tools, typically made out of stones or wood. Pounding on grains in the mortar using a pestle, made of a thick, long wood, with a good grip, can peel off the husk of the grains easily or just squash them. To make a delicious rice-cake, one must soak the rice in water and put it in the mortar, mill it, strain the rice flower multiple times through a sieve. Bearing all these difficult steps with pleasure, such a pure image of my mother praying after making the rice-cake for my birthday is still fresh in my memory.

When I remember such beautiful images of my mother's devotion in making rice-cakes, I think to myself that my rough words and behaviors should become finer in the mortar of life. And like delicious injeolmi cakes, I hope never to become someone like dduck-ohm that irritates the tongue, because I would not have been refined enough for this mysterious and profound life.

On a night with a bright full moon in the sky, I look for a milling white rabbit on the moon. Like the folklore in Korea where a white rabbit mills under a laurel tree on the night of a full moon, so I always look for such an image on the moon.

I used to refuse civilization for the destruction of the land of my dreams with the news of Apollo 11 landing on the moon in 1969. The world of childhood innocence imagined on the profound and mysterious lunar world is always pure and beautiful. On the contrary, my body and mind, living far away from such a pure place where my dreams live, have been stained and rugged from the greed of the world.

Wishing to live in the world of innocence, today I pluck the full moon in the sky and put it in the middle of the front yard of my mind. I mill on the mortar of life along with the mysterious white rabbit on the moon that has always captured the innocence of my youth. Inside the mortar, I put in my crude thoughts, acts, words, greed, and arrogance. I pound on them over and over with the help from God and strain a through a sieve of reason. The Creator would only be pleased with offerings of rice-cake made only with the finest flour. Cakes that contain dduck-ohm would be disapproved.

What a beautiful pain to be crushed into fine flour inside the mortar. What beautiful drudgery to be crushed to become sticky inside the mortar. I consider such beautiful pain and drudgery to be God's grace and use them in my prayers. As a common person, I walk the life of a pilgrim in this nomadic age where one's residence and work can be chosen without boundaries. For this reason, I live as a tiny part of this community meeting new people all the time.

Nowadays I wish to be refined with other people in the mortar of life as a part of a big community, rather than to be a special ohm that avoids the pounding and is hard to swallow in the mouth. Despite the crushing pain, I have an aspiration to become the finest flour in the distant future to ascend to heaven riding the wind. Therefore, I mill on the mortar of life, befriending the white rabbit that lives in the land of my dreams. Kung-dduck. Kung-dduck.

*Dduk-ohm = A lump that didn't become fine flour.

Father and a white heron

I am excited to hear on the news that the white herons are returning to a town in Korea. As hearing this good news, I can see my father in my eyes wearing the white beard and Hanbok, looking happy to see the white herons sitting on the green pine tree with their feathers slightly folded, like the ones in an oriental painting.

When a new year begins, we would see our father taking his quick steps early at dawn to the hill to greet the white herons. The white herons that are migratory birds that left our hometown as the weather cooled down were now coming back to return to their natural habitat. The white herons are a sign of good luck and are good friends to my father. When he meets his friends, the white herons, whom he had anxiously been waiting all winter, my father's face would be all smiles like a happy child. 'The white herons are back. They are back. This year will be a good year for us~.' My father would be so happy, his voice would crack with tears shaking the yard in the morning. With the excitement of my father's voice, our family would head out to the village hill, cheering and being excited.

It was one slow day. A little boy from our village runs to my father and tells him with a shaking voice, trembling and barely catching his breath. ' …. A hunter caught the big bird with a g… un. It fell on the rice field and bled a lot before it died.' He was already nervous to hear the gunshot, and he rushed to the hill as if he could see what had happened. '—Those damned hunters, killing innocent animals~ The white heron better be fine.' The next morning, my father announced the good news to our family, with a look of relief on his face. He told us that since one of the white herons was sitting still while the other was wandering around it flapping its wings, he suspects the mother bird was sitting on eggs.

I am a Korean living overseas. But my ears are always open to my home country and my heart wanders there as if it has never left. The sound and the smell of the pine trees are pulling me up to the hill near the river. The beautiful scenic hill of the river that oversees the spirit-filled Mt. Mo-ak and offers a peaceful view of the fields covered in snow. When will I ever hear the news that the white herons would be back to the hills of river I used to climb that are full of hopes and dreams? The village hill where my father was having delightful conversations with the white herons has long been turned into an orchard, so I know they would never come back there. But the hills near the river, whose nature is still well preserved, may become populated again by the white herons when the pine trees grow tall again.

I think of my future self, full of grey hair, sitting on the pine tree near the hills of the river and having a joyful conversation with the white herons. Just like my father did. Though it is mere a dream that may never come true, I become happy to even paint a picture of the beautiful scenery in which I am fascinated by the beauty of the bright white herons.

Earl-leh byt (Korean wide-tooth comb)

There was a space below the wardrobe my mother used to use, and there was always one thing that occupied its space. It was a bamboo plate containing combs, and inside it were earl-leh comb, cham (fine-tooth) comb, and a slick-looking bamboo stick to part one's hair.

Earl-leh comb has teeth that are thick and far apart from one another, and Cham comb has fine teeth on both sides of the balancing center piece made of bamboo.

My mother used to sit in front of a mirror and part her long hair right from the center of her head and from front to back over her shoulders, using a bamboo stick, and as if she was calming her complicated life she would comb her hair first using her earl-leh comb. Then, as if she wished to shine on her mundane life, she would put the camellia oil in her hands and rub it a number of times and apply it evenly to her hair and then finish it with a cham comb. Such process showed calmness and composure as if she was meditating.

After that, she would grab all of the carefully combed hair and twist it in a bundle to put it in the back of her head, holding it with a jade-binyeo, silver-binyeo, and gold-binyeo interchangeably. Her hair was so elegant and beautiful, it was almost a bright work of art by a woman with a slender build who has gone through a rough patch of her life. My mother, who combed her hair without a hitch to do a chignon, would check her hair carefully in the mirror. If my father happened to pass her by, the way she would say "How does your lady look?" and observe his expression looked even enchanting to me.

At some point, the earl-leh comb started to fall apart one tooth at a time and became barren, but mother would keep using it. "These teeth are getting old, decaying and falling out, just like my real teeth." "Mother, then please ask daddy to get a new one when he goes to the market." "Oh my little girl, why would I buy a new one when this one is still usable? We should use it as long as we can, and throwing old things away simply because they didn't cost us much would make us poor." While taking care of her many children, she had to endure the hardship of the Japanese colonial period as well as 6.25 Korean War, so 'saving' was her second nature and one secrete to her life.

After the Korean War, the Sae-maeul (new community) movement run by the government, based on conservation principles, to grow out of extreme poverty was followed by many products being produced using plastic. Of course, the hair combs made out of plastic, for their affordability, durability, as well as the ability to produce in as many colors and as many shapes, were no exceptions. A hair comb, which you can easily find whenever you go to the market or the front of the store, caught my attention one day while crossing a pedestrian overpass. Perhaps

I was drawn into his sales pitch, like a magic, that this would be the only comb I'd ever need in my life and that it couldn't ever be destroyed while he was 'pretending' to break it as hard as he could. I thought of my mother's earl-leh comb that was losing its teeth, and I immediately bought one for her.

And I also bought a small earl-leh comb for myself that I could carry in my purse. As he was saying that those combs would last forever, I thought this would be a perfect comb for her. When I gave her the comb, she looked happy but quickly I realized she wasn't using the new comb I gave her, continuing to use the old earl-leh comb made out of bamboo that lost many of its teeth. However, I did not ask her why she wouldn't use the new one I gave her. It was one day. Her face was full of joy and she looked extremely happy.

"Your father may seem indifferent, but he is actually very kind at heart. He could've just bought an earl-leh comb for me." At the local market day, which opened every 5 days, my father bought my mother a full set of combs. I first saw in my mother's cheerful mood the look of a happy wife who is being loved by her husband. With her middle part bangs showing her white head skin and wearing a beautiful skirt and coat hanbok made of white silk along with white beoseon (Korean socks) and the traditional white-colored rubber shoes, all perfectly in harmony, my clean and tidy mother was, to me, the most elegant woman in the world.

But one day, it was after my father passed away. It was a summer day that people in the village would typically describe it as "the day a male tiger got married" since it would shower for a short while on a bright sunny day. A mother, who had never been to a beauty salon, as if she was swayed by the new trend or as she couldn't stand the emptiness left by her late husband, she had cut her hair short and got a perm. As she had sensed the uncomfortableness in her daughter's eyes and her expression as if she was dumbfounded, she was stroking on her short hair awkwardly, saying "I am getting old and tired of doing the chignon every day. With this short hair, my head is cool on hot days and it is easy to brush my hair now." She quickly avoided any eye contact with me. Afterwards, she no longer used the bamboo earl-leh comb my father had bought for her and started using a new red-colored plastic comb. The so-called new style hair comb that had an earl-leh comb on one side and cham comb on the other.

My mother who had cut her chignon hair that used to stuck to her head, which made it look more black and shiny, and now with a short clumsy curly permed hair, on that day my heart broke as if I was watching her life and her beauty deteriorating due to her age.

Now her breath as well as her earl-leh comb that was used for her chignon hair are long gone, but I still use my small plastic earl-leh comb I had bought along with the one I gave to her as a present and gently comb my hair once in a while as to console my hurt life. Especially on days I miss my late mother.

Even now, my mother's hand-stained earl-leh comb, with its smell of a bamboo tree, saturated with camella oil that made it look shiny and whose teeth had sparsely fallen off, still flashes in my eyes, and her such lovely voice comes back to life. "A habit of throwing things always will always keep you poor." As she was saving even her old toothless hair comb, and as she would welcomed and cared for the hearts of the poor who would stop by our house, I am holding my old earl-leh comb that brings the footsteps of my mother and deeply reflect on how I have been living my life and what image of a beautiful life I have been showing to my daughter.

Ssari door

There is a ssari door that excites my eyes. Woven with the branches of the bush clover tree and attached by the fence, it is a low gate without bars to allow people to freely enter and exit. Only a ring made with a rope connects the door to the fence, for it is a gate only to make a slight distinction from the inside to the outside of a house. While keeping good manners with one's neighbors, it is a door full of affection where people can still see each other's precious faces. Well-suited with the roof of a thatched cottage in villages, it is the beloved ssari door of my hometown house that I always wanted to possess.

When the shimmering spring days come, the ssari door was the door that made my dreams possible like the forsythia flowers that bloomed yellow on the ssari fence. When the bright summer sun hovers the ssari fence, it allowed me to enter and exit the house with full of energy like the bees and butterfly that fly over pumpkin flowers. When autumn neared, it is the door that attracted people for the fallen leaves wallowing underneath it. Covered in large snowflakes during the winter time, the door snugly waiting for me, it held my emotions together when the scattered snow near the ssari door greeted the remaining snow on the peak of the Mt. Moack.

Containing the pure spirit of the nearby hill, the ssari door attached to the ssari fence was low enough so that people walking by could turn their heads and see the people inside the door. Then, the lovely door allowed people from inside to say hi with a friendly greeting. It was a door where a friend of mine, greeted by my dog, could invite herself in with a plate containing rice cake made with mugwort, full of generosity of the countryside. The low ssari door, which gently lets people know the boundaries between you and me, is a peaceful door that still holds a special place in my heart.

We moved to a city when I became older. The tall brick walls that caught my eyes, and broken pieces of glasses on top of the wall of cement blocks or the wooden or steel door along the barbed-wired wall were all terribly scary to me. As if it was telling the difference between the rich and poor families, the tall gated front doors to stop the intruders looked like people were getting cold-hearted, and that made me feel uneasy and cold-hearted too. Though I wanted to meet with the people living inside the houses with tile roofs and the gates tightly closed, I lacked the courage to knock on the doors only to miss the ssari door in my hometown.

Many years had passed, and I liked the fact that most houses in America did not have gates. I did not have to hear the sound of people locking their doors, and the vast open front yards with green lawns made me feel welcomed. I had thought such open space would be good for making people communicate better among the neighbors. But I had quickly found out that was not always the case. Pressed for time and with their hectic schedules, people had barely time to see their neighbors, and even when they did, they had barely anything to say to each other due to cultural differences. Since the yards are open, the neighborhood dogs passing by may use them as a bathroom. That is not all. There may not be physical gates, but their front doors would often be double locked, and most houses would have electronic security systems that protect their houses from intruders. When I found out about this, I thought it would be nice if I had a low-hanging ssari door made from ssari branches for my house. The cozy ssari door that only has a loop without a lock that would allow to talk friendly with neighbors. Similarly, for social life I can't help but think the life of a foreigner is such that having intimate conversations doesn't come easy even though an infinite amount of freedom seems to be granted to us.

It is still fresh in my memory of new ssari doors being made at my neighbors' places in my hometown when those pretty and fresh-smelling ssari flowers were in full bloom and fell. Though I am living in between two cultures, I dream of a day when I have a small ssari door for my house. There are boundaries for all of us, but I would hope for a ssari door in my immigrant life that would allow people to freely come in and go by. Instead of a heavy gate with the most secure lock on the door, how nice would it be if we all had ssari doors made with the branches of the ssari tree with just a small doorknob?

In my mind, I can see the warm sight of my neighbors looking for me over the ssari door. I can even hear the footsteps of people getting closer. I can hear the people talking delightfully.

When the wind blows, the sound of nature of the dry ssari branches bumping against each other will be heard. The ssari door, which does not have a bolt, teaches me a way to live happily with my beautiful neighbors making authentic and emotional connections. Installing the friendly ssari door in my mind from my youth, I feel such warmth and peacefulness.

Thinking about the ssari door brings a warm breath over my forehead and friendly laughter to my ears. The door that allows close connections while still allowing personal space between you and me. I become happy just thinking about the ssari door which brings me the joy of life.

The Wash Place

This is the place. The wash place. The source of our country being referred as a white-clad Korean people.

One of the beautiful sceneries of our country that has been disappearing is the wash place, which has been a home away from home for many of our women for centuries. It was a place near a community well, stream, or a pool, where women from the village would gather around and wash clothes or things to clean them. It was a beautiful scenery, which led us to be called a pure white-clad people. A pure and clean mind is a spiritual legacy from our ancestors who enjoyed wearing white Han-bok (Korean traditional clothes). No matter where you go in this world, there is no people like us who have created clean and elegant beauty. Wouldn't it be because our women washed dirty clothes at the wash places and boiled them in lye to finally dry them under bright sun light?

These days I miss the wash places where the women in the village would gather and gossip about their everyday lives. I would like to revisit the wash places, which was like a reception room for women. This becomes especially so when I want to cleanse my mind and soul. Where many village women would gather, sit down, and wash their clothes. I want to see the sight of white plain bedclothes, washed at the wash places along the Jeonju creek and boiled in lye in a big cauldron, and being dried in the sun when there is a cool breeze. I spent most of my school years in Jeonju, so I had many occaisions to be near the Jeonju creek. The fresh and pleasant feeling of the breeze inside my purple school uniform skirt while walking by myself along the banks of the Jeonju creek, watching the clean stream and the nearby wash places is one happiness that I would like to hold onto for the rest of my life.

I always think of the painting 'Wash place' by the painter Park, Soo-Geun, the painting of a scene of a group of women sitting together nearby a stream and doing the laundry. As it set the Korean records for the most expensive painting ever publicly auctioned, I am firmly in camp that this is the painting that best represents the characters of our people. Our proud painter, who painted Korean materials using the most Korean granite texture, perhaps he wanted to show the purity and the elegant minds of the Korean people through his painting 'Wash place.' If you look at the similar paintings by Dan-won. Kim, Hong Do or Hae-won. Shin, Yun-bok, their colorfulness and liveliness rather than depicting the joys and sorrows of the ordinary people, must tell that the wash place was a place where the women talked about many interesting things. The men must have tried their hardest to have a peek at the place since the women at the wash place would often wash their long hair or take a bath under the moon light. The wash place where the endless stores of their suffocating in-laws and the gossips in the reception rooms take place. This was the place for village women where both the body and mind tired from life were purified and the source of our people being called the white-clad people.

Our country, not only called the white-clad people, is a country is of courteous people, so there are etiquettes that are observed at the wash places. When the women choose stones to sit down on to do their laundry along the streams, they also care for other people at the site. The women who have clothes that are relatively clean to wash would sit towards the upper part of the stream while those with dirty clothes, such as ones with baby poop or clothes that may lose its color when being washed, would sit towards the bottom of the downstream. This is not all. When they hit on the laundry with a wooden laundry bat, they would be doing in a distance from the rest of the group so as not to cause accidental injury. When they were doing the laundry near wells, they would apply the soap on the clothes and scrub them on the washboard. The women would check the washed clothes with delight and the minds of these women whose clothes have been washed clean would now be cleaner than the clothes. These clean minds would take care of the households that form the backbone of our country and perhaps that is why we are called the people of white-clad.

Nowadays people would either use dry cleaner's or use washing machines in their households. While their clothes are being washed, the women can have quite time, but they could become lonely, missing out the fragrance of life that could be only felt at the wash places. While the laundry is being done, I would read books or listen to music to cleanse my soul, but because it lacks

The Loom

the rhythm that life presents to us, I miss the wash places. Though I am being told I am old-fashioned, I still prefer to use blankets made of white cotton balls. Every now and then, the sound of washing the cover of the cotton blankets, putting in the laundry detergent in the washing machine, the machine whirling, applying instant starch on the cover to iron it, the sound of the clothes brushing against the inserts of the blanket, all those sounds come alive as the sounds of drying clothes in the cool breeze at a wash place. The sound becomes friendly, full of the fragrance of life, and my heart becomes clean and pure again like a white cotton flower.

While the women at the wash places patiently wash the stains on their clothes with the tender loving hearts for their families, they also wash away the stains and makrs on their minds. When the minds come together at the wash places to clean dirty clothes over and over again, wouldn't that also make our lives pure and clean? As part of the white-clad people, I hope the body, mind, and our lives to be elegant. When I think of the wash place of the Jeonju creek that washes clothes that are stained in the harsh realities of life, my white blanket covers flutter in the wind, the sound of the wash bat, the chatters of the women all delight my ears. And my mind blooms like a white cotton flower.

I miss the wash place.

The lamp in a farming village

There is a lamp in a farming village that shines in the dark that makes someone's wish come true. During the day, it holds a beautiful image of waiting for someone in silence under the eaves of a thatched-roof house. It is a lighting fixture of a rectangular shape, covered with glass on all four sides, and a wooden support underneath it to support a horong light. Since those lamps were used mainly in farming villages over a half a century ago, it would now be hard to find one even in antique shops. Thinking about a beautiful life that is suitable for my age, which has always been my dream, I think to myself that I would like to have a life like that of the lamp in my childhood village, which is engraved in my heart as a beautiful mark of my childhood. I am talking about the beautiful lamp that gives a person wandering in the dark a beautiful, bright light to achieve his or her dream, and waits patiently, in silence, for someone to help him or her when it's not needed.

As the bright sunlight starts to set over the mountains in the west, darkness slowly approaches in the front yards of the countryside. At this moment, the lamp hanging under the eaves of the thatched-roof house, which has been taking a break during the day, now lights up for those in need of a bright light. For many of the farmers who are not able to finish their work by the evening, the lamps illuminate their large front yards. When the harvest season is in full swing and the sheaves of rice are being piled up in the yards needing to be threshed, the lamps in the farming villages are at the forefront of making the beautiful dreams of the farmers come true. When the rice crops are ripe in golden yellow and are harvested from the field, the farmers' dreams bloom along with the rice grains that are scooped up off the threshing floor by the farmers' hands. The farmers would laugh loudly with bright smiles on their faces during the day, but when darkness sets in they would become impatient and busy. At this moment, the lamps, which send out bright lights to the farmers, comforting them to achieving their dreams and guiding them in overcoming the darkness, are nothing short of being noble.

When there was no electricity, the rural lamps, which are now only in my memories, were such a valuable lighting tool. The rectangular lamp hanging under the eaves of my house was frequently used with a horong light inside it. This lamp was lit with a horong light whenever necessary and it was moved frequently from place to place. It would stay under the eaves most of the time, but other times it would be moved to the kitchen, or the bathroom, or sometimes over my desk. The lamp was the most useful when someone in the family did not return to home at night. To greet someone you love, you would hold the lamp in your hand and go to the village entrance. Especially on the day my father went to the Wonpyeong market, which holds every five days, my family would bring the two lamps under the leaves and fill horong with oil and turn on the light. And the family would split up in two groups to greet my father. Because there were two roads to the village and I wouldn't know which road he would be taking to come home. One road is following the new graveled, unpaved road into the valley of the market, and it would take a bit longer to come home this way. The other road is the path home by going along the winding path through the narrow trail near the ridge, and though it makes you out of breath going up the hills, but it is shortcut. My family would pick up the rectangular lamps and walk away from dangerous spots, over which we could potentially trip and fall, to greet our father who was coming late from the Wonpyeong market.

When the darkness creeps over our village, the lamp in my hand, which wishes to give off the scent of love, flashes on the hill of Gahangdaemi where Mt. Mo-ak can be seen. It is the top of a hill where low and vague-looking mountains would form a hilly area, and those hills would form another ridge that gives life like the rolling waves, on top of which Mt. Mo-ak, soaring high in the sky, can be seen during the day. It is such a beautiful place forming a natural environment, where the purple-red milkvetch flowers bloom in groups to make one's heart flutter in the field near the entrance of the village. On the hill facing Mt. Mo-ak that I used to climb up and down to grow strong without losing my smile, my mind was warm waiting for my father while holding the lamp in the dusk, as opposed to my trembling body due to the cold temperature. When my father saw the flickering light in the dark in the distance over the wide-open field, he would give us a big shout out of joy as he saw his family was waiting for him. That I could wait for my loving father and be in his warm arms as a happy kid was because there was that precious lamp that lit in the dark so I could avoide obstacles. The lamp in the farming village helped realize the dream of a safe reunion of loved ones.

I still remember the sight of my family waiting for my lovely father in the hill outside the eastern village, and I dream of a beautiful world in which people live together, who are like the lamps in the farming village that made me happy and that watched over one another. At this moment, I feel as if I am standing here with a lamp in my hand that shines in the dark, waiting for the sound of the footsteps of my loved ones. When it is dark around you and you are not sure which direction you should take, the lamp gives you comfort and hope by shining light on the road. The lamp also holds a beautiful figure of waiting to make someone's dream come true. The lamp gives me comfort when I am holding it for someone else or when I begin to think about someone potentially holding it for me.

I think to myself that a beautiful life that is suitable for my age would be letting someone realize his or her dream by shining light on them in darkness, and, when there is plenty of bright light, waiting under the eaves patiently in silence without revealing myself to those in need. It would be the life of the lamp in the farming village, which has become a mark of my old beautiful life in my heart, engraved in a pattern of love. How nice would it be if the rest of my remaining life can become like that of the lamp in the beautiful farming village?

| CHAPTER 3 |

The Snowflakes

It's okay!

The trembling voice of my friend, Moomyeongcho (the nameless pant) is touching my heart.

"Sorry, sorry, I am so sorry for having neglected you for so long. We've been together for over 30 years, yet I still do not know anything about you. Calling you a nameless plant."

Moomyeongcho tells me with a conviction that it still likes me and that it is satisfied no matter how indifferent I am or how I just gave it a random name, as long as I look at it every day. To come to think of it, I am a deplorable person, and yet I feel sorry and am deeply thankful to the plant for overlooking many of my faults and carelessness. The nameless plant is always with me and a friend who enjoys silent conversations with me. It lives in our garage, right next to the dracaena fragrans. I know of its name since someone told me so, but the person didn't know what my nameless plant was, so it still remains nameless.

I am positive this Moomyeongcho knows the history of my life as a Korean immigrant almost in its entirety. If I wanted to know its name, I guess I could have gone to a flower shop and ask around for its name. But I haven't felt the need to do so for over

30 years, so I have been inadvertently calling it Moomyeongcho, the nameless plant. It was never a flower tree that bloomed pretty flowers to entertain my eyes and flutter my heart, and it has never been a tree who grows delicious fruits that stimulate my appetite. It has always been an evergreen tree for all of its life, so perhaps I have been indifferent towards it for never having had to associate my hopes and dreams with it.

The nameless plant, which can easily be spotted in offices and buildings, resembles a bamboo tree, and without ever producing flowers, the beauty of the plant are the diverging white symmetrical lines, harmoniously stemming from the center of its green leaves. The nameless plant that is with me currently is in fact the second generation of the original plant. The first one is no longer with me. It was a house warming gift during my early days living as an immigrant. The plant, which came in pairs as if they were a married couple, were placed in the 2nd floor of our house in a well-lit place, and soon after we had to replace the base with a bigger one. Not long after, they had children of their own and grew as tall as the ceiling of our house. Every time I watered the plant, I would often be reminded that parents and their children are alike. Over the years, the two 2nd generation plants continued to flush, while their parents, in faded green, would tower over the room giving me insecure feelings as if it would break through the ceiling. At last, I had to cut down the parent plants to give room for the children to grow more freely. I would justify that decision that the parents must always sacrifice for their children. And when we moved to our next house, the plant moved with us to the new place, and I would put pretty clam shells inside the pot that someone gave me.

For some reason, the current second-generation plants did not produce any children. I would walk by them many times every day, and yet all I do now is I would just water them once a week along with some fertilizer. There is a reason why I would not try other methods to take care of the plant. I am not good at growing plants. Despite my good intentions, I have killed dozens of plants over the years from either over-watering them or giving too much fertilizers. And I would be devastated for my incompetence in providing livable conditions for the plants and would feel dejected as if my devotion and dreams had faded away. So, I have been trying not to give too much attention to this nameless plant, in the name of keeping it around longer and prolonging our daily silent conversations. But just today, after many months and years of negligence, I found a huge fault of mine. Decorating the plant with the clam shells that looked pretty to my eyes was blocking the airflow to the soil inside the pot and preventing them to have children. What to do with such carelessness and fault of mine that knows no boundaries!

But my friend, Moomyeongcho, who's been observing quitely the joys, angers, sorrows, and happiness of my immigrant life here in the States, understands my shyness in expressing inner feelings. So it just loves me from a distance not caring about what I call it or the never changing living conditions they've been in. As I was telling my plant friend in an abrupt, awkward way of all my indifferences and past faults, it comforts me by saying "It's okay." What consoling words. The nameless plant knows my peculiar way of expressing love, and perhaps its generosity was the reason why we have been together for over 30 years. I am so grateful that the nameless plant is just alive and keeping me company.

I carefully looked at the apple tree I planted five years ago, which I have been watering frequently with good fertilizers in hopes of seeing beautiful fruits someday. My goodness! Although it was right in season for apples, not a single apple could be find on the tree. There were three or four good ones last year, so I had expected to see more this year hoping I would share some of them with people I love. Without realizing, I uttered to myself "It doesn't care about me~," feeling deflated and my thoughtful love and dreams crushed. Soon after, however, I looked at the tree once more and realized that it was looking sad. At that moment, I thought of my Moomyeongcho, who is happy just to be around me, saying "It's okay" without faulting any of my indifferences and giant shortfalls. I felt ashamed about myself for obsessing over the fruits in the name of love. I was also ashamed about my narrow-mindedness that seeks forgiveness from others' generosities of my indifferences and faults, while doing the opposite myself to others.

Without hesitation, I tell the apple tree with my most lovable face,

"It's okay!"

These were the exact same words my nameless plant told me that touched my heart.

Christmas

It is December 25, the 2014th Christmas celebrating the birth of Christmas, commemorated by Christianity.

The modern calendar that we use currently was created based on the birth of Jesus. Instead of AD (After Death), in Christianity some people call it 'AC (After Christ)'. Thus, this Christmas would be AC 2014, December 25.

We are people who have committed sins, destined for eternal damnation, but Jesus atoned us from our sins with his blood borne on the cross.

God who created the heaven and Earth and sent his only son to Earth allowed us a new life, and led us to a path to heaven. Since humans cannot get to heaven, Jesus Christ came to Earth in the form of a human, which Christianity calls incarnation. That day is the Christmas, on which the world commonly celebrates.

Beyond the religious meaning of the day, Christmas is a world-wide holiday. If a store closed one day of a given year, it would be Christmas. That is because Christmas is a special day on which all humans celebrate.

Jesus was conceived by a holy spirit, and was born in a small stable in Bethlehem under his earthly parents, Joseph and Maria. His last days were love that was whole, on which he was falsely accused of and crucified on a cross for us, whose sacrifice cleansed the sins of the entire human race.

How about me nowadays welcoming Jesus? I feel nothing but shame.

Although I am fully aware that, instead of feeling happy from worldly honors or material goods, the true freedom and truthful happiness come from obeying the words of the Bible, which is the truth, and living in the arms of God, but I am ashamed to say that I haven't been fulfilling my role as a light and salt of the Earth.

The traditional colors of Christmas are red and green. Green represents the eternal life through Jesus, and red symbolizes the color of the blood of Jesus borne on the cross.

Poinsettia flowers with red and green leaves can be seen everywhere, but thinking that Jesus would not visit there due to my lack of praying for the unfortunate souls, I feel distressed of my guilt.

Greeting a merry Christmas on which Jesus was born on this Earth, I put together my life once more.

The Snowflakes

The white snowflakes, I feel the joy of life. The white snow that gently falls from the sky looks pretty, but the snowflakes that are pouring down from the sky forming colonies of snow all over the trees are immensely beautiful and holy, a prayer to the benevolent God is warranted. Since I am a fragile human being who would not be able to create such beautiful snowflakes even if I had tried my entire life, I think it is such a blessing being able to even observe the completed work of beauty created by God. Like the snowflakes that have been giving me joy in my life, can I ever become a white snowflake for someone else in my lifetime? Just like the humble and luscious snowflakes in my yard that were the culmination of my father's true love, which gave me joy to life when I was becoming a lady from a little girl.

The United States of America, which is the country I live in nowadays, is so vast and large, it enjoys four seasons simultaneously. A literary friend of mine who lives in Boston has recently texted me a number of beautiful pictures of snowy landscapes, while here in California, which is where I live, flowers are blooming even in these winter weathers. Wow, that looks amazing. Among the pictures of snowy scenes she has sent me that moved me enough to revive cells in my heart into jumping up and down, there was one particular picture that took my breath away, which was the one with snowflakes on an evergreen tree, staying humble and holy. Feeling mesmerized, I remembered the snowflakes that I saw in the season of love that gave me joy and hope of life. That year when the first snow fell down heavily, the white snowflakes in our front yard, that were holy and luscious, bloomed by my father's humble yet true love.

I remember the excitement at the unforgettable thatched house as well as the white tears I shed at the corner of my church. It is the menstrual cycles all women go through monthly, which is a bit embarrassing to say even at my old age. I had my first period with a thrill of excitement that struck the core of all my nerves as well as feeling shameful simultaneously. It was when my lower abdomen hurt and I couldn't fall asleep, the surprise in red color from my first period and the continual pounding of my heartbeats made me the grab on the door knob that was so cold, I felt like my hand was going to be stuck to it. When I got out of the room, the light snow, which started to fall little by little during the day, had turned into large flakes on our peaceful large front yard. As I was amazed by the large flakes falling from the sky and humbly growing on the winter trees to make snowflakes, feeling the joy of life, I heard the voice of my father. "Wow~ it's the first snow. I've never seen the first snow falling this much." My father said in an excited tone with his door only slightly open as I was going to the bathroom, since he must have sensed it and wanted to give me a sense of relief.

In rural houses where there were no lights or electricity, we had a seprate toilet house called 'Chit-Gahn' located away from the main house. The squat toilet with no way to flush, located on one corner of the front yard, was so scary enough to raise one's hair, a young girl like me would not dare to go there by herself at night time. So we would use a chamber pot, which was quite pretty, that looked like a small moon jar, so peeing was not an issue at night, but for the purpose of number 2, then our father would have to guard the toilet house outside. During my puberty, the day after my very first period, I felt the bloody tissues passing out of my body while I sat on the chamber pot. I felt embarrassed experiencing it for the first time, and I planned on emptying the pot early in the morning without anyone knowing, while trying to calm myself down, but my face was burning with shame and I had butterflies in my stomach while waiting for dawn.

As the paper covering of the door was getting brighter, signaling the arrival of morning, I quietly opened the ice-cold iron door and left the room quietly. Then I heard my father's cough. Before emptying the chamber pot, I headed to the toilet, listening to the sound of my feet walking on the snow. As it has the traditional squat toilet, I squatted down and with my knees bent, and I looked out the wooden door to see the snow while letting myself go. Gosh, my father! The first thing that I saw was my father. My father, wearing white Hanbok, was headed straight toward the toilet, with his hands holding the chamber pot and his head slightly lowered, across the yard covered fully in white snow. At that moment, I instinctively felt it. My father was heading to the area right next to the bathroom with grey ashes in order to empty the chamber pot there, which had urine with my blood in it. And in that moment, I saw white snowflakes that bloomed humbly with a warm and deep love of my father. Looking at my father holding the chamber pot, I felt ashamed for he was of different gender, but for some reason I felt happy and the joy of life, while looking at my father who looked like a humble snowflake, knowing I was truly loved. And the true love that did not reveal such incident to anyone has turned into a jewel shining beautifully in my heart.

How great would it be if I could bloom a beautiful flower of modesty before I die, like the snowflakes my father plant in my heart at that moment? I remember when I cried my hearts out in the corner of my church, missing my beloved father and for failing to tell him that I loved him while he was alive, who had passed away only one year after I had immigrated to the U.S. The humble white snowflake who had shown me in person what true love was in this world, and when I meet him in the afterlife I will tell him. "That day when it snowed a lot, I have seen the love deep in your heart, which did not reveal my shyness to anyone of having my very first period. On that cold, cringy winter day, in my shrunken heart from being shy, you became a white snowflake in the humblest form possible and that the true love has mysteriously given me the joy of life."

Happy Retirement

"Happy retirement! Congratulations on your retirement." "Yes, Thank you." An old gentleman cannot seem to stop smiling these days. "Should we celebrate his retirement? Well…" A young deaconess whispers in my years. Another deaconess hears the question and answers for me. "Of course." Some have faces that disagree with her. For me, I cannot say definitely whether it is something to celebrate and look at the face of the old gentleman. There are many opinions regarding retirement, but the old gentleman sure does look happy for not having to go to work every day and having all the free time in the world. He must be completely forgetting that he's retiring at this retirement age for being old and for his diminishing judgement skills. At any rate, a retirement embarks a second chapter in one's life. The old gentleman retired after having worked for his university for 35 years and 4 months. That's not all! Since he also worked as an educator for over 5 years from his home country, it is remarkable that he had worked in education for over 40 years for young people. The following is a poem written by him as he was retiring.

「**Retirement**」 *Lee, Byungho*

Been teaching at a university for 35 years and it is time for me to hang up my hat/ The stress and the tension accumulated all those years all seem to be melting always like snow/ Time flies too fast, like an arrow leaving a bow/ And I am sending away the agonies and difficulties of the past into the gentle breeze from the mountain/ I design the second chapter of my life/ Through the years of joy, anger, sorrow, and pleasure/ And in the midst of joy from teaching/ my hair must have turned grey/ I have walked along this path carrying health and hope on my two shoulders/ Moving forwards while never looking back/ Knowing patience is bitter but its fruit sweeter

He reminiscences the day, September 28th, 1978. It was a time when people were excited to emigrate to the United States. That day, the old gentleman left many that he had ever loved in Korea and got on a plane to the United States at the Kimpo International airport. Above all, his heart must have been heavy at the airport having to leave his barely one-year-old son to his parents. Fortunately, he had the conviction that God would be with him and his family, and he had the desire to fulfill his grand dreams in the vast land of opportunity. Rather than focusing on the suffering of living in an unknown world, he was optimistic, and his frontier spirit was never stronger. He took and passed a test in an office for education and started working as a supplementary English teacher near his place for over two years. A good opportunity knocked and he started working at the

Defense Language Institute. After working there for over 31 years as a professor, he is now retired.

Having retired as an old gentleman, the talk of the typical life of a retiree is mentioned frequently when they get together. Without a structured work schedule, he seems free. Without caring for his looks, he looks a bit hideous. As his hair becoming greyer, he has to choose between either going completely silver or dying his hair. Old retirees tend to have lots of dried dead skin, like dying trees with rugged bark. That's not even all. Instead of Mr. or Mrs., they would often be referred to as Grandma or Grandpa. With deteriorating health, they rely on devices, such as glasses, dentures, and hearing aids. Above all, they tend to suffer from loneliness. A male retiree, who is often called 'Sam-sik' for eating in all three of his meals every day, despises the back of his wife who cooks a beef bone soup. She would make the beef bone soup once and leave it in the refrigerator. And the wife would go out by herself for reunions or travelling abroad, without a care for him.

For this reason, the husband would feel lonely, spending most of his time alone. These days I think to myself. Not to feel lonely, a retiree must surrender thinking of only oneself and help others. To live happily as a member of a loving family, prayers should also be priority number one. Without nitpicking every aspect of others' words or action, he or she must act and talk that permeates a delicate scent of a human. One must pursue his hobbies to keep himself busy. The old gentleman seems to have a busy life, as if he hadn't retired yet. He says he does not have enough time to do all things he wishes to do, which are reading the bible, playing golf, practicing calligraphy, and reading books to become a better poet. Sometimes he grumbles that time goes by too fast. Perhaps he is fulfilling his self-worth and creating a happy life by actively pursuing things that make him happy. The old gentleman wearing an apron that says 'rice-distributing elder' and volunteering at the Church cafeteria is none other than my husband and poet Lee, Byungho. Each rice grain on the plate, turning into a white peony, seems to be saying "Happy retirement" in excitement.

Good writing

Where can I find good writing?

In order to find good writing, I become the tagger and search for it that seems to be a master at hiding. I am playing the hide-and-seek with good writing, the game I used to enjoy playing in my youth with my friends. "You have lots of ideas, and you will be a good writer," my mother, an old country woman, would tell me. This has become a trap and made me write essays ever since then. A literary friend of mine would boast she had become a writer after having taken literature lessons from renowned professors, but all my literature inspirations have come from my mother, who had spent all her life with soil. My mother, who taught me that soil is the womb for all life and the basis of love, always loved to watch me read. Many of the books I enjoyed reading, such as the Evergreen Tree by Shim, Hoon, Soil by Lee, Kwang-Soo, The Good Earth by Pear Buck, The Land by Park, Kyung-Rhee, were all based on soil, which must tell me that I was indeed born and raised in the country and a daughter of a farmer. The fact that I still can't write good essays means perhaps my character is still lacking, as my mother would say that good writing comes from good characters, which she has shown us all her life with her actions. Perhaps I should strive to live a beautiful life to write an essay that is like a flower that holds the scent of love in my ever-changing life…

Defining a good writing cannot be summed up in one sentence and many would profess their own opinions. Still, I lean towards the idea that a good writing is one that holds the spirit of the author as well as one that communicates well with its reader. No matter the fancy style or full of exquisite knowledge, if the reader couldn't understand the written piece it wouldn't be called a good writing. A flower truly becomes one when someone calls it, and a writing becomes a good one when someone reads the piece and be moved by it. When writers all over the world agonize to write a good piece, it must be to understand the meaning of life. What is the true meaning of life? I feel like I am beginning to find the answer little by little as I write more essays. A good writing would be materialized when one opens the eyes of the mind and observes the beautiful world with love.

No one could argue that a good writing is one that touches the reader and lets her feel the realization of life - such as a writing that moves, that has a sweet scent, that makes the reader feel deeply about the love of life, or that lets the reader feel graceful. I know in theory how to write, and on each of my essays I write I pour my heart and soul, but with little success so far. "Mother! How can I write good essays?" I have been asking her many times, but my mother only smiles. I do not know why I've been clinging to writing good essays that hold honest stores of my life, which is a bit anguishing. If I want to write good essays, my life first shall have a sweet scent, should be transparent, and should be beautiful.

Looking at myself in the mirror, I look back on my life for not having been able to write good pieces yet. I feel agony for my inability to write good essays for I have not had a pure and colorful life. All of this must be coming from my greed, so I try to rid of all things that are not necessary. When looking at myself in a clear mirror, I wish to write a piece with a soul as pure as the mirror. When looking at beautiful flowers, I wish to write an essay that is as beautiful and as fragrant as the flower. When looking at the blue ocean that embraces all kinds of filth without uttering a word, I wish to write a piece that lets people embrace the world. When looking up the blue sky, I want to write a piece that quenches one's mind. Will I ever be able to write a gentle piece like the white cotton flower? How nice would it be if I could write a piece that holds the soft sound from a distant bell or the mellow sound of a beautiful scenery? I am in agony wishing to write a good essay that is as tasty as the red pepper paste that has been well fermented. As I was born a daughter of a farmer, I would like to write about soil's generous love that absorbs warm light and gives birth to a new life. I would like to share with my readers the endless love of soil and the grace of light I have been receiving, despite not quite deserving them, through this genre of essay, and I would like to be used as a channel of unclogged communication. To achieve this, I shall practice writing essays with a passion and patience.

My writing shall improve if I can communicate with my readers by expressing naturally and honestly the flow of my life. As a genre of literature, the essay is a record of our lives and it would be useful if it can help us find the beauty and value of life as well as one's worth, and furthermore if it can express the emotions of life full of dreams in lively sentences. How great would it be if I could find many of the hidden beauties of life and be used as a channel to tell those stories to my readers through my essays? For this reason, many writers all over the world must be struggling, with their pens in their hand, to find ways to write good pieces. Sometimes they may ask themselves for what purpose they are being too hard on themselves. But the mind that keeps pushing them to continue to write, I believe that those minds are planting the seeds of love in corners of the world. These minds are working together to make this world more beautiful.

I feel ashamed that my life is not as beautiful as it should be to become a good writer as my mother believed I was. If I can, I shall try to live with only love in my heart and communicate with my readers capturing the feelings of many precious lives. I pray with a hope and with my hands holding together that God will allow the sweet rain of gratitude on my heart, which wants nothing more than becoming a good writer, a dream of my life.

The hidden truth in
'We have a big problem!'

We have a big problem~, says Choi, Soon-sill. The truth will eventually come out~, says the former president, Park, Guen-hae. These are the words by the two people, dubbed as Park, Geun-hae Choi, Sun-sill-gate, who have brought the storms to our country in recent years like a B-rated drama, for the state of affairs was controlled by an outsider. What is hidden in the phrase "We have a big problem!" uttered by these two people still puzzles me as to what it means. The meddling of national affairs by Choi, Soon-sill also began a chain of unprecedented events for the history of our nation, such as the national candlelight demonstrations, the official impeachment of then current president, Park, Geun-hae, and our current president Moon, Jae-in, who were elected shortly after, proclaiming 'People and hope should come first.'

What some politician said 'How dare to run our nation with some sloppy old woman, she deserved to be impeached.' and what the food researcher said at the Blue House, Ms. Kim, Mak-Up, who was close the president before she was impeached "She is less fortunate than someone like me who had no formal education." are wandering around my ears. The essence of this scandal is that the relationship between the two could have been that of a princess and her servant, or an even more mysterious one is that they shared secretes between them while the outsider, Ms. Choi, Soon-Sill, took massive personal profits by meddling with the state and national affairs with the president. In the middle of all this is Cheong, Yura, the daughter of Choi, Sun-Sill. Officially, she is the test-tube baby of her biological father, Cheong, Yoon-hoi, and her mother, Choi, Soon-Sill. But there is an unconfirmed rumor of Cheong, Yura being the daughter of Park, Guen-hae and Choi, Tae-min, the leader of the cult 'Forever life.' Cheong, Yura is at the center of the meddling of the state affairs with events such as winning a gold medal at an Asian Game in horse-back riding with the financial support coming from Samsung, illegal admission to Ewha Womans University, and her infamous quote "Money is talent," which she posted on SNS that angered many working people in Korea.

In Fall of 2016, the face of JTBC, Mr. Son, Suk-Hee, first broke the news of the illegal meddling in the state affairs. Afterwards, many who were associated with it, including the dean of Ewha university, were arrested, and I couldn't help but be surprised at the scope of the people who were involved in this, such as the former president Park, Geun-Hae, the main player, Choi, Soon-Sill, the vice president of Samsung, Mr. Lee, Jae-young who was arrested for an alleged bribery, Mr. Koh, Young-Tae who was questioned for an alleged affair, Mr. Noh, Seung-Il the whistle blower, Ms. Jang, Si-ho who is now nicknamed the helper to the special council Park, Yeong-Soo, the former secretary general Mr.

Kim, Ki-Choon who was the main figure in drafting the black list of celebrities who opposed the Park, Geun-Hae's regime, the former director of culture and sports Mr. Jo, Yoon-Seon, and a congressman Ahn, Min-Seok who are still perusing the truth for the case.

Rare and disorderly words have been flying around, like the male escort club, a shaman, exorcism, Botox procedures, burner phones, skin whitening injections, bribes, abuse of power..., the lost 7 hours of the Sewol Ferry, that have been souring the pride of the people of Korea. Against the candle rally that shouted, "Impeach Park!" there was another protest to protect the former president, flying the Korean flag. Taeguki is the national flag that is the face of our nation, which holds the sprits of Koreans, and it should be flying vigorously high in the sky for all the world to see, but I feel regretful as a Korean American that our flag is being used for such political turmoil.

Park, Geun-Hae, the first female leader of Korea in the Korean history since Queen Seonduk from the 5th century, was a president who refused to listen to the people of Korea. Being dubbed as a note princess, perhaps she is paying the heavy price of keeping a pretense relationship with Choi, Soon-Sill who was like her servant. As a daughter of a former president as well, it is tragic that someone who has lived all her life like a princess in wealth and who served as a president of Korea herself is now at the center of the issue and is shown to the people of Korea as well as to the world media in cuffs. Park, who became a president of Korea by the Constitution and thus should have followed the Constitution more rigorously than anyone in setting an example for her people, became the first president of Korea who was impeached by the constitutional court, unanimously in 8:0 votes, led by Ms. Lee, Jung-Mi, for failing to follow the spirit of the Constitution.

The former president, Park Geun-Hae, who was born as the first daughter of President Park Jung-Hee, famously known for his New Village Movement, and the first lady Yook, Young-Soo, known as the first mother, lived most of her life at the Blue House until her parents were killed, and many years later became the 18th president of the republic of Korea herself only to be impeached by the court without finishing her term. Seeing the former president, Park, Geun-Hae, who started with much fanfare proclaiming she is married to the country, and whose honor as the chief executive of the country was lost in such an unfathomable fashion, I feel sympathy as a fellow citizen who has lived through the same period as her. And I recall a passage from the Bible, the word of truth. Deeply engrained in my heart is the word of God spoken through the mouth of King Solomon who enjoyed wealth and prosperity, ' … Everything is meaningless! Meaningless!"

Mr. Woo, Byung-Woo, the former senior secretary to the President for civil affairs, recently angered the public by folding two arms in an arrogant manner while being investigated by the prosecutors. I wonder how much of honor to the president is left to people who are hurt by the recent chaotic political situations. If there was one wish as an ordinary citizen who believes that politics are to make the people happy, I hope our country will recover from this and our future generations can have beautiful dreams and hopes of becoming the president one day when they grow up. I also hope to see the president who once gave a speech in English with standing ovations from the U.S. Senate and the House of Representatives.

It still puzzles me to figure out the hidden truth behind the phrase "We have a big problem!" that became famous amid the Park-Choi gate of the meddling with the state affairs. In my mind, the people who supported the former president Park holding the Korean as well as the U.S. flags in the cold winter weather as well as the people who supported the impeachment of Park holding light candles in peaceful protests are all patriots of our country who dream of democracy. As I am hoping for a beautiful country where the knot of confusion can be untied quickly and justice to survive, I dream of the Republic of Korea full of happiness with love and compassion, and I send my heart across the Pacific Ocean to ask for the eternal grace of the Almighty.

The grateful
and always happy Sadons

I have sadons who are always grateful and happy. My sadons are folks I had always wanted to meet ever since I became a parent. Thanks to my own two daughters, Haemi and Haeryun, I am delighted that I get to meet the family of their husbands. Sadon is a Korean word referring to the parents of the son or daughter-in-law. As my two daughters got married, naturally I have now sadons. In March, 2015, I and my husband gave a prayer together withour our sadons and our daughters to God, who is the source of all good fortunes, and my heart became full of joy and my eyes full of tears. I wondered if I ever had such a joyful day like that day ever in my life.

The name of our first daughter is Haemi and the second daughter is Haeryun. Since they are not even two years apart, you could say that they were born within a year of each other. Perhaps for that reason, some have told us that they are like twins and could not tell apart one from the other. When I look at an old picture of them wearing the same Micky Mouse clothes, sometimes I become confused as to who is who, even though I am their biological mother. But deep down, there are still many different qualities that set them apart. First, my older daughter is small, and my younger daughter is tall. My first daughter adapts and concedes well, but my second one has a helping heart but at the same time she never fails to take care of herself. Even though they have their differences, the two sisters got married nearly at the same time. When we and the sadons were all hand in hand to form a circle and say graces to God, I was so grateful that I wished time had stopped altogether. I must have been working hard my whole life for that particular day. There is an old saying that "the farther the toilets and the sadons are from you, the better." Although toilets may smell and sadons uncomfortable to deal with, the saying means we still need them, but perhaps not too close to us.

Now with the shift in cultures geared towards being more comfortable, the bathrooms have moved inside our bedrooms and it is better that sadons stay friendly. As we married our older daughter off, she was absorbed into the Park family, and our younger daughter into a Ku family. Nowadays, the son-in-laws are referred to as sons who were born without the pains of labor. As our daughters got married, we received not one but two lovely sons as presents in our lives. The older son-in-law's name is Seungchan, and the younger son-in-law Joseph. We tell our sadons that "We sincerely thank you for allowing us with such a precious and well-mannered son-in-law." The sadons would also say the same. Our sadons also had a hard time adjusting their lives as the first generation of Korean Americans, and our son-in-laws are the second generations of Korean Americans who grew up proudly, juggling two cultures. For two families who grew up in similar situations to marry and become the sadons, it makes us feel easy and enjoyable.

The institution of marriage is a union of a man and a woman as a husband and a wife. Sometimes referred as a nuptial, it was not uncommon back in the days to hear a story of a husband and the wife meeting each other for the first time either during or only after their wedding ceremony. After the era of arranged marriages, which measured the pros and cons of each potential spouse, to a right to marry freely to now living together without being married to each other. Nowadays young couples prefer to not get married for convenience reasons, and I am not quite sure how the institution of marriage would evolve from here. I am thankful for our two daughters, who grew up facing numerous challenges while being raised in two cultures simultaneously, yet finding their life partners in their prime ages and getting married, and now they are the main characters of their lives. My heart fills with joy and gratefulness to see my daughters getting married and to hear the messages of their pastor that the two are becoming one as a married couple as God permits so they shall grow old happily together until their hair turns silver.

Our daughters had outdoor wedding ceremonies walking down the aisle with their mother and father like princesses on the petals full of delicate scent of fresh flowers. When the white veils, which were swaying like butterflies on their heads, were finally lifted, their pure faces were revealed so beautifully like those of angels. Wishing a happy and sacred marriage to love one another for eternity, my husband hands our daughters to our sons-in-law. When the sadons were giving our daughters a loving hug to welcome them as their daughters-in-law, I could feel the warmest affection from them.

Now I must leave everything to my sons-in-law except continuously praying for them. This is to be remembered as their best mother in the world who humbly prays in front of her daughters. As always, hearing the wedding march being played to announce the end of the ceremony excites every cell in my body and brings tears to my eyes. Her sweet voice saying "Mom, I will always be your daughter!~" echoes in my mind.

Feeling relieved and yet void at the same time, I wish for my two daughters, who in my mind are still little princesses wearing rainbow-striped dresses, to fulfill their beautiful dreams with wisdom and patience. At Pyebeak room outside, which was decorated with the Korean spirit and culture, we greet the newly-weds, who had just finished exchanging bows and thanking their parents, by throwing chestnuts and jujubes. "Here they are. We wish you many babies and a happy marriage.' The bride tries her best to catch all the blessings with the red cloth. The happy laughters of the sadons are music to my ears that congratulate the marriages of our children. The sadons we met around the time our daughters were dating were like an oasis we found during a rough, long journey in a desert. I would like us to spend the rest of our remaining journeys of life with the always grateful and happy sadons, enjoying friendly conversations with them.

I look up the sky and find the most clear and beautiful night sky.

These onions are making me cry.

I feel upset. The bridge of my nose is becoming irritated and my eyes are teary. My eyes have become sore and red, and my heart starts to cry from the inside. As I turn on the water in the kitchen, I begin to shout. These onions are making me cry! 'Please do cry with onions as an excuse~.' Such voice that makes me helpless; isn't it the person that makes my head spin and all my internal organs twisted? How did he know what I was going through, and what sort of consolation was it? My head becomes confused and out of control. I also feel that the salt grains are all tangling up in my heart as I stand in the midst of a test of my faith, struggling to save my soul.

As I was swallowing my salty tears, I look at the calendar hanging on the wall of the social room at my church. My eyes, blurred with the water from the red onion and my tears, notice the cross, which is the silent language. Ahh ~ the perfection of love! Such a thing that cannot become new unless it is reborn! I feel like the wind is howling, blowing past my heart as the salt grains in it are crushed. To function as the salt in the world, the white salt must be crushed and broken for it to taste good and to function as a preservative to prevent food from going bad. The salty water becomes holy and cleanses my annoyances that are dissolved in my tears and runny nose.

I know that in life one must let go of one's selfishness when living with others in this world in order to maintain beautiful human relationships. In particular, one needs consistent humility when ignored and be fearless when destroyed by the people around if he or she wishes to maintain a religious life and an ultimate eternal life. I would love to live while doing good deeds to have beautiful relationships with the people around me, which is a gift from God, but that's easier said than done. There are times when working in an organization you become blindsided by the events that were not planned ahead. When this happens, opinions can be divided, and voices become aggressive and loud. When opinions collide and disagreements arise, certain members would speak their minds unnecessarily stronger to put holes in the hearts of the other members. Even though we are all aware of the words of God from the Bible that emphasize the importance of how we treat each other, sometimes we fail to control our feelings only to hurt the hearts of the party involved.

Regardless of whether it's true or not, when one raises his or her voice and screams at the other person, the person on the receiving end will have his or her heartbeats elevated and become hurt with holes pierced in the heart. Physical pain can be forgotten with the passage of time, but the pain caused by words lingers and become hard to heal again. Because of the traces of scars, there is the wind of hurt emotions that penetrates into the gaps and nooks of our hearts. We all need to be careful not to make mistakes with words, since a broken heart cannot be undone no matter how hard we try to forget. Like flowers, there are color and fragrance in each word we speak, and I hope we can only say things that are beautiful and encouraging. How great would it be if we all could use a higher-level language that expresses all words with a warm heart that can comfort someone and have him or her live a life that can dream?

Because the characters of a believer become refined and harmonious through prayers within her community, it seems necessary to become wise and sensible to clean and forgive one's mind with tears and runny nose of a holy water broken down from salt. And let's assume the whole problem was due to the foolish fault of my own. If we want help, understanding, and warm love from one another, then there is no other way but to step back, be patient, and have reflection and humility. Compared to the sufferings of Jesus, who had no faults of his own, wouldn't the pains of our lives be a mere mole? Although the joy of ensuring happiness of an afterlife in a religious life, which desires a new life, cannot be greater, I can't fathom the life without happiness here on Earth that shares love with others with a warm heart. Wouldn't it be a role of salt to be helpful to others by educating oneself to be patient to live harmoniously among good people with humility and gentle hearts?

An onion is a round-shaped vegetable, that acts like a protective film for my mind and that brings out my inner cries in the form of tears and runny nose. The onion, which has the same shape even as one peels its layers over and over, is crispy, sweet, and has an unusual scent. There may be a varying degree of differences depending on the type, but they all contain enzymes called allyl propyl disulfide and allyl sulfide, which cause teary eyes and strong odor, so when one peels or cooks an onion with a knife, those substances stimulate the membrane of the eyes, which, needless to say, hurts very much. It is also a vegetable seasoning that creates various flavors harmoniously with all other seasonings. Of all the kinds available to purchase, I always try to find the kind that has the mildest taste, but I know in essence that all onions have sweet as well as peppery taste that comingle together. Just like people have their pros and cons. I think about the characters of believers and the roles of salt, when I try my hardest to peel onions, in order not to damage the image of the disciples of Christ who live by the principle of respecting the sky and loving people.

When the unhealthy emotions that have accumulated inside me over time and turned into white salt waiting to be crushed, changing its form to tears that roll down my cheeks, they bloom into the flowers of prayers of my humble soul. How grateful would it be if these flowers of prayer could be used to make this world a better and beautiful place to live in? It is easy to lose love in a little anger; if possible, wouldn't it be the role of salt in this world that overcomes pain in one's heart with patience and encompasses others? On a day I am scolded by people for my lack of good decisions and poor speech, I become disappointed in myself and begin to feel depressed, so it becomes hard to stay free from sins. When I am at my maximum patience and cannot endure the silence anymore, I let go of my emotions and release them in tears and runny nose. So, I have decided to thank the saints of my church for making me cry, on the pretext of onions, to fulfill my dreams as a true Christian. I then open my mind and shout out loud.

"These onions are making me cry!

The Loom

Mugunghwa (Rose of Haron)

Mugunghwa is the national flower of South Korea designated as the official government of Republic of Korea was formed in 1948. As I was born in Korea, I have always been fond of and loved Mugunghwa wholeheartedly with no conditions whatsoever. Mugunghwa has been a friend of mine and a partner of life. I have lived with Mugunghwa ever since I was a fetus till now in my sixties.

Ever since I was a child, the fence of our garden in the country was Mugunghwa trees. The Mugunghwa fence, through which my mother entered and exited many times every day, always looked fresh and beautiful as if it was telling us the joy of life. It must have been the water from the small stream that was running underneath the fence by the Mugunghwa trees providing moisture to the soil. The Mugunghwa flowers that hold early morning dew in them always gave me hope in life and made me feel refreshed. The yellowish green Mugunghwa leaves early in the spring gave us pollution-free materials we could use to make healthy side dishes. Mugunghwa belongs to a family of flowering plant called Malvaceae, and it has a sweet delicious taste when the soft leaves are washed until they form white bubbles inside water and put into doenjang (bean paste) soup made with dried anchovies. The leaves of Mugunghwa gave us physical strengths and its flowers gave our souls a hope for brighter tomorrow in the Japanese colonial era as well as during the 6.25 Korean war, sharing the pains of our people.

At the onset of summer, the Mugunghwa flowers start to bloom, and the cycle of their birth and death repeats until the deep end of autumn. Thanks to the bees and butterflies who like to kiss the flower's male stamen, we see many colors of Mugunghwa flowers, such as pink, white, or purple, in harmony. Among them, the white Mugunghwa is the most elegant and noble-looking one like a noble lady of our people wearing Hanbok (Korean traditional dress) made of calico with its purple coat string firmly tied. And Mugunghwa symbolizes principle and honor to love and protect our people and nation with a single-hearted devotion. With its stamen full of golden powder, which looks like a trumpet that makes a mysterious sound, the flower seems to be trumpeting a future that our nation will proudly become the world's most economically affluent country in the future. That is not all. As you go inside the Mugunghwa, its color becomes darker, which shows the compactness and solidity of our people. For this reason, I firmly attest that Mugunghwa is the flower that represents our people the most properly.

Mugunghwa flowers bloom in the morning in the most purist form and contract in the evening, and as they bloom different flowers every day, we get the feeling that the flower never dies. Perhaps that is to make us to believe the almighty God, who is invisible to our eyes, continuously takes care of our people. The humble, yet bright Mugunghwa, that is neither fancy nor bland, can survive unceasingly under the scorching sun humbly and patiently. Since the flower resembles the nature of our Korean people who overcame the many sorrows and hardships, it must have been chosen as the national flower to symbolize our people and hope of the nation's everlasting prosperity.

It was when I emigrated my home country with a hope of the American dream. My father-in-law, who has devoted his entire life in educating younger generations, gifted us with an oriental painting. Although it was a painting with simple lyrics on it, which said "Mugunghwa, Mugunghwa, a flower of our nation..' I had a heavy heart knowing the full meanings of the words. Though I would be living in a foreign country, he was telling us to live with the spirit of the Korean people, and his message has been deeply engrained in my mind over the years. I have never lost the strong impression I had at the moment, and I've been reminding my children, as well as myself, at any chance I get, that Mugunghwa is the flower that represents our home country, the Republic of Korea. I have since moved the Mugunghwa painting to the living room from where I could see with the door open. I wanted everyone who visit my home to see the painting more closely, and I believe I have succeeded in attracting people's interest. I never miss a chance to boast to people who live here how Mugunghwa is such a beautiful flower and how it is such beneficial to us humans.

These days my heart is beyond happy to see Mugunghwa trees being planted where I live. Korean people no longer live just in the land of Korea but all over the world. Thus, I think to myself that we should especially care, love, and distribute Mugunghwa, which contains the nature of Korean people. As I have raised our children with a beautiful dream, I am growing Mugunghwa in hopes of 'multiplying' the flowers of our people. Just like the Mugunghwa that lives and breathes the sprits and vigor of the Korean people, I can survive this life as a Korean American with the help of its soul. As Mugunghwa is never fancy nor shallow but rather plain, perhaps I am fond of it due to its resemblance of me. I feel happy to live with Mugunghwa every day.

Our peoples are still technically at a state of truce after the 6.25 Korean War. As people of one nation possessing the spirits of Mugunghwa, we shall come true the dream of being a unified country in the near future and dance together holding and hugging each other in the colorful garden of Mugunghwa. Mugunghwa flowers that can be seen near the rivers and the mountains of our nation can now be seen all over the global villages, and this makes me extremely happy and abysmally joyful. As long as I am on this earth, I would hope to live harmoniously with people who are plain, simple, yet beautiful with subtle and delicate scent just like the Mugunghwa. While I am putting down my roots on this vast and fertile land and becoming one Mugunghwa tree who possess the soul of the Korean people. Breathing with the loving people who have been the light, water, and air for me.

That was why!

"Ahhh - That was why! That's why I never liked candles in the first place."

As I was clapping my hands while mumbling in an excited tone, as though I had discovered something amazing, I felt this draining feeling that had been clogging up in my mind.

I had forgotten about it for many decades, but by chance I had discovered the very reason why I do not like candles.

"Look, come smell this candle. Umm~ it smells amazing. It is a lilac smell." My dear friend, seemingly enjoying the smell of the candle with her small roundish nose, suddenly offered me to smell it. "I don't know how to tell candle smells. Not to mention I don't actually like them." As soon as she was trying to place the candle in front of my nose, I pushed her away, while making those mean comments, not caring my friend's excitements from the fragrant smell of the candle.

Then, I glanced at my ugly scar on my right hand, which looks like the wax from a piece of candle had fallen on it and hardened. "That was why!" Having listened to my story about what happened, the friend, making a sheepish face, forgave me for my rude behavior.

There is another, similar episode. An older sister of mine visited my house one time and she brought a candle for us as a gift. I told her unenthusiastically "Oh, you brought candles. I don't particular care for them" "Is that so?" Why did I say such things to her? I regretted almost immediately when I saw her sad face, but the train has already left the station. It was a terrible mistake of mine. "But the candles are really pretty. Did you make them yourself? I'll put them where people can see, and I'll cherish them forever." I tried to change the subject, quibbling about candles. I know now. Although she lives far away, she would be understanding of my remarks made back then, once she knows what had happened to my hand and the scar in my hand. "That was why~."

It was a time when electricity wasn't widely available. It was the most boring time of my life, being in a graduating class in an all-female high school. At the time, studying late with lights on was something only rich people could afford to do, and it was considered to be unpatriotic to do so for the whole country that was trying to conserve energy. So, we would sometimes study with candles on, which was more convenient than a kerosene lamp.

That day was just like any other day. The day I hurt my right hand from a burning candle. I was studying for an exam, tired as usual, and I must have fallen asleep on the desk. When I woke up from a burning smell, the body of the candle was mostly gone, and it was about to burn the wooden table. Not knowing what to do, I tried to turn it off with my hand. The hot candle

The Loom

then stuck to the palm of my hand, burning most of the skin. After the incident, I must have developed a deep resentment towards candles for having left such painful scars. To the point that anytime I encounter candles I would immediately shun from them, instinctively sparing myself from any potential troubles.

But these days, when I look at the scars on my right hand, I would ruminate on my life to that of a candle. Just like candles, there are many people in this world who are brightening the lives of others by burning themselves until the last minute of their lives. Though I may live short of that degree of sacrifice, I should become someone who is able to say "That was why~" and develop generosity to understand situations that others are in as well as their reasons. At worst, I should never hurt others' feelings with complete misunderstandings.

At any moment and under many circumstances, people make mistakes or do what they think are the best options for them and for everyone, and I shall always try to put myself in their shoes and understand with an open mind, saying "That was why~." Just like when I make mistakes I would want others to understand and forgive me.

If I wish to become a loving person who tries to make this world a better and brighter place.

| CHAPTER 4 |

Monterey Arirang

Monterey Cypress tree

There is an old tree, which I named "Monterey Cypress tree," that has been a friend to me for the past twenty years. It is a good friend who always welcomes me with its open arms and offers me wisdom of life whenever I need it.

It points towards the sky with its long pointy branches with dense dark green needles, and although many years have passed it still shows its deep green.

If you look at the pine trees in the Monterey area, they are actually of all different types. In my estimation, there must be at most 5 or 6 different types of pines trees in this area. Even within the same type, the soil, temperature, and the wind conditions could change its shapes quite a bit. There is the "Monterey Pine" type just like the ones in the mountains from my hometown with big cones and pointy needles. On the other hand, there is also the "Monterey Cypress" type, which is a nut pine tree, with smaller leaves pointing upwards in an organized fashion with smaller cones, like my friend.

My old tree friend of the type "Monterey Cypress" is a creature from God, proud of itself to live in the Monterey area offering excitements to the tourists here. As the tree becomes more good-looking all the while the rough and twisted traces of life are added to it, we are all in awe of its posture that refuses to yield to its environment. I wonder to myself "Could I become someone who could make someone happy as I become older?" as this tree has been.

The Cypress tree is the tree that symbolizes the city of Monterey. Thus, a public office makes a great effort in managing and properly maintaining them. I also discovered on my friend, Monterey Cypress, a number '2200' inscribed on a small coin-like plate. I could sense that my tree friend is also being protected by an agency of some sort. At the same time, the plate with its number even looked like a medal of honor for surviving the long-lasting storms of life and for lifting the status of the city.

My friend "Monterey Cypress" is mature, so it is a troubleshooter for my problems of all sorts. When I am faced with a difficult situation I would ask it for solutions. "What should I do?" I would ask this giant tree that would require five of me to wrap around completely, leaning gently to its trunk and listening to the tree carefully as if being held in mother's arms. Then a voice is heard within my heart.

"Could you be more patient and wait for it? I'd like you to become more generous. Could you be more loving than you are now? Am I not staying put here after having overcome numerous difficulties that came at me all these years? I've welcomed all the scars that have been formed due to the rains and the winds, all the foreign substances that are corroding my body, even all the plants that have nothing to do with me that have claimed my weakest part of my body as their homes."

I can feel the history of my living here in the States is rooted along with Monterey Cypress tree. Perhaps that's why my tree friend seems to understand us celebrating the 100 years of the history of Korean immigration. First working as farmers working in sugar cane farms in Hawaii and never forgetting the pains of the L.A. riot, my tree friend, Monterey Cypress, seems to be proud of us for never giving up and getting up repeatedly and steadfastly to face the future. Today, our second generations make their ways into various parts of the society proudly and with a passion. I feel like my tree friend has always participated in sharing my proud feelings for our younger generations starting their careers in journalism, medical fields, or even in politics.

One day I was on my way to see my old tree friend, but a barricade was set up with yellow tapes around it, and within the barricade were the branches that had been cut that day. The old branches that had gone through its cornification and lost its vitality could have caused harm those who come to see it, so they were being proactive lopping off the dying branches in advance. At that moment, I realized a fact of life that all living things get old and they will eventually need care from other people.

Monterey is a small, yet beautiful tourist city, and one might just be tricked into thinking that it could be the most attractive city to live in. The seasons seldom change, and the air quality is top notch, and perhaps because of these, people living here are generally mild-mannered with pure hearts. The ever-green Cypress trees, all seemingly ready to fly spreading their wings at any moment with the force of vitality, and the antique houses rows after rows that look like palaces of dreams make up this charming small city. The rock cliffs following the coastline and the magnificent magic carpet flowers as if the whole city is painted in pink, and the mysterious glow of the setting sun in the middle of the vast Pacific are the ultimate beauty of Monterey.

Among all the countless qualities of the city that make the city beautiful, the reason why I care for my friend 'Monterey Cypress' the most is because we live in harmony, touching each other and having constant conversations to the point the tree is used to my smell of Kimchi and I am to its cheese smell.

One day I notice a water bird sitting on a dead branch of an old tree. I felt a lump in my throat as the bird looked weak with its skinny shoulders down to its bones and yet it was trying its hardest to stay afloat. It reminded me of us 1st generation of immigrants who have sacrificed themselves for their children as well as of the people who work hard in the background for the Korean community in Monterey.

Today I visit my old friend 'Monterey Cypress' again. Although my tree friend has been losing its green needles and its skin has become ragged and rough every year, like an old person with her receding hairline, it stands firm with its root put down deep in the ground, raising the status of the city of Monterey. I touch my trusty old friend, take a look at it with my head raised up, and hug it with my open arms.

Then the sound of the pulse of the pine tree, resonating strongly with me, gave me a hope of life. And it seemed like 'Monterey Cypress' was telling me the following.

"I will live young. You should live young. We all shall live young."

Life

There is life in everything that lives and moves. The Bible says God created the universe with words and he created us humans in his own image from dust and gave us the breath of life to make us living beings. Life is the realm of the mysterious God that us humans cannot understand. No one on this earth can create a life. Life is a unique gift from God for us, the living creatures, to be able to live on this planet. Since life is the one and only precious gift given to us which allows us to be alive, we should cherish it with great appreciation.

Life is a channel of time. The fact that there is a channel that connects the past, present and the future gives us the driving force in developing our characters. By reminiscing the past and trying to focus on the present, one can hope for tomorrow. At this moment of a precious life and caring for the poor on this plant, I wish to live a beautiful life along with beautiful people. Until the day I stand before the noble being who will allow me with a new life, life is fresh and beautiful. In Spring, green shoots lift heavy lumps of dirt while making loud noises to hold a festival of life. During summer, the world praises life in deep green. In fall, life holds a festival of splendid fruition and sings in a variety of beautiful colors. During winter times, life keeps its beauty in silence. Life has a refreshing beauty all throughout the year.

Life is mysterious. I feel a mystery when a baby looks for mother's breast. Isn't it mysterious when an earthworm is cut in half and yet still wriggles itself for survival? I feel mysterious when a small seed sprouts a new bud, blooms flowers, and bears fruits with just the right amount of water and nutrition. The wriggling of life is the mystery of life that cannot be observed in inorganic objects. The well-known mysteries such as the pyramids in Egypt or Angkor Wat in Cambodia are grand and wonderful, but they are immobile, and we do not feel the mystique of life that moves like when a wild flower bursts the eyes of a pink flower from a small green flower bed. Life is mysterious and it can only be felt in living things.

Life is about being thankful and happy. When I wake up in the morning and open my eyes, how grateful and happy is it to be able to detect the sound of the breathing air in the lungs and the pulse in the beating heart? How grateful and happy is it that I can think and feel my loved ones? How grateful is it that we can remember yesterday and plan for tomorrow? How grateful and happy is it that life gives us an opportunity to live with a pure heart? Life is constantly moving and changing itself. Where there is life, things always move and have a different look every time. Inorganic matter can be changed by others, but living things can change within themselves. I am a person who is alive, and I always try my best, pray to God for his help, and try to change myself so my soul can become beautiful. As long as I am breathing, I shall have to grind hard to have a soul that shines. Since there is life in me, I like that there is hope in myself capable of becoming a truthful person on a whim.

Life is fragrant. The smell of fresh life makes me feel good. The fragrance of life stemming from living honestly each and every day is the flower of life. The fragrance of love stemming from helping others in need stays in one's heart for a long period of time, adding joy to life. The fragrance of life that is created from movements becomes an energizer and gives us hope for the future. The smell of fresh grass and the fragrance of flowers become the fragrance of life, making the world that much more lively. There is a sound in life. It is such a mysterious sound. The life in my blood flutters and makes a sound. And it acts like a health care worker. It tells me to love my neighbors. It tells me to forgive those whom I hate. It tells me to be more embracing. It tells me to work on more humane projects. The sound of water flowing, the sound of a cumulus cloud dispersing, and the sound of wind…, it tells me to make a more fabulous sound of life than the sounds of nature.

Life is full of joys. The life chosen at the crossroads of life and death would be the ultimate joy. The love of life when one feels his or her breath after escaping the valley of death, it would be the natural pleasure to know that it is life that is more precious than the entire world. Life is joy that excites our hearts, but death is despair. Who would refuse joy and prefer despair? Life is finite. There are mayflies that live only a day, humans who live about 100 years, and trees living 1000 years, but they all become inanimate objects and fade away in time. To achieve eternal life, the only way is to live in faith. If people believe the creator who gave us life, we would all be given a new life forever after our life here on earth is finished and go to the other world. Life naturally makes us finite beings and it makes us feel the importance of the present moment.

As I have this precious life I shall live among my neighbors with love and enjoy the feast of life happily as long as I am here on earth. At this moment, I lift my blessed eyes and look up the sky, sensing, with my body and soul, life flowing freely through in my blood.

Monterey Arirang

Arirang Arirang Arariyo.
Arirang lovely diaspora
We are the Korean people brightening the world
We love the seashore with Mugung flower.
(Chrous) Arirang Arirang Arariyo.
Arirang I am walking along the Montrery seashore
Arirang Arirang Arariyo.
Arirang Diaspora Komeria
We are the Korean people beatifying the world
We love the seashore with garden balsam
Arirang Arirang Arariyo.
Arirang full of dreams like the diaspora of stars
We are the Korean people aromatizing the world
We love the seashore with pink flowers

I walk along the seashore of the Monterey beach humming along the 'Monterey Arirang' which I came up with my own lyrics. The Monterey Arirang is a song of longing for my hometown country, and the self-respect of my soul that enables me to live, feeling proud to be from Korea.

Even to these days, I sing Monterey Arirang every day, which contains the soul of Korea, here at the seashore of the Pacific. When I sing Arirang by myself, the familiar voices sing with me through the waves of the ocean. I feel that the souls of the Koreans all come out and sing along with me. This way, singing Monterey Arirang gives me the energy that enables me to live actively. At the shore of the Monterey beach that brings the voices of the people I love through these waves.

The number of years I have lived here as a Korean immigrant, which started with a dream of living a beautiful life, has surpassed the number of years I lived in my home country. However, I still feel uneasiness living here every now and then. Although I have lived my life to the fullest, I still feel pain deep in my heart due to the language barrier and the unfairness of subtle racism and being fired because of it. Sometimes I lament on my own weakness for not being able to confront these unfair treatments. I have turned in a lonely and empty soul and had the thirst to fill my void with love but having failed to meet anyone who would open up their hearts, I only depend on the ever-lasting water of life from time to time. Perhaps I struggle to write essays in order to be with those who are just like me, who suffer from pains, loneliness, and the void for a lack of love. Could I not write ever that can be like a cool breeze that eases the suffering and worries in us?

In the age of digital nomads with new patterns of life in which people find their work and place to live freely, sometimes I feel lonely, as a Korean American, even when I am surrounded by people. Not only from feeling lonely but losing someone dear to me, the screams of the soul pouring out blood from the unbearable pain and sorrow permeated in one's heart can be truly miserable. The edges of my eyes become filled with tears when I think about the joys, angers, sorrows, and pleasures of living as an immigrant who lacks day-to-day communication, trying her best to transcends her lonely nature, national borders, and the language barrier, like the wild grass that have been knocked down in the field. Nonetheless, I continue to walk the path of a Korean-American without losing courage or hope to live a happy life. Singing Monterey Arirang that contains my sorrows as well as my dreams(vision).

Nowadays, we are living in a global age. Although we can now visit many beautiful sites all over the world through many means and methods, Monterey provides the tourists who visit this place with delight pleasures that can only be experienced with naked eyes through beautiful flowers. People may drive on the 17-mile drive course, which is touted as one of the most beautiful courses in the world, decorated with beautiful light pink flowers, while looking over at the fantastic Big Bear mountain full of wild flowers. That fantasy leads to the Sokuri town in my home country that bears Arirang with the legendary fork tale that people whom you wish to meet dearly would always walk through the road in Sochunjae and becomes the Han River that you can pour out all your sorrows in your heart into it. However, I try not to dwell on the memories of the past and go about my life holding on to the dreams of a beautiful life as a Korean American. Since I understand the importance of right here and right now.

As usual, I walk on the seashore of the Pacific today singing Monterey Arirang. Though I have sung this song countlessly many times, I do not understand why today the name of this city I am standing on feels awkward. How many more years will it take before I can forget about the original Arirang song I used to enjoy singing in my hometown? The fading faces of the people I loved in my home country enter into my mind with the Ari Ari sound of the Arirang song.

I am thankful every day that I can sing my Monterey Arirang, which was arranged by me with new words from the original Arirang song from my home country that has always been in my heart. But today I feel somewhat foolish with a plaintive thought that I am not a smart person. Me who lives painfully as a Korean-American with a dream of leaving loving memories of a life here in the States.

This is what I think of while singing Monterey Arirang and longing for my hometown.

Sir. Rain is coming.

"Oh! Finally, Sir. Rain is coming~"

Pitter-patter! I still remember the sound of the rain drops on our tin rooftop making our parents rush out the front yard barefoot and shout with their arms pointing towards the sky. They must have been overanxious to hear the sound of raindrops; my usually taciturn dad was smiling with joys saying "We are now saved."

The sound of raindrops after a long period of drought is the sound of life that saves lives for farmers like our parents. It wasn't just rain, but called as 'Sir. Rain,' and I can still feel the overjoyed sound of my satisfied parents, which was more like crying, coming down from the sky and rolling down towards my toes. At that moment, I felt an area of God, that cannot be controlled by us humans.

When such Sir. Rain starts to roar and fall down on the ground, there was a list of things we were supposed to do. We were to gather all bowls and containers that could contain water and place them under the eaves. The water gathered under the eaves would then be used for washing clothes or other cleaning purposes.

When we could hear the rain drops from Sir. Rain, everything seemed abundant and came alive. A well that people used a bucket to draw its water would be filled with rain water, and people in the village would get soaked in rain gladly and head to the field with their hands full of farming tools. Sometimes I think about myself remembering about the sound of rain drops in a drought. Have I ever made someone suffer for having not made the sound that I should've definitely made for them?

The sound of Sir. Rain also announces new seasons. In spring, sprinkles of rain open the eyes of the mountains, streams, plants, and grass. In summer, summer showers fuel our mother nature. In autumn, drizzles give us poetic emotions with beautiful autumn colors. During winter times, sleets on naked bare trees allow us become patient that is needed to wait for the coming season. As such, the much-needed, welcoming rain in each season gives us the cozy, snug, as well as romantic feelings, mellowing our minds and hearts. When we hear the sound of rain, we turn on good music and lose ourselves in thought or remember the sweet words whispered with our loved ones in the rain under an umbrella. The sound of rain pouring down calms our minds and gives us the feeling of being purified of our bodies and the minds. The sound of rain streaming down is such a good one to hear. I wish to be such a beautiful sound for other people.

When Sir. Rain becomes engulfed with thunder and lightning as well as the raging wind, it turns into heavy rain. When rain pours down, then it eventually causes a flood. When the sound of rain is too abundant, a loss of lives or properties would surely ensue. In my hometown I used to live, a flood meant some poorly-built huts would lose their roofs, or worse the muddy water would collapse entire houses and carry them away. Floods would turn streams into small rivers that are too wide to cross, and schools would close until the sound of rain stops. At any rate, when the sound of rain prolongs, it means the rainy season had started, all outdoor activities would be minimized and hence we would soon get tired of the rain sound. What about the sound of me? Have I ever caused harm because I made too much of a sound? Too much of a rain sound would cause floods and it is no better situation than the drought which has no rain sound. It would mean that my non-stop voice, which bores other people, could be worse than a voice that people are anxiously waiting to hear.

Nowadays, many places on Earth, including here in Monterey, USA, are suffering from severe droughts with very little water to go around. In this circumstance, I am beyond thankful for my new friend, a cactus in my garden, who only eats dew and yet provides such pleasure by producing beautiful flowers in red, yellow, and white colors. The media has been busy to report the sufferings of the droughts from all parts of the world to console those who wish things would improve. When I read newspaper articles with pictures of an old farmer painfully looking at his crops in the dry field, I find myself not being able to read anymore due to the tears in my eyes. The old farmer in the pictures is after all our fathers. I have trouble breathing even thinking of how desperate those farmers in the country would need water for their crops.

Farmers in the mountain villages who solely depend on the rain from the sky live looking at the sky most of their lives. Farmlands near puddles deep enough to draw water with a well bucket to water their crops would be the highest-class lands. For farmers who draw water from the puddles with two giant buckets, one on each of their shoulders, connected by nothing but a cord, the sound of rain, that is Sir. Rain, under the scorching sun that causes extreme sunburns, would be equivalent to the voice from God.

As though I am lovesick with rain, I love the sound of the much-needed rain that falls down in my mind. I wish to make such sound for others as well like that sound from the welcoming rain, that is just between a drought and a flood, that can provide emotions for people. Was I ever a person that gave a much-needed voice for others in need? I think of all I've said in my life in this drought that is severe enough to dry all emotions. That is, have I been silent when I should have said something for others, or was I ever too loud when I should've kept my quiet and not disturb others?

How exciting would it be if I can become the sound for others like the sound of welcoming rain that falls at opportune intervals that grows mountains, streams, grass, and trees, and gives us hope and emotions? At any way, when can we hear the rain sound ever again here? I sincerely pray that my sound can fall upon someone in this generation as Elijah from the Bible prayed to God and gathered clouds and rain.

Oh my goodness, really? Sir. rain is coming.

A love that is like the wind

There is love inside me that is like the wind. It is a source of my being that has kept me alive like a never-ending stimulus. It is love like the wind that has grazed over my body every single day of my life. You may not see it with physical eyes, but you know it's there since you can feel it, hear it, and even see its traces. As you see from the traces of the wind that flattens the grass in the field.

Love, like a wind, visits the deepest part of my heart in the form of fragrance of flowers in spring, in showers during summer, as the aroma of rice ripening during autumn, and as large snowflakes during the winter. For this reason, my heart sees the pattern of mysterious yet gorgeous life that is being created by love that is like a wind. Sometimes loves visits me in different ways. It comes to me like a breeze in spring, like a tornado during summer, like a west wind in autumn, and like a piercing wind that strikes bare trees in the winter time. As such, love comes and goes like a wind between and throughout the four seasons, leaving marks as if it enjoys painting all over my body and my life.

There is more. Love sometimes goes through every joint in my body and makes large holes in them. As I let go of my ego and search for love only to get lost and discouraged and lie in my bed, love, which is like the wind, goes through the joints of my body poking and causing unbearable pain and proclaims that it wishes to reside in my body. Then, from time to time, the wind-like love pierces through my heart like a sharp awl passing through the cells in my heart. Then, an ill feeling darker than blood rocks my body. Not caring one bit of my body suffering from unbearable pains. At this moment, I feel the pattern of my life turning red near the heart area.

The wind-like love also tells me the following. "I have an attribute of not being able to stay in one place." And it goes on again. "It is the desire of yours that wants me to stay in one place permanently, and your desire comes from your obsession." Though it won't stay in one place, how can I possibly get rid of my obsession of wanting it to stay? The obsession is the desire to possess it forever, so even a life of worries and restraints cannot help but to feel that way. The wind-like love also tells me "Don't ever try to possess love, and become truly free by letting go of it completely." But I still try to hold onto it, albeit temporarily, with my skirt. And I become antsy to circle around with the wind-like love that can be felt with feelings.

I want love to be like a wind that has the scent of a flower. Or I want it to be like a tornado that wraps around my body. But it won't be just love that is like the wind that keeps moving around, since is there anything in this universe that does not move around or stay in one place? That is the truth. All things move and change. So is my heart. There is no such thing in this world that is forever or that doesn't change. If there is one such thing, it would be God in heaven.

The wind-like love does not always wish to show its form. It cannot be seen with eyes but with feelings and sounds, and it stays around for a short while only to disappear permanently. Perhaps I long for it even more because, like the wind, it can't be seen or touched. As if holding the keys to magic, love mercilessly pokes and penetrates my body on days I open my heart.

Sometimes, I feel out of breath and bewildered when love penetrates deep in my lungs. I shout at it to quickly go away for already feeling as sensitive as I am. For the capillaries in my body could congested, swell up, and explode when the blood in my heart boils up and becomes uncontrollable. Sometimes love penetrates even the cerebral nerves and the cells in my brain and ultimately rocks even my dreams. After all, it was as if it was trying to engrave in me that it will never leave me.

I look deep in my heart and assign many words and adjectives in front of the word 'love.' The love of parents, the love of friends, the love of one's child, and ... the first love. Since love tends to not stay in one place, I say love is like the wind. As soon as life came through my nose I could not have lived without love, had I not had close relationships. When I try to catch it thinking that it will be a treasure that will make my life happy, love like a wind steps aside and disappears from me. If it were to escape me eventually, I think that perhaps I should gracefully let it go. I should perhaps wish that it could enjoy life and roam freely and happily.

It was on a day when love ran through the pickets on my throat like the wind. While weighing the merits of families and education backgrounds, love left me again heartlessly showing its back, but for some reason it came back with one million roses. Perhaps it was roaming by the roses by chance and wanted to show me the true love.

I welcome it back but silently, since the marks of wandering around with my two arms stirring up the air still pains my heart. Perhaps it has realized from the scent of the million roses that all I want now is to write beautiful essays in this beautiful world and leave this long journey behind with the wind-like love. But what good is to know all this? After all, this love won't stay with me forever. But what can I do but to love such love that is like the wind? I still like love that danced on the field of white reeds in Moack Mountain.

But the fact that I can still hold on to my life is because this love, like the wind, always visits me and stimulates my life. The love that I cannot hold onto forever, and yet it's a true relationship that cannot be parted with my life. As usual, love grazes over my body today like the wind with a scent of million roses.

I feel love, like the wind, is drawing mysteriously the shape of my life that is elegant and graceful.

Diaspora nomadic age

Age is not something that wanders. However, my age as someone who lives as a Korean American diaspora is a wandering one. Thus, I gave it a new word, a nomadic age. As I live between two cultures, my age has become dynamic and nomadic. Thinking my age has become nomadic, I feel sad for it not being able to stay static, though it is somewhat free. The nomadic age moves constantly to paint beautifully the age of a foreigner. The nomadic age, which contains the history of Korean immigration, which started with dreams of the Korean diaspora, must play a role in being aged beautifully in different shapes, like the rings of trees planted on different lands. The nomadic age of the diaspora that exists due to different cultures possesses various beautiful colors and nutritive materials that creates the mysterious rings of age of a diaspora. It possesses the freedom of a foreigner, and the treasure of the immigration history of the Korean Americans.

Since it is important to ask the patient's name and the birthdate to understand her identity as well as her mental state, one day a doctor of a European descent asked me questions. How old are you? Umm, do you know the Korean war? With his eyes wide open, he started asking me not just my age, but the totally unrelated question of whether I remembered the Korean war. And he asks me again. "I asked you how old you were." "Did you not learn about the Korean war at school?" "No?" I tell the doctor that "I probably learned it in school, but I forgot about it. The war started in 1950. I was born in that year. Thus, I am becoming 66 years old, but legally I am 65 years old. Oh wait, since my birthday isn't in two days, I am 64 years old in American age. My Korean age is 67. The fact that I am alive is since the United States intervened in the Korean war. I am thankful that I am currently living in a country that participated in the Korean war.

The doctor who seemed to have more questions for me for further treatment wanted to say something, but rather he just smiled. Perhaps he sensed that I wanted to firmly establish my identity as a Korean. I believe it is my nomadic age as to why I tell an agent at the immigration office who barely knew the existence of our country and show my gratitude to the descendants of our allied nations how thankful I was of their help in the Korean War. I've lived here in the States longer than I did in my home country, I feel that the sentiments of my home country and those of a new one are meeting at the nomadic age. The nomadic age exists inside the mind of this traveler who wants to hold on to the sentiments of the Korean people.

Due to the confusion of cultural differences of counting ages in the Korean way as well as the American way, sometimes I become someone who is not even aware of one's age. I also realized that there are other Korean Americans from the Korean diaspora who are as confused as I am about their nomadic ages. Due to late registration during the war, due to clerical errors, and so on, there were many reasons of having different ages for different occasions. When people started to arrive in Hawaii during the early years, people's ages would sometimes be mixed up in marriage certificates. Due to cultural differences, people would report ages differently as well. Whatever the reasons, I am as surprised to find there are many who have nomadic ages as me in our Korean American community. The existence of nomadic ages from the Korea diaspora is the proof that the culture of one's own country and that of a foreign one are meeting one another.

Any one person is born once in this world, naked, so one should have only one birthday. But the nomadic age is dynamical and thus cannot stay in one place. Since my birth month is February, which sometimes overlaps in both solar and lunar calendar years, there are times I cannot tell my age quickly due to my age in my family register being different. But as time went by, and the history of myself of living as a Korean American of the Korean diaspora knows that I am getting wiser and more experienced. Having had naps of only a few minutes in the bathroom due to the lack of sleep at night to achieve my dream of the Korean diaspora, having had to drive to my other job while eating a piece of dried bread mixed with drops of my salty tears, they all coexist radiating beautiful mysterious colors.

A time of precarious living without having one's clear birth date to achieve an American dream while licking the floor of a foreign life. A time of consoling and being patient telling oneself that everything would be ok no matter the difficulties. A time of feeling like one was desperately searching for an oasis in an endless desert. The emotions of one's past struggles to have a better and beautiful life and the colors of joy, anger, sorrow, and pleasure all mixed together creating the rings of age of an immigrant; wouldn't all this make the mysterious history of the Korean Americans that will be lasting forever? The nomadic age of the Korean diaspora has been constantly moving in time that connects and communicates the past, the present, and the future, and has become the nutrition that has been drawing the rings of age. Turning into a mysterious color that culminates life's drawing every year as an experience of time on the history of the immigrants living as Korean Americans. The nomadic age of the Korean diaspora has freedom and contains the history of immigration of the Korean Americans. What a such treasure it is.

The Flower Grass

The flower grass! My heart flutters for such a beautiful name. I can't describe how joyful I was when I first learned of the name of this beautiful flower from a literary friend of mine. The flower grass is also known as the ice plant flower or the magic carpet flower. When the writer Mr. Gilbert Khang first said of the name, I was fascinated by the beauty of the Korean language and its linguistic aesthetics. I am thankful for the literary friend of mine who let me know of such a beautiful name whenever I see the flower grass from the coast of Monterey.

Mr. Gilbert Khang, who has told me of the name 'the flower grass' is the 7th president of the Korean Writers' Association (KWAUS) here in the United States. Started as a literary organization, unfamiliar even to writers in the early days because of its feeble activities, he has been putting all his efforts into managing KWAUS like an active volcano to invigorate the organization. He is known for keeping promises under all conditions and is trustworthy. About ten years ago on a summer day, it was when I got off the plane at an airport to attend a literature event, I first met him, who at the time was the chairman of the essay department of the KWAUS, and we have been working together ever since in the garden of literature.

At a literary event, it is often talked about among writers that there is no such multi-faceted person among Korean American writers, who possesses as broad knowledge in literature as Mr. Khang. An essayist, a photographer… Now, he is actively working as a literary critic. He is also known for his recent book of travel essays which explores new lives called <The Digital Nomad through Lenses>. He gives numerous literary lectures and is a pioneer in the publication of many literary magazines both in Korean and American. He is a rare scholar who gives a helping hand to those who have a desire for literature and dream about the journey of becoming a writer. For being such a witty literary scholar, I believed he could have coined such beautiful terms, "flower grass." For my lack of creativity having lived without knowing such a beautiful and comforting name for the flower, I feel ashamed as a literary person who creates work of art with the tools called language.

The flower grass is so beautiful that many fall in love at the first sight, and they always come back for more. Sunny days would temp people to lie on the flower grass and whisper in love. These flowers here in Monterey still continue to bloom decades later. The flowers may be new, but it's surprising to think that the roots have been the same. They live in the same area as they always have been, never disappearing nor growing in size. The flower grass in Monterey beach shows a stem with such cute green leaves gently covering the ground throughout the seasons. During the flower season, countless small flowers, soft and delicate in pink, bloom along their stems, and its beauty takes the breath away of those who admire them. It only rains briefly during the winter here in Monterey, and yet the fact that we can still see these beautiful flower grass makes me sense that there is an invisible hand looking after these flowers. Who else would it be except the benevolent creator of the universe who pulls the salty sea at night with his hand to save the flowers with the water fog?

Whenever I want to taste the joy of life, I visit the Lover's Point Park, a tourist destination at the Monterey Beach, and enjoy looking at the flower grass. During the flower season, I always have a good time due to the laughter of the flowers, and when the flowers fall, I feel warm to see them waiting patiently with a new hope for the future. One can say that the pretty flower grass, which is full of life, is my life companion. I feel like I have been living with the flower grass laughing and crying together. As time goes by my wrinkles are getting deeper and deeper, but the flower grass continues to entertain those who stop by with its forever-young body. Appearances may change over time according the provision of nature, but I learn from these flower grasses that our inside should remain truthful as well as beautiful.

When I am around the lovely flower grass, I feel like becoming a lovely person as well. I wish to live with the flower grass that blooms beautiful pink flowers every year and become a person myself who is always loved like these flowers. I wish to live honestly today as well as tomorrow, appreciating the fact that the grass flower is still with me. As the flower grass makes the earth more beautiful with its beauty and fragrance, I shall grow flowers in my heart and embrace the people around me. I am truly glad that I have the flower grass living around me. And I am always thankful to my fellow literary friend who gave the flower a new beautiful name. The 'flower grass' because it looks like grass that blooms flowers at the same time. What a beautiful and precious name, the flower grass.

The Loom

The Flower Garden

The flower garden is calling me. It's calling me day and night. The heaven and earth are urging me to listen to the sound of unity (harmony). I head out to see the garden of flower with a pleasant mind. The flower garden makes the sound of the universe being in complete harmony with such a scenic beauty. In this mysterious and beautiful harmony, it is making a joyful and loving sound that encompasses the entire universe. As I stand in this midst of such sound that unites the heaven and earth, I become truly happy. The flower garden exists in space between the blue sky and the earth. The fresh air and cool breeze are glazing over the flower garden. When the spring arrives with the soft haze dancing on one's eyes, new life blooms as flower trees sprout in light green from the ground that had been frozen throughout the winter. When summer comes, the season of freshness, the leaves of all kinds of trees turn green and flowers bloom full of fragrances. When fall arrives, the flowers lose their petals. In winter, the flower trees become barren and wait silently for the coming spring. The flower garden holds the changes of the four seasons. The flower garden with such a vital force of life, which allows us to love nature, provides us with mental stability and gentle feelings. Caring for a flower garden is caring for one's mind.

There are many flowers in my flower garden that make me happy. The smell of the roses, which reminds me of my sister-in-law, grabs my attention. This year, I started growing the garden balsam, which I used to color my finger nails in my childhood, and this is giving me the joy I once felt in my youth. The national flower of Korea, Mugunghwa, comforts me from my garden, and the cosmos flowers, which would decorate the streets of Song-jeong that my father used to watch with teary eyes thinking of his lost love, are in my backyard smiling big smiles. There are pink moss phlox plants that delight the coast of Monterey and the resurrection lily, which comes with a sad story of the leaves and the flower longing for but never having the chance to meet one another. Above all, there are also the peach flowers and the apricot flowers with their soft petals that form a palace of flowers, and these flowers make me happy because they are all growing in my garden. When I have a lovely conversation with the flowers, thinking of someone, the flowers tell me that they already love me.

The flower garden lets me meet with people from the past in my memories. It lets me meet with my parents and my siblings and hear their voices and smell their flesh. The worlds of flesh and spirits meet in this one place. At the Whittier dock in Anchorage, Alaska, there is an anonymous poem called 'A Thousand Winds' written on a stone cairn. This poem was written for the fishermen who had died in the sea to console their lost souls, and I feel those souls were revived as a thousand winds and come to see my garden flower. I feel in my heart the souls of the beautiful flowers in Sewol ferry, who unfortunately lost a chance to bloom at all, would come back again as pretty flowers with beautiful scents. I feel the ghosts of the comfort women who were forced into sexual slavery during the Japanese occupation would also come back as butterflies flapping their wings to my amours flower garden. The wish of the boat people living in the floating village, whose only wish is to live on land, touching and feeling the soft soil, is coming back to me as the fragrance of soil, penetrating deep into my lungs. As I water the flowers I think of my mother who said of the power of soil that brings life together. The flower garden is always full of mysterious joy and fragrance of new life and the sound of uniting all things in the universe.

Besides the bees, butterflies, or birds, I also see the earthworms and voles living in my garden under the ground when digging the soil with a hoe or a spade. The flower garden is a good living place for many lives. Perhaps it is so because it is a paradise with soil, which is a source of life, air, a source of peace, and the fragrance of the flowers, an energizer for life. As life was formed with soil and we are all going back to it eventually, I feel easy and snugged whenever working on soil. In the flower garden, where humans live harmoniously with the nature, the sunlight during the daytime and starlight at night gently touch down. The flower garden is a living space where I have been always with since I was young. For this reason, I can hear it calling me when I close my eyes. When darkness prevents me from going to the garden, I bring the flower garden to my eyes and have a conversation with it. I can smell the scent of the flowers and see the movement of the leaves of the flowers while lying down on my bed. They move to a suitable place to make it easy to breath and to get along with one another. On a calm, quiet morning, silence and the fragrance from the flowers cleanse my soul. It makes me think about my precious life and gives me the posture of meditation to make my life meaningful. Perhaps I enjoy staying in the flower garden all the time because I hope to live in this life with a modest attitude. The desire to make my flower garden beautiful has become a prayer of my life. While growing and taking care of my garden, my heart turns into one along the way.

In my flower garden, the sound of all things in the universe uniting in harmony flourishes. The world of God and human, the present life and the eternal life, the past and the present, the joy, anger, sorrow, and happiness of life, the body and the mind, changes that occur in nature... all of this can be found in my flower garden. How beautiful and mysterious are the sounds of all things in the universe uniting in harmony with such an open sky and earth? Three to four hours would fly by quickly when I am planting the seeds with wonder and excitement, watering the flowers, and plucking out the weeds. The flower garden is alive and well, and it lets me hear frequently the sound of the heaven and earth being united in harmony, which makes my life much more affluent and lively. I am thankful that I can frequently touch the soft soil that is the source of life and that I can enjoy my life along with my flower garden freely and peacefully. I would want to stay intoxicated with the scent of the flowers with everyone I love in the world. How wonderful would it be if everyone in this world could hear the beautiful sounds of the heaven and earth being in perfect harmony created in my flower garden?

Missionary and dentures

Through missionary work and dentures, we can see mysterious miracles of a new life being created from nothing. That is because in both of them there is love that lets something exist where it is absolutely needed to help them live a normal life. Upon careful reflection, it is this beautiful touch of hands that helps them restore their lost original form, which used to be there but gone for some unknown reasons. Missionary and dentures have the power of magic that can please someone, so I am happy to think about those two these days. When I think about the time we were implanting dentures in our mission field, I become so happy I can even laugh all day by myself. The mission to preach the gospel to places where Jesus, our savior, is unheard of, and implanting dentures where there are no teeth are essential things to live a happy life because of their mysterious nature of giving hope and dreams for a new life.

On July 24, 2017, the earnest prayer by pastor Lim, JinTae from the early worship at dawn, with the vision 'May the land we walk on become divine and may the people we meet become holy,' warms my heart. Our missionary team, who believes that the gospel that is as little in size of a mustard seed can grow into a new life, places its hope of missionary work in heaven with loving hearts. 'Monterey Presbyterian Church,' which I have been serving for over 40 years, is a beautiful church whose garden is essentially the Pacific Ocean. When the church door is wide open, one can see the birds flying peacefully over the vast wide blue ocean together with the high blue sky, all from the church platform, and I cannot help but praise the Lord for creating such a beautiful heaven and Earth.

Since one can easily drive to Mexico from California, the missionary teams from our church, including the youth members who are growing their religious dreams, were able to travel by cars. As soon as we entered the border of Mexico, however, we lost all communications via our cell phones as well as our GPS devices, and the car I was travelling with ended up in a wrong place. Since we were in panic and had to ask for directions with our limited Spanish, we ended up meeting people who were from gangs or who were only interested in our money. Fortunately, due to the grace of God for listening to Deaconess Eddie's prayer, what a pleasure it was to meet a good person who could help us in the right direction and we could finally join the missionary team safely-. Deaconess Yoon, the leader of the short-term missionary team to Mexico, cried, like it was a reunion of the families separated by the Korean War. Even though she is a doctor, wasn't it her who had to miss church for months when she became ill? As she was able to come back to church and became the proud leader of this missionary team as if she was full of the happy hormones for the missionary work she was doing in Mexico, what else could it be but God's way and grace of healing the sick?

In Ensenada, Mexico, when we met Pastor Lee, Dong-hoon, who has been serving missionary work by introducing Tae-Kwon-Do to the world and showing the healthy beauty of Korea, all problems were resolved. After the daily worship, we wanted to take a shower, but most of the faucets were broken and we quickly found out there would be no water available to us. I have been told that they had been out of water for two years due to a severe drought. For drinking water, they would purchase it from stores while some of it was rationed from the government, and for all other waters, they would bring them from the city. Taking a bath in this city would be out of the question, and since there is no water in the bathroom, we would have to bring a bowl of water to the bathroom to take care after ourselves, which was such a chore every time. Taking care of urine wasn't such a big issue, but feces posed a big hurdle. Without water, there is nothing we could do about the stools filling up the toilets.

At the camp, I had a chance to be alone with Deaconess Eddie, who never seemed to run out of jokes to share. She wanted to tell me the story about poop~. It was when her friend was not aware of bidet toilets. She was travelling in Europe, and one night she was staying at a hotel, and there were two toilets in the bathroom. She pooped in the toilet that was cleaner and more pretty, but since she had a sever constipation that night, her stool was like hard little rocks that wouldn't flush. When she woke up the next morning, she found her poop still floating inside the toilet. So she scooped them up, by making a little bowl out of her hands, and move them to the other toilet to flush them. She was so embarrassed to call the hotel staff, thinking it would give them the impression of a dumb Asian person, so she had to scoop it up from the bidet toilet using nothing but her hands and moved them to a regular toilet. As I was looking her mouth while she was telling me the story with all smiles like it was the funniest thing she has ever told in her life, I saw that she had absolutely no teeth on the front side. When I saw her removing her dentures, it was so funny I had to hold my stomach while laughing out loud, but in that moment, I was in awe of the Deaconess who took the lead in the difficult the missionary work despite her age, who was old enough to wear dentures, so that she would not regret later in her life

What we learn and feel at mission fields is consideration for others. Those who consider others first always make people happy and feel joyous. Since Ensenada, Mexico, where our short-term missionary team visited, is such an economically deprived area, the government must distribute their rations for the people in the city. But surprisingly some locals would bring their rations to church for those who live in conditions that are worse than their own. The missionary says he is moved to tears by the gestures of the people here who consider the needs of others over their own. Listening to this story of the locals considering others first, the eyes of our mission team lit up with new hopes.

The missionary missions that preach the gospel to strangers and implant dentures for those who lost teeth are two things that make things exist where they are absolutely needed, enabling them a beautiful, normal life. I envied the missionaries whom I met in my home country after the Korean war, but now I thank God for allowing someone like me to play such an important role. I am also grateful to God for dentures that allow people to laugh freely and loudly. They are such fun and exciting things. In order to make the rest of my life more beautiful, I shall continue my missionary work that is planting a seed to save new souls one at a time with a heart that cares for other people first and makes people happy and joyous, even when I become older and lose my teeth, that will eventually supported by those dentures.

The Loom

I saw

Of all the sounds, I saw people overjoyed by the sound of salvation and of the seed of gospel sprouting buds.

Our church formed a short overseas mission team of 7 people under the name of "Vision Trip" including Pastor Lim, who has had a firm vision of missionary. As it was determined that we would go to Thailand and Vietnam for our destinations after many years of prayers of visiting other nations, we started to learn the gospel songs as well as the accompanying dances in the native tongues. We decided to sing "Praise Jesus Praise Jesus" in Thailand and "Good God" in Cambodia. I was also given an opportunity for the first time in my life of writing a testimony of faith. At the same time, it was going to be an uncomfortable trip flying in an airplane for over 17 hours since I suffer from all kinds of motion sickness. For this reason, I have always had to secretly carry a motion sickness bag with me every time I travel. Though I did feel nauseous a bit in the plane, the fact that I didn't throw up even once until I landed at the airport in Chiangmai, Thailand must have been the miracle from the almighty God.

Thailand, the country I had never visited in my life until then, seemed like a relaxed and peaceful place. As reported in the world happiness report and ranked one of the top nations, people seemed calm, gentle, and peaceful. As it is warm and humid throughout most of the year and as they were entering a rainy season, all the falling rain made me feel jealous for their mountains, streams, plants, and grass looked fresh and moist with rain drops. This feeling must have been amplified since we were from California, USA, which was suffering one of the most severe droughts ever recorded in history. Their traditional greeting ritual called 'Wai' where they bow slightly with their palms pressed together under their chins in a prayer-like fashion was quite familiar to me and was a joy to watch. As a Buddhist nation, I encountered many Buddhist cultures flourishing such as golden pagodas everywhere we go. I met missionary Hwang who sermons messages of salvation to people who are firmly instilled with the Buddhist conventions and cultures of sacrificing the current life for an afterlife.

Looking at the young boys and girls living at the rehabilitation center called 'Jasper' who had to overcome their dark pasts and search for the news of salvation, I remember the prayers Mr. Hwang gave to God every day in tears. I was seeing in that moment the seed of gospel budding and growing while his prayers are being answered. I am grateful to Mr. Hwang for praying patiently pouring his heart and soul to plant the seeds of gospel in Thailand, which I believe might be harder than a trainer training an elephant to paint with a brush. Only after walking up the red clay steps for what seemed to be forever deep in the mountains, one can see the first-ever church build in this country, where the pastor resides. His face shines bright light with happiness when the church bell rings of love far out to the country.

I feel pity to know there is still a country in this day and age that cries silently to struggle for freedom in an ideological turmoil. It is Cambodia, a nation suffering from the pains of War, full of tears of blood, houses without toilet systems, whose people as their animals reduced to just skin and bone. I believe there is the providence of Heaven here on earth. We all have a god we believe in and serve. Some would even proclaim to be a god themselves. Looking at the style of architecture, which resembles the tails of cobras pointing and flying towards the sky, at the Angkor Wat temple, a jewel of Cambodia, so amazing to even believe it was actually built by humans, I thought of the life of Jesus Christ who sacrificed himself to save the humankind, as well as of those in power who sacrificed men just for themselves. During this trip, I met Mr. Kim, a missionary who is scarifying his life to preach the gospel and to live like Jesus. Going through difficulties of having to pray earnestly for a miracle even to make another step, he has served as a missionary in this country for almost all his life because he enjoys watching the sprouts of gospel grow like grains of wheat.

As if they were telling us it has not been that long ago in history when humans were treated like animals, there are sites in Cambodia called 'Killing fields' where one can still step over the clothes of the victims sticking over the grounds. Nowadays, they have changed the name and call them 'healing fields.' In 1975, the

Khmer Rouge regime were established and in the name of 're-education campaign' numerous people who opposed him during the Cambodian Civil War were killed, whose remaining white skulls are currently displayed in various museums. It is even said that kids, grabbed by their ankles, were smashed against a tree. Such tree that once was full of the horrendous sights of red blood still stands tall without saying a word. I see an image of Jesus on a cross who died a gruesome death to cleanse our sins.

Formed by lack of drainage of the waters flowing from the Mekong river near the city of Siem Reap is a giant swamp-lake called 'Boeung Tonie Sap' where the Vietnamese refugees referred to as the 'boat people' are currently living who still carries the wounds of the Vietnam war. They must live on the boats for the rest of their lives since as soon as they set foot on the land they would become illegal immigrants. They can live on the floating houses since the local lotus flowers living in the lake purifies the water for the people. What a breath of fresh air to see our Korean church to lend a helping hand to the unfortunate people who are surviving by catching the local fish from the lake. Through the sounds of throat-cutting of pigs, the chirping sounds of lizards, and the reading of Buddhist scriptures – the sound of gospel springing up can be heard. And where my interest lies, I see the faces of the missionaries who are happy to hear those sounds.

Growing the Flower of Life
as an Angel in White

Growing the Flower of Life as an Angel in White
– Chung, Soon-Ok's essays

•Cheong, Mok-Il
(Essayist, Vice chairman of Korean Writers' Association)

1 ————————————————————————————————

What an act of providence to have a chance to read Mrs. Cheong, Soon-Ok's third essay book 『The Loom』 . Mrs. Chung, Soon-Ok was the recipient of a literary award for new writers in 2009 from the monthly magazine <Korea Essays>, which propelled her journey as an essayist. At the time I was the chairman of the Korean Writers' Association and a publisher of <Korea Essays>, so I remember participating as one of the judges for her awards. Perhaps it is not a coincidence that I am writing the review of her third essay book. I feel reverence and gratitude for the life she's lived as a nurse and an essayist.

As a nurse who protects the lives of patients suffering from diseases, I feel a great deal of warmth and compassion for her life for taking the time to write essays by lighting a candle of self-consciousness. I can also feel humanity and bright smiles from her life as a nurse who has worked all her entire life healing patients from their diseases and pains. Her essays certainly convey responsibility and prayers of performing her duties as a nurse. Her essays come as a peaceful reminder of longing and contain the confessions of her life and prayers written by a warm, loving hand.

To write essays, one has to light a candle in his or her mind. Where the candle is lit is the central point where one finds herself. As a writer, she must examine her life as if she is the main character. She sits in the middle of her thoughts. Only there, she will find the mirror of her mind that allows her to see her inner true self. Thus, the mirror of the mind must be kept clean and pure to be able to see one's soul. If she fails to write essays due to distractions and pleasures of her insignificant day-to-day life, she won't be able to see her inner side, and subsequently she will miss out on the discoveries as well as the meaning of life.

Mrs. Chung, Soon-ok has devoted all of her life as a nurse, often referred to as an angel in white, curing the minds and the bodies of her patients. Her essays are perhaps then an extension of such a helping hand for healing the minds of the readers. The essay is not just a record of one's own experiences. It is a discovery of life through experiences and creation of the enlightenment of life. To capture one's reflection, one must wash off one's dead skin called 'greed', spots called 'anger' and the dust called 'stupidity.' The mind must be clear as well as pure to see one's soul. Writing essays is discovering the truth of life that looks into one's mind and soul. For the mind to be fragrant, the life must be so as well. Being in such a state of mind would be the only way to write an essay that is fragrant.

The basis of an essay is truth and purity. An essayist should constantly clean the dirt, stains, and dust of her mind. Only with the polishing of the mind and the cultivation of life, she can see clearly of her own image. There is no friend like essays that extends one's life, that leads to enlightenment, and communicates with eternity. Essays clear the mind and bring stability and peace. Through confession and revelation, essays can be a healer of the mind and removes conflicts, antagonism, enmity, as well as inferiority complexity.

The joy of writing essays is that by observing time and space one can be conscious of the discovery of his or her life. How fortunate is it to be able to hear the beatings of one's heart while writing an essay and to be able to recognize the breath of eternity? Writing essays is the perception of being alive and its expression. An essayist does not brag about one's grand dreams or ambitions. He or she would just try to grow the flower of simple yet true meaning of life. Isn't writing essays a breath of truth, discovery of life, creation of aesthetics, and the granting of meanings? The producing of a single flower that represents life.

2 ———————————————————————————

When I read essays written by Korean-American writers, I see that a big part of their writing is devoted to showing nostalgia and the longing for their hometown. Though the body lives abroad, how could they ever forget their own country and their hometown where they were born and raised? They will not be able to let go of their nostalgia for their country and hometown even to their last breath.

Garden Balsam

Why is that these days I am missing the garden balsams in my hometown so much? It is the flower that I long for the most among all things I have left behind in my hometown. When I close my eyes and think about the hometown from my childhood, the garden balsam pops and even the sound of them popping can be heard when I open my eyes and grab a spoon. These days are all about the garden balsam that pops its ovary even with the slightest touch expressing its happiness.

I began my immigrant life here in the United States many years ago, and I have lived it patiently, despite the harsh reality of the Korean diaspora and never forgetting my hometown, with a motto "Live your life with your mouth clenched" preached by my mother. I imagine the source of such resilience came from the garden balsams that suffer miserably throughout the day from the scorching summer sun, only to rejuvenate at night with the help of evening dew. The garden balsams that bloomed beautiful flowers and dyed my fingernails red. Perhaps the sprits of the garden balsam from my hometown that captured my childhood curiosity has always resided in me throughout the years.

As usual, today I am looking for the garden balsams from my hometown, that are not native to here, that bloom humble flowers at all the joints along its stems. I search for them everywhere with my ears wide open like a horn. My wish is to grow the garden balsams from my native country here in my back yard and live happily everyday looking at the faces of the red, scarlet, and white flowers.

My hometown was surrounded by low hills and mountains, so it was more like a mountain village rather than a countryside. Due to the abundance of trees and weeds, we would sometimes encounter centipedes or snakes in our yards. But I never heard of the snakes sneaking into our crocks. Like mother always said, the reptiles and the insects would never dare to be near the garden balsams. For that reason, in each household we could see the garden balsams blossoming near the crocks or under the fences. In a sense, the entire town would be dyed with the garden balsam flowers.

Our house, which has provided me with warm feelings throughout my childhood years, would become busy each year with my father's heart and dedication to prepare for the upcoming spring. Before spring arrives, the firewood and sheaves of rice that had been sitting by the mud walls all winter would be removed, and under his command, my older brother would plow the ground to make it more fluffy.

When the remaining now starts to melt away under the mud walls, mother would bring out the garden balsam seeds as well as from other flowers' that had been stored carefully inside her drawer. Then she would hand them to my older sister and tell her to plant them in the flower garden. She would make both of us hold a short half-moon hoe in our hands. In no time, we would plow the moist ground with the hoe and make a small valley. We would separate the garden balsam seeds from the rest and plant them side by side.

- Excerpts from <Garden Balsam>

In <Garden Balsam> there is nostalgia for her hometown. When she thinks of her 'lovely hometown' the first thing that came to her mind was 'garden balsam.' I would think that is more so when it comes to women. Other flowers are meant to be enjoyed by the eye, but the garden balsam flower can also be experienced by dying one's nails with it. It is a flower with which she recalls clearly her hometown and her childhood. I see the first expression of her feminine side from her experience of grinding of the leaves of the garden balsam flower and dying her finger nails with it. Dying her nails in red with the garden balsam would have been the first step towards decorating herself as a beautiful woman. Memories of those days remind her of her childhood and hometown.

In <Garden Balsam> the author depicts the spring of her hometown. Not as a colorful, decorative spring, but as a spring in nature that she experienced as a child in her hometown. In spring, she recollects the scene of planting the seeds of the flower in the ground with her sister.

In <Garden Balsam> not only there is a scene of planting flowers, it also contains the memories of her hometown and the longing for the spring from her childhood. It is an essay that captures the fragrance and the longing of spring she experienced in her old house from her home country, which she hasn't experienced since her move to the U.S.

3 ————————————————————————————

Mrs. Chung's essays capture the memories of her native home country rather than the experiences and reasons of her modern American life. How does she describe enlightenment through the discovery of life and her experiences as an immigrant in the United States? The author clearly shows in her essay 'The Loom' the answers to this very question.

Clink Clank.
Today as usual, I sit in front of my loom and continue to weave a piece of an immigrant life in a forieign country apart from my own. I weave proudly a piece of fabric with my Korean root in the longitude and an immigrant life in the latitude. Singing my favorite loom song 'Korean American.'
Clink Clank.
In my early days as a new immigrant, I wove fabrics using thread made of rough skin from a Samdae tree. Using the yellow, strong, and durable thread from Samdae tree in the basket, I started weaving the beginning of the life as a Korean-American. More ofen than not, I was at a loss not knowing what to do and how to find better methods. Sometimes the strings would break only to be reconnected creating knots, and the fabrics would be stained with my sighs and tears resulting from hard labor.
Due to the language barrier, I went through significant hardship in getting a new certification, and I had to try extra hard during the orientation at my job. Many times, I felt like my heart would burst out, and due to the pain of my soul

huddling itself up, the fabrics were never pretty or even.

That's not all! Removing myself from the people who enjoy hamburgers and coffee and coming back from my hometown searching for Kimchi and red pepper taste, the fabrics woven by the longing, love, tears, and loneliness for my hometown were indefinitely loose.

When I had my children, who are my hopes and dreams, and they began to go to school, other problems began to prop up. When they came home from school, they would often show depression and tears in their eyes. They wanted to play with friends in school, but they would say everyone was avoiding them. When I asked them what was going on, they would say that their parents told them to not play with oriental kids with "Asian Eyes." Oh my poor kids, hurt from their own friends. In the first years of living in the States as immigrants having to make ends meet every day, we had to be financially stable first above anything else.

With what my children told me, I lost control of the loom, and the hemp thread broke when too much force was applied to it. My hands that were connecting the thread again trembled and another knot was created. With the news, I couldn't possibly continue to make fine cloths with the trembling hands and my feet in the way, but I had to march on and continue on with my weaving loom with the sweat, patience, hope, dreaming the dreams of a rainbow.

- Excerpts from <The Loom>

The life as an immigrant in the United States is the life of a pioneer. One must concentrate all her mind to settle down in an exotic, foreign land. One would have to learn everything again to adapt to the ways of a foreign country. The author makes a confession of her life, in which she made every effort to overcome the difficulties of living as an immigrant family. As I was reading the essay 'The Loom' I realized the hard work and the efforts for independence put forth by many Korean Americans. They had to be recognized in the workplace for their diligence and sincerity and do their absolute best to settle down and take root by showing the life that lives up to the norm of the American society. The Korean Americans who have settled down in the American society are showing continuous efforts based on diligence and sincerity to form a foundation for stability.

4 ───────────────────────────────────────

Mrs. Chung's essays clearly depict the landscape and the experiences of the agricultural age of Korea. The life that disappeared after having gone through the agricultural and the industrial revolutions is shown through her essays like black and white pictures. Perhaps because she is a Korean American who was born in Korea, her experiences remain in her memory clearly. The young generations nowadays have probably never seen the scenery and the life of the early days in the agricultural and industrial era. The biggest transformation in the author's life was immigrating to America. It must have been possible since she had her vocation of being a 'nurse.' No hand is more sacred than that of a nurse. Perhaps I picture that a nurse who is genuine to herself would recite the 'hand's prayer' all her life.

Please let my hand be clean.
Let my hand not be one that is impatient
Blinded by greed wishing to hold on to anything
In the morning, not just washing my hand
Let me wash the hand of my mind.
Let that hand wash my soul.
Let my hand be the one
That knows how to touch the forehead of the wounded.

- From the reviewer's 'The prayer of the hand.'

I feel that the author's life, who is a nurse and an essayist having lived all her life to her fullest as an angel in white helping patients who were suffering from diseases, is deeply moving and full of gratitude. Her new life, as a Korean American pioneer and as a nurse fulfilling her noble duty, shows beautifully in her essays. In particular, she stands out as an essayist who captures her life and journeys. She knows that the essay is the only eternal device in this finite life. I wish the writer, who has been growing the flower of her awoken senses of identity and the meaning of life in the form of essays, a blessing as well as a literary luck in her future, and I hope her third essay book 『The Loom』 will be widely loved by her readers.